fiercely PROTECTIVE

R. LEIGH

fiercely PROTECTIVE

R. LEIGH

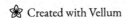 Created with Vellum

CHAPTER
one

ROGUE

There was a numbing, almost disorienting feeling of monotony sinking into my bones. It was making me both restless and irritable. My world was seldom tedious, but lately, nothing seemed to stir my blood, nothing excited me, challenged me. The loud music, the flashing bright lights, and buzz of the crowd were beginning to have an anesthetizing effect on me. My life was becoming boring and predictable. Everything around me seemed dull and nothing had motivated me for some time. As I sat alone in my private booth at the nightclub I co-owned with my friend and mafia don, Alessio Messina, the familiarity of the scene made me weary. While I enjoyed having a hand in my many business dealings and showing my face at the club tended to make things run smoother, there was a part of me that wasn't satisfied. I craved more. But what? I felt a deep embedded longing inside me to seek out and immerse myself in sin. Did I long for more wickedness, more of an adrenaline rush, or was it the hunger for danger that drove me?

It had been much too long since I had been tested, and even longer since I had relished in seeing fear in the eyes of those who were foolish enough to oppose me, and when the occasion called for it, I couldn't deny the feeling of euphoria that accompanied bringing death to those reckless enough to cross me. Lately, my life had been quieter than I liked, and I kept waiting, hoping, even longing for the peacefulness to shatter. There was a driving force inside me, urging me to do something, anything to ignite some sort of fire within me to relieve the tension coursing through my body before I went mad with boredom.

It wasn't the seclusion that bothered me. In my world solitude was an expectation. You didn't make too many close connections. It was dangerous to let people into your life. They would either betray you, or you would lose them. Although, I did have a few men that I trusted, those I would call friends. We had met as children growing up in the streets and formed strong bonds into adulthood as well as the men that I had encountered when I was older that helped forge me into who I was today. Men that lived life as I did, unafraid and unperturbed by the darkness that surrounded us. We each controlled and ruled our portions of the cities in which we resided. One of the men that I would trust with my life was walking in my direction with an uncharacteristic grin on his face. The sadistic part of my brain instantly awoke at the thought of finally being able to quench my thirst for malevolence.

"Why are you smiling? It usually doesn't bode well for others when you are in a good mood. Whatever it is, I hope it will bring some much-needed excitement to the night and end my boredom."

As Blaze took a seat, a buxom waitress wearing way too much make-up and an overpowering perfume instantly appeared with his favorite drink, bourbon.

"I brought some information that I think you will find interesting."

I rolled my eyes in disappointment as I finished off the rest of my drink. "News that makes you smile, makes me wary. What is it?"

He drank the bourbon in one gulp and closed his eyes relishing the burn as the liquid slid down his throat. "Someone is trying to make trouble and asking questions. I have been told that he is claiming to be Russian."

My eyebrows rose marginally with this revelation. "Bratva?"

He shrugged his shoulders. "Not sure yet. I suppose he could be.

Throwing his weight around, making demands and threats, doesn't sound like Bratva. They are usually more subtle until things don't go the way they want. He could just be an imposter hiding behind the Bratva name, using it as a tactic to intimidate people."

"I don't fucking intimidate easily. Chicago is my territory. It is unlike the Bratva to come into my domain and make a commotion without letting me know ahead of time. And they typically don't make blind threats; they carry them out. Have you called Nickolai? He will know if there is someone connected to the Bratva in Chicago."

Blaze raised his hand in the air and the waitress serving us immediately was at his side. He gave her a lust-filled gaze as his smile slipped and his eyes turned icy as she leaned forward, brushing her breasts across his shoulder. His arm snaked around her hip, his hand resting casually just above the curve of her ass as he told her what he desired.

"Another bourbon?" She practically rubbed herself against him like a damn cat in heat.

When she straightened, I sent her a look that communicated that I was not amused at her obvious flirtation, and since I was conducting business, I just wanted her to deliver the drinks and get the fuck back to work.

Blaze watched as she walked away, swishing her hips more than normal and glancing back over her shoulder to draw his attention.

"If you are going to screw her, just do so when she is off the clock. Now, did you call Nickolai, or have you been too preoccupied with finding somewhere to stick your dick tonight?"

His eyes narrowed as his face hardened and the familiar frown that sent most people running in the other direction was back in place. "Fuck you, Rogue. Need I remind you that I don't take orders from you? We are equals. I thought I would tell you first before I got Nik involved. You are always bragging about this being your damn city, maybe someone wants to take it away from you."

I smiled at his comment, glad to have someone with enough balls to defy me. It was the reason our friendship had lasted through the years. Neither one of us was afraid of the other and any challenge issued would be met, but in truth, there was no one I trusted more on this earth than Blaze.

"Trying to take what is mine, what belongs to me, would be an automatic death sentence. I don't feel this man is a threat, an annoyance perhaps, but nothing to fear." I sighed heavily as I drummed my fingers against the table. "The waitress ends her shift at midnight. Feel free to use one of the private rooms upstairs if you decide to entertain her further."

A faint light twinkled in the depths of his dark eyes as his attention drifted to someone else across the room.

"I think I have found other prey for the night."

My eyes narrowed as I followed his line of vision. The first thought that went through my mind when I saw her, was that she didn't belong here. She was wearing a simple lavender spaghetti strap sundress that came just above her knees. Her long chocolate-colored hair hung down almost to her waist in loose waves. She was wearing wedge sandals and if she wore any make-up at all, it was natural, not the heavy black eyeliner and multicolored eyeshadows worn by most of the women I saw in the club. She was an outstanding beauty compared to any other woman I had seen before, but it wasn't just her appearance that set her apart from the others. She was out of place, unsure of what to do, as if being in a place like this was unnatural.

It was as if an angel took a wrong turn and accidentally walked through the gates of hell by mistake and suddenly, my boredom disappeared.

I heard the low predatory growl emitted from Blaze as he gave her body a slow raking perusal. When he tried to stand, I put my hand on his arm, effectively restraining him from going after what I wanted.

"No, she's mine."

I didn't wait for an argument. I drank the remainder of the whiskey in my glass and stood up to make my way across the room to where she stood casually leaning against the bar, twisting her hands nervously in front of her. She kept her head lowered and her eyes diverted as the chaos moved around her. Most of the people who stood between us had no idea as to my identity, nor how close they came to being thrown out of my way as I moved toward the lost angel I was about to claim.

A man was standing by her side. He handed her a drink and smiled down at her as she sipped it, her eyes squinting at the bitter taste of the alcohol. He laughed scornfully at her as she covered her mouth and coughed softly. I had always been a selfish person and had never been particularly fond of sharing, so I wasn't surprised when an intense feeling of possession swept over me. When he stepped closer to her, his body brushing against hers, that feeling intensified. I stepped through a couple dancing near the stage and was at her side the moment she leaned back to avoid his touch.

She bumped into me, and my hand instantly shot to her waist to steady her.

"I'm so sorry," she said in a soft voice as she tried to move away.

I kept my hold on her waist and took the drink from her hand before giving her a disarming smile hoping to ease her nervousness. "No need to be sorry, love. That drink is bitter. Let me get you something smoother that I think you will enjoy more." I looked toward the bartender, who immediately stopped whatever he was doing and rushed over. "Champagne, the best." As if I had to state the obvious. I always insisted upon the best.

He nodded his head and rushed to get the drink I requested, and I turned back to her. "Without running the risk of spouting some nonsensical cliché, what's a girl like you doing in a place like this?"

Her lips curved into a smile, and I sensed that some of the unease she was feeling when I first approached was dissipating.

"Wow, that is terribly cliché. Do you say that to every girl that comes in here?"

"No, just the ones that look like you."

Her grin was irresistible, and I found myself drawn to her.

"Nice come back, but in answer to your question, I have an interview here tomorrow for a job, a waitress position."

Her voice was strangely melodic and soft, and I found myself wanting to hear her speak my name.

I leaned closer to her, the space between us felt like a chasm I had to cross.

She bit her lips to stifle her shy grin. "A few of my friends, well more like work acquaintances, from my previous place of employment, suggested I come here with them tonight and check the place out. They thought it might help with my interview."

The predator in me sprang to life at her words. "A job? Well, I hear the guy that owns the place can be a real asshole. I hope you are prepared to deal with a man like that."

She laughed softly again, and I found myself unable to pull my gaze from her perfectly kissable pink lips. I had a strong urge to touch her, to discover if her skin was as soft as it looked.

"I have heard that too, but it is also rumored that he pays well, and with tips, I could make twice as much as I was making working at my previous job, working as a hotel night clerk. For a decent job, I can put up with quite a lot. No matter how big an asshole the boss can be."

"Interesting. Why did you leave your former place of employment? Was the pay that bad that you would choose to work in an environment like this instead?"

She looked down and shifted from one foot to the other, then turned back to where the group she had arrived with was talking and drinking. Completely oblivious to her.

"There were other factors, but sometimes change can be good. Right?"

I nodded as the bartender returned with the Dom Perignon I suggested. I handed her the glass. "Try this, it's not as bitter as the drink your friend bought you."

Just speaking his existence caused the man to materialize at her side once again, and I felt the possessive asshole in me come to life once more.

He leaned closer to her before narrowing his eyes at me. "Hey buddy, you need to move on, the lady is with me."

Stains of scarlet appeared on her cheeks as embarrassment rushed over her. She tucked a stray curl behind her ear and looked down, avoiding the scrutiny in my eyes. "Brad, it's ok. He just bought me a drink, and it's not like we came here on a date. We came in a group as friends." She glanced back up at me with an apology on her face.

The man beside her squared his shoulders, as anger flared in his eyes. "It doesn't matter that we came in a group, you are with me, and this guy needs to go look somewhere else for a piece of ass."

I heard her sharp intake of breath and congratulated myself for maintaining my composure, something I was rather proud of since my inner beast wanted nothing more than to cave in this asshole's face. I stepped forward ready to do just that when she moved between us.

"Brad, you are kind of being a dick. He just bought me a drink and was being nice, and as I said before, we aren't here together on a date."

My hands clenched into fists and my security was already walking toward us to intercede. But when he reached forward and grabbed her wrist, causing her to shriek and suck in a breath of air, my arm shot out, and my hand wrapped around his throat. The people that surrounded us were watching intently, some out of morbid curiosity, and others hoping to have something to gossip about tomorrow. I pushed him back against the bar and leaned in closer, struggling to control the rage building inside me. I had put up with this asshole longer than was normal simply because I did not want her involved in an altercation.

"Don't. Fucking. Touch. Her. Again."

As I squeezed harder, he reached up, clutching at my fingers as they dug deeper into his flesh. I was hoping to draw blood, to see the panic in his eyes as he struggled to draw breath. Even though his mouth was open, he couldn't speak, his eyes begging for mercy and pleading for release.

My hold tightened, the urge to end his life right now growing stronger by the second, but suddenly Blaze was beside me. His deep familiar voice broke through my fury. "Let him go."

"Get this piece of shit out of here and make sure he knows not to come back."

When I released the douchebag, he would have fallen to the ground if Blaze had not been there to catch him and drag him from the club. The people around us, some stunned, resumed their frivolities. I turned back to my lost little angel standing behind me, her face had gone pale, her eyes wide, and she had placed a hand over her chest to calm her rapid heartbeat. The shock of what she had witnessed had wiped her smile away.

I took a step forward and she retreated. *Fuck.*

"I'm sorry. I didn't mean to frighten you."

She blinked and then stammered in bewilderment. "I have never seen…anything like that before. You moved incredibly fast."

I grinned and took another step toward her. This time she didn't back away.

"What's your name?"

She watched me cautiously. "Brielle, but everyone calls me Bri."

I held my hand out to her. "Bri, would you like to go somewhere more private and quieter?"

She arched her eyebrows and smiled tentatively. "And end up as a missing person? Or the subject of an Amber Alert that no one pays attention to. I don't think so."

My laughter was low and throaty, causing her emerald-green eyes to narrow. "I wasn't trying to abduct you. We don't even have to leave the club. There are private rooms upstairs where people can have a drink, talk, and get to know each other better without all the noise and crowds down here on the floor." I pointed to the stairs that led to the second floor where the rooms, all encased in glass, could be seen. Some of the rooms remained visible and it was easy to see groups of people mingling and partying inside; while other rooms had darkened the glass for a more intimate setting.

She looked at me skeptically. "I'm not sure that would be a wise move on my part. It seems a little reckless and more than a little stupid for me to go to a private room with a man I just met. Perhaps it would be best if I just thanked you for the drink and called it a night. I do have an important interview tomorrow."

Blaze's deep mocking laughter was coming from somewhere

behind me. Women never denied me, and my friend was finding it rather amusing. "I promise I will not keep you long, and I can give you some tips that might help with your interview tomorrow. I am familiar with Mr. Kent, the manager."

I knew the minute she was about to accept. Her eyes were so expressive. She would never be able to be devious or hide anything from me, and that thought excited me.

"Alright, but just for a few minutes, and we keep the door open."

She placed her hand in mine and when my fingers closed around hers, I felt a tremor at the contact, something I had never felt before.

"Tonight, you can call the shots."

But after tonight, sweet angel, you will be in my world where I maintain absolute control.

Bri

Hot was the only word I could think of to describe him. Incredibly hot. The kind of hot that you usually only see on TV and find yourself wondering where the hell you find guys that look like this. The type of man that women found deliciously appealing. He was dressed in a dark blue button-up shirt with the first three buttons undone, sleeves rolled up to his elbows showing a brief glimpse of the tattoo on his arms, and jeans...jeans that hugged his ass. It was obvious he was accustomed to having money. The kind of man who wore designer clothes tailored just for him. But it wasn't just his clothes that made me think that there was much more to this guy than I originally thought. There was a self-confidence about him that bordered on arrogance. He had an air of authority and the appearance of someone who demanded instant obedience. You could see it in the way he walked, the way he had wrapped his hand around Brad's throat, and the way he didn't seem to care about anything going on around him. He showed no fear. No concern for anything. He radiated money and power. Everything about him screamed at me to run far away. But for some reason, I gravitated toward dangerous men.

He was tall with wide strong shoulders, a perfectly proportioned body, dark brown hair, and deep coffee-brown eyes. The smokin' hot masculinity vibe he was sending out suited him. Yeah, this was not the typical guy I ran into every day. But I still should not have accepted his offer to join him upstairs. I came here to scope the place out, so I would be more prepared for my interview tomorrow, not for a quick hookup. I wasn't interested in meeting a guy or dating right now, not after the trouble I left behind in Colorado.

When we neared the stairs, I hesitated; I looked back over my shoulder to the group I came with and saw that none of them had even noticed my absence. It wasn't surprising. The only one who had insisted that I come with them tonight was Brad, and he had already made an ass of himself and been thrown out by security, so I was technically on my own. The thought made me pause. I didn't even know this guy's name. Past experiences told me that I should be wary. I pulled back before my foot reached the second step.

"Wait...I really shouldn't...I don't know anything about you. I don't even know your name."

"Rogue."

My lips trembled as I tried to hold back a smile. "Rogue? Is that your name or a description of your character?"

One corner of his mouth twisted upward and the warmth of his smile, as odd as it may seem, made me feel safer. I allowed him to lead me the rest of the way to the second floor where the private rooms were located. We walked to the end and entered one of the larger rooms that was set apart from the others. It was unexpectedly roomy inside with its own stocked bar, leather sofa, poker table, and plush chairs around the room. A pretty chandelier hung from the ceiling, and the décor was dark, mostly black, but surprisingly elegant for a nightclub.

"Are we going to be in trouble for being here? This doesn't look like a room that just anyone can use. It must be reserved for...well... not us."

He strolled forward, a drink in his hand. "Don't be nervous. It will be fine. Like I said, I'm familiar with the management. Can I get you something to drink?"

"No, thanks. I'm not much of a drinker and to be honest, I'm thinking I will need a clear head when dealing with you."

His left brow rose a fraction. "You don't drink and if my guess is correct, you haven't been in many places like this, but yet you want a job here serving drinks to a crowd that can get a bit unruly on occasion."

There was a critical tone to his voice, and I couldn't help but feel a little irritated at his obvious censure.

"The job description said nothing of being able to drink copious amounts of alcohol as a requirement, and just because I don't frequently spend my nights in clubs like this shouldn't be a deterrent for hiring me. I am a hard worker and while I have not been a waitress in a bar, I have waited tables before. You shouldn't make assumptions."

He stretched his hand out toward the sofa.

"I didn't mean for my examination of your character to offend you. Please, have a seat and relax."

I looked back toward the open door before taking a seat, once again questioning the wisdom of being alone with this man. *What could it possibly hurt? It's not as if you are going home with the guy.* I was still having a conversation in my head when he walked over and sat beside me.

I nervously looked up, finding myself entranced by his warm brown eyes. "So, is your supermodel girlfriend out of town this weekend?"

Amusement flickered in his eyes as a chuckle came from deep within his chest. "Now who is making assumptions? But in answer to your question, there is no girlfriend, supermodel or otherwise. What about you? Is there a guy out there somewhere wishing he was with you right now?"

He moved closer, the warmth of his body touching mine. "No, it's just me."

"Tell me about yourself."

I had never been one to share my personal life with too many people, and while this guy was sexy and unbelievably intense, he seemed to be nice enough, but I was still cautious. "There isn't much to tell."

He reached over and lightly traced his finger along the curve of my cheek sending shockwaves through my body.

"Oh, let me see if I can guess. You tell me if I am close."

He took my hand and raised it to his lips as he pressed a kiss to the inside of my palm, virtually paralyzing me. I should have pulled away; any rational woman would have sensed the danger. Red flags were waving everywhere, but his eyes seemed to hold me captive.

The huskiness of his voice seemed to move over me like velvet. "I think you are always careful, to the point that you never take chances. You color in the lines, never drive over the speed limit, never cross the street until the crosswalk gives you the go ahead, always follow the rules, and never disappear anywhere with strange men you just met." He traced circles softly over my skin from my wrist to my elbow. The warmth of his touch made my skin tingle.

He leaned closer, and I could feel his warm breath as his lips neared my ear.

"Even now you are more worried about being caught in a room where you are not supposed to be than you are with the fact that I am about to kiss you."

Kiss me? Did he just say what I thought he said? He was going to kiss me. The words didn't pierce through the fog in my brain in time for me to resist and when his lips pressed against mine, my body decided my brain needed to take a vacation...a long vacation. I leaned in as he deepened the kiss. His hand moved up to cup my cheek as his thumb gently pressed against my chin, so my mouth would open, and when it did, he took full advantage. His tongue swiftly swept inside and tangled with mine. I was shocked at my body's eager response to his kiss.

I heard a soft moan pass from my lips and the sound seemed to excite him. He pressed my body back, and I felt his hands glide up my arms to the straps of my dress. My body shivered as he slid the strap down my arm, exposing my shoulder, and I felt the heady sensation as his lips moved against my neck where he feathered kisses down to the curve of my shoulder and along my collarbone. My eyes drifted closed, and I shivered as an unfamiliar sensation began to move through me. I had been kissed before, but nothing like this.

I tightly squeezed my legs together as I felt the warm moisture building there. His hands moved to the other strap, sliding it down farther till the tops of my breasts were exposed. *I should stop this now before it goes any further. I really should. Shouldn't I? Ok, just a few more minutes. As soon as he has finished kissing me, I definitely will stop him.*

He shifted me, so I was lying completely on the sofa as he hovered above me, his eyes were compelling, magnetic, as they stared into mine. He pulled my dress down farther exposing my breasts to his hungry view. He took a moment to allow his gaze to focus on me, and I felt my cheeks burning crimson as he continued to rake his eyes over my bare skin. I raised my arms to cover myself, but he shook his head, a silent command in his expression, and just like that, I obediently moved them back to my sides.

"Beautiful. Absolutely perfect." There was a sensual drawl to his voice that was both seductive and carnal.

The warmth of his palm, as he cupped my breasts before dipping his head lower, caused an involuntary tremor of arousal to pulse through me. His tongue flicked over my nipple; my back arched urging him to continue. The achy yearning I felt as his tongue continued to lave over my tender flesh surprised me. I cried out as his teeth nipped the skin on the side of my breast before sucking hard, no doubt leaving a bruise, a memento to remember this one night of recklessness.

The heat continued to build between my thighs, and I felt as if I might explode. I placed my hands against his chest, intending to push him away, but instead, I found myself wanting to feel him, to explore the firmness beneath his shirt.

He sat up and unbuttoned a few more buttons before whipping

the shirt over his head. *Holy crap, the guy was ripped.* I chewed my bottom lip as my hands glided over his rippled abs and firm chest, my pulse quickening.

"Go ahead, love. I'm all yours." His voice was deep and sensual, sending a ripple of awareness through me.

I wanted more than to touch him; I wanted to taste. I leaned forward, hesitantly pressing my open lips to his warm skin. I had never done anything like this before and wasn't sure what to do, but when I let my tongue lick him, taste him, he emitted a growl that reverberated through my body and like a cold glass of water tossed in my face, I came back to reality. I pushed against him, and he moved away from me. I quickly pulled my dress back into place and sat up, my hands shaking slightly as I brushed my hair aside.

"I...I'm sorry. I really should be going."

"Why? You liked dipping your toes into the darkness, didn't you, sweetheart?"

He let his fingers, once again, trace the curve of my cheek and I began questioning my reasons. "Inside the perfect, rule-following angel, there is a little part of you that likes being wicked. You crave it."

I blinked a few times, trying to keep from falling under his trance again. "You don't know me, and this was a mistake." *A very pleasant... no...a very hot mistake.* "This isn't me. I...I need to go. The interview tomorrow."

He smiled as he stood from the sofa, grabbing his shirt and putting it back on. "Oh yes, the interview. I'll have a car take you home."

I pushed back the disappointment I felt when he didn't try to coerce me to stay.

Something was wrong with me. I was disheartened that a strange man who I allowed to feel me up in a club didn't try forcing me to stay longer.

I stood from the sofa, my knees a bit wobbly. He reached out and put a hand on my waist, the warmth and pressure of his fingertips nearly making me toss all my inhibitions aside.

"That isn't necessary. I can just call Uber or take a taxi."

His smile faltered a little. "No, my driver will take you home. I insist."

The silent command in his expression returned, and I knew there was no use declining again. I nodded unable to form another refusal. He walked me back down the stairs and through the crowds. The blaring music and flashing bright lights seemed distant and fuzzy as we made our way to the club's entrance. He raised his hand in the air and a man in a suit stepped forward.

"Take her home."

The guy nodded and then stepped off to the side, giving us a moment. I ran my tongue along my lips, a habit I had developed when I was nervous.

"Thank you for the ride home, but it wasn't necessary. I feel like I should say something along the lines of I have never done anything like that before, but you probably wouldn't believe me. But it's the truth, I don't know what came over me."

He leaned closer and kissed my cheek softly. "I know exactly what came over you, sweetheart." He gave me a wink and turned to walk away.

His words held an underlying sensuality that was captivating. But I couldn't help but feel like the world's biggest idiot. Thankfully, I came to my senses before I did something I would regret even more. I took a deep steadying breath and turned to where the driver was waiting for me. I had to put this night behind me, forget about the mesmerizing hunky stranger I had allowed to take way too many liberties, and focus on the interview tomorrow because if I didn't find a decent-paying job soon, I would have more trouble than I could handle.

Rogue

. . .

When I returned to my private booth at the back of the club, I found Blaze already there, an annoying half-smirk on his face.

"It didn't take her long to get sick of you. Honestly, I thought you would have been able to last a bit longer. Disappointing."

I reached for the bottle sitting in front of him and filled my glass. "Mind your own business. Have you seen Mr. Kent?"

"No, but he is probably in the office."

"The girl applied for a job here. I want her application, and I want to know her interview time."

Blaze grunted. "That girl? She won't survive here. I can tell that from looking at her. She is too sweet, too innocent." He took a sip of his drink and then narrowed his eyes as he stared across the table at me. "But that isn't going to stop you from hiring her, is it?"

"No and isn't going to stop the plans I have for her."

Blaze stood from the booth. "She isn't your type, Rogue."

My brow furrowed as we glared at each other, the tension becoming thick. It was unlike Blaze to be so vocal and rarely did he give a shit about anyone or anything. So, it was puzzling to me that he had shown so much interest in the girl and my intentions. A sharp sense of selfishness coursed through me, and I felt the need to stake my claim.

"She is off-limits, Blaze."

The left corner of his lips turned up slightly, and his smile was more predatory than humorous. "But for how long? If you remember, I did see her first."

I wasn't sure if he was issuing a challenge, or if he was merely trying to provoke me.

"I'll tell Kent you are looking for him." He drank the remainder of the whiskey in his glass and walked toward the back office, slapping the flirtatious waitress from earlier on the ass as he passed her.

I sat back in the booth, trying to tune out the music and noise surrounding me. Images of Bri lying beneath me passed through my head. There was something about her, something that made me look forward to the games I had planned for her. I normally didn't get involved in the hiring of staff for the club, nor did a woman rarely hold my interest for longer than it took to fuck her, but this woman was different. It would be interesting to see her reaction tomorrow when she discovers exactly the type of man I am.

CHAPTER
two

BRI

The reflection staring back at me in the mirror did not scream confidence. It may be simply an interview for a waitress job at a nightclub, but *Sinners* was the most exclusive club in Chicago, owned by one of the most elusive and richest men in the country. It was rumored that the pay and benefits couldn't be matched anywhere, so I needed to make the best impression possible. So, I opted for a crisp white blouse, with a navy-blue blazer, new pants, and navy ballet flats. Nothing overly fancy, yet something that stated that I was serious about obtaining the position.

With my bills piling up, I needed this job. After the cutbacks at the hotel, I haven't been able to find anything that paid enough for me to afford my small apartment and the necessities I needed without giving up things like food or electricity. My pantry shelves were almost empty and my TV had so many white lines running across the screen, that it was pointless to try and watch it.

So, when one of the girls I worked with mentioned getting a job at the club, I immediately googled it, applied online, and was called for an interview two days later. Last night, when I went there with a group from work, I thought it would give me an opportunity to check it out. I thought it might be helpful during the interview if I knew something about the place, at least I could say that I had been there. But instead of thinking about my interview, I ended up doing something completely reckless. Making out in a private room with the sexiest guy I had ever seen was completely out of character. Now, I would have to go into the interview and try to push those wicked but delicious images from my brain.

To make matters worse, if I was lucky enough to get the job, there was a high possibility that the guy from last night frequented the club and I would see him again. Of course, those kinds of guys didn't have relationships with the help. He might not even recognize me. I might have been just one of many girls that he lured to a private room. *How humiliating would that be?*

I shook my head and tried to forget about it. It was a stupid mistake that I would not let happen again. After taking one last look in the mirror, making certain my hair and makeup were good, I knew I needed to make my way downstairs to catch a cab. This interview was important, and I would rather arrive early than late. I was swiftly running out of options. If I didn't get this job, I could lose my apartment and I would be faced with moving back to Colorado. I squeezed my eyes shut tighter as flashes from that night came back to me.

After coming close to being sexually assaulted and having the shit beat out of me by a crazy and abusive stalker, I fled my hometown and moved to Chicago. Tony, a guy I had only been on a couple of dates with, started giving off these weird and scary vibes. He became insistent on having sex and was handsy all the time. It was like fighting off an octopus whenever I was with him. When I refused, he became agitated and aggressive. On the last night that I had gone out with him, he slapped me a few times and shoved me into the wall when I refused him again. He kept screaming that I had no idea who he was and that I would be sorry for spurning him. Thankfully, my neighbor had been home and called the cops.

After that night, I filed a restraining order against him, but that wasn't enough to stop the harassing phone calls or his stalking me everywhere I went. Then one night I came home late after seeing a movie with my friend Allison, and he was waiting for me. He beat me nearly unconscious, broke one of my ribs, and left my whole body bruised. He would have raped me had Allison not forgotten her purse in my car and come back for it. When she heard the noises coming from inside the house, she started pounding on the door, and he ran out the back. She finally broke a window to get inside, but I was barely conscious and don't remember much after that. That encounter put me in the hospital for a week.

When I got out of the hospital, the judge had already released Tony on bond. Knowing that it wasn't safe for me to stay there, I left that same day. Allison had paid for my bus ticket and gave me enough money to stay in a hotel until I found a job. She was the only friend I had and the only one that knew of my location. It was safer that way. She had called me a few times saying that Tony was looking for me and swore he would find me, but I had no relatives in Chicago or any other connections to the city, so it was a safe bet that he wouldn't think of looking for me here. It was a big city anyway and easy for a girl like me to remain invisible which made it the perfect place for me to move on with my life. So, this interview and getting this job was important. I needed it to stay focused so I would be able to stay in Chicago and put my past behind me.

When I got downstairs, a black Jaguar was waiting by the curb and the driver was holding a sign with my name on it.

Confused, I stepped toward him.

"Brielle Rogers?"

I nodded. "I'm Brielle, but I didn't send for a car. There must be a mistake."

"No mistake. You have an interview at *Sinners* today at noon?"

"Yes, but..."

"I am here to escort you to that interview." He stepped back and opened the car door for me.

I hesitated for a second, thinking that this couldn't be real. I knew the club was high-end, but to send a car to collect job applicants was unheard of. But, once again, I went against my more cautious nature and took a seat in the luxurious car and allowed myself a few peaceful moments to compose my thoughts and get my nerves under control.

My eyes closed as I leaned back against the soft leather, noting the new car smell, and tried to mentally focus and get ready for the interview. I had practiced my smile in the mirror and googled some common interview questions that might be asked, now I just needed to appear confident and prepared.

When the car came to a stop outside the club, the driver came around quickly and opened the door for me. I grabbed the folder with my resume and walked toward the door.

"Just go inside, there will be someone to walk you back to the office. They are expecting you."

I looked back and smiled at him. "Thanks."

I took one more steadying breath, put a small smile on my face, and walked through the front doors. The club was very different in the light of day. The lights were on, and there was no loud music or flashing colored lights. The staff that were there were busy either cleaning or preparing for the next shift. I stepped toward the bar when a lady came over to me.

"Miss Rogers?"

"Yes."

"You are here for an interview with Mr. Kent. Unfortunately, Mr. Kent had some other business to attend to."

The sense of disappointment was almost crushing. "Should I reschedule?"

"Oh no, that won't be necessary. Mr. Delaney is here and will conduct your interview. If you would please follow me, I will escort you to the back office."

I followed behind her briefly allowing my eyes to stray toward the stairs that led to the private rooms above, and I couldn't help but wonder if *Mr. Handsome* managed to entice some other girl upstairs after I left.

The older lady stopped outside a solid black door. "Wait here and I will see if Mr. Delaney is ready for you."

I nodded but was much too nervous to reply.

When she returned, she opened the door wide and stood to the side. "He is ready, Miss Rogers, and good luck."

I took a deep breath, pasted a small smile on my face, and walked through the door only to come to a halt when I saw the man standing before me. *This can't be happening.*

"You?"

The smirk on his face said that he was rather pleased with himself and at the fact that I was shocked at seeing him. "Good morning, Bri."

I felt as if the world was conspiring against me. Of all the things that could have occurred to sabotage this interview, I never imagined this. How could this be the same guy from last night? Was he the same Mr. Delaney who owned the club? My cheeks blushed as I remembered that I had agreed with him when he mentioned the club owner was an asshole.

"Would you like to have a seat or conduct this interview standing?"

I stepped forward to take a seat in the chair situated in front of his large mahogany desk, ignoring the voice in my head screaming at me to run in the opposite direction.

He was even more strikingly handsome in the light of day than he had been in the dim darkness and flashing lights of the club last night; only this time, he looked more threatening, more wicked. He was dressed in a crisp white shirt and black dress pants, his arms crossed over his broad chest as he leaned back casually against the desk as if he were testing me to see if I was brave enough to be in the same room as him.

I raised my chin a notch higher and summoned what little courage I possessed. If he brought me here to humiliate or degrade me, I would not give him the satisfaction of seeing how unsettled his presence had made me.

"Why didn't you tell me last night who you were?" I hated the way my voice cracked when I was finally able to speak.

He looked at me intently then walked back around to take a seat behind the desk. "I saw no need in it. Besides, where would the fun be in that?"

I may have been impulsive last night, but I had been through too much to allow this man, a man I barely knew, to humiliate or frighten me. "I am sorry for any inconvenience this may have caused you, but I feel that this is a waste of time, and I don't have the luxury of time to waste." I rose from my seat, but his deep authoritative voice caused me to freeze in place.

"Sit down." It was more of a command than a suggestion.

I immediately sank back into the seat I had just vacated, mentally chastising myself for being so easily controlled.

I looked up to see his lips curve in a one-sided sexy as hell grin. "I am not going to bite unless that is what you came for. I was under the impression that you were here for an interview and an interview is what you shall have."

"Very well." I sat up a little straighter then handed him my resume across the desk. "I uploaded a copy with my application online, but I brought a hard copy in case it was needed."

I watched as he took the paper from me and scanned over it before tossing it in the trash can beside his desk.

"You went to a lot of trouble for a waitress position, but I don't need to read your resume to know that you are more than qualified for the opportunity I am about to offer you." He interlaced his fingers as he regarded me, a crooked smile on his face. "It is quite an important position and one that requires someone with your... skillset. Would you care to hear more about it?"

"I came here to interview for the waitress position."

"It would not be a good fit for you. Besides, the club has plenty of waitresses. Do you truly think that serving drinks would be reaching your full...potential." A faint light twinkled in the depths of his eyes as he stared at me from behind the desk. "You are the type of woman who could have so much more. And I am the type of man that can offer it to you. It just so happens that I am looking for someone to fill a different role. It will require 100% devotion to the job. There could be travel involved as well as long hours. But it does include housing, a clothing allowance, as well as a substantial salary. If you think you would be interested and can meet these requirements, we will discuss it further."

My eyes narrowed wondering what those requirements would be. "What exactly is this opportunity you are offering?"

"I won't lie to you. It is a very demanding position and will require you to be at my disposal 24 hours a day, 7 days a week. As I mentioned before, I travel for business from time to time, and you may be asked to accompany me if I deem it necessary. You will be asked to attend charity or business functions with me. But you must know and understand upfront that I can be very difficult at times. That fact I will not try to hide from you. I require someone that will be devoted solely to me and only me. So, if you have a boyfriend or someone that would require your attention, you should think seriously about it because I am not the type of man that will share."

I narrowed my eyes slightly as he laid out his proposal. "That doesn't exactly sound like a position for which I am qualified. I think you have the wrong girl. I came here to interview for a waitress position, not to be a paid escort."

He leaned forward. "You didn't let me finish, but if you feel that is the case, you may leave now. But before you go..." He handed me a folded piece of paper. "This is the weekly salary I will pay you and of course, there will be bonuses. It does not include your housing, clothing, travel, and any miscellaneous purchases. Those will be paid for you and will not be taken from your salary."

I took the paper from him, my curiosity getting the better of me. When I saw the numbers written out in ink before me, I felt a little dizzy. This would not only solve all my problems but also allow me to put some money aside for the future. I would no longer be living check-to-check, nor would I have to worry about finding a way to keep the lights on or food in the fridge.

"Interested?"

I looked up from where I had been staring at the numbers swimming before my eyes. "I'm still here." *Regardless of the warning bells going off in my head.*

"The offer will not be on the table long. I'm afraid I am an impatient man and will require your answer today. If you decide to accept my proposal, you can start right now. I need someone bright enough to learn what I like and anticipate those needs. Someone that I desire to spend time with. I will also expect you to be friendly and congenial to the clients I entertain."

I raised my eyes to find him watching me. "Friendly? How friendly? If you mean I should fall into bed with them, then we can stop right now."

I watched his eyes darken, and I could almost feel the fury radiating from him.

"No one will touch you. I can promise you that. I'm not trying to pimp you out, Bri. I am offering you an opportunity that most women would kill for, one with lots of possibilities."

"You are offering me a position as a highly paid escort. Prostitution is a nasty word, but the meaning is the same unless you are including yourself in that promise not to touch me. I highly doubt you would offer me the salary written on that paper if this was to be a purely platonic arrangement?"

He stood from his seat and walked back to stand in front of me. "First of all, I have more than enough money to pay you whatever I wish. Secondly, I will not make you a promise I have no intention of keeping. After having already touched you... kissed you...tasted you...I will not deny myself the privilege to do so again. I have thought of little else since last night. But I can promise that I will never do anything you do not...desire." He reached out and placed a finger under my chin to lift my face higher. "I can see the yearning in your eyes even now, Angel."

The man must have some sort of enchanting or sorcerer-like qualities, because I found myself wanting to give in, wanting to do whatever he asked of me. It was like being under a spell. *What the fuck was wrong with me?*

"Before you accept the offer, you need to know that I am indeed the asshole you believe me to be. I am also possessive, dangerous, and a little bit of a monster. If you accept, I will touch you whenever I wish and eventually you will be in my bed, because since you walked through the door, I have had trouble thinking of anything else. The only thing I will guarantee is that it will be consensual and extremely pleasurable."

The last word dripped off his tongue, and I had to clamp my thighs tighter together. I knew this was something I would regret later, but the money was just too tempting. I could at least give it a try. What did I have to lose?

"I will need time to think before I accept the offer."

"I already told you that I am not a patient man. I will require your answer now. If you do not wish to accept, you will be allowed to leave. I will have my driver take you back to your apartment. If you do accept, your new life will start immediately."

Was I considering this? And if I did accept his proposition, what's the worst that could happen? I could always back out later if my senses returned, and this job wasn't the only thing keeping me from being thrown out of my apartment. My rent was due in a week, and I didn't have the money to cover it.

"Fine, I will accept the offer but just so we are clear. I will be your companion, the girl on your arm at charity or business functions, but I will not grace your bed, no matter how confident you seem to be."

He smiled with satisfaction, and I couldn't help but wonder if I had walked into some kind of trap. The offer was too good to be true and how often did those kinds of things work out? He held out his hand to me and he helped me to my feet.

"I admire your confidence, Bri, but you may be surprised at how far I will go to get my way. It will give me such gratification to prove you wrong. But we can discuss your resistance later. Now that we have reached an agreement, in a few minutes Brenda will give you a brief tour of the club; we will spend a great deal of time here. After I have finished up a few details and you have finished your tour, we will go shopping to get you something to wear tonight. I will be conducting business here at the club, and you will be required to join me upstairs in my private suite." He dared to wink at me. "I'm sure you will remember the way there."

He pressed a button on the desk and the lady that had escorted me inside walked back into the room.

"Brenda, Miss Rogers has accepted my proposal. Do you have the contract for her to sign?"

"I do, Mr. Delaney."

I turned quickly at his words. "A contract? Why does there have to be a contract?"

"I always protect my investments. Let's say that you have it in your pretty little head to accept my offer and then after a week or two you decide to bail. This protects me from that possibility."

Brenda walked farther into the room, placed a thick packet of papers on the desk, and handed me a pen. I looked over the first page and flipped through it, even though something in my brain told me I should read every line carefully; it was a bit unnerving doing so with two sets of eyes peering down at me. I flipped to the last page and signed. As soon as I set the pen on the desk, Brenda took out her notary stamp and made it official.

"Excellent, if you go with Brenda, she will give you a quick tour then you can wait for me by the bar. I will finish things up here and we can go purchase you some acceptable clothing."

I turned and looked back over my shoulder before following the older lady from the room. He had a smug smirk on his face that made me think that this job might be more than I expected. Despite everything, the job was a godsend that couldn't have come at a better time, so I would accept the challenge regardless of the burning feeling I had inside that said my new boss had more planned for me than I expected.

Rogue

I was honestly surprised that she so readily accepted my offer. She must be more desperate for money than I first thought. I would have Blaze investigate her circumstances more thoroughly, but for now, I was eager to take her from the club to some of the boutiques and exclusive designer shops around Chicago and see her outfitted in

clothing that would accentuate her glorious figure. The modest jeans
and oversized blazer she had worn to the interview hid her perfection
from me. I longed to see her in clothes made just for her, something
that would showcase her luscious long legs and tight little ass.

The door to my office opened, and I knew that the only soul
brave and daring enough to enter without announcing himself or
knocking was Blaze.

"What are you doing here this early? The waitresses will not arrive
for a few more hours yet."

He lifted his eyebrows as he took a step closer. "I'm not here to
appease my appetites; I'm just curious about yours. Did your newest
obsession take the job that you offered her? I saw her sitting at the bar
when I came in. She was looking rather...regretful."

I wanted to tell him to fuck off and keep his hands to himself
when it came to her, but if I demanded he leave her alone that would
be an open invitation for him to do whatever he could to piss me off
and get under my skin.

"She accepted the position without much hesitation, I might
add."

His brow furrowed. "You plan on having her on the floor serving
drinks?"

I knew he would find out soon enough, but the desire I had to
keep everything about Brielle to myself was strong. I didn't want him
interfering in the plans I had for her, and I damn sure didn't want
him anywhere near her.

"No, I have something much different in mind for my lost little
angel."

His eyes widened and a smirk formed on his lips. "Hmm, I have
something that keeps popping up in my mind for her as well. Tell me
your fantasy and I'll tell you mine, that is if you plan on sharing."

I slammed my fist down hard on my desk. "Don't! Don't speak of
her as if she is about to be another one of your conquests. I have
already told you that she is off-limits. Leave her alone."

The expression on his face never changed with my outburst, but I
knew he understood.

"You should take your own advice. She isn't the kind of girl that can survive in a place like this. It will swallow her, corrupt her, and then you will lose interest."

I changed the subject. Blaze giving me advice on women was new, and it was beginning to irk me. I didn't even want him to mention her name again. "What did you learn from Nickolai?"

He stepped farther into the room, his massive frame taking a seat in the chair by the bar.

"It wasn't shocking that he already knew about the man in town claiming ties to the Bratva and has some news that you will find interesting. He and a few of his men will be joining us tonight, here."

My frown deepened.

"What a great on-the-job training opportunity for your new... what are we calling her...your new personal attendant? It will be interesting to see what Nickolai thinks of your new little toy. Or do you plan on locking her away solely for your pleasure?"

I narrowed my eyes as he smirked at me from across the room. "The only thing that anyone needs to know is that she is mine. I am claiming her, and I will fiercely protect what belongs to me. Feel free to communicate that ahead of time to anyone who needs a reminder of how selfish and brutal I can be when provoked."

He shook his head as an annoying grin spread across his face. "No, I don't believe I will. Things have been too quiet lately. We could use the entertainment. A little competition between you and Nik for the girl might be exciting to watch."

My frown deepened as I stared at my friend. He knew exactly what to say to get under my skin, but there was no one I trusted more with my life. Blaze was borderline psychotic, a natural-born killer. He took pride in bringing the most pain imaginable to anyone that crossed him. He enjoyed the hunt and didn't mind getting his hands bloody. His enemies feared him and rightly so. But he was loyal, and when some serious shit hit the fan, I was happy to have him on my side.

"Just make certain you remember to be here on time tonight and keep your hands off the waitresses."

"If I were you, it wouldn't be the waitresses I was worried about."
He grumbled something else under his breath and slammed the door
on his way out. But I didn't have the time nor the inclination to be
pulled into a dick measuring contest with Blaze. I had more important things to do, and first on my list was to go find what he had
rightly called my newest obsession.

Bri

After I left Mr. Delaney's office, Brenda gave me a quick tour of the
club, showing me the upper rooms and the private room used only by
Mr. Delaney. I couldn't stop the blush that formed on my cheeks as I
looked around the owner's private suite in the light of day. Of course,
it was the same one that he had taken me to last night. The same one
where he had kissed me, touched me, made me feel things I had never
felt before. Just the thought of his touch made me smolder, as if I
were standing too close to a flame.

After her tour, I went to the bar where I could quietly wait and
contemplate the terrible life choices I had made lately. Sure, the
money was good; no, it was great, but I couldn't stop the nagging
feeling that this was something I would come to regret. I was getting
the impression that there was quite a bit more to Rogue Delaney than
one would see at first glance and that instead of agreeing to be his
employee, I should run...run far and fast.

I nervously drummed my fingers along the bar. Perhaps I made a
mistake. I had never done anything like this before, and the more I sat
and thought about it, the more ridiculous it sounded. I had basically
signed a contract as a paid escort. And while he had honestly stated
that he wanted me in his bed, he did say it would be consensual, so he
wouldn't force me. Could I believe that? It could be something he
says to every girl he has offered this opportunity. For all I knew, he
could be a serial killer, and this was how he got his jollies. But if that
was the case, why make me sign a contract, why introduce me to

Brenda and give me a tour of the club? And the money...I would make more in a week than I would make in a month working anywhere else. I rolled my eyes to the ceiling and huffed out a ragged breath. How did I come to this point where I would try to rationalize accepting such an offer? *I knew the reason why; I just didn't want to admit it.*

"Are you ready?"

I jumped at the sound of his deep, sensual voice behind me. "I wasn't sure if you would take me or if you had people to do these sorts of things for you. Forgive me for not knowing how an arrangement like this works. Don't you have other things to do, more important things than shopping for my wardrobe?"

He placed a hand at the small of my back, forcing me to repress a shiver, and guided me toward the club's exit.

"I trust very few people when it comes to things that I deem important. Besides, who better to know what I like than myself."

Well, I couldn't deny that logic. I did accept a job where the only requirement was to please him. Even as the thought raced through my head, my body warmed, and I slowly released the breath I had been holding.

We walked outside and headed toward a new blacked-out Jaquar where a driver was waiting for us. He opened the door and Mr. Delaney held out his hand to assist me into the back seat. After closing the door, he gave the driver instructions then walked around and climbed in on the other side.

"I have already made arrangements for you at a few exclusive boutiques and shops downtown. This certainly will not be the extent of your wardrobe needs, but it will give us a nice start."

His eyes roved over the outfit I was wearing, and my cheeks flushed before the reality of what he said had time to sink in. I turned sharply back to him. "You had already made arrangements? How did you know I would accept?"

He turned his head to the side quizzically as if he couldn't contemplate anyone doing anything except what he wanted. It was obvious that this man was not told "no" often.

"Let's just say I had a hunch."

I turned my head away from his magnetic smile and looked out the window as the city went past. When the car came to a stop outside a small but exclusive boutique with only the letter J on the door, he took my hand and brought it to his lips. A shiver crept up my spine.

"There is no limit to what you may purchase. I will also select a few things for you to try on, but feel free to pick out what you would like."

This was starting to feel very much like a *Pretty Woman* scenario, except he looked much more dangerous than Richard Gere.

"I can't help thinking that I am going to regret this, and I should just have you take me back to my apartment. Is there anyone else, anyone who would be a better fit for you? I mean, I'm just a girl from a small town in Colorado. I'm not one of those high-class fashion models or glamorous ladies who frequent your club. I'm not the kind of woman you are used to being around."

He leaned a bit closer and the air around me crackled with intensity.

"That is one of the reasons I want you. You worry too much, Angel, and in case you still aren't convinced, I think you will fit me perfectly...or rather I will fit inside you perfectly."

I rolled my eyes at his comment. *Did he really just say that out loud?*

His fingers brushed against my elbow and an involuntary tremor moved over me. I thought he was about to kiss me again, a ridiculous thought. Wasn't this guy one of the richest men in the city? He probably had a plethora of women on standby ready for his call to fulfill any wish he desired. I felt my temperature rising at the thought of his cravings, his yearnings. While he might be handsome as sin and look like a guy from the pages of a magazine, he was not the kind of man who was interested in girls like me, at least not seriously. This entire arrangement was outrageous and if my instincts were right, perilous. But desperate times called for desperate measures, right?

The car door was opened by his driver, and he nodded his head.

"Go on inside. They are waiting for you. I have a few calls to make before I can join you."

I stepped out of the car onto the sidewalk and his driver escorted me inside the shop where a lady with a bright eager smile was waiting for me by the door.

"Miss Rogers, we are so pleased to have you as a patron of our boutique. We offer the finest fashion in Chicago. If you will follow me, I have a fitting room prepared for you with some dresses and other items already selected for you to peruse."

My lips turned up into a slight smile, her cheeriness rather contagious, but when I looked around the shop, I was surprised to find it empty. "I guess this is not your busiest time of day."

She turned around and the look she gave me was puzzling. "We are rather busy all the time. We are the finest boutique in the city. Today, however, Mr. Delaney reserved the entire shop just for you. He didn't want you to have to wait for anything."

He reserved the entire shop. What kind of man was he?

I followed her into a large room where several dresses and other things were displayed for my perusal. There were evening gowns, cocktail dresses, shoes, and casual clothes, along with intimates such as panties, bras, and silk pajamas.

"Mr. Delaney will not be purchasing my underwear." I half laughed when I said it, but her eyes narrowed slightly.

"Mr. Delaney gave us strict instructions as to what he required."

I pushed aside the irritation I felt at this man that I barely knew presuming that I would allow him to purchase panties and lingerie for me, but how could I seriously be upset over that when I had agreed to his outrageous proposal? It was rather silly I suppose to quibble about undergarments at this point. If I wanted to adjust the terms of our agreement, I could do so later. It wasn't her fault I had foolishly gotten myself into this situation, and I was not the type of person to take out my frustrations on someone who was completely innocent and was only doing what she was told. It was her job and she probably worked on commission, so I'm sure she was hoping we would buy everything in sight.

I spent the first hour trying on formal and cocktail dresses. Then moved on to more casual clothes. There were so many things that I loved, but I only picked out a few of each style.

I never thought it possible to get tired of shopping, but when Gwen brought in one more cocktail dress, I sighed heavily and sank into a chair. "I truly do have everything I need Gwen."

"Mr. Delaney requests that you try this on."

It was a short silky black-beaded cocktail dress with a low back and spaghetti straps. I ran my fingers over it and then looked at the price tag. This one dress was more than what I used to make in two months. I took off my bra and slipped it over my head then zipped it up.

"Well, what do you think, Gwen?"

"I think it is perfect. I think you are perfect."

My body froze when I heard his deep husky voice behind me.

I should remind him that being in my dressing room was not part of the arrangement. No matter what he had in his mind, I would not be his plaything. But when he stepped closer, wrapping his arms around my waist and pulling me back into him, every protest I had formed in my head vanished.

He moved my hair to the side and my eyes closed as his fingers glided along my spine from the nape of my neck to the base of my ass.

"Your skin is so soft, sweetheart."

He pressed his lips against the skin right below my ear, and I leaned my head to the side giving him better access. The arm he had wrapped around my waist tightened as he pressed against me.

"I want you to wear this tonight."

He feathered kisses down my neck, and I felt my knees growing weaker. "Don't kiss me."

He quickly spun me around and pinned my body against the wall. I felt his hard dick pressed into my belly, and it took all my strength not to rub myself against him. *Damn, this man was sin personified.*

He gripped my chin and forced me to look up at him. "Oh, my

sweet lost angel, kissing is only the beginning of what I have planned for you."

His lips claimed mine in a possessive kiss that lifted me on my toes. I shouldn't want him, and I should be appalled that I was, once again, allowing this man to reduce me to a puddle whenever he touched me.

If this arrangement was going to work, I needed to get control of myself and let him know in no uncertain terms that I would not permit him to use me.

I pushed against his chest, and he released me. "I know I signed a contract, but I am not going to allow you to take advantage of me. This is strictly a business relationship, and if you continue to kiss me, I can't continue to do this."

He raised his hands in the air in defeat and stepped back. "Hmm, I'm impressed. Your will is stronger than I thought it would be. But it's too late to back out now. Know this, Angel, your resistance only makes me want you more. I will tear down any walls you build to keep me away. I never lose and I have never not gotten what I truly wanted." He stepped back and looked me over from head to toe. "There are a few other places Steven will take you to and then return you to the club. Wear this dress tonight, we will be entertaining business associates."

"Mr. Delaney."

He arched his eyebrows. "I would like to discuss something else with you." I pointed to the assortment of lingerie on the table. "I don't think you should be purchasing things like this for me."

He shrugged his shoulders. "To be honest, I prefer you not to wear them at all. That dress, with no panties, hmm." His eyes darkened with desire. "That would please me and isn't that the whole point of this position? So, if wearing nothing at all underneath your dresses makes you happy, by all means, go right ahead, Bri. It will just save me time."

I narrowed my eyes at the comment and put my hands on my hips, but before I could respond, his eyes turned serious, and he gave me a look that made my blood turn cold.

His hand came up and gripped my chin firmly forcing me to look up at him. "Don't think of running away, Bri. I meant what I said. There is no backing out or escape now. I will expect you at the club by ten. Steven will drive you, and if there is anything you need, let him know. Anything else you purchase will be on my accounts. Do you have any questions?"

I shook my head too stunned to think.

"Very well, have fun spending my money, and I will see you later at *Sinners*."

He stepped out of the dressing room, leaving me alone again, and I couldn't help but think that I might have made the biggest mistake of my life, and if my fears turned out to be true, I had no idea what would happen next.

CHAPTER
three

ROGUE

I looked down at my watch for the third time, wondering if Bri would defy me right away by being late or if she was foolish enough not to come at all. Having second thoughts about what I had offered her this morning was foreseeable. She was nervous, afraid, unsure of what she had agreed to, and her fear roused something in me. It excited me more than anything I had experienced in a long time.

Steven had kept me informed throughout the rest of her day and had sent me a text as soon as the car pulled up in front of the club, but Bri had yet to appear. I watched for her, eagerly waiting to see her transformation. Thoughts of her had distracted me most of the day. I had imagined her wearing the new designer clothes I had purchased for her and me taking them off later when I had her all to myself. An image of her lying naked on my bed popped into my head, and I narrowed my eyes as I continued to watch the door for her to make an appearance.

Blaze was entertaining my guests upstairs in my private suite, and I was anxious to join them. I took out my phone to call Steven to see what the hell was keeping her when I finally caught a glimpse of my sweet little obsession as she moved through the crowd. The mass of people parted for her and rightly so. She was stunning. The dress I had selected for her to wear tonight hugged the curves of her body and showcased her extra-long firm legs. Her hair was styled in long chocolate-colored locks down her back. She was every man's vision. A fantasy that could easily drive a man to madness.

As she walked through the crowd toward me, a guy stepped in front of her blocking her path. I watched as she glanced at me over his shoulder and then gave him a small smile. The monster inside me roared and a fierce possessiveness surged through me. My hands clenched into fists, but I maintained my control until she made to move around him until he made the dangerous mistake of reaching out and grabbing her wrist to keep her from moving past him. That I would not tolerate. Nobody touched her, nobody was allowed to put their hands on what belonged to me.

I stepped forward quickly, gripping his hand and yanking it away from her. "Do not touch her again, and if you value your life, you will get the fuck out of my club."

For a minute, I thought he would disregard my warning. I leveled my gaze and let my eyes communicate what would happen if he didn't decide to back off. He must have sensed the danger and his courage quickly melted away. He held up his hands and backed away. I nodded toward one of the club bouncers who would make certain that he left the premises and was not allowed admittance again. I did not have a forgiving nature and touching my angel was unpardonable.

I turned to see her standing just a few feet away, her arms crossed over her chest and a disapproving look on her face. "That was uncalled for. I could have dealt with him myself, and you really should stop acting as if I belong to you, I only work for you...whatever this arrangement is between us, it is strictly professional. I don't need you following me around wreaking vengeance on anyone that talks to me."

This was not the time or the place to discuss the fact that, yes, she did indeed belong to me; she signed a fucking contract to that effect. She had just not accepted it yet.

"Wreaking vengeance is kind of my thing, Angel, and he didn't just talk to you, he grabbed your wrist and tried to prevent you from walking past, and you are late."

Her look of censure immediately turned contrite. She shifted from one foot to another. "It wasn't Steven's fault, so don't do anything like fire him or something. I was waiting out in the line too nervous to come inside. I still don't think this is right for me. You haven't told me what I am supposed to do, other than being the girl on your arm for the night, and the only job training I have received so far is learning how to swipe your credit card."

I stepped closer to her, close enough that I could smell her perfume. God, I needed this meeting to be over with so I could have her all to myself. "You are worrying again, Angel. And what's this about you waiting in line? Darling, you don't wait in line...anywhere. You don't wait for anything. Not anymore. Come with me."

I took her hand, interlaced my fingers with hers, and walked toward the stairs as I sent piercing glares to anyone stupid enough to look in her direction.

We took the stairs toward my private suite. When we entered, I watched as every eye in the room feasted on her. The hungry looks and grins from the other men caused me to feel very protective. I had an almost overpowering urge to claim her before them all, to mark my territory, to brand her. It was unsettling. I was still holding her hand, so I raised it to my lips to press a kiss to it before releasing her.

I walked purposefully toward the table where Blaze was already sitting with Nickolai, and I motioned for Bri to have a seat on the other side of the room while I conducted business and got some answers from the Bratva leader. I wasn't sure she was prepared to know the types of businesses I was involved in or the dealings I had with the Russian mafia.

"Blaze said you had some information for me. Tell me what you know about the man in town. He claims to be Russian, but we both know that can't be true. Why would he be here drawing attention to himself and causing trouble in my city?"

Nickolai Volkov glanced at Bri before turning his icy blue stare to me from across the table. We have been friends and business associates for many years now; however, he still regarded me with caution. It was the way of the Bratva and as the leader of the Volkov Bratva, he had to always be on alert. He was flanked by two of his men while another three were in the room standing along the glass windows where they could watch and vigilantly monitor the activity in the club. I'm certain there were more downstairs, mixing in with the crowd.

Blaze sat beside me and watched all of them carefully. That was the thing with Blaze, he never fully trusted anyone.

Nickolai raised an eyebrow at my request. "The man you speak of is not associated with any family that I am aware of. He most likely isn't even Russian. Possibly just someone foolish enough to run his mouth hoping people will think he has powerful connections." He shrugged his shoulders. "But using the Bratva name, especially when you aren't Bratva, to intimidate people is signing your death warrant. If it continues, we will handle it."

"The man is in my city, making trouble in my territory, since he is not Bratva, I will handle it myself."

Nickolai's lips turned up just a fraction on one side of his mouth. "If I allow you to handle it, things might get messy." He looked pointedly at Blaze. "Especially, if our bloodthirsty friend here has anything to do with it. But as long as whatever you do doesn't interfere in my affairs, I will allow it."

My eyes narrowed. "Allow it? Have you forgotten who runs this city?"

His smile widened. "Don't let my choice of words annoy you. I realize Chicago is your territory. But don't be mistaken about how powerful and far-reaching the Bratva can be, my friend. To do so could be deadly." He then broke eye contact with me and looked around the room. "Business looks to be good. It seems as if the club has become more than profitable. But I shouldn't be especially surprised since you are partnered with Alessio Messina. Anything the man touches turns a profit."

The grin that formed on my lips was not one of mirth. "You underestimate me, Nik. You know everything I touch turns into a fucking gold mine. Don't believe for a minute that I required

Alessio's assistance to turn a profit. Besides, I didn't know our partnership was public knowledge."

"Public, no, but I do try to keep an eye on my competition."

I leaned forward, keeping my voice low and controlled. "Are we in competition, Nickolai?"

"We are all in competition, my friend. Luckily, our competition has been affable so far, and if you stay out of Las Vegas, it will remain so."

I watched as his eyes shifted back toward where Bri was sitting looking like every man's dream. The dress she was wearing had risen higher up her thigh as she crossed her legs. Her legs had a silky sheen to them that made me want to run my hands from her ankles to the juncture of her thighs. I had been around many women in my lifetime, but none of them looked like her. And none of them made me feel hot burning jealousy when I saw the eyes of the other men in the room rake over her body. I frowned when I noticed one of Nic's men watching her appreciatively, his eyes lingering on certain parts of her body.

She stood and walked toward me, her hips swaying pertly from side to side, and a nervous smile played on her lips. "Is there anything I can get for you? Something to drink perhaps?"

I looked at the bottle that was already sitting on the table and picked it up to pour myself a glass. She shouldn't be here, and I didn't like the way Nickolai was watching her. I opened my mouth and was about to tell her to go back downstairs and wait in my office, but the Russian Bratva leader spoke up before I had the chance.

"You are new here. I haven't seen you before, ptichka"

Bri turned to face him, and her smile brightened. "Today is my first day." She glanced back to me and then hastily replied, "I'll go mingle."

She walked away toward the other men standing along the wall and my eyes followed every movement.

"I'll make you a deal."

My eyes moved back to Nickolai, curious as to what deal he was about to offer.

"Give me the girl, and I'll handle your problem with the masquerading Russian for you. You won't even have to hear about it. I'll make it quick and neat; there won't even be a body, nothing to link it back to you."

My eyes narrowed as I leaned a bit closer, keeping my voice low. "The girl isn't for sale, Nickolai. I don't operate like that. And I don't need your help getting rid of my problem. I am more than capable of handling an errant Russian on my own without the help of the Bratva."

Nickolai grinned as his eyes darted back to where Bri was standing beside one of his men. "Have you claimed her then?"

"She is off-limits."

I heard one of his men speaking in Russian and while my knowledge of the language was limited, I did understand the meaning behind the words he uttered. I drank the remainder of the whiskey, then slammed the glass down hard on the table.

"Let it go, Rogue," Blaze murmured as he sat beside me.

I heard the words Blaze uttered as I pushed myself from my seat, but I had seen and heard enough. I stormed over to where Bri had moved to the other side of the room. I heard her politely ask the men surrounding her if this was their first time in Chicago, but she did not get a chance to hear their reply.

When I reached her, I bent lower and swept her up, tossing her over my shoulder. She shrieked as I began carrying her from the room. I was done having her body, a body meant only for me, on display for other men to see, and I was not going to have her subjected to Nickolai's men's comments and leering stares. If I had to make a statement so everyone in the whole fucking world knew that she belonged to me, so be it.

I carried her down the stairs toward my office, ignoring the people we passed along the way. Thankfully, she didn't draw any more attention than was necessary by yelling or screaming, but from the tension I felt in her body, I was certain she would have plenty to say once I got her back into my office.

Once I had her behind closed doors, I leaned forward and let her slide from my shoulder back to her feet. The shock on her face was evident and the firm set of her jaw and the flashing of her eyes let me know she was more than a little angry.

"What the hell are you doing?"

Her question was asked in a low, calm voice, but her clenched fists hanging by her side as she waited for my answer showed she was anything but calm.

"I am removing you from the situation. I never should have let Nickolai see you."

She narrowed her eyes confused with my statement. "You were the one that brought me upstairs, and since I was hired to be your... companion or whatever I'm supposed to be, I thought I was doing what you would want. You did tell me that part of my job was to be congenial to the people you are doing business with, not to just sit in a corner while you do whatever it is that you do." She waved her hand in the air flippantly. "I don't understand why you felt the need to behave like some kind of caveman and carry me out of there. Do you plan on doing that anytime a man looks in my direction?"

"If men are foolish enough to look in your direction and I feel it is necessary, then yes."

She slapped her arms at her sides in exasperation. "You know what, I knew this was a mistake. I never should have come to this club or accepted your offer. I will go change or better yet, I will have the dress returned here in the morning, and I will go wait for a ride. There is no need for you to send me home in your car; the bartender offered to drive me home after the club closes, or I can just take a cab."

She turned to walk away from me, and I allowed it because I knew she wasn't going anywhere. Her hand reached for the doorknob, but the door wouldn't open. She turned the handle again and started pulling on the door before she turned back around to face me.

"Unlock the door."

I leaned back against the edge of my desk and waited for her reaction.

"We aren't finished yet, Angel. Would you like a drink?"

She put her hands on her hips and looked so magnificent in her fury.

"No, I don't want a drink. I want you to unlock the door."

"Are you certain? Whiskey can be quite calming."

She moved away from the door to stand before me and took a deep breath. "Mr. Delaney, I am trying to be calm, but the way you have behaved tonight, and the fact that you will not allow me to leave is quite disturbing. There is nothing you can say that will make me stay."

Since there wasn't anything I could say, that would convince her, perhaps more intimate methods would be more persuasive. I wanted her to let go of her anger and accept everything I was offering. I was about to reach for her when shots fired outside the club got my attention.

"Was that...?"

I shoved my hands into my pants pockets and studied her reaction.

"Gunshots? Yes."

"And you are not concerned?"

I leaned back against the desk. "Of course I am concerned. Gunshots are always taken seriously."

The way her expression changed from fear to disbelief and then to irritation was almost comical.

"There are gunshots outside your club, and you aren't going to investigate?"

I shrugged my shoulders. "Is that what you want me to do?"

She put her hands of her hips. "It does seem like an appropriate action to take."

"Very well, stay here."

Before I could reach the door, Blaze pushed it open, the deep frown on his face was indicative of the seriousness of the situation.

"Someone took shots at Nickolai as he was leaving the club. One of his guards was injured, and Nickolai is understandably pissed."

"The shooter?"

"Dead, but there was another one that got away." He looked over my shoulder to where Bri was standing. "She needs to leave."

I turned around and frowned at the way her complexion had paled. "Sit down, Angel, before you fall."

I watched as she sank into the chair near my desk and then turned back to Blaze. "She stays. No arguments about it. Do you know anything about the shooter?"

Blaze's eyes narrowed as his gaze moved from her back to me. "He wasn't wearing a t-shirt advertising who was working for, but perhaps Nik will know something."

"The body?"

His lips lifted on one corner. "The Bratva has already taken care of it."

I nodded. "Make the necessary calls so that the police don't show up here. I don't want any unnecessary attention here at the club. Offer a free round of drinks on the house. Let's keep it business as usual."

"I will see that it's done, but you need to do something with her."

I looked back over my shoulder to where Bri was intensely listening to our conversation, the fear evident on her face. "I will take care of it, and then I will call Nik. Something doesn't feel right. He rarely leaves Las Vegas, so who would even know that he is in town?"

"For someone to make a move against the Bratva, it is always serious and I'm certain Nik has many enemies. He has never been a fucking Boy Scout."

He turned and walked out of the room, leaving me alone with Bri. I walked past her to my desk, opened a drawer, took out a bottle of whiskey, and poured a small amount into a glass before walking over and handing it to her.

"Here drink this."

She shook her head. "I'm not sure what is happening, but I am more convinced than ever that I made a mistake by coming here. Will you take me home now?"

"There are things I need to take care of first and when I get back, we can continue our discussion."

She jumped to her feet. "There is no discussion. I don't want to be a part of this. Take. Me. Home."

I pushed her back into the seat and leaned down close to her face. "You are already a part of this."

Her lips clamped together as she stared up at me.

"Now is not the time to be brave, Angel. Don't try and defy me. There will be time to talk about your future once I have made certain it is safe for us to leave. Now sit down and stay quiet."

Bri

I waited a total of five seconds after he left before I jumped from my seat and looked around the room for another way out. How could I have been so stupid to get involved with a man like Rogue Delaney? A man was just killed outside his club, and he behaved as if it were just an ordinary day. Now I understood why his club was aptly named *Sinners*. I moved over to the desk and looked for anything that might help me escape. I rummaged through the drawers, not caring if I made a mess, but I didn't find anything other than another bottle of whiskey and two glasses along with your typical office supplies, pens, notepads, etc. none of which looked as if they had ever been used. It was as if this wasn't a real working office, just a room made to look like one, like a movie set.

I started pacing the room, my brain conjuring up all sorts of horrible things that could happen once he returned. My heart began to beat faster. I still had my cell phone, and I contemplated calling Allison and asking her to come help me, but that would more than likely just get her into trouble, and I couldn't keep relying on someone else to rescue me. I had to find a way out of this mess myself.

Surely, he wasn't going to kill me. What if he planned on selling me? Young women went missing all the time and were never found. The thought made me a bit nauseous. No, if he was going to kill me, he would just do it or have one of his goons do it for him.

Whatever he had planned, I didn't come this far escaping a deranged stalker in Colorado just for this guy to attempt to hold me hostage or to get killed by getting mixed up in some kind of war between criminals. There had to be a way out of this, and to find it, I had to be smart. I took a few deep calming breaths and slowly moved about the room, taking in as much of it as I could. The room itself was very sparse. A desk containing nothing significant, with a black chair behind it, and two black leather chairs in front. A small bar on one side of the room, but nothing else of importance. No pictures of him, no pictures of anyone or anything. The walls were bare, and the room was well-lit.

After realizing that I would find nothing here that would help me get out of this situation, I sank back down into the seat and covered my face with my hands, knowing there was nothing I could do but wait. Wait to see what this arrogant devil of a man had in store for me. But he couldn't watch me 24/7. There would be an opportunity to escape, and once I found it, I would not hesitate to take it.

Rogue

After leaving Bri in my office, I went back upstairs to find that most of the patrons in the club had no idea what had gone on outside. My employees had done a good job of offering distractions, so no one became aware of the attempted assassination or shooting that occurred just a few feet from where they were all drinking, dancing, and performing more intimate acts. Blaze was standing by the stairs, his phone in his hand and a glass of bourbon close by.

I walked toward him and took a seat at a table nearby. "Any news from Nickolai?"

Blaze turned the glass up and finished off the contents before pouring another. "He said that he would be seeing you soon. I imagine that after your little possessive display with the girl, he thought you might be otherwise occupied for some time, and he obviously had other things to do." He took a sip of bourbon. "If you aren't going to send her on her way, you need to think of ways to protect her. It would be very easy for someone like her to be hurt, caught up in a world she knows nothing about. What is she to you? Is she just another employee, a fling you have taken interest in, or is it more?"

I poured my drink and leaned back in the chair. "For now, she belongs with me; I am claiming her. That is all anyone needs to know."

"And is she accepting?"

I smirked as I drained the glass of liquor, letting it burn my throat. "Since I had to lock her in my office to return here, I would say no."

Blaze closed his eyes and leaned his head back against the cushion of the chair. "Hmm, taking advice on women from Alessio?"

"Alessio blackmailed and married his beautiful Cara Mia. He was concerned with cementing his legacy and protecting the Messina family from Benedict Russo. I just want to have her in my bed. She will be well compensated for the time she spends with me and once I have had my fill, I will let her go."

Blaze stood from his seat. "Hmm, we will see. I have never known you to stay interested in a woman for more than a night and with an assassin trying to take out the Bratva leadership, now might not be the best time to play around with the girl."

He spoke the truth. I had never had any kind of relationship that lasted longer than a one-night stand, but this woman was different. I had been instantly drawn to her, and after getting a small taste of her last night when she first wandered into the club, I knew I wanted more, much more, and I always got what I wanted. But Blaze was right, I needed to find a way to protect her for as long as she remained with me. How long that would be was still uncertain.

CHAPTER
four

BRI

When I heard the lock turn on the door, I jumped from the seat and moved to stand on the opposite side of the room. The slight bit of hope I had thinking it might be someone that could help me was dashed when Rogue Delaney strolled back into the room.

"I'm sorry the night didn't go as expected."

I couldn't believe how nonchalant he was acting. "Didn't go as expected? How can you be so calm? Your friend, who I suspect is a member of the Russian mob, was shot at, the would-be assassin was killed, and your grumpy friend is covering it up. I would say, didn't go as expected is a bit of an understatement."

His lips turned up slightly, but otherwise, he seemed completely unaffected by my words. He held out his hand. "Come, I'll take you home."

Thank God. He must have come to his senses. Perhaps his broody looking friend convinced him that my being here would only bring trouble. With caution, I moved across the room toward him, intentionally sidestepping his outreached hand. The deep growl that escaped him indicated his disapproval.

Once outside the office, he gripped my hand tightly, interlaced his fingers with mine, and began tugging me behind him as we moved through the crowd. It surprised me that even with the incident that had happened outside the club, everything was as it was before. People were dancing, the music was loud, and the noise of voices and laughter was buzzing around me. When we reached the waiting car outside the club, I looked around expecting to see police cars and a crime scene unit, but the only thing was a line of people waiting to get inside the most popular hedonistic club in Chicago. I felt Mr. Delaney's hand on my lower back as he urged me forward. He opened the door for me to get into the back seat then climbed in to sit beside me.

"This isn't necessary. I could have found my way home on my own, and I don't need an escort."

He tilted his head in my direction but made no effort to touch me. "I will determine what is necessary."

I scooted as far away from him as possible and looked out the window as the car moved through the busy city streets, but it didn't take me long to discover we were not headed in the direction of my small apartment.

"I thought you said that you were taking me home. Where are we going?"

He turned to look at me, his face serious, and his eyes seemed to pierce through me. "I am taking you home, just not your old apartment."

"What the hell? Where are you taking me?" The fury I had initially felt was soon replaced with fear. Had he grown so tired and bored with my petulance that he was planning something much more sinister? He had already proven that he was a dangerous man, and that violence was nothing new to him.

I switched tactics. "Just take me home and we can forget that we ever met. I will not tell anyone about what transpired at the club tonight. I won't call the cops, and we can pretend this day never happened. I promise. Or you can just stop the car and I will either walk or take the bus from here. Either way, you will not have to worry about me talking about you or what occurred tonight. You will never see me again."

He reached across the car and pulled me onto his lap. I thought about fighting him, but that may cause more harm than good. He turned my face toward him.

His brow furrowed as he studied me. "You are afraid, Angel. Your whole body is shivering."

I tried to turn away, but he held my chin firm.

"Do you think I could so easily forget meeting you, Bri? Do you believe that I could let you walk away, never to see you again? That you would be a passing thought, just another girl that wandered into my club?"

His warm lips moved to my bare shoulder, and I closed my eyes willing my traitorous body not to react. "What are you going to do to me?"

"I told you. I am taking you home, just not your home. After what happened tonight, I want to make certain you are safe, and the only way I can do that is to keep you close. Until I have more information about the incident that occurred outside the club, you will stay with me."

His arm wrapped around my waist. "But that is not what you are afraid of, is it, Angel?"

I held my tongue, refusing to answer.

"You can relax. I have plans but none of them include hurting you."

His fingers slipped lower as he traced circles on my thigh just below the hem of my dress. "But that assurance still doesn't ease your mind. There is something else that is worrying you."

I pushed his hand away. "The only thing that will ease my mind is being away from you and whatever crazy shit you have going on in your life. I am not your responsibility anymore. In case you have forgotten, I quit. I am no longer your employee. I know I signed a contract but after tonight I'm sure you aren't going to try and hold me to it. So, stop telling me to calm down and stop trying to make me accept this as normal. It isn't making me feel any better. I'm sorry if me being a bit freaked out over this displeases you. A man was killed tonight, and you and your friends are involved in things I don't even want to know about. I just don't understand why you won't let me go home." My hand flew up to cover my mouth. "Oh my God!! Are you holding me captive?"

My body shivered as a deep rumble vibrated from his chest.

"Hmmm, is that what you think I'm doing? Holding you as my sweet little hostage? Keeping you all to myself so you can play out my deepest, darkest fantasies. I must say, I like the sound of that."

I rolled my eyes not certain if he was serious or not. "Just take me home. I don't have time for this. I have too many responsibilities to play games. If I don't get a job soon, I will be evicted from my apartment, and I won't have anywhere else to go."

His eyes widened. "You no longer need to worry about trivial matters, love. I will be taking care of things for you from now on."

The man was exasperating. "Needing money for food and rent is not trivial for most people. Not everyone is wealthy. So, I can't accept your help. I don't want your help. You expect more from me than I am willing to give."

He shrugged his shoulders and smirked. "I did warn you that I was demanding and would expect your full attention."

He had me there. "That's exactly why I can't accept your help. I'll think of something. Needing money and running away from a dangerous man is not exactly new to me."

The tremor in my voice as well as my words must have tipped him off. He tilted his head to the side and his face turned serious. "Are you running from something, Angel? Has someone hurt you?"

I looked away quickly. "No, I just need the money. Like I said earlier, if you weren't listening, some of us in the real world find it difficult to pay our bills."

The car came to a stop outside a large skyscraper. "Where are we?"

"This is where you will be staying, at least until I deem it safe for you to be elsewhere."

The driver came around and opened the door for us. Mr. Delaney gave me a boost from his lap and then followed behind me.

"An office building?"

He chuckled. "There is a penthouse on the 21st floor. I hope you will find it adequate."

We walked through the glass doors into the building and two security guards at the front desk jumped to attention.

"Good evening, Mr. Delaney."

"Good evening, Craig, Brian."

We continued walking to the elevator, he took a card from inside his coat and swiped it. The elevator doors closed, and we began moving up to the 21st floor.

"Let me try to explain this to you again. Apparently, you are having difficulty understanding me. I have rent to pay. If I don't have a job, I will lose my apartment, and I can't just move without giving notice to my landlord. Besides, I have things at my apartment that I need. I wasn't thinking when I left for my interview this morning that I would not be returning. I don't have time for this."

"I will deal with your landlord and hire a moving company to pack your things. Any more concerns?"

I put my hands on my hips. "I need to tell my friends where I am. I don't want them to worry about me."

"The same friends from the club that allowed you to disappear with a man you didn't know? The friends that never bothered to look for you when you didn't return? If so, you don't need them."

I clenched my teeth tighter, hoping he would notice my frustration. "I have other friends."

The elevator stopped and the doors opened directly into the luxurious penthouse. He held his arm out for me to enter first. The only sound was the echo of my heels clicking across the marble floors. My eyes widened as I took in the expansive rooms before me. I shouldn't be surprised that a man like him would have access to such luxury, but after living in a small one-bedroom apartment that was just barely large enough for me and the few things I owned, this seemed like a mansion, and I suppose it was.

I stopped and watched as he walked farther into the room, his steps slowed as he removed the jacket he had been wearing and casually draped it across the back of the leather sofa. The interior and furnishings were reminiscent of his office. Everything was black or white, with dark color schemes, leather, sparkling crystal chandeliers, and cold expensive tile and marble.

"Shall I give you a tour?"

My feet felt heavy, but I managed to cross the room to where he was waiting for me.

"There is a large kitchen equipped with everything you could need, well...except food. If you make a list, I will have someone do the shopping for you."

I looked around at the extra-large professional kitchen with shiny stainless-steel appliances that appeared to have never been used. "I can do my own shopping."

"You won't have time for things like that. As I mentioned before, you no longer have to worry about trivial matters. I will take care of you."

He stepped closer and I got a whiff of his cologne and perhaps a touch of brandy.

"There is coffee here and the bakery down the street delivers. They do have the best cinnamon rolls in the city."

He gripped my elbow softly before letting his fingers slide down my arm to take my hand and then pulled me through to the dining room where a large table for eight dominated the space. A crystal chandelier hung above it with an ostentatious fresh flower arrangement as the centerpiece.

"Feel free to order any flowers you like. The florist in the building changes them out weekly. If you have a preference, simply let me know." He continued pulling me forward. "There are two bedrooms and two bathrooms."

We stepped into one of the bedrooms. There was a king-size bed along the wall with a thick white down comforter and at least a dozen pillows.

"This is to be your room. Through those doors is a large closet where you will find the purchases you made today. The bathroom is on the opposite side, and I feel you will find it more than adequate. I had it stocked with products and what I felt you may need, but of course, you need only make a list if there is anything else you wish for."

As I moved around the room, looking at the designer style closet and enormous bathroom, I wondered what he would call grand. The closet alone could be an extra bedroom and the bathroom looked like one of those you would see in a fantasy home show.

"My bedroom is across the hall." There was an underlying sensuality to his words that captivated me and caused me to feel a little warmer.

He didn't ask me to follow him, but I got the feeling it was expected. When we stepped into the master suite, I couldn't stop the sharp intake of breath. It was much larger and decidedly more masculine. The bed was along the side of the windows. There was a fireplace on the opposite wall. The bathroom had a huge whirlpool tub, and the shower was big enough and designed for more than one person. As I looked around, I started to get an uneasy feeling in my stomach.

"How long do you expect me to be here? I mean, the clothes I purchased today are already in the closet, which leads me to believe that you had every intention of moving me in before the incident tonight."

He removed his tie and threw it on the bed. "What better place for you to be than here with me? When you accepted the job I offered, I did tell you that I was demanding. But after the incident tonight. I feel it is the only way for me to make certain you are protected, and I'm not going to lie, having you at my disposal both day and night is a rather exhilarating prospect."

My eyes narrowed as I watched him begin to unbutton his shirt, the hint of a tattoo on his chest peeking through. I found it difficult to pull my eyes away. I finally broke free of the trance I had voluntarily slipped into and found my voice again.

"Like I said earlier, I quit. I don't want the job. Contract or no contract. And as far as you doing this as some kind gesture just to keep me safe, I don't believe you. And I don't need protection. I am not connected to you or your friends. I am a nobody. Someone who was simply in the wrong place at the wrong time. So, you can keep your money and your protection, I don't need it. And I am certainly not moving in with you. The farther away from you I can get, the better off I will be. You may have everyone else jumping through hoops to do your bidding, but I'm not going to be one of them. I am going back to my apartment."

I turned, half expecting him to physically stop me, and walked back to the elevator. Surprised when I didn't hear his footsteps coming behind me. Once the doors closed, I felt a sense of relief and finally let out the breath I was holding. The man was controlling and arrogant, but those coffee brown eyes and crooked smile still made me weak in the knees. I had to put some distance between us so that I could think clearly.

When the elevator stopped and the doors opened, I took a step out but was surprised to see the two security guards from earlier blocking my path. I tried to move around them, but they effectively stepped in my way, stopping me from going any farther.

"Miss Rogers, I'm afraid you can't leave."

I stepped forward and once again tried to get past them. "Get the hell out of my way! What do you mean I can't leave?"

"Mr. Delaney asks that you return upstairs."

"Mr. Delaney can fuck off, and so can you. I am going home, and you are going to get out of the way."

I tried to push through them, and one of the men grabbed my arm. He twisted it back in some sort of submission hold, causing me to cry out.

"Please, Miss Rogers, we don't want to hurt you."

I heard the clink of handcuffs and when the man holding me reached for my other arm, I started fighting harder. There was no way I would get away if they managed to get the cuffs on me.

My head jerked up at the sound of the elevator doors opening, and I hoped it would be someone who would intervene on my behalf, but disappointment made my heart sink when I saw who was walking toward me. His face, hard and severe, held no hint of the teasing tone he had taken with me earlier. He was pissed, and I shivered when his eyes raked over me and then back to the men holding me.

"Take your hands off of her now, or I will kill both of you."

He didn't yell, but there was a chill to his voice that was frightening. The two men who had managed to get the cuffs on me immediately released their hold and took a step backward.

"She wouldn't listen, Mr. Delaney. If we hadn't detained her, she would have left the building."

I stepped back into the elevator as my captor moved between me and the two security guards. His rage making the two men standing before him quake in their shoes.

"I told you to keep her from leaving the building. I never gave you permission to touch her. If you ever put a hand on her again, I'll kill you both. Do I make myself clear?"

"Yes, Mr. Delaney."

Their faces both paled, fear evident in their eyes. I should feel sorry for them, but I didn't. If they hadn't been following their boss' orders, I would have had a chance of getting away.

Mr. Delaney continued holding them with his cold stare before turning toward me, but his face did not soften. "That was stupid, Bri."

"No, I was stupid for ever going to that interview and even more so for accepting an offer from a man like you." I turned around and showed him the handcuffs. "Is there nothing in an HR handbook for your 'organization' that says handcuffs are not meant to be used in the workplace?"

His left eyebrow arched upward. "Do you need a reminder, sweetheart? You quit. You don't work for me anymore, but if it will make you feel better, you can file a complaint."

He pushed me backward, swiped his card, and again the elevator slowly took us to his penthouse on the 21st floor. When the doors opened, he gripped my elbow, led me over to the sofa and shoved me down on it.

"Would you like a drink?"

"I would like for you to take these cuffs off."

He walked over to the bar, poured a glass of some kind of amber-colored liquor, and strolled back to sit by me on the sofa. I watched as he took a sip of his drink and then casually leaned back as if he were about to read a book or watch a movie. As if everything that had happened tonight was just normal day-to-day stuff.

"You can't keep me here."

He took another sip of his drink before answering. "Darling, you have no idea what I can do. You are here because I wish you to be, and you will stay for as long as I want you. Regardless, this is the safest place for you." His voice was soft but alarming and held the certainty of a man who was never deprived of anything.

I blew out a heavy breath, knowing that arguing with him would get me nowhere. "Please, take the cuffs off. They are too tight and cutting into my wrists." I saw a spark of concern in his eyes before he pushed me forward, and I heard metal clicking and then the cuffs were released from my wrists. I immediately began rubbing the red marks left behind on my skin from the restraints while staring at the man sitting beside me.

He picked up the glass and took another drink. "The man I was meeting with tonight was Nickolai Volkoff. I don't expect you to know who he is or what he does, but he is one of the most dangerous men in the country. When he saw you tonight, he wanted you."

"He wanted me?"

His lips turned up slightly in a mocking grin. "That was the reason for the dramatic display when I got you out of the room. Nickolai is the leader of the Volkoff Bratva. He usually takes what he wants."

My eyes rolled. "Unlike you?" From the slight grin he gave me I knew my sarcasm had not been missed. Then I shook my head in confusion. "Why would he want me?"

His brow furrowed as he studied me. "It amazes me that a woman that looks like you can't see your sex appeal. That you can't recognize the desire men have in their eyes when they look over your body." He stood up and walked to the other side of the room, then turned to face me, his hands in his pockets as he leaned back against the wall. "Nik might not have been the original target tonight outside the club, and until I know for certain who was behind the attack and the reason for it, you will stay here with me where I can protect you."

"Why do I need protection? I don't know him, and if I'm honest, I don't know you either. I don't know anything. So, if I am not the target and not in any way connected to either of you, why would you insist that I stay here, against my will, no less? I am beginning to think that you are using that as an excuse to keep me here."

His smile held no humor. "Darling, I don't need an excuse. Like I said before, if I want you to be here, that is where you will be, and you will stay until I say you can leave. There aren't many who would oppose me. Do I make myself clear, Angel? You have nothing to fear as you are under my protection, but don't try running from me again, Bri. I have already allowed you to test my patience to its limits."

I met his eyes without flinching. "You expect me to just accept all of this? To allow you to keep me here against my wishes?"

He grinned as if he thought the defiance in my tone was a subtle challenge, and he liked it. "Is it truly against your will? Last night at the club you seemed willing enough, and I would bet money that with a little bit of coercion on my part, you would be willing right now."

I wanted to slap his smug face. "Last night was a mistake." My voice was soft, and I looked away from the intensity in his eyes.

"No." He crossed the room quickly, gripped my chin, and turned my face back to his. "Last night was not a mistake, Bri. It was destiny. You walked into my club, into my life, and from the moment I saw you, I knew you were supposed to be mine. I was hoping for an easier transition for you, but as it is, your entrance into my world, into my life, will not be as simple as I would have hoped."

I tried to pull my eyes from his, but no matter how hard I tried, I couldn't. "What kind of man are you? What kind of life do you lead?"

I watched his eyes darken and instantly wondered if the question angered him.

Regardless of the icy expression on his face, I continued probing for answers. "I know you are in business with the Russian mob, and I suspect you are involved in other criminal enterprises. But taking me and keeping me here when I have so clearly stated that I want no part of this, is asinine. What kind of a man even thinks this is acceptable?"

He finished off his drink and then moved to stand in front of me. "I will tell you the kind of man I am. When I saw you walk into my club last night, I knew I wanted you before I even stepped forward and offered to take you upstairs. You looked out of place, like you were lost, as if an innocent angel had walked through the wrong door. I have not been innocent for a long time, Bri, if I have ever been innocent at all, and I felt the need to pull you into the darkness with me, even if my doing so steals that innocence away from you. So, you can see little angel, there is nowhere you can run to escape me; this is my city. I control almost everything that goes on here. Trying to leave is just foolish and will only make me angry. You should enjoy what I can give you and be happy for the protection I offer. Because as long as you are with me, no one would dare touch you."

His words left me speechless. My hands trembled as I pressed back against the sofa, trying to put as much distance between us as possible. "You said you wouldn't hurt me." My voice was barely audible, almost a shaky whisper.

His hand cupped my cheek, his touch soft. "Darling, I am indeed the monster you perceive me to be, but I meant what I said, I will not hurt you. I will, however, have you in my bed."

Even though the man scared the shit out of me, I still felt my anger building inside me. He thinks he can snap his fingers and get whatever he wants, but I was not going to give in that easily. And to be honest, I was pissed at myself for feeling desire whenever he mentioned having me in his bed or the longing that pulsed through me at his touch.

"I disagree. You may control this city and you may have a plethora of people willing to do your bidding, but I am not one of them. So, I will play your little game until you give up and decide to let me go. I assure you there is easier prey out there for you to hunt."

He moved back to the bar and refilled his glass before walking across the room and handing it to me.

"Oh, I am aware that there are other women who would easily fall into my bed. Who would be much more appreciative of the offer you have received, but where is the challenge in that? The fact that you continue to deny the obvious attraction and desire you have intrigues me. And I like a good challenge."

I rolled my eyes at his arrogance. "You would think that, but there is nothing you can do to make me want you, to want this. Now, if we are finished, I would like to go to my room."

He blocked my path and when I went to move around him, he gripped my arm and pulled me closer. "Tsk, tsk, tsk. Do you think that after the little stunt you pulled earlier, I would allow you to have the freedom of your own room? That offer has been rescinded, sweetheart. You will stay with me."

I jerked my arm back, trying to free myself from his grip. "If you think that is going to happen, then you are not nearly as smart as I thought."

His hand shot out and gripped my chin, not enough to hurt, but it got my attention. "I have given you more leeway than I have given to anyone before, but don't try to take advantage of my leniency." He looked over to where he had tossed the discarded handcuffs. My eyes followed his and I lunged for them, but he was faster. He gripped my arm and pulled me closer to him before dangling them in front of my face. "Since you are planning on fighting your arrangements, I suppose these will come in handy."

My eyes narrowed and I tried to pull away. "Let me go."

"Never."

He leaned closer and let his fingers brush my hair away from the side of my neck before he leaned over and pressed a small kiss just below my ear, making me tremble slightly. *What the hell was wrong with me?* Even after everything he has done, I can't stop my body from reacting to his touch. His fingers dipped lower and grazed the side of my breast, causing me to suck in a breath. Then before I could protest, he tossed me over his shoulder and carried me down the hallway to his bedroom. I shrieked, but there was no one to hear me, and even if they did, this was his building, and I knew no one would dare to challenge him.

I thrashed around, pummeling his back with my fists, earning a rather hard smack to my ass, causing me to suck in a deep breath of air.

"If you don't stop moving around so much, I'm going to drop you."

"Go to hell! I hate you!"

"Now is that any way for us to start a new relationship?"

He tossed me on the bed, momentarily stealing my breath, and quickly moved over me, gripping one hand over my head and snapping the handcuffs over my wrist before securing the other cuff to the headboard. I kicked at him and pulled, trying to free myself, but he simply gave me that one-sided grin that made him look like sin itself, which in turn made my anger intensify.

His gaze lingered on me with seductive intensity. "If you would stop fighting long enough, you might take a minute to appreciate how we could take this situation and turn it into something much more pleasurable."

I glared at him. "Fuck. You. The only thing that would give me pleasure right now is seeing your heart ripped from your chest."

He pulled on my wrist again and moved to stand closer to me. "Ooh, violent, I like it." He chuckled before turning serious again. "Stop fighting the restraints, love. You can't free yourself and pulling against them will only damage the skin on your wrist." He picked up my free hand and turned it over to press a kiss on the inside of my wrist before tracing over the lines on my palm. The feel of his warm fingers against my skin instantly made my body grow warmer.

"Has chaining me to your bed been your plan all along?"

He tilted his head to the side as he traced over the curve of my cheek. "Hmm, keep talking like that, love, and you will find out much sooner exactly what plans I have for you."

He removed his jacket and tossed it on the other side of the bed. "I am going to shower and get ready for bed. If you had been more polite, you could have joined me. As it is, you can sit there and think about what you are missing."

He whipped his shirt over his head and try as I may, I couldn't pull my eyes from him. He was so damn sculpted and despite my best efforts, I looked my fill. He removed his pants and stood before me naked. The sight made my throat dry. He was the most magnificent specimen of a man I had ever seen. His cock jutted out hard, thick, and long. Our little altercation must have turned him on, and he was unashamed at showing me the evidence of his desire. I felt the heat building between my thighs and my panties grew damp despite my best efforts to push his image from my mind. I looked away and closed my eyes, hoping to squash the burning fire that had ignited inside me at the sight of him. I took one more peek through my hooded eyelids to see him grip his dick and stroke once before turning his back to me and walking into the bathroom. I heard the shower running and tried to shut out the erotic images that kept popping up in my imagination.

I had to think of something, some way to turn things in my favor...and I had to get out of these damn cuffs. Once he was out of the shower, I had a feeling that he had every intention of continuing what we started the night I met him at the club, and while I had adamantly stated that I would not give into his wants and desires, I wasn't so confident in my abilities to do so. While the man infuriated me, I didn't understand the desire that I was feeling, the desire to throw caution to the wind and give in and take what he was offering.

Rogue

Bri's anger wasn't unexpected. However, I was disappointed that she tried to run from me and even more so that I didn't anticipate it. When I called downstairs and told the guards to stop her, I should have been more specific and told them to do so without touching her. The fury I felt when I saw her being manhandled and restrained almost made me lose control. I wanted to kill them when I saw how tightly they were gripping her arms; nobody would touch her but me. And while I was hoping that would be a great deal more touching of her tonight, it seems as if my lost little angel was not as receptive to the idea as I was hoping.

There was no doubt that with some effort, I could make her forget the anger she was feeling. I stared into the bathroom mirror, trying not to think about her lying cuffed to my bed. I had never had a woman that haunted my thoughts like this before. This was new to me. Women had always been forgettable and convenient for the time I had them in my company, but once I grew bored, I found it easy to walk away and never look back.

But not with Bri. I wanted her here with me now. There was an intense need for her to want me. I craved her acceptance of me, all of me, and everything that I am, both man and monster. I turned the shower on and stepped inside, letting the hot water run over me. Pressing my hands against the tile, I lowered my head. My dick was hard as steel, and it ached for relief. It had been many years since I had sought release by my own hand. Never had a need to. There had always been a woman willing to part her legs or open her mouth for me. Whether it was for my money, the power I possess, or simply the allure to danger, I had never been denied the pleasure a woman could give, until now.

Many of the women I had dated were attracted to the sparkle of the parties and society functions that I attended. Being the lady on my arm brought them the attention they craved. Their pictures taken by the many photographers who stalked the events attended by the rich and powerful of Chicago, being on the society pages of the newspapers and magazines as my newest conquest. All of them wanted what I could give them, but none of them could handle the real monster I kept hidden from most of the world. As soon as the slightest beastly part of me came to light, I knew what they would do. That was one of the reasons I never kept a woman for more than one night, none of them had ever made me want to do so until I saw Bri.

Fuck! I wanted her. I turned off the shower and grabbed a towel with every intention of doing my best to make her see the stupidity of her refusing me and the pleasure I was longing to bring her. I wrapped the towel around my waist and had only taken two steps when the buzz of my cell phone broke through the haze of lust in my brain.

"What the fuck do you want?"

There was a short moment of silence and then a deep grunt before he spoke. "You can meet me at the warehouse, or I can come to the penthouse, either way, we need to talk...now."

"I'll be at the warehouse in half an hour."

I walked back into the bedroom and threw the phone on the bed before moving to the closet to get dressed. I knew from the tone of Blaze's voice that it was something important, but right now even the urge to commit violence was not nearly as strong as my need for her. It angered me that this woman was so embedded under my skin, and I hoped that whatever Blaze had at the warehouse would allow me to work off some of my frustrations because if I didn't get some sort of relief soon, there would not be anything to keep me from taking what I wanted so desperately.

I walked out of the closet fully dressed to see Bri trying to squeeze her wrist through the cuffs. "I told you that you will hurt yourself if you don't stop."

Her eyes flashed fire as she yanked her hand one more time. "I would rather hurt you."

I smiled as I walked closer to her. "There will be time for that later, I promise, sweetheart."

Her eyes narrowed as she took in the clothes I was wearing. "Are you going back to the club?"

I sat beside her and was happy to see that she didn't shrink away in fear. "Why? Will you miss me?"

She rolled her eyes. "Hardly, but surely you aren't going to leave me here like this." She tugged on her arm again as if to remind me of her predicament.

"But if I let you free, how can I be certain you will still be here when I get back? My guess is that you will run as soon as possible." I reached up and gripped her wrist that was cuffed to the bed.

"You can't be serious! What if there is an emergency...a fire or armed intruders? I would have no way to save myself."

I laughed at her, which caused her to reach across her body with her free hand and try to hit me. "Fine, I will release you, but it will cost you. If I do you a favor, I will expect one in return."

"Releasing me from where you have me handcuffed to your bed isn't exactly a favor. You are only righting a wrong that you inflicted upon me."

I shrugged my shoulders. "Well, if that is how you feel..." I stood from the bed and started walking to the door.

"Wait!" There was a shrill urgency to her voice.

I glanced over my shoulder. "Yes?"

"You win. If you will release me, I promise to not run away."

I turned back to her and leisurely strolled over to the bed, fighting the urge to push her skirt higher and part her legs so I could taste her. "Not good enough. I can easily make assurances that you won't be able to leave the building. I want something else."

Her fierce stare nearly burned and if looks could kill, I would have already burst into flames.

"Fine, what favor do you want?" Her nostrils flared with fury.

"When I return, I want you to share my bed with me. Willingly."

"Are you insane?" Shock seemed to cause the words to become wedged in her throat.

I turned back toward the door, ignoring her comment.

"Wait!"

There was the urgency again.

"I don't have time to wait, Bri. I should have already left. The business I must attend to is quite urgent," I replied impatiently.

"I'm sure you can spare me a minute or two." Her voice dripped heavy with sarcasm.

I looked at my watch. "You have one minute to convince me."

"If I agree to share your bed, does that mean you will expect me to...you know."

I frowned as I took a step closer. "It means that I want you in bed beside me."

She glanced over at the handcuff on her wrist. "I just don't want you to get the wrong idea. I do not want to have sex with you."

My eyebrows had risen as I watched her. "Times up, Angel. I will see you when I get back."

"I'll do it! Just please don't leave me here like this."

I walked over to the bed, took the key from my pocket, and released her. She rubbed the red and raw marks on her wrist while looking up at me.

"You don't have to worry, Angel. I would never force myself on you. I simply want to share my bed with you. If anything, other than sleeping occurs, it will be because you want it as much as I do. Perhaps you will even instigate it."

"Don't hold your breath."

I reached out and let my finger glide over her cheek. "Get some rest. I don't know how long I will be."

When I walked out of the bedroom, I grinned as I locked the door behind me. I heard her yell my name. While I was willing to release her, I was not stupid enough to give her complete freedom. I knew she would try and find a way to leave the penthouse if I didn't lock her in the room, but I did get her to agree to share my bed, and I cursed Blaze for disturbing what could have been a very pleasurable evening.

CHAPTER
five

ROGUE

The argument with Bri had caused me to be later to my impromptu meeting with Blaze than I had intended. When my driver stopped the car out in front of the dark metal warehouse building in a more industrialized part of the city where we conducted our more clandestine meetings and slightly less than legal activities, I motioned for him to stay behind. I did not know what Blaze had waiting for me inside, and there were some parts of my business that I kept strictly between Blaze and me.

"Took you long enough."

Blaze unhurriedly stepped out of the dark shadows of the mostly empty building. A smoke circle passed from his lips as he emerged into the moonlight before tossing the cigarette he had been smoking on the ground at his feet.

"I wasn't expecting to have to leave the confines of the penthouse again tonight so you will have to excuse my tardiness."

Blaze stepped closer, and I could see his hands were already covered in blood.

"From the extra surly look on your face, I would venture to guess that you were not successful convincing your newest plaything to join you in your bed tonight." His lips curved up slightly in a sarcastic grin. "Or maybe leaving her alone naked in your bed is the reason for your annoyance. Either way, I'm glad to oblige."

A low growl passed from my lips as I stalked forward. "I don't recall it being any of your business who I have in my bed or in what state of undress they are in. But regardless of the inconvenience of your call, here I am, shivering in the cold and looking at your ugly face instead of enjoying what could have turned into a pleasurable evening. Not exactly the delightful turn of events I was hoping for, thus the reason I seem disagreeable. Now, why the fuck am I here? I know you did not drag me down here just to chat."

"I have a present for you." He walked back toward the warehouse.

I followed the smell of blood, piss, and fear growing stronger the farther we went into the building. Blaze stopped in front of a man tied to a chair. His face was beaten and bloody, his shirt had been torn open and there were cuts along his chest still oozing blood from where Blaze's knife had carved into his skin. Knives and blades had always been his preferred method of inflicting pain when he was "playing" with his victims.

"There were two men outside the club tonight, the shooter, and this unfortunate fellow. He was lucky enough to escape on foot but not smart enough to keep running. I caught up with him a few blocks away, hiding behind a dumpster and waiting for someone to come pick him up, but I have a feeling that since he and his dead friend fucked things up so spectacularly, whoever sent him decided that he wasn't worth the trouble and left him to fend for himself. One of our men working security recognized him as being with the would-be assassin tonight outside the club before all the chaos occurred. All he has done since I caught him is make threats and feign courage."

I leaned forward to glare into the swollen and bruised eyes of the man Blaze had strapped to the chair before me. I studied the tattoo on his neck. "Not Russian. This looks to be Armenian." I gripped his chin and forced his face up to mine. "My question is why would a member of the Armenian mafia be in my city, and why would you try to attack the leader of the most powerful Russian crime organization in the country? If you are so eager to meet death, you have come to the right place."

I watched as the man's teeth clenched and his chin jutted out in defiance, and I smiled. This was exactly the distraction I was needing right now.

I took off my coat, not wanting it to get ruined, and handed it to Blaze before putting on the thick leather gloves I had with me. I tilted my head slightly as I examined the man sitting before me.

"Most men are brave until they realize that there is no escape from death. I have seen it before many times. You think you can block out the pain, the fear. You think you are strong enough to withstand it. But there comes a point when death is not what one fears the most."

His eyes flicked up to watch Blaze circle behind him. The anticipation of what was to come made his body begin to tremble.

"I can see the wheels turning in your mind. You think that if you talk to me and tell me what is being planned, your boss, whoever that might be, will do far worse than what I am about to do." I leaned closer, my voice lowering as I spoke to him, adding to his fear. "But that isn't true. I can make your suffering linger. I have spent years studying the art of bringing the maximum amount of pain with minimal blood loss. It allows me to play with my victims for longer before they bleed out or lose consciousness. I can do this for days until you tell me everything you know. When I am done with you, you will be willing to sell out your mother just so the pain will end. And I am not squeamish, so shall we get started?"

I could see my words were starting to affect him. Perspiration mixed with blood began to drip into his eyes. I had a reputation, one that I had proudly cultivated over the years, and whoever had sent him had to know what would occur if he was caught. While the thoughts of what was about to happen to him began to sink into his brain, Blaze rolled over a small table with everything I would need to cause the agony necessary to get the information I needed. Just the sight of the implements made his eyes widen.

I walked over to the table and let my fingers glide over each piece.

There were knives of all shapes and sizes, some jagged and others sharp as razors. Screwdrivers, drills, poisons, and alcohol to pour over the wounds to make them burn. Speaking of burning, there was a butane torch, pliers, a hammer, and all sorts of fun tools. I finally settled on the nail gun. It would be a nice slow start. I picked it up and walked toward him before pressing it to his shoulder.

"Since I do have somewhere I would much rather be right now, I will give you an opportunity to stop this before it begins. Tell me who sent you and why you tried to assassinate Nickolai Volkoff at my club tonight?"

A sudden flash of defiance appeared in his eyes, and I knew it wouldn't be that easy. He squared his shoulders and lifted his chin. "Fuck you! Soon all of you will die and this city will be free of your stench."

I squeezed the trigger, sending the nail into his shoulder at the joint. He screamed before spitting blood on the floor at my feet from where he had bitten through his lip.

I kept my voice calm and steady as I watched a glazed look of pain and anguish begin to spread over his face. "Such vulgar language and spite for someone in such a precarious position, my friend. Let's try this again. Who sent you?"

I pressed the nail gun to the side of his knee at a place that would create optimum pain.

"Kakes ger merakoun!" *Eat shit motherfucker!*

I pulled the trigger again. His screams echoed around us. "I speak several different languages, and Armenian is one of them. You should learn to think before you speak."

The sound of Blaze cracking his knuckles echoed around the room as he stepped forward, drawing my attention. "While you might have your reasons for dragging this out, I would like to get at least a couple of hours of sleep tonight. So, stop playing around. Just get on with it. Nail his balls to the chair or cut off his dick. I don't care which, just speed this up."

My voice dripped with cynicism. "That's easy for you to say, you have already had a bit of fun with him."

I raised an eyebrow as I turned back to our victim and gave Blaze's suggestion a bit more thought. "Hmm, I imagine you are right. He isn't going to need his dick after tonight anyway." I moved over to the table, selected a scalpel, and stepped closer. That was all it took for our Armenian friend to start talking, and I found it rather disappointing that he didn't have the stamina to endure more.

Two Hours Later

I stepped out of the warehouse, the cold-biting wind whipping around me along with the smell of sulfur as Blaze struck a match to light his cigarette.

"Send a message to Nik. I want to talk with him as soon as possible."

"And the Armenian?" Blaze asked, his voice hard and cold.

"Dispose of the body. I don't want it found. I need to let Nik know what is being planned so appropriate measures can be taken before the Armenians make their next move."

Blaze nodded automatically. "Do you believe everything he said in there?"

"No, but there could be some truth to it. Whoever is behind this knows the connection between the Bratva and our organization. The shooting taking place at the club was not a coincidence. Taking on both the Bratva and our organization is ambitious. It makes me wonder if there is more behind this than what our dead friend back there knew. He was just following orders, hoping for notoriety by killing Nickolai. He was just a pawn, not the brains behind this."

"I'll take care of the body and call you with the details later. You should go back to the penthouse and hope your sweet little houseguest doesn't kill you before the Armenians get the chance."

I watched as he walked back inside the warehouse, and I made my way back to where my driver was waiting for me. I wasn't exactly sure what the Armenians were planning. If they were attempting to steal from me or the Volkoff Bratva, they would fail, but my instincts told me there was more to it than that. Whatever they had planned, I knew trouble would soon be coming. Unless Nik and I could put a stop to it before it started. Their attempt at assassinating Nik had failed, and the men directly involved were all dead now. But I had a feeling this was just the beginning. Things would only get more dangerous.

This was a bad time for me to bring a woman into my world. Things were about to heat up quickly, and I would have to be vigilant to keep her safe, which meant that she would have to stop fighting me. I didn't have the time or patience to deal with a testy female, no matter how beautiful and alluring she could be. Her defiance was not simply annoying now, it could get her killed. Perhaps Blaze was right, I should rethink our arrangement and either let her go or put her on a plane out of Chicago. As the car drew closer to the penthouse, I knew that was something I wasn't willing to do. The challenge now would be to get her to accept her fate.

Bri

Once I was alone and sure that Mr. Delaney had finally left the apartment, I began moving around the room, trying to find anything that would pry open the lock on the door. The arrogant asshole may have released me from the cuffs, but I was still locked in the room. After searching for a few minutes, I realized it was useless. The place was like a damn fortress. I thought about throwing something through the window and drawing attention to me, but we were twenty-one floors up and the windows looked pretty thick. I wouldn't be strong enough to break them and there was no way anyone would notice me this far up without a major distraction. Once the realization sunk in that there was no way I was getting out of his bedroom until he returned, I figured I might as well take advantage of my captor's hospitality.

The dress I had worn to the club was not exactly something

anyone would want to lounge around in, so I moved to his closet and rummaged around until I found an extremely soft and what looked to be a very expensive silk shirt. A part of me hoped that it was one of his favorites. I slipped it on and rolled up the long sleeves to my elbows. The material hung down to the middle of my thighs and would be adequate until I could leave the room and get my own sleepwear.

I snooped around the rest of the room, and I had to give it to the man, he had style. His clothes were all designer and if my guess was correct, they were all tailored to fit him. Everything he possessed screamed luxury, wealth, and power. I moved from the closet and walked to the bathroom. There was a huge shower and a large whirlpool tub on the other side of the room that seemed to be calling my name, and since I was alone, I thought I would take advantage of it while I could.

I turned on the faucet and undressed as the tub filled. As I sank into the hot water, steam rising around me, I couldn't help but think that a girl could get used to this kind of luxury. My tiny apartment only had a shower that was barely big enough to turn around in; the water pressure was weak, and the water would barely get warm. It was nothing like this.

After soaking until my skin grew pruney and the water cooled, I stepped out of the tub onto the plush bathmat and wrapped myself up into one of the thick cotton towels I had found in the linen closet before moving back into the bedroom. The penthouse was eerily quiet. I slipped his shirt back over my head, the silk caressing my skin, and climbed into his bed, the bed that I had agreed to share with him.

I propped up a few of the thick pillows and watched the door, wondering when he would return. It was surprising that a part of me was looking forward to another encounter. The man was as infuriating as he was stimulating, but I wasn't the type of girl to sit around and whine when things got tough. So, I plumped up the pillows behind my back, crossed my arms over my chest, and prepared for him to walk back through the door.

. . .

The Next Morning

"Do you plan on sleeping the day away?"

A rich husky voice penetrated through my sleepy haze. I blinked my eyes, my lids heavy from sleep, to allow them to adjust to the light streaming in through the windows. A few strands of hair hung down in my face, and I brushed them away before pushing myself into more of a sitting position. It took a moment for me to become aware of his presence beside me. I must have fallen asleep while waiting for him to return last night. He wasn't wearing a shirt, and the sheets had slipped low over his hips, really low, barely covering the lower portion of his body. I forced my gaze back up to his face.

"When did you get back? Why didn't I hear you come in?"

"You were sleeping peacefully, and I was quiet so as not to disturb you."

He smiled as I scooted toward the edge of the bed. "No need to be shy now, kitten. You weren't that eager to get away from me an hour or so ago."

I gripped the sheets and pulled them up to my chest as if they would shield me from his teasing eyes. "What are you talking about?"

He smugly turned onto his side to face me and pressed back into the pillows. "You sleep soundly and didn't even flinch when I crawled into bed beside you in the wee hours of the morning, but it didn't take long for you to seek my warmth. I have to say, I enjoyed waking up to find your tight little ass snuggled against my side."

The slight grin on his face was incredibly irritating.

"I never would have guessed that you would be such a bed hog."

"You are a liar and so full of yourself that it is nauseating." I twisted away quickly, but before I could swing my legs to the floor, I felt his strong arm wrap around my waist and pull me roughly to him before he pressed me down onto the mattress and covered my body with his own, making me ever so conscious of where his warm flesh touched mine.

"Not so fast, sweetheart." His fingers traced over the silk of the shirt I was wearing. "You have good taste, this shirt is my favorite, even more so now."

His hand slipped lower, and his fingers seared a path over my bare thigh, causing my body to shiver with delight. "Although, I would prefer that you sleep naked. Skin against skin is much more sensual, don't you agree?"

A gasp slipped past my lips as the hardness of his thigh brushed against mine, but I pushed back the desire building inside me. "I would prefer to be back in my apartment, but we don't always get what we want, do we?"

He narrowed his eyes as he leaned closer to me, his warm breath teasing my naked flesh. "Speak for yourself, sweetheart. I always get what I want."

Before I could offer any kind of protest, he ripped the shirt open. The sound of tearing silk and buttons pinging against the tile floor should have spurred me into action. I should have fought against him, pushed him away, screamed, but I didn't. Whether it was from shock or that inner part of me that wanted him to touch me, I wasn't sure. Either way, I didn't move, and I didn't fight, and when his warm hands skimmed over my naked breasts, every nerve came alive. How could this man make my skin burn and shiver at the same time as if my body was half ice and half flame?

"We shouldn't be doing this."

His nose pressed into the crook of my neck and my eyes nearly rolled back in my head when his tongue flicked over the skin just beneath my ear.

"This is exactly what we should be doing." There was a cool authority in his voice.

His hand seared a path down my side and over my abdomen, causing the war raging inside me to intensify. I barely knew this man and what I had learned about him so far, was definitely sending up some red flags. It wouldn't be wise to allow myself to fall for a man like him...no matter how gorgeous he was. No matter how much I wanted him to kiss me, to touch me. He had hand-cuffed me to the bed, locked me in his bedroom, and refused to let me leave. How could I still want him? I had to have something wrong with me.

His hand slipped lower, between my thighs, parting my folds. I heard a soft sigh pass from my lips, but the pleasure I was feeling was short-lived. A sudden pounding on the door brought back my sanity. He was surprisingly swift as he moved away from me, a pistol suddenly appearing in his hand.

"Stay here!"

I pulled together the ripped material of the shirt I was wearing, or what was left of it, and jumped from the bed. "Wait...don't go out there."

He looked back over his shoulder as he moved to the door. His face was hard and serious, causing me to freeze. "This is not the time to disobey me, Bri. Stay here!"

I took a step back at the harshness in his voice. He slipped on the pants he had discarded before he had gotten into bed and held the pistol at his side before leaving the room and slamming the door behind him.

Rogue

My anger at having my time with Bri once again disturbed was near the boiling point when I walked out of the bedroom to find Blaze waiting for me. I was beginning to think that he was doing it on purpose.

"Why the hell are you here?"

He was making himself right at home standing by the bar pouring himself a glass of whiskey, my best bottle no doubt.

"I didn't know I needed a reason, but as it were, I thought I would come by and introduce myself to your lost little angel. With things heating up and becoming more dangerous, it would be wise for her to become familiar with me."

I walked over and took the glass from his hand before turning it up and draining the whiskey. "You don't think I had already thought of that? But as noble as your intentions sound, coming by for a surprise visit is not why you are here. So, tell me the real reason you have chosen to disturb me again."

I watched as he took the bottle from in front of me and turned it up. He closed his eyes and a low growl of satisfaction rumbled from his chest. Blaze has always enjoyed a good whiskey, almost as much as he enjoyed the women he had in his bed.

He sat the bottle back down and strolled over to take a seat on my sofa. "I talked to Nik. He wants to meet before he leaves Chicago to return to Las Vegas. He will contact you with a place and time."

"Is that all? You could have texted that."

His expression didn't change. "I was hoping I could reason with you about the girl."

I crossed my arms over my chest. "You? The voice of reason?"

He shrugged his shoulders, the slight grin he had worn when he came in disappeared. "Think what you want, but the girl shouldn't be here. Especially now. There is no doubt the Armenians have you under surveillance or at least they did until the two fools from the club fucked up their assignment. Even so, if they have seen her and think she is more than just a casual fuck toy, they could try to use her. Send her away before something happens to her, or she hears and sees more than you want her to. We both know you have the city in your pocket, but you still don't need some innocent young girl telling everyone the things she has seen while with you. Don't let your dick make decisions that could hurt the business. You can give her a settlement that will make her happy, and she can be on her way before she gets involved. There is a war coming. We should all prepare for it. Send the girl away. When all of this is over, you can go find her again or better yet, find another beauty to grace your bed."

My eyes narrowed as I contemplated his words. "You certainly have a lot to say on the matter. Why the sudden interest in what I do?"

He shrugged his shoulders in mock resignation. "I am feeling uncharacteristically charitable. Take it for what it is, it won't last long."

"I prefer you better as a psychotic asshole. Get the hell out before I decide to shoot you myself."

He stood from the sofa, adjusted his jacket, and nodded toward the hallway where I could see the bedroom door cracked open and Bri peering out. "The longer you let this game play out, the harder it will be for her to leave. I will see you at the club and you should prepare her to meet me. If things continue on this path, she will need to trust me as much as she does you. It might be what keeps her alive, especially if you are too stubborn to let her go. We both know you will tire of her soon enough, Rogue. End it now before she gets hurt."

The truth of his words did nothing to improve my mood. He was right. If the Armenian mob was about to make a move against us, the city would become embroiled in a war and Bri was in danger of becoming collateral damage. But with me being under surveillance, she might already be a target. Her life may already inadvertently be in danger.

I turned to walk back toward the bedroom and watched her close the bedroom door with lightning-fast speed. Blaze was right, but unlike my normally bad-tempered friend, I was not the least bit charitable. I always got what I wanted and right now, I wanted the blue-eyed lost angel that walked into my club two nights ago. Unfortunately for her, the life she once had was about to change forever.

CHAPTER
six

BRI

I listened to the conversation Mr. Delaney was having with his associate, the scary guy from the club, and my heart beat faster with every word that they spoke. When he turned and saw me listening, I quickly closed the door and backed away. I needed to get the hell out of here. I didn't belong here. I didn't want to be embroiled in whatever dangerous life he led.

When he walked through the door, I jumped back.

"Listening at doors is an unattractive habit." He stalked toward me as I backed farther into the room, matching my retreating steps with his own. "It can also be hazardous."

A wave of apprehension swept over me. "I didn't hear anything."

The smile in his eyes held a sensuous flame. "Oh, I think you heard quite a bit. If you didn't overhear anything, you wouldn't be shirking away from me like a frightened rabbit." He gave my body a raking gaze. "I'm not going to hurt you, Bri, but I am tired, and I am going to take a hot shower, and I want you to join me."

"I...I...don't think..."

I watched as he rolled his eyes, but before I could finish the thought forming in my head, he stepped forward and scooped me into his arms.

"While I enjoy our little arguments, I don't have time for it this morning."

He placed me on my feet, and I stood there frozen as he turned on the shower and removed his clothes.

Damn, resisting him was going to be harder than I thought. He was freaking magnificent. A chiseled chest and rippled abs were just the icing on the cake. And the tattoos, good grief. They just made him look that much hotter.

He held his hand out to me and when I hesitated, he raised his brows and tilted his head to the side.

His invitation was beginning to be a challenge that I was struggling to resist. Logically everything was telling me to refuse, to run in the opposite direction. But no matter what my brain was telling me, I wanted more. I needed to feel something I couldn't explain. My body hummed with a deep yearning that grew stronger the longer I was with him. I blew out a deep slow breath and slipped the torn silk shirt I was wearing to the floor. My skin tingled as his gaze dropped from my eyes to my shoulders, then to my breasts and lower. He crooked his finger at me, and I stepped forward, placing my hand in his. He radiated a vitality that drew me to him like a magnet. He pulled me into the shower with him, but I immediately stepped back against the wall as far away from him as I could get, not quite prepared for the intensity of my feelings. I crossed my arms over my chest as the hot water streamed over his body. *Holy shit!* The man was sculpted like a freaking *Magic Mike* dancer and the water running down his sinewy body caused the desire that was burning on a slow flame inside me to flare. I bit down on my lip as I allowed myself the pleasure of ogling him...thoroughly. For the most part, he ignored my presence, and all I could do was stare as the steam began to rise around me.

"You know instead of standing there shivering against the cold tile you could enjoy the show while being an active participant."

I shook my head. "I'll wait till you're done. Besides, I don't think this is within the rules."

His laughter was low and throaty. "Rules? I wasn't aware that we had rules."

"I thought it would be best, so I set some of my own."

He moved toward me and put his hands on either side of my head effectively caging me in with his arms. "You want to fill me in on some of those little rules you made up in your head."

His body wasn't touching mine, but he was close enough that I could feel the heat of his wet skin against my own. "Well, I think we should avoid situations like this."

"Showering together?"

"Anything that requires us to both be naked...yes."

He leaned closer and his lips pressed against the skin on my neck just below my ear. "I have never been a fan of rules." He pulled me away from the wall underneath the hot stream of water.

"Rules are for those too afraid to take chances or risks. Rules make life rigid."

He dragged me against his body, his erection pressed against my belly, and I gasped even as my hands moved over his shoulders marveling at how firm he felt beneath my fingers.

"Rules....rules...are necessary for survival."

His hands began a lust-arousing exploration of my flesh as he trailed a line down my spine to the base of my ass. His other hand traced over the side of my breast and back over the curve of my neck as it arched to the side before gripping my hair in his fist and pulling my head back hard.

"I suppose in some cases rules are a necessity to survive. Tell me the rest of these...rules."

He lowered his head again, this time his teeth nipped lightly at my throat, and I clamped my thighs together tighter as moisture began to build. His fingers glided across my belly before sweeping between my legs, cupping me, and making my knees buckle.

"Are there rules against this? Tell me. What other rules are you trying to impose on me, Bri?"

His warm breath caressed my skin as he whispered near my ear, and I had to put my hands against his chest to keep myself from leaning in.

"We shouldn't kiss. We should avoid touching each other as much as possible and we shouldn't...." Even as I spoke the words, my hands had drifted lower down his chest and over his taut abs.

"What? What else has your pretty little head decided that we shouldn't do?"

I swallowed hard. "We shouldn't have sex."

His arm tightened around me, and he walked me backward until I felt my back hit the opposite wall, the coolness of the tile was shocking against my warm wet skin.

"It seems as if we have broken all of those rules except one."

My breathing increased, my heart jolted, and my pulse pounded as I stared up into his deep brown eyes that held so much promise of what was to come.

His hand gripped my chin tightly.

"I don't do rules, Bri. I don't take orders. I don't have a lot of patience, and I do not share what belongs to me with anyone."

His lips claimed mine fiercely, punishingly, and I found myself clinging to him, surprised by my eager response to the touch of his lips. One minute I was thinking of pushing him away and the next minute, I found myself surrendering...completely.

I returned his kiss fervently and when his tongue swooped inside my mouth to twist and tangle with mine, shivers of desire raced through me.

He turned off the water then gripped my ass as he lifted me and wrapped my legs around his waist before carrying me from the shower never stopping until he roughly deposited me on the bed. Both of us dripping wet, both of our bodies hot to the touch. The cool sheets clung to my body as I scooted back against the pillows.

His eyes had grown darker and more serious as they raked over my body. "I have waited for you longer than I have any other woman." He hovered over me before taking his hand and pushing my legs apart. I closed my eyes as the sensation of his lips moving slowly up my legs from my ankles to the backs of my knees made me quiver. His tongue began licking and kissing up my inner thighs until he pressed his mouth against my folds. My hips arched off the covers as his tongue swiped over me. His teeth lightly nipped my clit before his tongue flicked over me again. My fists gripped the covers on the bed as sensations that I was unfamiliar with swept over me. His hands gripped my hips, pushing me back down so he could further his exploration of my most intimate areas with his mouth and tongue.

"I knew you would taste sweet."

The moan that escaped my lips was much louder than I intended, and my hand moved to cover my mouth. A low groan of appreciation slipped past his lips and the vibrations against my sex nearly made me come undone. He continued licking and sucking my clit until my body began to convulse. The ferocity of my orgasm shocked me and I closed my eyes and bit down so hard on my lip that the copper taste of blood was on my tongue.

"That's it, my innocent little angel. I want you to cum on my tongue. I want to taste you."

My cheeks burned with embarrassment. I had never felt anything like this before and the fact that his words were turning me on was shocking. I tried to scoot backward but his fingers tightened on my hips.

"Be still, love. I'm not done, yet."

Before I could blink, he flipped me over onto my stomach and his body covered mine, pressing me deeper into the mattress. He gripped my wrists and pulled my arms over my head. "Don't move."

I tried to rise on my elbows and turned my head to look back at him. I immediately received a sharp smack on my ass.

"Were you not listening? I said don't move."

He leaned down near my ear. "Since you seem to like rules so much, I'll make a few of my own, sweetheart. One of them is to always do what I say, especially when we are in bed."

My ass was still stinging, and I was sure his palm had left a red mark. His hands moved from my wrists down my arms to my sides. He began feathering a series of slow shivery kisses down my spine.

"Open your legs for me."

When I hesitated, he bit down hard on my right ass cheek. "I can leave marks all over you, baby, but I would prefer to give you more pleasure than pain, as much pleasure as your body can handle."

I opened my legs just a bit, but he pressed them wider. His fingers slipped between my legs, and I sucked in a sharp intake of air when he entered me.

"Fuck! You're so goddamn tight. I want to drive into your sweet, tight little pussy and feel your body clench around my cock while I fuck you."

After working magic with his fingers, he roughly flipped me onto my back and lay between my thighs, his throbbing erection pressing at my entrance. He leaned down and sucked my nipple into his mouth, the pain was both surprising and exhilarating.

"I want you to scream, Bri. Don't hold back, baby."

His eyes locked with mine and a silent communication passed between us, demanding to know if I was willing, if this was what I wanted. My voice wouldn't work, but the slight incline of my head was all he needed.

He slowly pressed into me just a fraction of an inch. "Lift your hips, love."

I did as he said and cried out loudly when he roughly thrust deep inside me. He stilled while I tried to get my breathing under control. My eyes closed tightly as my body adjusted to his intrusion.

His deep husky voice cut through the silence. "Open your eyes and look at me, Bri."

I did as he asked, and the look on his face chilled me to the bone. Was he angry? Why the hell would he be angry? I was the one feeling like I had been ripped apart.

"Why didn't you tell me that you were a virgin?"

I blinked away the moisture gathering in my eyes. "It isn't something that usually comes up in casual conversation and things between us moved much faster than a normal relationship."

He leaned down and brushed a gentle kiss across my forehead before softly kissing my lips.

"If I had known, I would have taken you slower."

I looked away, embarrassed by his sudden tenderness. "I'm fine."

His brow furrowed as his frown intensified. He pulled out of me and pressed back in more slowly allowing my body to stretch around him. My hips shifted so I could take more of him. His thrusts gradually grew in intensity and became faster, more frenzied, rougher, and I let my hands move over his chest, my nails leaving red streaks on his skin as they raked over his flesh. My muscles tightened as another orgasm began building inside me. My hips began to rock with his and his thrusts became more urgent, harder. I cried out again as he began to pound into me furiously. My whole body trembled as a rush of release came over me and he thrust again, and I felt him empty himself inside me.

The ramifications of what I had allowed him to do, what I wanted him to do, began to race through my mind.

"We just broke all my rules." It was the only thing I could think of saying.

He leaned up on his elbows with an irresistibly devastating grin on his face. "Yes, we did, and I can see another round of rule-breaking in our near future."

His smile slipped a bit as he stared into my eyes. "There is a new set of rules now, Bri, rules that will not be broken."

My brow furrowed as I looked up at him. "What do you mean?"

He shook his head. "There will be time to talk about it later. Get dressed. I have some business to take care of this morning and another meeting at the club tonight. All the clothes you purchased are in the other bedroom, wear a dress."

"Why a dress?"

He stood from the bed. "Because we are far from finished, and a dress will give me easier access to you."

Rogue

The fact that she had been a virgin, that no other man had been with her before, ignited an almost primal instinct within me. A desire to claim her so everyone knew that she was mine, to protect her, and to keep her. There would never be another man in my angel's bed. No other man would know her sweet taste or see the perfection of her naked body. I now knew that she was made just for me and after today, after taking what no other man would ever know, she truly was mine. Whether she liked the idea or not, I would not give her up.

I turned as she stepped out of the bedroom wearing a flowy pastel pink dress that came just to her knees. The black belt she was wearing showcasing her tiny waist and the sleek black heels she had on made her legs appear even longer. Long loose chocolate-colored curls hung down her back, and it took all my willpower not to toss her over my shoulder and take her back to my bed.

She sighed heavily as I stepped forward. "I wasn't sure if this meets your specifications."

"You look stunning."

Her eyes immediately fell to the floor and her cheeks pinkened as if she were not used to hearing compliments.

"I'm not sure what we are doing here. I am not your employee, and I'm starting to think that was never your intention from the beginning. Yet, you refuse to let me return to my apartment. And after what just happened between us, I need some clarification. Just tell me why you have taken me and what plans you have. I think I would rather know than let my imagination keep coming up with different scenarios."

I arched my brows. "Very well. I'll talk, you listen. I truly did have intentions of keeping you as my employee. It was quite a lucrative offer if you will remember, but since things have taken an unexpected turn and you quit, most adamantly, I have revised my plans. As far as what happened between us, I would think it was simple. We fucked, and I have every intention of doing so again just as soon as the opportunity presents itself. That is one of the reasons I asked you to wear a dress. If it were not for the fact that other men will be present today, I would have you remove your panties so that there would be fewer barriers between us."

She put her hands on her hips and popped her right leg out looking entirely too tempting.

"Why do you have to say things like that? Do you do it to shock me? To take my mind off my original question, why the fuck am I still here? Just tell me and as far as what we just did, I don't think we should continue...with...I don't think we should do it again. Sex tends to complicate relationships and well, we don't even have a relationship. I honestly don't know what this is."

I stepped closer and she backed away. "How do you know sex complicates things, Bri? You were a virgin up until an hour ago."

She rolled her eyes. "Don't try to make me feel bad for not giving it out freely to every man I dated. I was always so busy in high school with track and dance that I never had a serious boyfriend. In college, I just wanted to go to class and go home. I was always waiting."

"You were waiting for me, Angel."

She turned away from me. "I knew you would make this difficult."

"You want me to simplify things for you? Fine, you were made for me and only me, Bri, and while I may be an arrogant asshole that you hate at the moment, I am the only man that will ever lie between your legs. You can forget about ever leaving because after tasting you, after sheathing my dick to the hilt up inside your tight warm body, I will never let you go. If you run, I will find you. So, all thoughts of returning to your old life can be forgotten, all thoughts of fighting me are useless. You are mine. Now, reach under your skirt and slip your panties down your legs."

The shocked expression on her face would have been comical if my mind had not been so filled with lust for this woman.

"You can't be serious!"

"I am always serious. Do it, or I will do it for you...with my teeth."

I watched her jaw tighten as she reached up underneath her dress and slid down the white lacy thong she had been wearing. I dodged as she tossed it at my face.

"Are you happy now?"

I walked forward and put my hands on her waist. "I will be when my face is buried between your thighs as I lick your pussy. Go sit on the couch and spread your legs."

"No."

"How long are you going to lie to yourself? You know as well as I that you enjoyed every second of my tongue on your flesh." My fingers slowly moved up her arms, causing her flesh to prickle with excitement. "But if you truly want to pretend defiance, I can find other methods to make you comply."

Her face turned a delightful shade of red, but she did as I instructed and moved to sit on the sofa.

"Lift your dress to your hips and spread your legs wide. I want you on full display."

She hesitated, but when I arched an eyebrow, she complied, and holy fuck was she gorgeous. I moved forward, keeping my steps slow even though my pulse was pounding with anticipation.

I knelt before her and placed my hands on her knees, pushing them apart even wider before sliding my hands up her hips and pulling her down so she was perched on the edge. I dipped my head between her legs and immediately heard the soft groan come from her lips as my tongue worked its way over her folds. I would never get tired of her taste. I could spend the entire day in bed with her, tasting every inch of her body, marking her for everyone to see, before fucking her so hard that she would forget ever trying to leave me. I was obsessed. Obsessed with her skin, her smell, the sound of her voice, the tightness of her body...and the way she trembled when I made her cum on my tongue.

I lifted my head to look into her heavily lidded eyes. The look of satisfaction on her face was enticing. I pulled her skirt back down over her knees, then stood and walked back to where she had tossed her panties a few minutes ago.

"Here, put these back on. I don't want to kill anyone today for accidentally getting a glimpse of heaven."

I watched as she stood on shaking legs and slipped the panties back up over her hips. I wiped my mouth on a handkerchief and walked over to take her hand.

"Shall we go?"

She pulled away from me. "No, I want to use my phone."

"I will buy you a new one."

Her brow furrowed with irritation. "It's not about getting the newest model; I want to make a call."

I wasn't sure why, but the thought of her calling another man made me furious. "Who?"

"Does it matter?"

I stepped toward her, closing the small space that had been between us. "I asked you a question, Bri." I could hear the bridled anger in my voice, and I clenched my hands into fists, resisting the urge to wrap my fingers around her pretty little neck.

She walked away to stand by the windows and looked down at the street below. "I want to call my friend, Allison. She knew I was going for a job interview and will be wondering why I have not called her to tell her about it. I never expected to take a job working for some kind of crime boss and then to be taken against my will and kept prisoner at his penthouse suite." She turned back to face me. "She will be worried, and I need to talk to her."

"Crime boss? Are you placing me in some kind of *Goodfellas* fantasy? I assure you, darling, I am much worse than anything you can imagine. But to most of the world, I am just a well-connected businessman with some very questionable alliances." I reached into my pocket and took out the phone I had taken from her last night. "Is there anyone else you need to contact besides your friend?"

She shook her head. "No, Allison is the only friend or family I have."

A look of sadness crossed her face. "Make the call but watch what you say. I have many friends in the police department here in Chicago, most of them on my payroll, but that does not mean I want unnecessary trouble with them."

She jerked the phone from my hand.

"I won't tell her anything about you. She doesn't need to know that I am being held against my will by a crazy psychopath or that I was dumb enough to sleep with you. I wouldn't want her to get hurt trying to get me out of this mess."

"Do you really think I would hurt your friend?"

She shrugged her shoulders. "I heard enough of the conversation between you and the guy that was here earlier that I wouldn't want to take the chance. You already told me the kind of man that you are, and I can only imagine the things you do. You are claiming that you will never let me leave and don't seem to think anything is wrong with keeping me captive. I don't want my one friend in this whole world to get hurt simply because I decided to try and get a job at your club. Believe me, if I could, I would turn back the clock and stay far away from you."

The speed at which I moved surprised her. I wrapped an arm around her waist and pulled her into my chest. "You don't mean that. Lie to yourself all you want, but not to me. You wanted me to fuck you, I could see it in your eyes and when I make you cum on my tongue the sounds from your lips are not of pain or torture; they are pure pleasure. I told you before that I will not hurt you. You must learn to trust me. Call your friend, she will be safe."

Bri

My whole body was trembling, and I felt like I was on a roller coaster ride of conflicted emotions. I was mad at myself because I knew he was speaking the truth. I had wanted him, but I was also afraid. Could he seriously mean that he would never let me leave or was this just another game he was playing, and why was the thought not nearly as terrifying as it should be? Right now, I couldn't think of that. He had given me my phone and I needed to talk to Allison. I meant what I had said about not telling her everything that was going on; I wouldn't want her to be involved. I walked into the kitchen, wanting some privacy, and looked back over my shoulder to see if he had followed me before dialing Allison's number. She picked up on the first ring.

"Where the hell have you been, Bri? I have been worried sick." Her voice was filled with worry and concern, and I felt terrible for putting her through this.

I kept my voice low. "I know, I know, I'm sorry. Things have been really...hectic lately."

"Did you get the job?"

"It's complicated, but I wanted to let you know that I am alright and I'm sorry for not calling sooner."

"You need to leave Chicago, Bri, as soon as possible."

An involuntary shiver ran up my spine at the urgency in her voice. "Why?"

She hesitated. "He knows where you are, Bri. Tony came to my house and told me that he was aware that I was in contact with you and wanted me to deliver a message. He said he is coming for you and that you better be ready."

My stomach clenched tighter as fear swept over me and I gripped the counter to steady myself. The ringing in my ears grew louder, creating a piercing pain behind my eyes as my heart beat faster. I felt as if I would be sick.

"Bri? Did you hear me? You have got to leave now! He is probably already there, and it gets worse."

The urgency in her voice brought me out of my stupor. I closed my eyes and found my voice. "How can it be worse?"

"He told me that he knows people, that he has connections, and from the sound of it, they are not the kind of men you want to find you. I'm scared for you, Bri. He put you in the hospital before and I'm afraid it will be much worse if he catches you now."

I swallowed hard. "I can't leave Chicago just yet."

"If you need money, I will wire it to you. You can come back here, or you can go stay with my brother in California. He is ex-military so he can keep you safe."

I felt my hands start to shake. "I can't. I told you that things were complicated but I...I will think of something, but I just can't leave."

"Is it the new job? For God's sake, this is your life. Tell your new boss to take his two weeks' notice and shove it up his ass. Do I need to come there?"

"No! No, I will handle it. Things are complex, but I will call you again in a day or so. Don't worry, Allison."

I didn't wait to hear another argument. I hung up and placed the phone on the marble island before rushing to the sink. I turned on the faucet and ran some cold water over my hands before pressing them to my cheeks. Hearing that Tony had discovered where I was and was coming to find me made me cringe. Now, not only was I being held hostage by a rich but incredibly sexy badass, but I had a psycho stalker trying to find me. How in the hell did I get mixed up in something like this and more importantly, how would I survive it?

I heard Rogue's footsteps growing closer, and I realized that for the time being, living here and being close to him might be the safest place for me.

I could feel his presence standing behind me, but he had yet to touch me.

"I just need a minute and then we can leave." I tried to whirl around him, hoping to get to the bathroom and freshen up before he noticed anything was wrong, but I wasn't that lucky. His hand shot out and gripped my arm to stop me.

"Who are you running from, Angel?"

I sucked in a short breath. "You listened to my conversation? Did you not just say a few minutes ago that listening behind doors could be a hazardous and unattractive habit?" I tried to pull out of his grip again, but he held me firm.

"Don't try to turn this around. Never lie to me, Bri. Your face is too easy to read, and I will always be able to tell when you aren't being truthful. Now, tell me, what, or who are you so afraid of? Your face is pale, and you are still shaking, so I will ask again, who are you running from?"

I sighed heavily in desperation. "This isn't any of your business, but there was a man I met in Colorado where I lived before moving to Chicago."

His expression clouded with anger. "What is your connection to this man and why are you afraid of him?"

I looked away from the furious expression on his face. "He isn't anyone to me. We went out on a few dates, but he became really creepy and quite insistent on having sex right away. I told him I didn't want to see him again after date three when he got aggressively handsy in the movie theater. He slapped me around a little but one of my neighbors stopped him. I thought that was the end of it, but he started stalking me."

"Is there more? From the way you are trembling, I am assuming it gets worse."

I closed my eyes, not wanting to relive the nightmare again. "I can handle it. It doesn't concern you."

He pulled me roughly, almost violently to him. "Anything involving you concerns me!"

"Why?" His eyes narrowed even further, and I knew he was waiting for me to continue. "One night I went out with Allison. When I came home, he was waiting for me and after beating the shit out of me, he tried to rape me. If Allison had not left her purse in my car, he would have succeeded. When she came back after it, she heard my screams and interrupted him before he could follow through with what he intended. I was in the hospital for a few days and when the doctor released me, I moved to Chicago, hoping that he would forget about me, and I could start a new life here. Unfortunately, it doesn't look like that will happen."

He reached up and gently tucked a stray curl behind my ear, causing a shudder to pass through me.

"Give me his name." The command was given in a low but serious voice.

I shook my head resolutely. "Why? I told you that this is none of your business. Allison said he has connections to some very nasty men and there is no need for you to get involved. I am not sure what I will do. She suggested I go stay with her brother in California. He is ex-military, special forces, and would be able to protect me. But I prefer to handle this myself."

I watched as his face grew angrier. "Do you think I would allow you to go to another man for protection? I meant what I said earlier. You belong to me now, Bri. You can keep denying it and fighting it, but it will not change things. I will be the one to keep you safe, to protect you, and I will be the one to kill the bastard that hurt you."

"Threatening to kill people is not the normal way to solve problems. And I don't belong to you. You keep saying that, but it isn't true. Once you've tired of whatever little game you are playing with me, I will be on my own again."

His eyes hardened. "Is that what you think?"

"You can't make me believe that this is anything more. I am just a plaything. Someone that caught your attention, an anomaly in the circles in which you move. But it won't last. Men like you...don't fall for girls like me."

He grinned and my stomach flipped upside down. He was possibly the sexiest man I had ever seen.

"Hmm, you will soon learn, sweet Bri, that I am not like most men. Don't underestimate me. Now, there is much to do today and our activities this morning, while pleasurable, have already made us late."

He grasped my hand as we walked to the elevator, but I had a feeling he was still very angry. There was a tension in his body that wasn't there before and the arrogant sneer on his face was even more intimidating than usual, causing a cold shiver to creep over my skin. Hopefully, today will bring me the answers I was seeking. Could it be safer to stay with Rogue Delaney, a man who had proved to be dangerous and unpredictable, than it was to run the risk of bumping into Tony and whatever bad people he was mixed up with? The elevator door opened, and I made my decision, no matter what kind of man he was or what kind of criminal shit he was mixed up in, Rogue had never hurt me. He pissed me off and made me feel things I had not felt before. He had touched me and made my skin burn with need. One look from him made my knees weak and my panties wet, but he had never caused me physical pain. I closed my eyes and breathed in deeply. While one man had the power to destroy me physically, the other could very easily destroy my soul, either way, I was in trouble.

CHAPTER
seven

ROGUE

Seeing the way her face paled as well as the stark fear and anxiety in her eyes after her conversation with her friend confirmed my suspicions that she was running from someone. But now that I knew that it was a man, a man that had beaten and nearly raped her, I was filled with a murderous rage so intense that my knuckles were white from clenching my fists at my side. It angered me that I didn't find her sooner, that I wasn't there to protect her. To know that she went through something so traumatic made me feel an even stronger need to shield her from all things that could cause her pain or hurt her. I never wanted her to feel that powerless or afraid again. The fact that she refused to give me a name did not help assuage my fury. I would find the man responsible for making my angel tremble in fear if I had to scour every part of this earth, every hole in which he would try to hide, every back alley in every filthy city. And when I found him, he would then know true terror, true fear, and I would take delight in seeing him suffer.

Bri sat next to me in the back seat as my driver took us to the club. Thoughts of her, the sweet smell of the perfume she was wearing, and the reminder of the softness of her skin were the only things breaking through my anger. The woman was going to drive me mad with lust. I wanted to touch her, pull her onto my lap, and lift her skirt so I could drive into her. I wanted to ease her fears and those worry lines between her eyes. I wanted to assure her that I would never let her be hurt again, that she was safe with me and would never have to handle things alone. She had me now. I would protect her. She would never want for anything. Every wish, every desire, I would grant, if it were in my power to do so.

My fingers itched to touch her, but with the fury I was feeling now, I was afraid that I would hurt her. Although, a part of me wanted to bring her a small measure of pain just so that I could take it away again, ease the sting so that she would finally understand that she was mine, that no other man would have her in their bed. My rage was so intense that I barely heard the notification on my phone. I looked down to see a text from Blaze telling me that Nik wanted to meet at his favorite restaurant as soon as possible. I responded then tossed my phone on the seat beside me.

"Why are you so angry?"

I couldn't look at her. The wrath I was feeling toward a man I didn't know and the desire to fuck her until she could think of nothing or no one but me was almost overpowering.

"What tipped you off, Angel? Tell me, why do you think I am angry?"

I heard her sigh loudly and could almost feel the roll of her eyes.

"Well, the frown on your face is typical but today it is more severe than usual. You haven't tried to touch me since I told you about ... about him...about what he did. I suppose I should be grateful for that, but I know it's because you are upset about something. As to why, I don't know. I told you the truth, I didn't say anything to Allison that would cause you problems, and I haven't tried to run again since last night."

I clenched my jaw. "Are you certain you want to have this conversation with me right now?"

"I don't want to have this conversation at all, but since you seem to be brooding over it, I thought I would ask. It's not as if you were the one beaten and almost sexually assaulted by a crazed stalker."

Once again, my anger threatened to singe the corners of my self-control. "He hurt you, Bri, and he will pay for that with his life. I promise you that."

Her luminous eyes widened in astonishment. "You can't just appoint yourself as my guardian or my personal avenger for anyone that dares to wrong me." Her brows rose slightly. "And why would you?"

She still didn't understand, still so reluctant to accept her fate. "You will learn very soon, Angel, that I can do whatever I want. You have no idea how far I will go or the drastic steps I will take to protect what belongs to me. But you will find out shortly and then you will no longer be in doubt about where you belong."

I watched her eyes widen and decided to change the subject. "We will be having lunch with Nickolai today."

"The man we are meeting, is he the same one that was almost killed outside your club? Will that not be dangerous? Especially if the ones that shot at him return to finish the job."

"Nickolai faces threats regularly. As head of the Bratva, he has many enemies. Last night wasn't even serious enough to make him increase his security detail, and we are meeting on his turf. They will not be so foolish as to try and attack him there so soon after their first failed attempt. He is much more powerful than the men who want to see him dead."

Her eyes searched mine. "And you? How powerful are you? Powerful enough to be well-protected?"

I found her obvious concern amusing. "Worried about me now, love?"

The concerned expression she was wearing quickly turned into one of irritation. "Never mind, I shouldn't have asked. Being shot at is probably an everyday thing for you. I can certainly see why. Sometimes I want to shoot you myself."

Her cheeky nature and quick wits amused me. I continued to look out the window, knowing that if I looked at her now, I would not be able to keep my hands to myself, and while I had every intention of throwing her skirt over her head and devouring every inch of her before fucking her until she could barely walk, Nik's favorite restaurant was only a few minutes away. There would be time for that later.

Bri

Rogue remained quiet, but I could tell from the hard set of his jaw and the rigidness of his body that he was angry. I didn't know much about the kind of life that he lived and while I imagined being shot at and being friends with people who were vicious criminals could make anyone's nerves on edge, he was not the type of man to be intimidated. To say that my nerves were a bit frayed would be a monumental understatement. My foot continuously tapped against the floor, a gesture I often did when I was nervous; my palms were sweaty, and my stomach fluttered. We were about to meet with the leader of the Russian mob. Would we be searched when we entered? Would there be guys with guns everywhere? I had only met the man once before Rogue threw me over his shoulder and carted me away. But he did say that his friend Nickolai was dangerous, as if I couldn't have figured that much out on my own.

The car came to a stop in front of a small Italian restaurant that was nothing like what I expected. It was very simple, almost like a family café, nothing like the fancy expensive restaurants that seemed to be everywhere in Chicago, the ones I could never afford to eat at, the ones where you had to have reservations weeks ahead of time or know someone important to get in.

The driver came around to open the door for Rogue. He stepped out and adjusted his suit jacket before extending his hand to me. When I got out of the car, the only familiar face I recognized was that of his scowling and sulky friend that I had seen at the club and again at the penthouse.

He stepped closer and even though he was wearing dark sunglasses that hid his eyes, I knew he was staring at me; I could almost feel it.

"Hello, little one."

It was the first time he had spoken to me directly. I was too nervous to speak so I just gave him a timid smile, and I felt Rogue tighten his hold on my hand.

"Blaze will be by your side anytime I am not. If anything happens and you can't find me, he will find you. He will protect you at all costs."

I looked from one man to the other and wondered how two obvious alpha males could coexist peacefully. Then the words he had spoken began to pierce through the stupor my brain seemed to be in.

"Do I need protecting?"

He turned back to look at me briefly. "You are my woman, and I will not take any chances with your safety."

Those four words, *you are my woman*, sent a chill down my spine and seemed so final, as if that was all I needed to know.

I didn't have any more time to argue that statement with him as he immediately began tugging me behind him as we entered the restaurant. I heard a deep brief chuckle from behind me, and I wondered if Blaze found this entire situation entertaining. It made me speculate how many women he had said that to before and if any of them were held captive as I found myself to be. I imagined I am the only woman who did not run to his bed the minute he looked in their direction. Although I kept referring to my predicament as captivity, I had to admit that I hadn't tried very hard to escape since the first night. There was something wrong with me.

When an unintentional sigh slipped past my lips, Blaze stepped forward and whispered near my ear, "Bored so soon or were you thinking of the more pleasurable aspects of being Rogue's woman?"

I turned my head and met his gaze. "Jealous? I will trade places with you if that's what you want." I was about to also let him know in no uncertain terms that I wasn't anyone's woman when a very large and burly-looking man stepped out of the shadows.

"You all have to be searched before you go any farther." His Russian accent was thick.

Blaze stepped past me. "The fuck we do! Nickolai knows we are coming."

"Yes, he does, and he left strict orders that everyone was to be searched."

Blaze's expression became even more severe. "Let me save you fuckers the time. I have three pistols on me and about five different knives and not one of you is capable of relieving me of them."

Rogue released my hand and opened his coat. "We are both carrying weapons and Nickolai knows it. What kind of game is this?"

One of the men stepped between me and Rogue separating us. I took several steps back as a small grin crossed his lips.

"Touch her and I'll cut off both your hands."

I was surprised at how relieved I was to hear Rogue's voice through the buzzing in my ears and even more glad to feel his arm around my waist.

"She is with me, and nobody touches her. Do I make myself clear?"

For a minute I thought a fight would break out before we were even allowed admittance into the restaurant, but a deep laugh came from one of the tables inside.

"Let them pass, Yuri, and for God's sake, don't touch the girl. I do believe Rogue is serious with his threat." He stood up from behind the table and held a glass in his hand. "I can't say that I would fault him, should I ever possess something so lovely, I would be protective of her too."

My feet seemed rooted to the floor, but Rogue was pulling me alongside him as we moved to the large round table at the back of the restaurant to take a seat with the Russian mob boss.

Rogue sat to my left and Blaze to my right while Nickoli and one of his men sat across from us.

"It is good to see that you have decided to stick around, Miss Rogers. After Rogue's rather barbaric display, I had my doubts."

I wanted to ask how he knew my name, but Rogue's hand instantly went to my knee and squeezed softly. I took that as my cue to keep my mouth shut.

Blaze leaned forward. "For someone that has an army of assassins trying to kill you, I have to say that you seem rather calm, Nickolai."

The Russian's lips lifted into a slight smile that seemed more deadly than it did humorous.

"When you are the leader of the Volkoff Bratva, you get accustomed to attempts on your life. To me, it is just another day." His eyes lifted and held mine. "Besides, there are times that a man needs something that challenges him both in business...and in the bedroom."

The Russian had the most penetrating ice-blue eyes I had ever seen. There was a glass of water in front of me and I picked it up and drank half of it.

Was every bad guy in this city sexy as hell or was it just me?

"What do you know of the Armenian threat?"

Thankfully, Nickolai broke his gaze with me to focus on what Rogue had just asked. "Little more than you I imagine. Although I am not sure that I believe the confession you extracted from the Armenian that Blaze captured outside the club the night of the assassination attempt. He was much too far down the food chain to have any real details. But I do believe they want to weaken the hold you have on the city. Perhaps they are seeking to draw your focus onto something else, thinking it will be easier to seize control if you are otherwise...preoccupied." His gaze turned back to me. "They want Chicago and everything within your empire. Once they have taken out your organization, there is no doubt that their greed and stupidity will cause them to move on to Vegas and Los Angeles and try to take from the Bratva. The attempt on my life was just a bonus. They never expected me to be in Chicago. Someone was just trying to take advantage of the situation and became ballsy. I imagine the original target was you."

"The man Blaze tortured in the warehouse said that they wanted to start a war between us. I had already determined that he was too far down the line to be the one making the decisions. He wouldn't give up a name and we were quite insistent on it. I don't think he knew who was pulling his strings. Do you have any ideas?"

I watched as Nickoli shrugged as if none of this was a big deal.

Did I just hear Mr. Delaney talk about torturing a man?! What the hell had I become mixed up in?

I twisted my hands on my lap as Rogue moved the material of my dress up so he could touch my skin just above my knee. The slow circles he drew with his fingers caused me to shiver but were not as comforting as I imagined he thought they would be.

The Russian's lips curled into a smile. "Creating a division between us would be a waste of time, but like I said before, I do not think that is their intention. I feel they are trying to create a distraction that will put you off guard. It will require more digging to discover who is behind it. I will, however, offer my support and help if the need arises. If you and Blaze find the situation more than you can handle, that is."

I turned my head to see Rogue's face darken.

"While I appreciate your help, I assure you that I am more than capable of protecting and securing everything that is mine."

Nickolai nodded. "I never doubted you. I will be returning to Vegas tomorrow, but you know where to find me if you need anything. I will also send out feelers and speak to my contacts to see if I can discover anything else that would be helpful. But since I am here in Chicago and rented out the entire restaurant, we should at least eat."

His eyes met mine again. "They have the best pizza in town. You should try it."

I was startled when Rogue's phone buzzed with a notification and bumped my knee against the table, causing the glasses to rattle. I saw Nickolai's smile widen and I could tell that it amused him to see me frightened. It was all I could do not to kick him under the table.

Rogue leaned over, pressed a kiss to my cheek, and whispered in my ear. "Don't be afraid, Angel." He then glanced at Blaze before turning to address Nickolai again. "If you will excuse me, I need to step out and handle this."

I wanted to reach out to him and had to clasp my hands together to keep from doing so. Rogue may have done some despicable things, namely handcuffing me to his bed, and keeping me against my will, but he was the one man in this room who did not make me shy away in fear. Even my so-called protector Blaze made me anxious.

"Would you like some wine, Miss Rogers?"

I nodded and he poured some in a glass for me.

"It's odd being the only ones in a restaurant." It was something that popped into my head and suddenly my mouth decided to speak it aloud.

"It makes it easier for me to manage who is allowed entrance that way." His smile faded. "I was speaking the truth when I said I receive death threats and assassination attempts routinely."

I felt as if something was stuck in my throat. I took a sip of the wine as I let my eyes move around the room, taking note of the security he had stationed at every window, every entrance, and I didn't see how anyone would be able to get to this man.

"I need to use the restroom."

Nickolai stood from his seat as did Blaze.

"It is down the hall to your left."

Blaze took my arm. "I will escort you."

I shook my head desperately, just wanting a few minutes to myself, time to clear my head and think. "That will not be necessary."

Nickolai moved from around the table. "The room has no windows and there is only one way out. She will be safe to go alone."

Blaze nodded, but I could sense his reluctance. "I will be watching for you, little one."

I turned and made my way past two of Nickolai's rather large guards and down the narrow and dark hallway to the ladies' restroom. Once inside I immediately went to the sink and turned on the water. I only needed a few minutes away from the table, away from the dangerous men surrounding me, and away from the ominous threats that surrounded them.

My chest heaved as I breathed in and out, almost on the verge of hyperventilating. My heart was pounding, but if I didn't get back out there soon, there was no doubt in my mind that someone would be coming to retrieve me. So, I washed my hands and took a few more deep steadying breaths to calm myself before opening the door.

I stopped suddenly when I was met by a rather large and intimidating force. Nickolai was leaning against the wall waiting for me.

"I thought we could have a few minutes alone to...talk."

I instantly became more alert. "Where is Blaze?"

"He is being detained for the moment; a feat not easily done I might add. And I am not sure how long my men will be able to hold him."

"What do you want to talk about?"

He stepped closer, looking down at me intensely. "You."

He began closing the space between us so that I was trapped between his body and the only exit. My eyes darted past him, expecting to see Blaze or Rogue coming to my defense at any time, but right now, I was alone.

"I assure you that I am not at all interesting nor am I worth your time."

He leaned closer and studied me as if he were sizing me up. "I can see where Rogue finds your innocence appealing. It is both fascinating and enchanting. But will a woman as pure and guileless as you be able to withstand this world? Are you strong enough to belong to a man with so much power, a man who can easily crush his enemies and anyone who makes the mistake of crossing him? Or are you here for some other purpose? Is all this sweetness just an act to get close to him? Could it be that you are the distraction meant to bring him down?"

He was baiting me. I tried to swallow the lump that seemed to be stuck in my throat. "That's a lot of questions."

"I am just trying to make certain that you aren't hiding something behind that beautiful smile and sexy body."

He leaned closer and regarded me with curiosity. "Fuck, I can almost smell your purity. Are you truly so virtuous, Miss Rogers? Or is it all make-believe?"

Warning spasms of alarm moved through me, and I pulled away. "Don't touch me."

He tilted his head to the side, his voice dipping an octave lower. "I am not accustomed to people telling me what to do, *ptichka*, but I assure you that I have no wish to anger my friend by touching what is his, no matter how tempting you may be."

I had already had a hell of a morning and I had enough of this man trying to frighten me, or intimidate me, or whatever he was doing. I pushed against his chest, and he took a step back. "I am stronger than you think, and I do not belong to anyone. The past few days have been very long, more than a bit disturbing, and quite frankly I have grown tired of everything. So, get the hell out of my way or do whatever it is that you came here to do."

His dark frown turned up slightly at the corners of his mouth, and I moved past him and walked back to the table where I saw Blaze being physically restrained. Rogue walked back inside at the same time, his eyes moving from Blaze to where Nickolai followed me from the hallway. His eyes seemed to burn with anger as he came to me.

"Trying to intimidate her? You should know better, Nik. Don't make me kill you."

Nickolai's men immediately pulled out their pistols, but he held up his hand and they quickly lowered them.

"No worries, my friend. I was the perfect gentleman. I did not touch her."

Rogue put an arm around my waist and anchored me to his side. "If that is the only information you have for me, I will leave you to your lunch. I have more important things to do today, but I will keep you informed if anything happens that concerns you or the Bratva."

He nodded routinely. "And I will do the same."

Nickolai stepped closer to me. "It was a pleasure to meet you, *ptichka*, and I am glad that we had our talk. If it means anything to you, I think you just might be strong enough to be in our world, even if you don't plan on staying long."

I heard a loud scuffle behind us and turned to see Blaze pull free of the men that had restrained him and immediately punched them, causing both men to drop to the ground. "Put your hands on me again and I will fucking kill you!"

Nickolai shook his head slightly, telling his men to stand down when they shot to their feet ready to fight.

Rogue pushed me forward. "Go with Blaze. He will escort you back to the car. I need to speak with Nickolai."

I glanced back over my shoulder, glad to finally be leaving. Blaze gripped my elbow and the other men parted to let us pass.

When we got to the car, Blaze opened the door. "I didn't expect Nik to do something so bold and stupid. Next time I will be ready."

He shut the car door before I could respond, and I leaned back against the seat glad to have some time alone.

Rogue

"You shouldn't have done that, Nik. Blaze will not easily forget, and your men are lucky they aren't dead."

Nickolai waved a hand and his men instantly disappeared to leave us alone. "I will make it up to him the next time he is in Vegas."

"What did you say to her?"

"I merely wanted to get a better feel for her character. I have seen you with many women over the years, but never have you been so enamored with one. I simply wanted to find out if she was hiding something behind that innocent facade you find so attractive. You can't be too careful, Rogue. What if she was sent to infiltrate your organization? A pretty face like hers would be easy to lower your guard around. But after speaking with her, I feel her innocence is genuine. She also showed me that she possesses an unexpected strength. It will be an asset. A weak woman can be a liability. You know that as well as I do. But it appears as if Miss Rogers is much more than what you see on the surface. I honestly think she would have tried to fight me if I had not let her pass when she asked me. She has a fire in her eyes that I find appealing. But I am not certain you will be able to hold her. She is quite adamant that she does not belong to you. Perhaps you should just cut your losses and allow someone else a chance to tame her."

"Fuck you, Nik."

His mocking laughter was deep and low.

"Before you leave, I have a gift for you."

He nodded to one of his men who left the room.

"What have you done, Nik?"

A sinister grin crossed his face. "Just doing you a favor."

I turned as two of Nik's men came back into the room dragging a bloodied and beaten man between them. His head was hanging down so I couldn't see his face.

Nik walked over and pulled his hair to hold his head up. His men had done a number on him.

"Who is he?"

Nik dropped his head. "This is your masquerading Russian."

My eyes narrowed. "I told you that I would handle it, Nik. This is Chicago, not Vegas."

"His deception was a slap in the face to the Bratva. I couldn't let an insult to me, and my family, go unpunished. Besides, before he passed out from the pain, he was able to give us important information on his reason for being here in Chicago causing trouble."

Bri was waiting for me in the car, and I had more important shit to take care of today, I didn't have time to play Nik's games. "Are you going to tell me or are we going to play charades?"

"Impatience is a flaw, my friend. Your lovely little captive can wait a few more minutes."

He walked back over to the table and casually took a drink of his wine. I was beginning to believe he was purposefully dragging this out just to piss me off.

Nik sighed. "He was paid to masquerade as a member of the Russian Bratva. He doesn't know the name of the man who gave him the money, but he was told to go around the city, demand money from shop owners, vandalize property, etc. But he had to make certain that he claimed to be doing all these things in the name of the Bratva."

"That doesn't make sense. Why would he do something that undoubtedly would bring the attention of the Bratva on him?"

"Money. They paid him rather well. He did say that the men who met with him all wore the same tattoo on their necks. Sound familiar?"

"You think whoever is behind the Armenian threat is also the one that paid him? They certainly are going to a lot of trouble."

Nik took another sip of his drink. "Whoever is behind it is a fool. None of this makes sense and none of it is statistically beneficial to a takeover. It's very amateurish and stupid. To be honest, I do not think there is much to fear."

"They tried to assassinate you."

Nik shrugged his shoulders. "But they didn't succeed. Besides, why should I fear when you and Blaze are the main targets? And I don't have a beautiful long-legged distraction as you do."

"What are you going to do with him?"

"I haven't decided yet."

I nodded as I walked toward the door.

"Rogue."

I turned back to see Nik smiling. "Do try and stay alive. I would hate to have to deal with just Blaze anytime I visit Chicago."

While I was angry at Nik for what he had done to Bri, I knew his reasons. As I walked to the car, I wondered how she would react to my next move and smiled. It was the reason for the phone call I received while at the table with Nik. Even before he questioned my motives, I had already decided what I needed to do. She would be furious and turning every ounce of her anger into passion would be a pleasure.

Blaze was waiting for me beside the car, his hands clenched into tight fists as he paced. Bri was seated in the backseat.

"I should have killed every one of those fuckers!"

I arched an eyebrow. "Nik meant no harm."

"What did he do to her?"

"He just asked questions. Nik knows better than to hurt her. I need you to plan on attending the gala with us tonight and then go to the club, I have other plans for the evening."

Blaze's frown intensified. "Something that involves her, no doubt. Why can't you just let her go, Rogue? Things are too dangerous. If you don't focus on the damn Armenians or whoever else is behind the recent takeover attempts, you won't have a dick to fuck her with. Get your head together. Women are meant to be fucked and discarded, nothing more."

I moved around him toward the car. "Not this one. Will you be at the club or not?"

"I'll be there, but heed the warnings you have been given, Rogue."

I watched as he walked away and for a minute I wondered if I should listen to his advice and send her away, not for good, but at least until the danger had passed. I could send her to Alessio in New York. He would keep her from running as well as protect her. I opened the door and sat beside her. The driver had already been given instructions as to our next stop.

I looked over to see her sitting as close to the opposite door as possible. Her arms were crossed over her chest, and she refused to look in my direction.

"I'm sorry if Nik frightened you."

"I wasn't afraid."

"That is admirable of you and says a great deal about your fortitude and courage. I have seen grown men break down into tears when forced to kneel in front of Nik."

She looked over at me but did not uncross her arms. "He didn't force me to my knees, all he did was ask questions. I think he believes me to be some sort of spy."

An image popped into my head of her being forced to her knees in front of me and my cock instantly stiffened as I thought of her pretty pink lips wrapping around my throbbing dick. I wanted to touch her. I reached over and pulled her toward me. My hand cradled her neck as I pressed her back against the seat. I wanted to taste her. I wanted to strip her naked and let my fingers pave the way for my tongue. She pressed against my chest, but I wasn't ready to release her. I wanted to brand her, mark her, claim her as mine. The thought was driving me mad. I moved from her lips and sank my teeth into the side of her neck, eliciting a cry of surprise from her sweet lips. I sucked hard and then licked over the spot where my teeth marks were still evident.

"Soon everyone will know that you are mine, Angel."

I moved back to her lips and swallowed the cry of protest before she could argue that point. Soon there would be no escape. I had already made the arrangements and then she would forever be trapped in the darkness and danger that was my life. A part of me felt guilty at what I was about to do, but then I remembered how it felt when I sank my cock into her virgin pussy, and the red-hot possessiveness that came over me earlier returned full force. She was made for me, and only me. The thought of any other man touching her and taking her to their bed made me homicidal. There was nothing else I could do to ease the fire inside me. No, I would not feel guilty for wanting her; I would not feel guilty for tying her to me forever. My hand moved up her skirt to touch the smooth silky skin of her thigh. I wanted to feel the warmth of her core; I wanted to thrust my fingers inside her and bring her pleasure, to feel her come on me.

I roughly pushed her legs farther apart and slid her panties aside before rubbing my fingers against her folds. My mouth swallowed her cries as I thrust two fingers inside her. My thumb rubbed over her clit, making her squirm against my hand. She was very passionate, and I looked forward to pushing her boundaries, to making her experience things she had not before.

She continued to ride my hand as my fingers moved inside her until I felt a rush of her essence over my fingers as she trembled. Her eyes were slightly glazed, and her cheeks flushed when I pulled my hand free. I placed the two fingers in my mouth and licked them clean as she watched.

"The only man you will ever be on your knees before is me, love. And I can't tell you how much I look forward to seeing your lips wrapped around my cock." I gripped the back of her neck and pulled her mouth to mine, knowing she could still taste herself on my tongue. "But first, I have a surprise for you."

CHAPTER *eight*

BRI

The desire I had for this man was almost like a craving, an addiction I couldn't deny, and I hated myself for allowing it to overpower my good sense. The thought of resisting never crossed my mind when his hands touched me. Although I still protested when he claimed that I belonged solely to him, the idea of being in his bed was not nearly as disturbing as it should be. There was something about him, something that was almost as magnetic as it was alarming. Whenever he kissed me or touched me in places no one had before, it was as if I was in a drugged stupor unable to fight against the hold he had on me.

Even the danger surrounding him did not detract from the sexual appeal that radiated from his every pore. I had to get control of my emotions, of my desires. I couldn't let my body betray me. The man was a threat and I had to find a way to walk away. I couldn't continue to allow him to control me, to use me, no matter how much pleasure his touch brought me.

The car came to a stop in front of a large cathedral.

"Why are we stopping here?"

He reached over and took my hand. "There is something that needs to be done."

"If we are here for the priest to listen to your confession, we will be here all day."

The driver opened the door for him, and he stepped out of the car tugging me behind him. "Confession is not my thing, Angel. We are here for something entirely different."

I followed behind, not really paying attention until we entered the sanctuary and saw a priest standing at the end of the aisle, wearing his long robes and holding a bible in his hand. An ominous feeling swept over me, and my nerve endings began to tingle as my brain started sending out warning signals to the rest of my body.

I stopped suddenly and pulled my hand from his grasp. "What's going on? Why are we here?"

I wasn't sure why my instincts were sending me red alert warnings. Surely, he had not brought me here to have a priest give me last rites before he killed me. I shook the absurd thought from my head. I was being ridiculous. No, I wasn't here because he wanted to kill me.

I felt his hand reach for mine again, this time holding me tighter. He stood in front of me, blocking my view of the priest who was still standing and waiting.

"Do not make a scene. I will caution you about what you say. Father Michael is a friend of mine and while he knows what I do, I still do not wish for him to think the absolute worst of me."

"Great. I'll just wait here in this pew while you conduct whatever business you and the good Father must do."

He squeezed my upper arms a little firmer. "I'm afraid your presence will be required."

The increased intensity in his eyes made my pulse quicken. "Stop being cryptic. There is a reason you brought me here, what is it?"

It was easy to see from the arrogant tilt of his chin that I would not like what he was about to say.

"When you first walked into the club, I knew at that moment that I would have you in my bed. At first, that was enough. But after touching you and tasting you, after learning that I was the only man to have ever had you, I knew a few nights would not suffice. But as you have already learned, the world in which I live is dangerous. I am surrounded by it. It isn't safe for you to be around me, in my life, without protection. Not to mention the fact that you are running from a man that tried to rape and kill you. This way I know you will be safe, and you will receive the respect you deserve; other men will not even entertain the thought of having you for themselves, and it will make it easier for me to protect you." He gave me a crooked smile. "Not to mention the added benefit of no longer having to listen to your constant insistence that you don't belong to me."

I listened but still wasn't sure of what he was trying to tell me. "So, are you going to leave me here with the priest? Why not just let me go home?"

My face must have given away my confusion. He leaned closer, his voice was at the same time soft yet firm as steel.

"No, my plans do not include leaving you here. You are mine, Bri. I have already claimed you. You can deny it, you can try to fight me on it, but nothing will change that fact. If you try to run, I will chase you. You can try to hide, but I will always find you. You can scream and rage at me, but the inevitable will happen. You will become my wife on this day." He shrugged his shoulders nonchalantly. "And as my wife, you will be protected from both your enemies and mine."

I couldn't have heard what I thought I did. I must have misunderstood or maybe this whole thing was some weird dream. There was no way in hell he thought I would agree to marry him. "You brought me here to marry me? Are you delusional?"

I put a hand over my mouth as a burst of laughter sprang forth. "This is a joke, some sort of trick or game you are playing. Trying to shock me or cause me to panic? Because I know you can't be serious." I laughed again and his eyes narrowed slightly. "You can't think that I would agree to something so ridiculous, so incredibly bizarre. We haven't even known each other for a week."

"I know how hard you come for me when I am deep inside you. I know the seductive sounds you make when you reach the point where you can't hold back anymore. I know what it feels like to have your body against mine. I know you like the way my tongue feels when it licks your folds before I suck your clit. I savor the sweetness of your taste, your smell, the feel of your skin, and every curve of your body. I know I was the first and only man that will know those things about you."

From the way his eyes had narrowed, and his lips had thinned into a firm hard line, I was beginning to think that he was indeed serious.

"This can't be real. I'm not going to marry you."

"I am quite serious, and I don't have time to indulge you in another argument. So, shall we get on with it? Father Michael was gracious enough to work us into his schedule today."

He gripped my arm and pulled me to my feet. "You are crazy! I'm not doing this. There isn't a priest in this country that will marry someone that adamantly refuses. And I will not agree to this."

He began pulling me forward. "Like I said before. You can fight, kick, scream. I can drag you up the aisle, no doubt causing great embarrassment to both you and Father Michael, but the result will be the same. So, what will it be? Will you walk on your own or shall I carry you?"

I took a deep breath. Perhaps if I calmly and rationally tried to reason with him. "Please try and pay attention to me, I am not going to marry you."

He came to a sudden stop, turned, and loomed over me and a shiver of fear moved up my spine. "Do you know what could happen to you if I give in to your demands and release you now? Let you walk out of here to return to your old apartment and your old life."

I shook my head slowly.

"There are some very bad men looking to take from me. I suspect that I have been under surveillance for some time now, which means they have seen you. They already know you are someone important to me, someone they can use to hurt me or get whatever it is they want. Believe me, Bri, they will. If I release you, if you are no longer under my protection, they will not hesitate to take you and use you as a bargaining chip to get to me."

He leaned closer and I swallowed hard.

"They will not be as kind as I have been to you. Do you honestly think you could withstand the torture they would inflict upon you?

The cuts to your tender flesh, the breaking of your bones, or the removal of your nails. Perhaps they would let their men use you in ways that would destroy both your body and soul, or they could simply kill you. And if that isn't enough to convince you, what about the man hunting you? He could have already found out where your old apartment is and just be waiting for your return. Do you think marriage to me is worse than either of those two fates?"

I reached for the pew behind me. My knees grew weaker with every word he spoke. He pushed me down to sit, then gripped my chin, turning my face up to his.

"As my wife, you will have the respect and protection of my organization and those who work for me, not to mention the use of my name. The choice is yours, Bri. I will allow you to walk out of this church right now, free of me, free of this life, but without my protection. Stay, agree to be my wife, and I will use my power and influence to keep you safe, to keep you alive and free from the danger that surrounds us both."

"But couldn't you protect me without taking such drastic and permanent measures?"

He shrugged his shoulders again. "That wasn't one of the options you were given. I have presented you with your choices, Bri. Now you must decide."

My heart was pounding, my breathing erratic, and I was sweating. He didn't touch me, or say anything else; he just waited and watched. His eyes seemed to peer inside my soul. If I stayed, I would be forever tied to a man that scared the shit out of me but had never hurt me. If I left and took the freedom he was offering, I could be tortured and killed by whoever was trying to hurt him or face Tony again. Was that really the only two options I had?

I saw him look at his watch and I knew he was running out of patience. I glanced up at the priest who was still waiting in front of the altar. His face was sympathetic, but he appeared to be ready to perform this sham of a ceremony anyway.

"Why me?" The question was quiet, my voice wobbly as I pushed back the tears that threatened to fall.

He leaned closer to me. His lips only an inch or so away from mine. "Because I have never wanted something so bad in my life. You are my obsession, a need I can't explain. I am not sure why or the reason behind it, but I want you."

"But you would still let me leave if I chose to?"

He narrowed his eyes and while he may theoretically have given me a choice, I'm not so certain he would abide by that promise.

"It seems as if I don't have much of a choice, do I?"

Rogue stepped off to the side, giving me a free path to run, to escape the fate that loomed before me. "We always have choices, Angel. Now is the time for you to make yours."

I took a deep breath, wiped a stray tear away that had slipped past my lashes, and stood. "You say I have a choice, but I truly do not." I brushed a hand through my hair and smoothed out the dress I was wearing. "Well, this isn't exactly how I pictured meeting the man I would marry. But I suppose being married to you is a step up from being tortured."

I pushed past him and walked toward the priest on my own. Each step heavier than the last. I could feel his presence behind me, but he didn't try to stop me. When I came face to face with Father Michael, Rogue caught up to me and took my hand. I didn't try to pull away. His thumb glided over my knuckles as if he were trying to bring me some comfort.

Father Michael gave me a sad, concerned smile as he inclined his head toward me.

"Are you alright, Miss Rogers?"

My head shot up and just for a moment I contemplated begging him for his help, but if he was friends with Rogue, it would be useless to try.

"I am fine, thank you."

He then turned his gaze back to Rogue, his eyes showing his disapproval. "Are you certain this is something you both wish to do?"

"Just perform the ceremony, Michael." Rogue's voice was curt, and I could detect a hint of annoyance in his tone.

The priest opened the bible he held in his hands before shooting daggers in Rogue's direction. "It's Father Michael to you, and I will thank you to remember that. I don't usually perform marriage ceremonies under duress so you will give me a few minutes to make certain the bride is going to be alright. Right now, she looks as if she could kill you, and I have no wish to perform a wedding and administer last rites in one day."

Rogue sighed heavily as if he knew that any more insistence on his part would not speed things along as he had hoped.

Father Michael looked back at me, a mixture of sympathy and kindness mingled in his glance. "I don't know the circumstances behind this rushed marriage. I didn't ask, but if this is something you don't wish to do...."

"Michael," Rogue said in a harsh voice.

I tried to give him a small smile, but I couldn't muster more than just a slight curve of my lips. "I will be alright. Can we please just get this over with?"

He sighed heavily and nodded his head before beginning the ceremony. I don't believe I heard most of the words that were spoken. I repeated what was asked of me, but tuned out the rest of the ceremony. I do remember shivering and feeling dizzy as Rogue slipped a plain platinum band over my finger and wondered where he had procured a ring on such short notice. When his arm wrapped around my waist, I couldn't help but be thankful for his strength because I wasn't sure how much longer I could remain standing. He turned me to face him, and I could see the concern on his face.

"Are you going to faint?"

I blinked a few times. "Is it over?"

"Yes, it's over."

"But you didn't kiss me."

He led me over to the first pew to take a seat. "With the way your face had gone ghostly pale, I was afraid you were about to hit the floor. Sit here with Father Michael, I will go get you something to drink."

He walked away and I lowered my head, hoping the dizzy feeling I was experiencing would subside. I felt Father Michael sit beside me.

He placed his hand over mine. He seemed quite at odds with the situation.

"I am sorry for my part in this."

"It's alright. Does Rogue have something he is holding over your head, blackmailing you to do his bidding, hoping you will pray for his dark soul?"

He chuckled softly. "Sadly, it isn't salvation that Rogue seeks."

His words and the tone of his voice sparked my curiosity. "How do know him?"

"I'm not sure Rogue wants me to share his secrets."

I rolled my eyes, wondering how a man like Rogue Delaney commanded such loyalty. "It is not like you are telling just anyone. I am his wife now...thanks to you."

I could still tell that he was torn as to how much was acceptable to tell me and for a minute, I thought he wouldn't respond.

"We grew up together. Both of us from the wrong side of the tracks, so to speak. My father died in prison, and I'm not even sure if Rogue knows who his father is. He never talks about him or any family. We were around eleven years old when we met. I was picking pockets on the streets in one of the fashionable districts of Chicago. I was pretty good, but one day I got caught, and the man grabbed my shirt collar and started punching me. Rogue saw what was happening, picked up a metal rod from somewhere, and cracked it across the man's knees and then over his back. The man released me, and we both ran. We became close friends after that. Rogue watched after me, he took care of his friends. He was a born leader. I knew he was meant for more than just petty thievery. He was smart. By the time we were teenagers, Rogue had built up quite an enterprise. Stealing cars and other merchandise, but it was all petty stuff. Then one day he met Alessio Messina. Alessio was the heir to the Messina crime family in New York. Alessio admired Rogue and taught him how to use his brains to create a powerful organization. He taught him how to be a businessman. By the time he reached his early twenties, he had grown very powerful and already controlled much of the city. I still worked for him at that time."

"You used to be a part of Rogue's organization?"

"I was his second in command. He trusted me with his life."

"What happened?"

"The more Rogue grew in power and wealth, the more enemies he had. One day there was an assassination attempt by another bad element in town. He failed and Rogue captured him and killed him to send a message. I was there. The next day, I told him that I couldn't be involved with the death and danger anymore. I didn't have what it took to be a part of his world. I knew where his life was headed, and I didn't want to live in fear or surrounded by danger at every turn."

"Was he angry with you?"

An almost playful smile overtook his features. "Angry? No, he had already picked my replacement. Somehow, he knew I wasn't strong enough for this life, and he was ambitious. His power would only grow stronger. He was destined to be just as big as any other crime family in the country, and he has earned his place."

I listened intently, knowing there was more he wasn't saying. "You became a priest?"

"I did. And a damn good one too."

I shook my head slightly. "But you have remained friends. Do you condone what he does?"

"I never said I condoned what he does, but I am his friend and while he resides in darkness, I know there is good in him."

I heard heavy footsteps approaching and was disappointed that I couldn't find out more about the man I was irrevocably tied to now.

"Fuck, Michael. We aren't in a confessional."

Father Michael stood from his seat, his eyes narrowed in disapproval and censure. Rogue moved closer to hand me a bottle of water.

I took the water from him and felt the backs of his fingers glide over my cheek.

"Feeling better, Angel?"

I sipped the water slowly. "As good as can be expected. I don't suppose you have any other surprises like this for me today."

"Don't sound so melancholy, love. I have plans for later that you will enjoy, but I don't wish to discuss them in front of my priest. But before that, tonight, we have a society function to attend. The mayor is expecting us and there will be other government officials present. It will be the perfect venue to make an official announcement regarding our spontaneous marriage."

He then turned to Father Michael. "Thank you again, Michael."

Father Michael nodded. "I wish you both happiness." He held out his hand for me and helped me to my feet. "For what it is worth, I hope that you can forgive me, Brielle."

"Thank you for the conversation. I hope we have another opportunity to speak again."

Rogue took hold of my arm and pulled me toward him. "Michael talks too much, but you will see him again. We have a standing dinner engagement once a month."

Another infectious grin ruffled the corners of Father Michael's mouth. "Don't hype it up." He looked over at me. "Rogue joins us for a spaghetti supper once a month. Proceeds feed the less fortunate and it also provides funds for the children's choir. Rogue is a generous donor."

Rogue's features were set in irritation. "You are talking too much again, Michael. If she listens to your nonsense for much longer, she will think I am some sort of philanthropist."

Father Michael ignored him and moved once again toward me. "I was very happy to meet you, Brielle. And I am sincere when I wish you well."

"It was an unusual way to meet someone but thank you for your kindness."

Rogue slipped his hand into mine and began walking out of the church to the car waiting for us. The driver opened the door, and I slid into the back seat with Rogue following behind me.

Once the door was closed, he placed his hand on the back of my neck, his thumb gently stroking my skin. "Your coloring is better, but you are still a bit pale. Tell me the truth, you aren't about to faint or get sick, are you?"

I sighed, still in somewhat of a state of shock. "No. I don't know how to feel, but I am not going to faint or throw up all over your car if that's what you are worried about."

His hand came down possessively on mine. "I don't give a fuck about the car. I was worried about you. I know this was a shock, but it is the best way for me to make certain no harm comes to you. I'm glad you are feeling better."

I lifted my chin, meeting his sensual gaze straight on. "I know this is an arranged marriage, a dupe to trick your enemies into believing I am more than what I am. Maybe it is the best way you can think of to protect me, regardless of how bizarre it sounds. Whatever it is, it's not real." I hoped my voice sounded more confident than I felt.

I watched as his face darkened and his eyes turned serious as if he were accepting a challenge. He moved quickly, wrapping his hand in my hair and jerking my head back enough to make a soft gasp escape my lips. "Stop! Stop trying to deny what you feel for me, Bri. You are my wife now, not an actress playing a part, not a game or trick to throw my enemies off guard. My wife, Bri! And if you are still in doubt, tonight I will make you a believer." He pressed his lips to mine, his kiss brutal, hard, and painful. When he released me, my lips were swollen and stinging from his assault.

"My driver will take you back to the penthouse. Blaze will be waiting to escort you. I thought you might like some time to relax before the evening."

I turned toward him and felt a slight tremor of fear at being left alone. "Where are you going?"

He looked behind us. "I'm going to find out why that car, the one parked three cars back, has been following us this morning. I want to find out why they are still here. Then I have some legitimate business to take care of. I will meet you back at the penthouse later."

"But...won't confronting those men be dangerous?"

His grin even looked deadly. "For them, it will be."

He gently pulled me toward him and placed a softer kiss on my cheek. "I was hoping to spend more time with you today and show you more of the city, but I promise to make up for it later."

I didn't know what to say. The way his kiss could turn from

brutal to gentle in such a short time, the feel of his hand at the back of my neck, before it was cruel, now it was surprisingly comforting.

He opened the car door and stepped out. I quickly turned to watch from the back window as he strode purposely toward the car he had mentioned as my driver pulled away from the curb. I wanted to see what would happen, but the driver made a turn that prevented me from seeing anything else. I turned back around and clasped my hands together on my lap, trying to contain my nervousness. Would I feel this fear for the rest of my life, or would I become so numb to it that it would be the new normal? How ironic that I left Colorado out of fear, afraid of the violence that I had been exposed to and now I was drowning in something much more deadly, much more sinister. But this time, there was nowhere to run. Nowhere Rogue wouldn't find me. This time I would not escape from it.

CHAPTER
nine

ROGUE

The dark gray sedan first caught my attention as we were leaving the restaurant after the meeting with Nik, and I was aware that it stayed a consistent three car lengths back as we drove to the church. It did not take long for me to be certain that we were being followed, but whoever it was, they were not professional. The person driving was an amateur, making them very easy to spot. I was confident it wasn't anyone connected to whoever was behind the Armenian threat or any other crime family I was aware of; they were too sloppy, too easily noticed. I had texted Blaze to let him know about the situation and he had immediately said he would take care of it, but I called him off. I needed him to return to the penthouse and be there to escort Bri and protect her until I could deal with other business matters. I would handle this myself.

After the ceremony, I walked Bri to the car after already giving my driver instructions to take her back to the penthouse. No stops along the way.

Once the car began moving away from the curb, I walked toward the gray sedan parked along the street. From the short distance, I could see the two men inside reaching under their coats. I knew exactly what they were going for, strangely enough though, neither one of them made a move, at least not one quick enough.

I swiftly moved to the driver's side window, pulled the pistol I had under my coat, and slammed the butt of it into the middle of the window shattering the glass.

"Fuck!"

Before the man could utter another word, I pulled him through the shards of glass by his neck, halfway hanging out the window, and began pounding his head against the car door. The man in the passenger seat, jumped out, his hand on the pistol he should have already used. But it was too late now. I still held the pistol in my hand and was able to fire before he could even raise his toward me. The bullet penetrated the man's shoulder, causing the pistol in his hand to drop and clatter on the sidewalk. His hands moved to cover the hole the bullet had made as blood began to spurt out of the wound.

I pulled the driver the rest of the way out of the window. "You have about five seconds before I bash in your head and spill your brains all over the sidewalk to tell me why you are following me. And who the hell sent you?"

When no answer was forthcoming, I gripped his hair and slammed his head down on the pavement.

I could vaguely hear Michael's voice as he attended to the man bleeding from the gunshot wound.

"Tell me who sent you now! If you don't, I will kill you and let you bleed out all over the street." I pressed my hand around his throat. His eyes bulged in fear.

"Rogue! Rogue!"

I looked up to see Michael, his bloody hands holding a cell phone he had taken from the other man. "Here, look at the last text."

He tossed me the phone, and I looked down at the screen to read what had been sent, hoping it would lead me to the person responsible for sending these two idiots after me.

"He is just coming out of the church and the girl is still with him. What do you want us to do about her?"

Michael came to stand behind me. "You need to get these men off the street. There have already been some people peeking from their windows."

"There will be a crew here in two minutes. I had already notified Blaze of my intentions. They will make certain nobody talks to the cops or connects you to this incident."

"What about them? Are you going to let them live?"

I took out a handkerchief and wiped the blood from my hands. "For the time being, but not without sending a message to whoever sent them."

We both turned as an SUV carrying five of my men pulled up. They knew exactly what to do. Both men were loaded up without fanfare. Two of the men who worked for me came over to get instructions on how I wanted everything handled.

"Where do you want us to take them, boss?"

"Take them to the warehouse. I will be there shortly. Have two of the men stay here in case anyone who saw what happened tries to make trouble. I don't want Michael to be linked to any of this."

"Sure thing, Mr. Delaney. But the people in this neighborhood aren't going to say anything. They trust you more than the cops, but we will hang around just to make certain."

I watched as they walked away, ready to do whatever was necessary.

I turned to Michael who was frowning and looking at me with that judgmental face that made me want to punch him.

"My men will see to the rest of this mess and have it cleaned up before any of your parishioners see it."

"Thanks for that, but while I never wanted to be pulled back into this world, I have to know, is someone trying to kill you?"

I put a hand on his shoulder. "There is always someone trying to kill me, Michael."

"Don't! Don't try to play this off as just an ordinary day. Something is going on and you need to tell me. You show up here with a girl I have never seen you with before and ask me to perform a marriage ceremony. It was obvious she was not expecting it nor was she thrilled about it. Now, you have beaten the shit out of a man and almost killed another right in front of the church. This is not ordinary, Rogue. What the hell is going on?"

"The less you know the better."

"Bullshit!" He immediately raised his eyes to the heavens and said a quick prayer for forgiveness and most likely patience. "God forgive me. I swore an oath to you the day that you saved me when we were kids. I haven't forgotten it. If you need my help, I am always here."

I shook my head, not wanting Michael to be more involved than he was already. "You swore a greater oath after that, Michael, and I will not ask you to break it for me. Besides, these people were not here for me. Chances are they had no idea who they were dealing with. They were too inexperienced, too green. They were both armed but hesitated at my approach. No, these two dumbasses are small time."

A look of confusion crossed Michael's face. "If they weren't here for you, then who were they after?"

I took out my phone and dialed Blaze. "Has she arrived yet?"

"No, but I am waiting out front."

"Good. Get her up to the penthouse and stay with her. I'll call you back when I know more."

Michael's eyes narrowed. "They were after her, weren't they? That's the reason for the hasty marriage. You really are doing this for her, to protect her."

I shook my head in denial. "Don't make me out to be noble. You know me better than that. I always have selfish reasons for doing things. But in answer to your question, yes, I think they were here to take Bri, but I will know more when I extract some answers from our semi-conscious friend."

Michael's face twisted in disgust.

"Torture is one of the things I am glad not to witness again."

"Go back inside, Michael, and if things are not cleaned up to your standards, let me know. If anyone in the neighborhood says anything..."

"They won't. In this neighborhood, it will all be forgotten."

"Good."

Another car pulled up and I opened the door. "If you see anything that makes you uneasy, give me a call. I can have men stationed here to protect you."

He reached up and clasped the crucifix he was wearing around his neck tightly in his hand. "I am already protected."

I knew there was no use arguing with him; he was well-rooted in his faith. I sat in the backseat, clutching the bloody cell phone tightly in my hand. Could this incident be related to the phone call Bri made this morning? Could this be the man who had stalked her and beaten her back in Colorado? I would soon find out, and if that was the case, he had just signed his death warrant.

Bri

When the car came to a stop outside of the office building where Rogue's penthouse was located, I saw Blaze waiting for me just as Rogue had said. He stepped forward, opened the car door for me, and unceremoniously pulled me from the back seat, tugging me behind him as we moved inside the building.

"For heaven's sake, could you slow down a little? These heels are not meant for running."

I heard a deep grumble, but he did slow his pace a bit, allowing me to catch up. He pulled out a key card and the elevator took us back up to the penthouse. When we stepped inside, I expected him to excuse himself, but instead, he walked straight to the bar and poured himself a drink.

"You look like you could use one too, little one."

I shook my head. "No, thank you." I walked toward the sofa and took a seat. "You don't have to stay with me. I'm sure there are other things you would prefer to do than to babysit me."

He drank the whiskey in his glass in one gulp before refilling it. "There are a hundred things I would rather be doing, but Rogue told me to stay with you. So, I guess you will have to endure my company."

"Can I ask you a question?"

He sat the glass down on the bar and stepped closer, his eyes narrowed as he looked me over. "You can ask, but you may not get the answer you want if I even answer it at all."

I pushed my hair back and studied him. "I'll take my chances. Have there been other women that Rogue has taken and kept like me? And while my mind is cautioning me against asking this next question, what happens to me when he grows tired of all this?"

He didn't answer right away, the palm of his hand rubbed over the rough stubble on his face and his eyes seemed to stare right through me.

"I've never seen Rogue with a woman for more than a night or two. He grows bored with them rather fast or at least he has in the past. He surprised me today when he had Father Michael marry the two of you. That decision leads me to believe that you will be around for a bit longer. How long that will be is uncertain."

An odd twinge of disappointment moved through me. "Hmm, that doesn't leave me with a warm fuzzy feeling."

His lips turned up so slightly that it was hardly noticeable. "Do I look like the kind of man that is capable of giving you warm fuzzies?"

I sighed before kicking off my shoes and pulling my knees underneath me as I got comfortable on the sofa. "No, you don't. I was just hoping you could impart some wisdom, say something that would make me feel better."

He stood up and walked back to the bar and poured a drink before bringing it back over to me. "Drinking will make you feel better. Take a few sips."

I reluctantly took the glass from his hand and took a sip before coughing violently.

"This is repulsive."

He chuckled. "You will get used to it. Take another sip, the first one always burns the most."

I did as he suggested and while the liquor seemed to sear a path of fire down my throat, I didn't cough this time.

"Do you believe as Rogue does that I am truly in danger? Or was that just the reason he gave to scare me enough that I wouldn't fight the marriage he forced on me?"

He leaned back in the chair and seemed more relaxed than I had ever seen him before. "Forced? You don't look like a woman that was forced to do something."

I took another sip of the whiskey in the glass; it seemed to give me a bit of liquid courage. "Just because I'm not covered in bruises doesn't mean that I wasn't coerced. He told me that if I left, people who wanted to hurt him could take me and use me against him."

"They could try, but you are under Rogue's protection now. It would be a fool hearty move to lay a hand on Rogue Delaney's woman."

I took a larger sip from my glass; the whiskey was beginning to make me feel warm all over. "His protection or his control?"

He took the glass from my hand. "I'll order some food. If you keep drinking on an empty stomach, you're going to get drunk, and I don't want to listen to Rogue bitch because I got his new bride wasted on her wedding day."

A sudden pain squeezed my heart. "You know it doesn't feel like a wedding day. I didn't get a fancy dress, or the gifts from people I barely know. I didn't get to smash cake into my groom's face. There was no music, no speeches, no first dance."

He chuckled sardonically. "That sounds very dramatic, but I wouldn't mind seeing the cake smashing thing."

I blew out an exaggerated breath. "What will I tell my friend, Allison? She is never going to believe this."

"I would suggest a well-crafted lie."

I laughed a little. "Who goes to a job interview, ends up being held captive by the boss, and then married the next day? Hell, I can't believe it myself. It's like a weird dream that I can't wake up from."

"Chinese?"

I draped an arm over my eyes as I leaned back against the leather sofa. "What?"

"Chinese, do you eat Chinese food?"

"Oh, yeah. It doesn't matter." I groaned as I heard the whininess in my voice.

His frown deepened. "Stop. You are beginning to sound pathetic, and it is not appealing or attractive. It's fucking annoying."

I got up from the sofa a little quicker than intended and almost lost my balance. "I feel pathetic."

"Far from it, little one. You are now married to one of the richest men in the country. The whole world will be at your fingertips. Instead of whining and complaining about it, why don't you embrace it? Do you know how many women would love to be in your shoes?"

"Perhaps I can trade places with one of them."

"It doesn't work like that, sweetheart, not in this world. You were chosen. Go change into something comfortable while we wait for the food to be delivered. Then you can take a much-needed nap before it is time to get ready for the gala tonight."

I huffed out a shallow breath. "Oh yeah, I forgot about that. Will you be going?"

"Unfortunately, yes, at least until I leave for the club."

I didn't ask what he meant by that. I walked into the bedroom Rogue had first given me before he insisted that I share his bed. The closet was filled with all the things he had purchased for me. I rummaged through the closet, easily finding evening attire, dresses for every occasion, and some casual outfits, but nothing suitable for lounging on the couch and binging Netflix. I just wanted my favorite old t-shirt and comfortable leggings, the ones with a hole in the right knee from my apartment. But I settled for a pair of jeans and a soft white cotton T-shirt.

By the time I finally made it back into the living room, Blaze was already setting out a variety of Chinese food to eat.

"That was quick. I hope you didn't order all of this for me."

He was reading something on his phone, his expression darker than it had been earlier.

A sudden chill swept over me. "Is everything alright? What's happened?"

He looked up from his phone. "Nothing that can't be handled."

I walked closer and peeked inside the takeout boxes and felt my stomach rumble at the smell of the chicken fried rice. I sat down and grabbed some chopsticks. "Aren't you hungry?"

"No, I'm going downstairs to make a call. You will be safe here; no one can access the elevators that come up to the penthouse without a special key card. Rogue and I are the only two people with one, and I will be watching. Eat, watch television, take a nap, do whatever you wish. Just be ready to leave for the gala by eight. There is a dress waiting for you in the bedroom. Rogue had it delivered while you were out."

I rolled my eyes as I took another bite. "Will I ever be able to make my own decisions? Does he not trust me to do something as simple as picking out a dress?"

"It's not my place to say, little one. But it's good to see that you are still set on complaining."

I looked around for something to throw at him, but before I could find something, he was gone. I took another bite or two of the Chinese food. While it was delicious, I just wasn't hungry anymore. I walked back into the bedroom that I had shared with Rogue and found a garment bag lying on the bed. A part of me wanted not to care what was inside, but my curiosity got the best of me, and I unzipped it.

Inside was a stunning one-shoulder silver beaded gown. I ran my hand over the silk. I might be angry at having my decisions taken from me, at being forced to marry a man I barely knew, but I was still a woman. A woman who had never had the opportunity to own clothes this extravagant. Living in a small town in Colorado didn't exactly put me in the midst of high-class social circles. Never having the money for fine things growing up, I couldn't help but be a little excited at having the opportunity to wear a dress that looked like something I would have drooled over in a magazine or seen an actress wearing on the red carpet. I zipped the garment bag back up and climbed into bed. Exhaustion seemed to sweep over me. Stress tended to do that. And I couldn't remember a time when I had been more stressed than I am now. My eyes grew heavier as I nuzzled into the thick down comforter and incredibly fluffy pillows. The sheets were the softest I had ever felt. Knowing this was his bed made a part of me want to rebel against the contented feeling it gave me. I inhaled deeply, the scent of sandalwood with hints of oak lingered. I knew I should probably rest before tonight, and I was so tired, but the fear of knowing that Tony was in Chicago looking for me might trigger the nightmares to return.

For several months after the attack, I had terrible dreams almost every night forcing me to relive that terror. It was almost as if I could feel his fists hitting me until I was too weak to fight back any longer. I could feel my clothing being ripped and torn, his hands rough and hard against my skin. I fought harder when he tried to force my legs apart. I knew what he was after and even barely conscious I knew I had to keep fighting. That's when I would wake up. Covered in sweat, tears streaming from my eyes, and shaking almost uncontrollably. Allison had suggested that I see a therapist, but that was just another luxury I couldn't afford.

Gradually the nightmares became less frequent and shorter until they disappeared completely. But now with being faced with the possibility of Tony finding me, I felt like I was right back in that night. Sure, Rogue Delaney had married me to protect me, but once the danger he was facing passed, I was sure he would tire of me. Even his friend Blaze said he had never seen him with a woman for more than a night or two. And once he was through with me, I would be on my own again. Only this time if Tony found me, I knew he would kill me.

Rogue

I looked at the two men tied to chairs in front of me. The one with the gunshot wound in his shoulder was beyond asking questions, while the one unfortunate enough to still be conscious was crying so much that I was tempted to slit his throat just for some peace and quiet.

I walked around his chair slowly as I held his phone in my hand. From what I had discovered and from what he had willingly spilled on his own without me having to use any means of force confirmed exactly what I suspected. These two were members of a small-time inconsequential gang here in Chicago. Nothing that I would have ever deemed a threat or given two thoughts about. They were more concerned with selling drugs on the streets and petty theft. Nothing that involved me or any of my business dealings. But from the texts I had read they weren't there for me, they were after Bri. A mistake that would cost them dearly.

I moved in front of the man and stared down as he continued to weep and beg for mercy. It was truly nauseating to see someone with so little courage.

"I want to know why you and your piece of shit friend were following me."

"We weren't, Mr. Delaney, I swear."

I stood back as one of my men stepped forward to emphasize that I expected an answer to my question.

"Now, I will ask again. If I don't get the answers I want, I will have my associate start taking you apart piece by piece."

"We were told to follow your car, but just to see if the girl was still with you. We were just told to find her. Some guy came to our boss and wanted his help in finding her. The guy we work for owed him a favor."

I didn't have the time for this nonsense.

"Who was the man that wanted you to find her?"

The man's lips trembled pathetically. "I don't know. We were just told to find the girl. Once we found her, we were told to report back with her location. That's it. We weren't supposed to take her or hurt her, just find her."

I looked back to my men standing around the warehouse. They would kill both of these idiots if I commanded it, but they weren't the ones I wanted. I wanted the man who had hurt Bri, the man who had tried to take what was meant for me.

"I want his name and any other information your boss has on

him. Tell your boss he has until tomorrow night to appear at my club with the information I want. If he doesn't show or chooses not to share what he knows, I will shut down his entire operation. It won't even be difficult."

The man was sweating profusely, but he nodded in understanding. "Yes, sir."

"Take them back to the church. Drop them there." I walked away and Jason, one of my men, followed me. "After you drop them off, follow them. I want to know where they go."

"You don't trust their boss to show up at the club?"

"Trusting people is not how I got where I am. Follow him and report back to me, and if you find the one that paid them to find my wife...."

"Kill him?"

"No, I want him brought to me. Killing him quickly would be too easy."

CHAPTER
Ten

BRI

After soaking, once again, in Rogue's luxuriously large whirlpool tub, I lost track of time and now I was scurrying around trying to get dressed for the gala that he said we must attend this evening. I sat before the mirror with only a towel wrapped around me, trying to finish my make-up and deciding how to do my hair. I wanted to pin the curls up, but since my hair was so thick, I wasn't sure I had enough pins to do so. I wished I had my things from the apartment. Rogue had the bathroom stocked with everything a girl could dream of, but none of it felt as if it belonged to me. There was just something about having my own things.

After several failed attempts and almost giving up altogether, I finally managed to get my hair curled and pinned up the way I wanted. I glanced at the clock beside the bed. I had about ten minutes to finish getting ready. Blaze had said that Rogue would be here at eight o'clock and I was almost certain he would be the type of guy to be punctual.

I stepped into the dress, the soft silk caressing my skin, walked over to the mirror and took a minute to just admire my appearance. I had never had anything so nice, or so expensive in my life. I let my hands move over the beaded silk and watched how the light in the room caught the shimmer of the crystals sewn onto it. Despite the situation I was in, I still had to admit that I loved the way I looked in the dress.

I glanced at the clock again and seeing that it was now eight o'clock, I grabbed the heels that came with the dress, hoping I could walk in them without breaking my ankle, and headed to the living room, hoping Blaze would be there to zip my dress up the rest of the way.

When I stepped out into the hallway, I stopped short. Rogue was standing there and despite the deadly serious expression he wore on his face, he looked sexy as hell in the black tux he was wearing.

"Oh, you're already here. I hope you haven't been waiting long. I guess I lost track of time."

The ferocity of his gaze surprised me as he stalked forward. "Tell me the name of the man that you ran away from, the man that hurt you."

I shook my head, not wanting to have this discussion again. "No, there is no need for you to know."

He gripped my arm tightly. "Damn it, Bri! There is every reason for me to know! You are my wife now and as such I will protect you. Give me his name!"

Fire flashed in his eyes and for a second, I was reminded of how dangerous he could be and how terrifying it must be for those that find themselves on his bad side.

"Why? What are you going to do?"

He abruptly wrapped an arm around my waist and anchored me to his body while his free hand held my chin firm. "I am going to do whatever it takes to keep you safe."

I tried to look away. "And how are you going to do that? I thought marrying me was supposed to keep me safe, or was that just a ploy to get what you want?"

The corners of his lips turned up slightly, but it was not a pleasant smile. "You want to know what I will do to him once he is found? Alright, I will tell you. I have every intention of finding him and when I do, I am going to chain him to a wall in a place that I have set aside for just these kinds of things. I am going to bring him more pain than he could ever imagine. I want to watch him quake in fear and tremble with the realization that his life is about to end. I want him to feel the pain you felt when he tried to rape you. I want him to know that he fucked up when he dared try to take what belonged to me, Bri."

I pushed against his chest, needing to put some space between us. Whenever Rogue was near, he seemed to suck the oxygen from the room, and I found it difficult to breathe, to think. "You can't kill him for something that happened before I even met you."

"Have you still not learned, my sweet angel, that I can and will do whatever I want? Now tell me his name so we can enjoy the remainder of our evening."

The man may drive me mad with lust, but his arrogance was astounding. "No, I told you that he is dangerous and has connections to people who are just as bad as he is. So, do what you will, but you can't bully me into telling you his name."

For a second a sliver of fear rippled through me as I watched his eyes darken. His breathing increased just a hitch, but then a calm mask took over. I wasn't sure what was more terrifying.

"Very well, if that is what you wish."

He yanked me beside him and pulled me back to the bedroom.

"What are you doing?"

He walked over to the nightstand and pulled out the handcuffs he had used the first night I had tried to leave the building.

A panic began to settle over me. "You are not using those on me again!" I tried to pull away, but the grip he had on my arm tightened.

"I was hoping to have a more pleasurable evening, but you are so stubborn."

My mouth opened. "I'm stubborn? You are the one threatening to handcuff me to the bed again just because you didn't get your way." I pulled back and struggled as he clasped the cuff around my wrist.

"You are my wife, whether you want to be or not, and it is my job to keep you safe! Today, when we left the church, the car that was following us was not there for me, Bri. They were sent for you."

I felt the color leave my face and all the fight left my body. Rogue must have noticed and quickly wrapped his arms around me.

"He said he would kill me." My words were soft, barely audible.

Rogue's touch instantly gentled. "No one is going to hurt you, Angel. I will make sure of it, but I can't keep you safe if you don't trust me. Give me his name. I will find him eventually regardless. Your refusal only slows me down a bit. If you continue to be stubborn, I will handcuff you to the bed and keep you locked away until I find him myself. That is not a threat, Bri."

I glanced over at the metal on my wrist and then over to the bed. I couldn't stand the thought of being restrained again.

"Do you promise not to kill him?"

His eyes narrowed. "Why are you so hell bent on protecting a man that put you in the hospital, that tried to rape you?"

My eyes shot up. "I'm not trying to protect him! I just want to forget. I don't want to relive it again."

A tear rolled down my cheek, and I furiously wiped it away, ashamed to show the man before me any weakness.

When his arms tightened around me, I welcomed the warmth and steadiness he offered. He kissed the top of my head. "I will make you forget him, love. He will not be able to get close to you, but to keep you safe, I need you to tell me his name."

I sniffled and took a deep breath, determined not to let another tear fall. I was stronger than that. "Tony. Tony Galante." Rogue released me and typed something into his phone. Probably sending Tony's name to his friend Blaze. "Now that I told you, will you take off the handcuffs?"

He lifted my wrist and released the metal before placing a kiss on my skin. "I'm glad you told me." He dangled the cuffs in front of my face. "I prefer to use these for pleasure, not punishment."

"What are you going to do now?" I took a step back and wrapped my arms across my body.

"Whatever I need to do."

He stepped forward, the hard lines of his face even more pronounced as he moved into the light. "I have something for you."

He walked out of the room, but I didn't follow. When he came back inside, he held out his hand and I saw he was holding a jewelry gift box. He opened it and sitting on the black velvet glistening in the light was a stunning diamond necklace, matching earrings, and bracelet. My fingers itched to touch the stones. I had never seen anything so lovely in my life, and I knew it had to cost more than I made in a year, probably three.

My arm started to reach for it, but I pulled my hand back. "I shouldn't take things like this from you."

I saw his eyes narrow even more. "Why shouldn't you? You are my wife, Bri, and as my wife, I intend to give you gifts quite often. Now, turn around."

I did as he asked and shivered as he placed the diamonds around my neck, his fingers whispering over my flesh. "I think we should talk about that as well."

"What?"

He leaned closer, his lips near my ear. "The fact that you are my wife?"

He grabbed my wrist and fastened the bracelet around it.

I held it up and admired the perfection of the stones. For just a few seconds I was caught up in the moment, but the events of the morning came back in a rush. "Yes, everything happened so fast, I wasn't prepared for any of it. I don't know what to think. There is a rush of emotions I have felt and none of them made me feel any better about this."

He took my hand and placed the diamond teardrop earrings in my palm for me to place in my ears. "You are rambling, love. What do you want to know? You are my wife; it is legal and binding. Tonight, I will present you as such to the elite society circles that I move about in, and any enemies I might have, or you have, will know that you belong to me now and that you will be protected by me and everyone within my organization. I'm not sure what else there is to know."

I blew out a slow breath, trying not to react to his nearness or the smell of his cologne. "Yes, I suppose I should thank you for that anyway. You did say that I would not be safe unless I was tied to you, but when all the danger has passed, what then? Do we go about our lives and pretend this never happened? Get an annulment or a divorce?"

He stepped closer and I backed away until I hit the wall. "I know it's only been a few days, but do you think you could forget, Angel? That you could go back to your old life without a thought for me and the way I make you feel."

He kept coming closer until his body was flush against mine. He was taller, and I had to crane my neck to look up at him. His coffee-colored eyes peered into mine. "Because if that is the case...," He leaned down closer, his lips a breath away from the skin of my neck. "I will remedy that tonight."

His hands came up to grasp my hips as he pulled me into him. His erection was evident and despite myself, I couldn't help but feel aroused to know that I could make this man desire me so fervently.

Suddenly, he spun me around, I placed my hands against the wall and gasped as his fingers traced a path along my spine. His fingers toyed with the zipper as if he was trying to decide if he should zip it the rest of the way or tear it free from my body.

I blinked a few times, trying to make my brain focus on anything other than the man behind me. "I tried to zip it myself."

He moved my hair to the side and once again let his fingers trace over my skin. "I would much rather be helping you out of the dress than in it, but when I do relieve you of this dress, I want to take my time and if we are to make an appearance at the gala we should hurry."

I turned around, still unnerved by his close proximity. "I would rather stay here." I saw something flash in his eyes, and I knew he had misinterpreted what I meant. "Not for the reason that you are think-ing. I mean, I won't fit in. Last week I was working as a hotel clerk. You can't drape me in expensive jewelry and designer dresses and make me into something I'm not. Wouldn't you rather go alone or with someone else?"

He grabbed my hand and started pulling me behind him as he

walked toward the elevator. "No, Angel. There is no one else I would rather take than you."

I realized there was no use fighting or arguing anymore and followed him into the elevator. Once the doors closed, he pulled me into his chest and kissed me. His lips were warm and possessive, and I found myself melting against him.

"You look beautiful." His hand came up and a finger traced over the curve of my cheek. "I can see the worry on your face. Why do you look so afraid?"

"I don't know. Maybe it's because my life has been turned completely upside down over the course of just a few days. I was forced to marry a dangerous crime boss so that his enemies would not go after me. I'm sure you remember that conversation, don't you? The one where you suggested I could either marry you or be faced with extreme torture or death. And to make matters worse, the crazed stalker who almost killed me in Colorado has discovered my where-abouts and has sent other dangerous men to find me. Other than that, it's been a fairly normal week."

His deep chuckle made me want to hit him, but the elevator doors opened, and his friend Blaze was waiting for us.

"The car is here, and all security precautions have been taken."

He looked from Rogue to me without a hint of emotion in his eyes. "Have you talked to her?"

My eyes darted to Rogue's face. "Talked to me about what?"

He took my arm and led me to the car. "There are certain things that have been put into place to ensure your safety."

I climbed in the back seat followed by Rogue, and Blaze sat up front.

Rogue reached over and took my hand.

"I'm waiting. What sort of safety protocols have been put in place? From the way that your friend looked, I'm not so sure I will be happy about them."

I heard Blaze grunt from the front seat.

"You will always have an escort. You may not go anywhere without either myself or Blaze at your side."

I couldn't help but roll my eyes. "That seems a bit drastic. So, I am to have an escort to the ladies' room?"

"Yes." He said without hesitation.

"You are serious?"

"Most definitely. Alessio Messina's wife was accosted outside the restroom of the Guggenheim in New York at an event very similar to this one. He discovered her in a hallway fighting against a man whose hands were up her skirts"

My hand flew to my mouth, instantly feeling sympathy for a woman that had been through a situation similar to mine. "What happened?"

He raised my hand to his lips. "Alessio killed him. And since I have other plans for tonight, you will abide by these rules."

"Killed him?"

Rogue's eyes narrowed a fraction. "Do you still not understand? I am the type of man who takes what I want without apology, and I will mercilessly protect what belongs to me with violence if necessary. So, just as Alessio protected Eden, I will not hesitate to kill anyone who disrespects you."

I felt a lump in my throat and wasn't sure how to react to such a bold statement. I had never had anyone in my life to protect or care for me. I had been alone since I was six years old. Raised by an uncle who spent more time in a bottle than he did taking care of his niece. At twelve, I went to live with a cousin who provided a place to sleep and food to eat but ignored me completely. When I turned eighteen, I moved in with my friend Allison. Having someone want to care for me, and provide for me, was a foreign concept and hard to adjust to.

"Is the event we are going to dangerous?"

"Just because these people have money and are for the most part considered the diamonds of society doesn't mean that evil doesn't move about in their circles. I am proof of that."

Rogue

. . .

I knew my words had shocked her, as I had meant for them to do. It was important now that she obeyed and followed the guidelines that I set. I needed her to understand fully the type of man that I was.

"You are missing something."

She turned her face to mine, her eyes still wide, the passing lights of the city shining in them.

I took her hand; she was trembling. Frightening her had not been my intention. I wanted her to know that I was serious about the protection she would receive and the lengths I would go to shield her from anything that could hurt her, but I was not a man she should fear.

"Are you afraid of me?"

"Should I be?"

My hand instantly reached for her neck to pull her closer to me. "Anyone that dares to touch you, should fear me like the devil himself. But never you...my lost angel."

I had not meant to kiss her then, we were only a few minutes away from the gala, but when her pretty little tongue slipped over her bottom lip, I knew any restraint I had been holding onto when I first saw her tonight in her silver beaded gown was lost. I was not expecting the electrifying sensation that moved through me when my lips touched hers. I intensified the kiss pressing her back against the seat, my hand instinctively sought her warm flesh. My fingers slid up her dress to her knee and while I wanted to go higher, we were not alone. I wanted to have the driver turn the car around. I wanted to rip the designer dress from her body and bury myself deep inside her.

"Stop the car and get out!"

"We are only a block away from the gala," Blaze responded, but my driver was already slowing the car, knowing that it would be the end of his job not to follow orders.

"I don't give a fuck. Stop the goddamn car and get out!"

I heard Blaze grumble something under his breath about me being an impulsive asshole, but right now I didn't care what he thought. I wanted to feel more of her, I wanted to kiss more of her, and I didn't want anyone but me to hear the soft sighs of pleasure that slipped past her lips.

When I heard the doors to the car close behind them, my hand slipped farther up her leg, easily finding her panties and slipping them aside so I could slip my fingers inside her. She was already growing wet on my hand. I reached up and pulled the neckline of her dress lower until the peaks of her nipples came into view. I growled greedily as my tongue circled the tight little nubs before sucking them into my mouth.

"Rogue." The sound of my name, a sultry whisper on her lips, spurred me on. I pushed her dress up higher, fully intending on tasting her when her small hands pushed against my chest.

"We can't do this. Someone will see."

At this point, I was beyond caring. "There is limousine tint on the windows. No one could see in if they tried. Now, you have about three seconds to slide out of those panties before I tear them off you."

I watched as her hands moved up her dress and she slipped the tiny bit of silk and lace down her long legs. I unzipped my pants, my hard cock springing forth. "Come here."

She didn't move fast enough for my liking. I gripped her waist and lifted her, so she was straddling my dick. I pushed up the skirt of her dress so my hands could rest on the bare flesh of her hips.

"Slide down over me."

The slowness in which she moved was almost torture. I had to hold myself still. The urge to grip her hips and slam into her was stronger than anything I had felt before. I closed my eyes and gritted my teeth until I was fully sheathed inside her. The little vixen may have been a virgin yesterday, but when she wiggled her little bottom adjusting herself, I nearly came undone.

My hand went up and tangled in her hair as I yanked her head down and my lips crashed into hers. The kiss was brutal, there was some part of me that wanted it to be painful. I wanted her lips to be swollen from my kiss. The urgency was too much. I swiftly shifted positions until her back was pressed against the seat. My arms hooked her knees pushing her legs up and out farther as I slammed into her. Her cries should have caused me to be more tender, gentler, but they had the opposite effect. They drove me to the brink of insanity. What was it about this woman that made me want her, all of her? I wanted her to scream my name. I wanted to fuck her so hard that she would never again question that she was mine, that she belonged to me and with me.

I felt her body shiver beneath me, her hands clawing at my shoulders. I dipped my head lower and sank my teeth into her collarbone, leaving a mark that would be seen by everyone, which was exactly what I wanted.

I thrust into her, forcing her legs higher over my shoulders. Her tight pussy clenched around me as her orgasm came over her. I pumped once more filling her, my shoulders heaved with my heavy breathing, and my heart hammered in my chest. The intensity of the moment was almost alarming. I leaned down and kissed the red mark I left on her collarbone before gently kissing her swollen lips.

"You drive me mad, woman. My control breaks when you are near. The way you smell, the softness of your skin, the silkiness of your hair, everything about you drives me to the brink of madness. All I can think of is you lying naked beneath me." I looked down at her flushed cheeks. "A distraction, a curse, a thirst I cannot quench, a fire that burns me to my soul, I cannot, nor will I be without you."

I glanced down at her bare perfect breasts once more before pulling out of her. I helped her back into a sitting position. I watched as she pulled her bodice back into place and it took every ounce of control I possessed, not to rip it from her body. I wanted nothing between us.

The pounding outside on the window drew my attention away from the enchanting woman I held in my arms.

"I didn't get dressed in this monkey suit just to stand watch while you defile her in the back seat of the car."

Blaze's harsh voice broke through my lust. It wasn't just the gala, there were other reasons to attend tonight, and I needed to put aside the hunger I felt for Brielle for the time being and focus on business.

A man was to be in attendance tonight with information on the Armenian mafia and their next move. Blaze had done his research, and it appeared to be on the level. If the information would lead to the end of the Armenian threat, it would be well worth the price the man was asking.

I reluctantly sat up and pulled Bri up alongside me, still wanting to touch as much of her as possible. "I'm sorry for my lack of control, love. I would say that I never meant to hurt you, but it would be a lie."

She adjusted her dress and tried to fix her hair so it wouldn't look as if she had been manhandled. But there was nothing she could do for her lips or the marks I had left on her perfect skin. They were plump and swollen from my kiss and she looked so damn fuckable right now. My dick hardened, and I looked away before I told Blaze to handle the meeting himself, took her home, and fucked her until she couldn't move.

Her eyes were bright, and her cheeks still flushed when she turned to me. "Is there somewhere I can clean up."

"No, I want you to walk in there with my cum dripping down your legs, my scent lingering around you." My fingers brushed over the reddened mark on her collarbone that was impossible to hide. "I want everyone to know who you belong to; I want everyone to know that I just fucked my wife."

Her mouth fell open slightly as she was scandalized by my words. I knew I was a bastard but right now the beast inside me was roaring to possess her, to claim her for the world to see.

"I said earlier that you were missing something."

I reached into my coat pocket and pulled out a ring box. She was still in too much shock to open it, so I did the honors for her.

"If it is not what you want or the cut you prefer, we can look for something else later. But as my wife, you needed a ring."

I took her hand in mine before slipping the large twelve-carat emerald cut diamond solitaire surrounded by another two carats of smaller stones on her finger just above the plain platinum band I had placed earlier.

"Do you like it?"

I watched as she held it up to study the ring, her hand still trembling. "It's beautiful."

I smiled. "I'm glad you think so."

"But it is too much. It must have cost a fortune." She reached up and touched the diamonds around her neck before glancing at the bracelet on her wrist. "You don't have to do this you know."

"What?"

She shrugged her shoulders. "Give me expensive things. I never had things like this before, so it isn't expected."

She was a breath of fresh air. Most of the women I knew that's all they wanted, what my fortune could buy them. But not Bri, she was uncomfortable with gifts. That was something she would have to get over because I intended to give my angel much more than she could ever dream of. I wanted to see the worry lines leave her face and a smile stretch across her lips, the kind of smile she had on her face when I first met her at the club before the darkness that surrounded me encased her.

"The diamonds suit you, and I tend to do whatever I wish, so I'm afraid you will have to get used to me spoiling you."

She looked away, a mixture of irritation and uncertainty on her face.

The car came to a stop, and I interlaced my fingers with hers. The flash of the cameras was blinding as we stepped from the car. I squeezed Bri's hand, hoping to give her the encouragement she needed to get through the evening.

As we made our way through the throng of photographers and paparazzi, I felt Bri's hand tighten in mine. The thought that she was beginning to feel safer with me made me grin. My girl was starting to come around.

When we entered the gala, the first person to come forward to greet us was United States Senator Bentley O'Malley. He was a snake, but useful at times.

"Rogue Delaney, it has been too long." He held his hand out to me, but his eyes had locked on Bri.

I took his hand and squeezed a little harder than necessary to get his attention. "It's not an election year, Senator. What brings you to Chicago?"

His sleazy smile made me want to push Bri behind me and far away from the man. "I am here for my constituents...and campaign funds. You never stop campaigning, Rogue." His gaze moved back to Bri. "And who is your lovely companion for the evening?"

"Brielle, this is Senator O'Malley." As the Senator reached for her hand, I interceded. I didn't want anyone the likes of O'Malley touching her; I didn't want any other man to touch her. "She is my wife, Senator."

No more words were needed, the tone of my voice and my protective stance communicated easily that she was off-limits. Even a senator with as much power as O'Malley would not dare try to invoke my anger by touching my wife.

"It is nice to meet you, Senator."

Bri's soft voice cut through the haze of possessive fury I was beginning to feel and instantly calmed me.

I wrapped my hand around her waist to hold her against my side.

The senator's eyes wisely moved away from Bri. "Congratulations. I had not heard that you had married, Rogue."

"I never imagined you would, O'Malley. I don't disclose my private life to those not in my inner circle."

I watched the senator's eyes flash with a momentary spark of anger. I imagined he had grown accustomed to people kissing his ass wherever he went, but I would never be one of them. He should be begging for my favor, not the other way around. I was the king of this city.

"Have a good evening, Senator, and enjoy the short time you are in Chicago."

I took Bri's hand and led her to the dance floor and pulled her into my arms.

"Should you have done that? He looks pissed and making enemies of a senator could be detrimental to your career or whatever you do to make money."

The music had just started a slow dance. "I am not afraid of the senator. If I wanted him removed from office, he would be, and he knows it. My power and influence are far more reaching than his, love."

She looked over her shoulder to where the senator was speaking to someone else. "He gives me the creeps."

I couldn't help but laugh. "You are a good judge of character."

"I wouldn't say so."

Before I could argue the point with her, I saw Blaze standing across the room. He inclined his head slightly, then looked toward the bar where our informant was drinking while trying to coax his way into the pants of a girl much younger than him.

I gripped Bri's arm. "I would take offense at that if I thought you were speaking of me."

"Who says I wasn't? Where are we going?"

"I have someone I need to speak to alone. You are going to wait with Blaze. Have a drink, enjoy the music, perhaps he will delight you with stories."

She sighed softly. "Delight me with stories? Are we talking about the same guy?"

I knew Blaze was not much of a conversationalist, but he was trusted, and I would only leave my most prized possession with him. "Stay here. I'll be back when I can."

"How long will you be?"

I heard the change in the tone of her voice. "Miss me already?"

"No, I just wanted to know how long I would be free of you."

I leaned closer to her ear. "Just long enough for you to imagine all the things I am going to do to you tonight once I rip that dress and anything you are wearing underneath from your body."

Her cheeks were still flushed from where I had fucked her in the car before we arrived at the gala, and I loved it. "I bet if I backed you up against the wall, and my fingers found their way to your pussy, you would be soaking wet."

"Stop talking to me like that."

She looked away, and I couldn't resist leaning over and kissing her cheek. "I enjoy seeing you flustered, baby."

Her eyes lowered. "Am I just to stand here with the grumpy giant? What if someone asks me to dance?"

My teasing smile instantly vanished. "No dancing unless you want to see me commit violence."

I glanced over at Blaze, who had heard her question and was grinning at my response. The two of us had always commented on how ridiculous we thought Alessio behaved when it came to his wife Eden, but now that I had Bri, I understood the feeling of intense possessiveness that coursed through my veins at the thought of another man touching her or thinking that they could take her from me.

"Keep her in your sight at all times. As soon as I have what I want from Sevan Avagyan, we will get the hell out of here. I have already grown bored with this."

CHAPTER
eleven

BRI

As Rogue walked away, I observed how the women in the room immediately tried to gain his notice, either by a sly smile, a casual wink, a louder than necessary laugh, or the even bolder approach of walking into his path. I couldn't blame them. He was sexy as hell, and in that tux, with the way he exuded money and power, it was enough to make any woman do a double take. A few weeks ago, if I had seen him in the same situation, I would have ogled him too. Now, after being in his bed, I felt as if there was a hypnotic force drawing me to him. I had said time and again that I would leave when given the chance, that I didn't belong to him. I repeated it in my head over and over, just waiting for the right moment, but now I wasn't sure if I would take the opportunity if it was given to me. The man was captivating in a strange perilous sort of way.

I pulled my eyes away from him and instead turned to Blaze. "Why does he come to these things? He doesn't mingle well. He doesn't dance. He doesn't seem to enjoy any of it. And he wants to leave early. I just don't understand. Why not avoid it all?"

My grumpy bodyguard stepped a little closer to loom over me when it looked as if a gentleman was getting ready to approach us.

"It's business, little one. He makes an appearance to let everyone know that he is still in power and that this is still his city. To remind his enemies and anyone foolish enough to confront him, that they will not succeed. It is a show of supremacy and lets people know what he will do to keep it. And you."

I looked at him sharply. "Me?"

"Yep, you don't think he brought you here tonight just to show you a good time. He is letting everyone know that you are his now." He looked down and his lips turned up for just a second. "Marking his territory...so to speak." His eyes flicked over the red teeth mark embedded on my collarbone.

I scanned the crowd until I saw him again. He was speaking to a man at the bar, his stance, his mannerisms, and everything about him radiated authority and dominance. The man he was speaking with was older and appeared to be nervous. I couldn't deny my curiosity.

"Are we here because of what happened at the club? Because someone tried to kill your friend Nickolai? Does this man have information or ...." I paused as another more disturbing thought crossed my mind. "Are we here because of the men that were following us today, the ones that were after me?"

I reached for his arm to steady myself and the look of panic on his face was almost comical.

"Are you alright? Don't you dare faint!"

I closed my eyes briefly. "I'm not going to faint. Why does everyone think I'm going to faint? After everything I have been through, you should know by now that I am not that fragile. I just needed a moment. So, will you tell me? Is that the reason he is here tonight, to find out who was following us? Was it...Tony?"

Blaze frowned and grumbled something under his breath. "He is here for another reason, little one. Not for the man that was after you, not tonight anyway."

I tried to turn my attention back to the gala and the people in attendance. I had always been a people watcher, but tonight my eyes kept drifting to only one man. Even with my giant lurking bodyguard blocking my view, I still managed to catch a glimpse of him again. The conversation he was having was turning serious, the man he was speaking with began sweating profusely and took out a handkerchief to wipe his brow, but Rogue maintained his casual, yet superior demeanor.

As if he could sense me watching, his head turned in my direction. I stepped back and turned away, hoping he didn't think I had been staring at him the entire time, which for the most part I had.

Blaze's deep voice startled me. "Would you like a drink?"

I couldn't stop the snarky reply that slipped out. "Am I allowed?"

"I just thought you might be thirsty. Staring at Rogue the way you have been doing the past few minutes has to have made your mouth dry. Not to mention your extracurricular activities in the car."

I took a step away. "I wasn't staring. And I wasn't looking at him anyway. I was watching someone else."

"I would watch my words if I were you, little one. Rogue has proven to be quite jealous. I have never seen that part of him before, but if his jealousy is like everything else about him, it will be intense and consuming. Games can prove to be dangerous."

I glanced back toward the bar, but Rogue was no longer there. He was walking back in our direction, and from the look on his face, the news or information he had received was not good.

Rogue

"You are being paid well for what you are about to tell me, Sevan. It had better be worth it. Why is the Armenian mob making a move on my city?"

Sevan took a drink and looked toward the door as if he were afraid someone would walk in at any moment and discover him talking to me. "It is not a unified effort and not supported by most of us in the family. It's these young men coming into power. They don't want to work for anything anymore. Their fathers built up their empires and they are burning them to the ground as soon as they come into power."

He took another drink. "Petros Sargsyan took over the family business after his father Hayk's death last year. His father was a friend of mine. He worked hard to build up his family business; he was ruthless but fair. Petros is nothing like him. He doesn't want to put in the work and is too busy running around trying to pretend he is *Scarface*. He is arrogant, foolish, and merciless. He was always cruel as a child but is worse now that he is the leader of the family. He was Hayk's only son, so he has no one to challenge his authority."

"None of which is my business. But coming into my city and trying to make trouble with the intention of taking from me and my organization is beyond foolish."

He shook his head in agreement. "Many of us close to the family believe so as well. But Petros wants to take it all: Chicago, Vegas, even the Italians in New York. To say he is ambitious is an understatement."

"Ambitious is the wrong word. Foolish and reckless is more apt. But you should not be concerned with the Bratva or the Italians. Petros will not survive me."

"There are a few of us that will be pleased to see him meet his end. That was why I came to you."

I looked across the room and saw that Blaze was keeping watch over Bri. "Do you know his next move?"

I listened as he detailed what Petros Sargsyan had planned. If the information Sevan had given me was correct, the young Armenian was not only preparing to attack my organization but Nickolai's as well. At least I now knew who specifically was behind the threat and a timeline for the next attack. The ambitious young fool was planning to burn my warehouses and my nightclubs to the ground, disrupt shipments, and of course, kill me as soon as the opportunity presented itself. Sevan also confirmed that I had been the original target at the club the night Nikolai was attacked.

I had been forced to eliminate threats before, that was nothing new. But this time it was different...because I had her. The thought of Bri being hurt or taken from me because of some ambitious young punk wanting to make a name for himself made me furious. So, I needed to end this before the danger got closer to her than it already was.

I would have to increase security more than I had already. Blaze would organize the men that worked for me and since Alessio was partners with me in our newest nightclub, I would need to inform him. Not that I needed his help, but it was his business interests that were threatened too. If the Armenian nuisance wasn't enough, I also had to find Tony Galante, the man who was searching for Bri and sent the car to follow us this morning. I can't deny that I would take great pleasure in bringing him death.

But all of that could wait. Tonight, I had more pressing matters. Blaze could start preparing for what needed to be done to thwart Petros and the threat he posed. I had restrained myself for as long as possible. My beautiful but reluctant wife stood off to the side of the ballroom, looking more tempting than any woman I had ever seen before, and she was all mine.

The crowd parted as I pushed through it. Her expressive eyes locked with mine, and I wasn't certain if I would permit her to walk out on her own accord or swoop her up into my arms. The latter would more than likely cause more of a stir than I was comfortable with, but at this point, I wasn't sure how much I cared.

Blaze had a drink in his hand, but when he saw me headed in his direction, he threw it back and swallowed the contents in one gulp.

"What did Sevan have to say?"

I grabbed Bri's hand. "Go speak with him, he is waiting for you. You will want to call Nik and make arrangements with him. We can talk tomorrow in the office at the penthouse. I am not certain the club is secure enough. I'll send the driver back for you."

"No need. I can find my way home."

I followed his line of vision and saw a woman in a short red cocktail dress seductively eating the olive off the toothpick in her martini. He had found his prey for the evening.

I pulled Bri closer to my side. "Come on, love. I have other plans for tonight that don't involve being surrounded by a hundred pretentious people."

"I don't understand. The only reason you came tonight was to meet with the old man at the bar. And now after doing so, you just want to leave?"

I stopped and she bumped into me. "Are you saying you want to stay?"

She shook her head. "No, I just don't understand. You bought me this dress, draped me in diamonds that cost more than what I could make working in three years, for what? So, I could stand with Blaze?"

"Believe it or not, my sweet angel, I enjoy buying things for you. I love seeing the diamonds that I bought for you wrapped around your neck. Being spoiled is something you will have to get used to. And I didn't leave you behind at the penthouse because I wanted others to see you and know that you are mine. Tomorrow morning your picture and the news that you are now my wife will be in every news-paper in Chicago. If that doesn't deter the man searching for you, he is a bigger idiot than I first imagined. And while I could tell you that I brought you with me because I didn't wish for you to be alone all evening at the penthouse, or I simply wanted us to spend time getting to know each other better, it would be a lie, my intentions were purely lecherous."

I pulled her a little closer and winked suggestively. Her cheeks turned a lovely shade of pink, and I had an intense desire to see if that blush would spread to other parts of her body. "So, with that being said, I will give you a choice. We can either leave right now, or I can find the nearest closet, bathroom, empty office, whatever, pull you into it, and fuck you until you are screaming my name so loud that everyone will hear. But before you decide, know that I am quite seri-ous, and I don't give a shit what people think."

Her eyes widened. "You say the most wicked things without regard for anyone that might hear them." She looked around at the people surrounding us.

"I know, it is one of my more endearing qualities. Are you ready to go now?"

The nod of her head was barely noticeable. We resumed our way through the path of people and I ignored anyone who tried to stop me.

When we reached the car, my driver jumped out and quickly opened the door. I helped her inside then walked to the other side of the car to get in beside her.

My hands clenched into fists, and I willed myself not to touch her again until we were back at the penthouse. But having her so close, knowing that I could easily have her on her back again was a temptation difficult to resist.

The car was silent and the tension between us was thick. After driving for a few minutes, she turned to me. "Has anyone ever told you that your behavior is wildly erratic, not to mention inappropriate? You are teasing me one minute, angry the next. You behave as if you are going to rip my clothes off in the middle of the gala and now you sit on the opposite side of the car as if you don't want to touch me. It's like you are made up of both fire and ice." She sighed and turned back toward the window. "It's as confusing as it is irritating."

I remained silent but couldn't keep the slight grin from my face.

When the car came to a stop, I opened the door and jumped out before the driver could come around. Bri was already getting out; I didn't waste a second. I scooped her up into my arms and carried her through the doors inside and moved quickly to the elevator. Once the elevator doors closed behind us, I sat her back on her feet and removed my bowtie. When my fingers went to the buttons of my shirt, she had backed away, obvious trepidation on her face.

The elevator doors opened, and I took her hand and pulled her down the hallway into the bedroom. "Stay right here and don't move. I have another surprise for you."

I walked to my closet and came back with a red silk blindfold. When she saw what I was holding in my hand, she took a step back.

"What are you going to do with that?"

"Be still and you will see."

I stepped forward and slowly slid the silk over her eyes and tied a knot securing it. "They say that when someone loses their sight, their other senses are heightened. I think we should test the theory. Will you be hypersensitive to my touch when you are blindfolded and can't see what my hands are doing?"

Bri

Rogue had spent so much time shocking me with the things he said he wanted to do to me, that when he made no move to touch me in the car or even speak, I found myself getting pissed off. *What the hell was wrong with me?* I should not want this man to touch me. I shouldn't have the feelings I felt. And there was no way I should feel a hot burning lust whenever he looked in my direction. A man who had taken me against my will, blackmailed me into sharing his bed, and the worst part...made me like it.

But when he pulled me from the car and swept me into his arms to carry me into the building, he ignited the fire I had been so quick to extinguish. The look in his eyes was both thrilling and frightening. When the silk moved over my eyes, sending me into darkness, I shivered with anticipation. The man may be dangerous, but my body burned for him, and while he may frighten me and make me furious, there was no denying the attraction I felt.

An involuntary shiver passed up my spine as his fingers slowly unzipped the back of my dress, letting it pool on the floor at my feet, the air felt cooler against my skin, and I wondered about his suggestion of my senses being heightened.

The warmth of his breath on my skin as he leaned over my shoulder made me shiver. I balled my hands into fists as his lips pressed against my bare skin.

"After tonight, there will be no more doubts in your pretty little head. Tonight, you will know exactly where you belong, Angel."

My breathing increased as his hands roamed over my breasts, his fingers tracing the lace edge of my bra before passing over my stomach.

His touch was soft and gentle, his scent surrounded me. I reached out my hand hoping to connect with his flesh. I wanted to touch him.

"Not yet, sweetheart."

I dropped my hand back to my side. I could sense his nearness, but not his touch.

"You are so incredibly beautiful. A rarity, a treasure to be guarded. My treasure."

His hands slid deliciously down my arms. "Tonight, I want you to discover new feelings. I will hold back my own ravenous desires to allow you to discover your own."

His warm moist breath caressed my ear as his fingers continued to burn a path across my skin and despite the way he made me feel heat wherever he touched, I still couldn't stop my body from shivering.

"You are nervous, Angel."

I shook my head wanting to deny it, but inside I knew he was right. But it wasn't fear. It was my reaction to his touch. He made me feel things I had never felt before and it made me uneasy. But I wanted to yield to the burning sweetness.

He took my hands in his and electricity seemed to pass through me. "Come with me, Bri. Allow yourself to trust me."

I took a step, allowing him to guide me. When he stopped moving, he placed his hand on my shoulders and turned me around. The back of my knees hit the soft plush comforter on his bed.

"Sit."

I reached behind me, placing my hands on the bed before scooting back.

"Now, lie back."

I did as he instructed, strangely aroused by the timbre of his voice.

I felt the mattress dip as he climbed on the bed; while I was blindfolded and couldn't see, I knew he hovered above me.

His fingers dipped just under the waistband of my panties, sending involuntary tremors of arousal through me before he pulled the silky lace down my legs agonizingly slow.

"Since the first time I had you in my arms, I have taken what I wanted, what I needed, what I craved. Tonight, I want you to tell me what you want. Tonight is about your desires, your cravings."

I reached for the blindfold, but he grabbed my wrist. "No. Tell me, Angel. What do you crave? What do you want me to do to you? Where do you want me to touch you, to kiss you?"

"I don't know."

"Yes, you do. I have already felt your desire, tasted it. Where should my fingers touch you next?"

I shook my head, self-conscious, nervous, but still longing for something. A part of me hated that he was putting me in a position where I was so uncomfortable while a bigger part of me felt an excitement like nothing I had ever felt before.

"Say something, Bri. Where shall I touch you next?"

"My breasts."

"Hmmm, excellent choice." His hand slipped behind my back and unsnapped my bra before he pulled it free. I was naked now, completely exposed. He outlined the tips of my breasts with his fingers before cupping them, and I forgot any shame I might have felt. My back arched as the backs of his fingers moved over my nipples, causing them to harden.

"What now, Brielle? Should my fingers explore elsewhere or would you like my mouth to join in our little game."

"Your mouth."

As soon as the words passed from my lips, I felt his tongue flick over me. The sensation was arousing, and I wanted more, needed more. "More."

He took me fully into his mouth, his teeth nibbling along the side of my breast before sucking harder on my nipples. "My fingers are bored, darling. Tell me what I should do to keep them occupied while my tongue is happily feasting on your tits."

"Touch me."

His deep chuckle reverberated through me. "I plan on it, but where sweet angel, do you want to be touched?"

I shook my head. I couldn't ask him to do that. I couldn't say the words.

"Come now, Angel. Where?"

"Just do it. Why do I have to say it?"

"Because I want you to be able to express all of your desires to me." He took one of my hands in his and pressed a kiss to my palm. "If you can't speak it, show me. Take my hand and show me."

His fingers interlaced with mine. A few weeks ago, I would have never imagined I could be this bold, but I found myself guiding his hand lower until it settled between my legs. When his fingers slipped over my folds, I opened my legs wider, biting my lip as each stroke drove me closer to the edge of ecstasy. When he pressed a finger inside me, the base of his palm ground against my clit as he worked magic with his fingers, moving in and out of me. My back arched and I cried out in torment. I wanted more; I wanted him. My hands reached out for him but this time when he tried to push them back down onto the mattress I pushed back.

"No! If this is supposed to be about me and what I want, then let me...let me touch you."

His hand released mine, and I reached out again, connecting with his bare chest. At some point during this seduction, he had removed his shirt. My hands explored his strong firm muscles, loving the way I felt him twitch as my hands dipped lower. My fingers followed the small trail of hair below his belly button.

How far did I dare go?

I stilled.

"Don't stop now, love." He inserted another finger inside me, and I felt a rush of moisture. I cried out again.

"Shh, Angel. We are just getting started. Go ahead, touch me."

My fingers dipped lower until they wrapped around his cock: hard, velvety smooth, and thick. I stroked him and smiled as he groaned loudly in approval. It was empowering to know that I had a similar effect on him as he had on me.

"Your touch makes me feel as if I am on fire, baby."

I rose up and pressed my cheek to his chest. I could hear his heart beating; his chest was warm. And I had an intense desire to feel his skin against mine. He must have sensed my desires and removed his fingers from where they were working magic inside me. I opened my legs wider, anticipating him to settle between them.

"Not this time, sweetheart."

He immediately flipped me onto my belly. "Get on your knees."

I did as he suggested. "Just your knees, sweetheart." He pressed my shoulders down until my head was on the pillow. His hands caressing the curves of my ass.

The blindfold was a blessing at this point and I was glad to be able to hide my uneasiness behind it as I lay there so exposed. I didn't know what to expect next, but when I felt his tongue lap over me, I could not hold back the shrieks of passion.

"I can't...."

"Yes, you can, baby." His tongue slipped over and then pressed inside me.

"Please..."

It was a pleading cry. I couldn't hold back any longer. I wanted him, I needed him.

"I've got you, sweetheart."

I couldn't hold back the shriek that passed from my lips as he plunged his cock into me from behind. His hands gripped my hips as he continued the powerful thrusts. He showed me no mercy. Each thrust brought me pain as well as overwhelming pleasure. I buried my face into the bedding and screamed louder as my orgasm began to build until it burst forth from me. My body grew limp as he continued to pound into me. With one more thrust, I felt him convulse and empty himself inside me. I didn't have the strength to think about any ramifications of falling for a man like him. It could be the biggest mistake of my life, but tonight I wanted everything he would give me.

When he pulled out of me, I lowered my hips back to the mattress but remained on my stomach. His hands moved over my spine. I felt him working the tie on the blindfold and the silk giving way. He then turned me over to my back.

"Open your eyes, Bri. Look at me."

My eyes opened to see him hovering over me. "Now you know,

Angel. And I want to hear you say it. I want to hear it from your sweet lips. You are mine, perfection made just for me, and after tonight, you know it to be true." He leaned down and kissed me. "Say it."

"I know." My voice was hoarse from screaming.

"What do you know, baby?"

"That I belong to you. I was made for you."

His smile stretched wider. "And you will never leave?"

I hesitated and his eyes narrowed. He settled over me and pushed my knees apart wider.

"Do I need to remind you again?"

"I am yours and...I will never leave."

As soon as the words left my mouth, he pushed inside me again. Any protest I would have formed was lost in the haze of lust that descended upon me as he fucked me again. The man was insatiable and I ...was lost.

CHAPTER
twelve

ROGUE

"No! Don't touch me!"

The panic and terror in Bri's voice woke me from a dead sleep and I reached for the pistol that I kept under my pillow.

"Get off me! Stop! No!"

She was thrashing about in her sleep, sweat beading on her forehead. I reached out to touch her, and her fists pounded against my chest as if she were fighting off an attacker.

"Angel! Wake up, it's me."

Tears streamed down her cheeks; her eyes still closed, fighting off an invisible demon in the hell she was trapped in. I grabbed her wrists and pinned them to her sides.

"Baby, it's ok. You're safe. I'm not going to let anyone hurt you."

She was sobbing now. I pulled her into my arms and held her, my hand caressing her back in slow calming circles. At first, she resisted the comfort I was trying to give, but her body soon began to relax against me.

"Shh, it's alright, love. Wake up and look at me, baby. You are safe with me." I softly kissed her forehead. "Whatever monster has hurt you; I will destroy it."

Her sobs softened to sniffles, her body clinging to me as she came back to the present. It took some time for her to completely relax and breathe normally again. She was still holding on tight to me but no longer shaking and her sobbing had stopped. She raised her head, her beautiful eyes swollen and red-rimmed from crying. I pushed back her hair and cupped her cheek.

"How often do you have nightmares, sweetheart?"

She tried to pull away, but I refused to release her.

"They aren't as common as they once were. I'm sorry that I woke you. I haven't had one like this in a long time. I guess after talking to Allison and knowing that Tony is in Chicago looking for me triggered something. I thought it was over, but I don't know if it will ever be over."

I kissed the top of her head as I held her, hoping to reassure her. "You no longer need to fear him. You are mine now, my wife, and I will protect you. Let me defeat your demons, fight your dragons. Trust me to do whatever it takes to save you, to protect you."

She sniffed again and I positioned us so I could hold her as she leaned against my chest, hoping she would be able to get some sleep tonight.

I didn't ask her to explain, but when her fears started pouring out of her, I listened.

"The dreams are always the same. I see his face and I run, but he always catches me. It's almost as if I can feel him hitting me. I hear the sound of him ripping my clothes, sometimes it is paralyzing. I can't move or fight back, other times, like tonight, I fight with all I have only to have him hit me until I can't breathe."

She snuggled closer, laying her head against my chest, her hand resting over my heart. "The nightmares started once I was released from the hospital. For months I relived the events of that night. There were times that I thought I would never be free of the fear and pain, but after being in Chicago for a few weeks, they started to become less frequent, but now..." Her voice broke. "He's back."

I rolled her to her back, then positioned myself so that I hovered over her. "Baby, I will find him, and I will end this. I will take away all your fears."

I leaned forward and kissed her lips softly. They were still a little swollen from the hours of sex we had before she fell asleep in my arms.

"I fought him that night and I fought the fear afterward. I didn't want what happened to me to make me weak, to make me hide from the world. But I don't think you can save me from him, I can feel it. He will find me. I had no connections, no friends, nothing in Chicago. That's why I came here, but he still found me. Eventually, I will have to face him again."

"You must trust me, darling. He hasn't come up against a force like me, protecting what is mine. He isn't a real man. He might have felt strong fighting against you, but I promise you, I will bring him to his knees. He will tremble in fear and know true terror before I send him to the devil. I will be your vengeance, Angel. I will be his reckoning as I am your salvation. That's one of the reasons I dragged you to that gala tonight. I want everyone to know. I want him to know the fury I will unleash upon him if he dares to hurt you. I want him to already be watching his back, knowing that I am coming for him and that there isn't a damn thing he can do to stop me." I wrapped my arms around her and held her close. "And when I am done and you come to accept that you are fully mine, he will no longer haunt your dreams."

She didn't argue or contradict me. But I could feel the wetness from her tears on my chest. Eventually, she did fall back asleep, but I lay awake staring at the ceiling, listening to her breathing gradually getting deeper, her body more relaxed. I continued to hold her close so that if her nightmares returned, I could quickly wake her before she had to relive the terror again. But as I lay there in the darkness holding her soft sweet body against mine, I was calculating every way I would make this man suffer. He would pay dearly for what he had done to her, and I was the man that would collect that debt.

Bri

. . .

My arms stretched out in the large bed and met nothing but cool sheets. I sat up quickly and seeing that I was alone, a little bit of panic coursed through me. The memories from last night came back to me. I remembered the nightmare, the way Rogue had held me, kissed me, and spoken soft words to calm me. Now I was alone, and the fear began to settle back in the pit of my stomach. I sat up, pulled the sheet over my body, and searched the room for any sign of Rogue. Had he left me? Had he decided that I was too damaged, too much of a burden to put up with? I was about to get up from the bed when the door opened, and Rogue walked back inside wearing a pair of blue sweatpants and nothing else. His chest was bare, and I could see a few of the places where I had bitten him last night during our frenzied lovemaking My cheeks heated as the images of what I had done and allowed him to do came to mind.

"Good morning. I thought I would let you sleep in since you had a restless night."

I watched as he came farther into the room. "I'm sorry about that. If you would allow me to sleep in the other room, I wouldn't disturb you."

His brows arched. "Are you trying to get on my bad side first thing this morning? You are my wife, and as my wife, you will sleep with me. As far as the demons that haunt your dreams, I will relieve you of them too."

"You know that you can't protect me from everything, but right now if you could save me from hunger, I would appreciate it. Is there anything for breakfast?"

His smile made my stomach flip. He was stunningly handsome.

"I had someone deliver an assortment of pastries, fruit, and some crepes. I wasn't sure what you would want, so I had them buy several things."

"Do you always have people do everything for you?"

He moved closer to the bed and looked down at me seductively. "Not everything." His gaze lingered on my breasts. "Some things I prefer to do myself."

Just the way his eyes raked over me made the temperature in the room go up at least twenty degrees.

"I should get dressed."

He leaned down and pressed a soft kiss to my lips. "No, you will stay right there. I'll bring you breakfast and then after that, I will help you shower."

"You don't have to do that. I have taken care of myself since I was fourteen."

For a second, I saw a hint of sadness, or was it pity come into his eyes? Whatever it was it was short-lived, replaced by the authoritarian look I had come to recognize when he was about to give an order.

"You are not alone anymore, Angel. You need to get used to the idea of me taking care of you."

I blew out a short breath and nodded, unsure why I even felt the need to argue the point with him. It was a nice feeling having someone be so attentive. As he walked from the room, I couldn't help but wonder if this could be real. Could this man truly be my savior, the one I had been waiting for to sweep me off my feet and rescue me from the fears and monsters that chase me? He was a monster himself, a criminal, a killer. How could he be my knight when he had so many flaws himself? Whatever he was, right now he was the only man I trusted, the only one to make me feel safe again. And if it didn't last, if he decided after a time that I was just a passing fling, something to hold his interest for a time, I would deal with that when the time came. I had faced heartbreak before. What scared me the most was that I was beginning to imagine a future with him. I was beginning to think of this as a forever life for me. I shook the thoughts from my head. I couldn't leave my heart open for that kind of hurt.

Rogue

"You are late," Blaze said as he sat behind my desk at my office in the same building where my penthouse was located. He looked irritated, but then again, when did he not?

I strolled forward, ignoring the fact that his feet were propped up on my desk as if he owned it. "Did you have a nice chat with Sevan last night?"

"Nice? No, but I did find out what I needed to know, and I communicated the consequences of betrayal, just in case his loyalty was in question. There is something about him that I don't trust."

Blaze trusted few people in his life, so I was not surprised by his comment. "And Nik?"

"He knows but his overconfidence prevents him from being concerned."

"That's typical of the Bratva, but make no mistake, Nik will be prepared. He didn't get where he is today by flagrantly disregarding threats."

Blaze stood from behind my desk and walked toward me. "I hope you are taking them seriously. Where is the little one?"

"She is taking some much-needed time to relax, taking a hot bath, and lounging in bed. She had a restless night."

"You trust her not to leave?"

I didn't want to discuss my feelings on that matter with Blaze. While I felt that Bri was finally beginning to trust me, I had still taken precautions against her running away. "I didn't come here to discuss her. I have been thinking that instead of waiting for Petros and his small gang of Armenian thugs to make their next move, we should be proactive and strike first."

"Go on the offensive. I like it. You know I am always ready to start a fight but taking him out might not be as easy as you think. From what I gather, he doesn't put himself in the line of fire. He is a ghost. Sends his men into the fight while he hides like the scared pussy he is. You would have to provoke him to draw him out."

"That's exactly what I plan to do. Cut off the head of the snake before he can strike. From what Sevan told me, many other members of his family and the organization have no interest in seeking reprisal. They want him gone as much as we do."

"Then they should have the balls to take him out themselves instead of letting him wage a war he can't win and get his men killed for nothing. Pisses me off that he is our problem now."

I understood Blaze's frustration. "Trust me, there will be consequences for our involvement. I am not removing him from power for free. I will expect some sort of payment and a measure of allegiance to whatever deal we agree to. What are your thoughts?"

"I think we should provoke him into making a stupid mistake, then take advantage of his immaturity and incompetence."

"And how do you suggest we do that? Any ideas other than just storming his house?"

"Not yet but give me time."

"Perhaps you should call Tomas. I'm certain Alessio will not object."

"Fuck you, Rogue. I don't need that bastard's help!"

I held up my hands in surrender. Tomas, Alessio's second in command, and Blaze disliked each other immensely. I suppose dislike was not a strong enough word to describe their relationship; they despised each other. The hate between them was deep, but so far, they had been able to put it aside whenever their services needed to be unified. While I trusted Blaze with my life, he was not as skilled at planning out an attack as Tomas. Blaze liked going in with guns blazing while Tomas carefully planned out each aspect of an assault, leaving nothing to chance.

"Relax, it was just a suggestion. I knew you would not happily accept help from anyone, especially Tomas."

His hands were still clenched tightly by his sides and his jaw set firm. "Damn right. But putting your bad sense of humor aside, I'm afraid you have bigger problems than Petros just being a pain in the ass."

I walked over to the bar on the other side of the room. If the expression on Blaze's face was any indication, I was going to need a drink. "Does it have to do with the man that is stalking Bri?"

"It does. I found out exactly who he is and if you kill him, you may very well start a different war. You will need to tread carefully."

I picked up one of the glasses from the bar and threw it against the wall shattering the glass. Blaze never even flinched.

"The fucker almost killed her! He stalked her, scared her, beat her, and nearly raped her. Do you think I am going to let that go? I held her in my arms last night while she fought against an invisible attacker in her dreams. I have never seen someone have such vivid nightmares. She clung to me, her body shivering as she recounted the details of that night. You think I will cower to that bastard. Allow him to walk this Earth freely while my wife looks over her shoulder constantly wondering when he will reappear, if he will come for her. No, he has to die. I don't give a shit what war starts because of it. It is the only way she will have peace and me the retribution I seek."

Blaze's lips lifted into a one-sided sardonic smile. "I was hoping you would say that."

"You have his name, who is he connected to?"

"Tony Galante is the stepson of Frankie Ballantine."

I filled my glass and drank down the bourbon. "Frankie Ballantine, the mafia hitman?"

"One and the same. They say he has had over three hundred hits. I'm sure that is an exaggeration, but his resume is still impressive. If you go after his stepson, he might take offense and you do not want to be on his list."

I walked toward my desk. "I don't give a fuck who he is or who his family is. He hurt her and will pay for it. I'm not afraid of Ballantine. If he makes trouble, I will kill him too."

Blaze walked over and poured himself a drink. "I thought you would feel that way, so I put in a call to Alessio. His father knew Frankie, perhaps Alessio can get more information."

"Alessio doesn't use hitmen. He prefers to handle matters himself."

Blaze's face darkened. "Or he has Tomas do it for him."

I frowned down into my empty glass. "You and Tomas really should put aside the dislike you have for each other. You work well together...when you aren't trying to kill each other."

"I didn't come here for you to lecture me. We have two problems that need to be addressed. My question is which one concerns you the most, the threat to your business and empire, or the one to your girl?"

I walked toward him. "I don't plan on losing either one."

"Then you should know that security at the club said there was a man there last night with a picture of Bri. He was asking people if she had been there lately. Of course, none of your employees gave him any information, but it sounds like Tony knows she has been there, or he wouldn't be looking."

My anger returned full force knowing that the son of a bitch was so close. The fact that he dared to come into my club looking for her showed that he was either overly confident or overly stupid.

"Keep this between the two of us. I don't want her to know. I gave the men who were following us yesterday an ultimatum. I expect their boss to present himself at the club tonight either with information about where to find Galante or if we are lucky, he will hand him over to us."

Blaze rolled his eyes as he took another drink. "You know it won't be that simple. We are never that lucky."

"Speak for yourself, my friend."

"Where are you going?"

I tried and failed to hide the smirk that formed on my lips. "I am going to spend the day spoiling my wife before I meet Michael for dinner. Care to join us there?"

His face took on an almost ashen look. "Dinner with the priest? No, I think I will shy away from all things sacred and saintly. You can seek redemption if you must, I will remain with the sinners."

"It's just dinner and Michael likes to see you from time to time."

Blaze moved to the door. "Then tell him to stop by the club after midnight. There will be plenty of people there needing salvation." He opened the door. "Once you have news from Alessio, let me know. If Tomas is going to be in town, I want advance notice. Don't fucking surprise me with that shit."

He shut the door a little more forcibly than expected, and I knew he was more concerned than he wanted me to see. Blaze was an asshole most of the time, but he was loyal to a fault, and I wouldn't want anyone else by my side when faced with any threat.

I walked over to the windows and looked outside; the skies were beginning to darken, and rain looked imminent. Gloomy weather typically delighted me, and fit my mood, but now that I had Bri in my life, I found myself longing for sunshine. I looked at my watch and my mind drifted to thoughts of her and what she could be doing right now. I felt an urge to go to her, a desire to touch her. I wanted to make certain she was still there.

I glanced back at the desk; there were proposals, financials, and investments that I needed to look over and approve, but all I wanted right now was her. I walked over to the desk and picked up the stack of files that my assistant had placed there for me to review, but it could wait. Right now, I needed her more than I did anything else. And with her this close, why wait?

Bri

I didn't know how long Rogue would be gone. After we had a delicious breakfast of the best crepes and strawberries I have had in my life, he insisted on drawing me a hot bath. Of course, it wasn't that simple, everything the man did was sensual. He slowly undressed me, his caress making my skin prickle, and then carried me to the tub. After making certain I had everything I needed, he left me alone to soak and relax. But being alone in the large penthouse, no matter how secure it was, didn't make me feel comfortable. Every creak, every noise made me jump. I hated this feeling. I hated feeling like a victim and it was time I did something about it. So, I got out, dried off, and went to the closet to put on a pair of jeans and a soft cotton top.

Now I sat on the sofa near the window, watching the busy streets of the city below, and while I wanted to forget, I wanted the nightmares to stop, I couldn't help but wonder if Tony was down there somewhere waiting for his chance. The thought made me a little nauseous. I brought my knees up to my chest and wrapped my arms around them. I glanced at the elevator doors. He had not warned me about leaving, but I had a feeling he had taken precautions against it. At least he hadn't handcuffed me again. Although, the urge to run was not as strong as before. I was more afraid of what waited for me outside his sphere than I was of the man himself.

When the elevator doors opened, I turned to see Rogue walking toward me. "I didn't think you would be back so soon."

"And I thought you would still be in the bath. I am disappointed."

I looked away from the obvious desire I saw in his eyes. "I know you told me to relax but I couldn't. It was just so quiet." The way he was looking at me made me feel uncomfortable.

"You still do not feel safe."

My head shot up at his words.

"How can I feel safe? With everything that has happened to me, you can't expect me to feel anything but a measure of uncertainty and fear."

"I can expect you to feel a great deal more than that."

I looked away. "I just wonder where I would be, what I would be doing if Tony had never come into my life. If I had never fled to Chicago to escape him. If I had never walked into your club that night? Would I have married a high school history teacher, drove a minivan, and maybe had three kids and volunteered with the PTA?"

He reached down, grabbed my wrist and pulled me to my feet. "Enough! None of that matters now. You did come to Chicago, and you did walk into my club. And the moment you did, you became mine and I want everything, every smile, your laughter, your tears, every thought, every dream, it all belongs to me." He leaned down and kissed me, his lips hard and consuming. "And I will conquer every fear and all your anxiety, but I will not have you ever imagining your life with another man, or him putting his babies in your belly."

A loud gasp came from my lips as he ripped open the shirt I was wearing. One hand gripping my wrists and pinning them behind my back.

"You still don't understand it. So I guess I will have to keep trying to make you comprehend. I won't deny that a part of me hopes you are a slow learner."

His lips came down on the side of my neck and I felt his teeth nipping lightly at the skin there before he picked me up in his arms and carried me back to the bedroom. Fighting him was no longer an option. I wanted him, I yearned for his touch and the sensations they elicited from me. I was fully aware of the kind of man that he was, and it didn't matter to me anymore. The biggest concern I had now was after he tired of me, and I was sure he would, how would I be able to move on with my life? I knew another man could never touch me and make me feel this way. I had been through hard times before, but could I survive a broken heart?

CHAPTER
thirteen

Rogue

I was waiting in the kitchen while Bri changed clothes. The white shirt and jeans she had been wearing earlier could not withstand the urgency with which I had to have her naked again and in my bed. But while I wanted nothing more than to spend the entire day with her long legs wrapped around my waist, some things needed to be done. Things that couldn't wait.

I poured myself a cup of coffee hoping it would help staunch the raging lust I had for my wife while I conducted business. Whiskey had not helped, and I was beginning to think there wasn't anything that would free me from her spell. Even after just fucking her, I found myself wanting her still.

The buzzing vibration of my phone drew my attention away from the fantasies my mind was eagerly creating. I saw the name on the screen and grinned. I had been wondering how long it would be before Alessio tried to insert himself into my troubles.

Bri had yet to make an appearance, so I decided it was best to go ahead and answer. No doubt he would keep calling until I did anyway.

"I was expecting a call from you sooner or later."

"And I thought you were smart enough not to antagonize a mafia hitman."

I frowned, not really in the mood for a lecture. "You have talked to Blaze?"

Men like us had very few friends or people in our inner circles. Alessio Messina was one of those that I trusted and considered a friend. He ruled New York with the same fierceness that I ruled Chicago.

"Blaze called me this morning. It seems that not only are you determined to piss off one of the world's most dangerous hitmen, but you seem to have gotten the attention of a young Armenian thug as well."

"I have no problem with Frankie Ballentine, but I have every intention of killing his stepson. You can communicate that information to him if you like. As far as the young Armenian, Petros Sargsyan, he is a threat that can easily be handled. From the information I have gathered, he only has a small number of men who still support him. His family and others in his late father's organization think he is unhinged."

I heard Alessio let out a deep breath. "Yes, I had figured that much out myself. And while you may not be concerned with him, I have a few interests in Chicago, and I don't like hearing that some young punk thinks he is powerful enough to take anything from me. I will be there by the end of the week to assist you in any way that you need."

"I don't need you to come here, Alessio. Like I said, Petros is nothing I can't handle on my own."

"Yes, I know, but it will give me an excuse to meet your new bride. I have to say, I was more than shocked when Tomas told me the news. I never saw you as the marriage type. You give off more of a playboy vibe than that of a doting husband."

I knew this was coming. "How the hell did Tomas find out about my marriage?"

"I have my sources too, just like you."

"It is not what you think. Marriage was necessary to keep her safe. It was not expected to be the love match you have with your Cara

Mia." *I didn't know why the lie fell so easily from my lips. Perhaps I didn't want to admit my deepest feelings even to myself.* "I am assuming Tomas will be arriving with you."

"Yes, Eden will be traveling with me as well, and I don't travel with her unless I have added security. I know you aren't suggesting I leave her with Blaze again, not after last time. Besides, she is anxious to meet the woman you were so interested in protecting that you forced her to marry you. I suppose they have something in common."

I took another sip of my coffee. "I will make preparations for you."

"No need. I will see you in a few days. If something changes and you need assistance earlier. Call."

I didn't bother to respond. Alessio may be as cold and as dangerous as any of us, but his friendship was true. And since friends were rare in our circle, I valued it.

When I walked out of the kitchen, I found Bri looking exceptionally sexy in a black dress and matching heels, but her face was solemn, and I wondered if she was still worried about Tony Galante or if it was something else.

The conversation I had with Alessio came to mind. I had told Bri that she was mine, that I would protect her, keep her, and that no other man would touch her, but I had never mentioned ...love. To be honest I wasn't certain if I was capable of love. It had not crossed my mind. I knew Alessio was deeply in love with his Cara Mia, but I had always thought that was a rarity for men like us.

"You look stunning, Angel." I took a step forward, but she retreated a step, brushed her hair back, and looked down.

"I am sorry it took me longer to get ready than I expected."

I tilted my head to the side wondering about the softness in her voice and the way she seemed suddenly uneasy with me. We had just spent the past two hours in bed where she had been far from reserved.

"What is bothering you, sweetheart?"

"Nothing, I'm fine."

She looked away, and I knew at that moment she was lying. I

could see in her eyes that she was hiding something from me. But if
we didn't leave soon, we would be late meeting Michael for dinner. I
took her hand and raised it to my lips. "I had planned on taking you
around Chicago and showing you the city today. I'm sorry we didn't
make it out of the bedroom. Let me make it up to you. Is there something you have always wanted to do while in Chicago but haven't had
the opportunity?"

I watched as her eyes met mine and for a minute, I thought she
wouldn't answer.

"I have never been to the Field Museum. When I was a little girl, I
read about it at school and when I got here, I thought about going
but never had the time or the money."

I moved quickly before she had a chance to back away from me
again and took both of her hands in mine. She tried to look away
again.

"Look at me, Angel!" When her eyes turned back to mine, I
leaned forward and pressed a soft kiss to her cheek. "Tell me what is
bothering you and I will fix it."

She looked down and pulled her hands from mine. "Shouldn't we
be going?"

I nodded and wondered what the hell had happened to make her
look so melancholy. She stepped into the elevator and while she didn't
move away from my touch, she didn't exactly melt against it either.
When the doors opened, Blaze was waiting for us, and I saw a smile
play on her lips when she saw him.

"Will you be joining us, Blaze?"

What the fuck?! Since when did the two of them get so chummy?

"No, little one. I avoid these dinners."

"Why? Do you not like Father Michael?"

"I don't like what he represents."

I took hold of Bri's arm and began leading her to the car. "Blaze is
afraid of bursting into flames should he get too close to anything
religious."

She smiled again, but it wasn't directed at me, and it was beginning to piss me off that her demeanor had changed so suddenly.

"Well, we will miss you. Have a good evening, Blaze."

I saw the slight tilt of his head and the smirk on his face and realized he was enjoying the fact that her sudden friendliness toward him was pissing me off.

"It seems as if you and Blaze are getting along better."

Her lips quirked up slightly. "He is gruff and surly, but he grows on you after a while."

I escorted her to the car and while I wanted to pull her to me, I kept my distance. If I touched her now, it would lead to me canceling dinner and going back to the penthouse where I would make her tell me what was bothering her, and I had already canceled on Michael enough. After what happened outside the church, I owed it to him to show up tonight. There would be time later to coax another smile out of my little angel.

Bri

I don't know why overhearing Rogue on the phone saying that he married me just for protection, that love had nothing to do with it had upset me the way that it did. I shouldn't be surprised. I had told myself that he would tire of me. I had told myself it was lust and desire I was feeling and at first it had been, but the fact that he held me after my terrible nightmare, and the gentle way he had kissed me made me hope for more.

This was ridiculous; how could I fall in love with a man like Rogue Delaney? I leaned my head against the window of the car as we drove through the city. My thoughts continued to drift. It was irrational and immature for me to think that this could be anything more. But if love was off the table, could I be content with just desire and lust? Would it ever be enough? I suppose it would have to be.

The car came to a stop outside of the church. "We are having dinner here?"

"Yes, Michael likes to cook almost as much as he likes to lecture me on frivolous spending at expensive restaurants." He took my hand. "Don't get excited. Most nights it is as simple as homemade pizza or pasta. He also makes a chicken and rice casserole from time to time."

"In addition to the spaghetti suppers once a month?"

"Yes, the spaghetti suppers are for the congregation and the unfortunate in the community. Tonight will be just us. He invites me at least once a week, but I typically don't have time for it. I'm sure he is more concerned about your welfare than seeing me. I am bound to receive another scolding about my behavior." He opened the door and got out of the car, then held out his hand to assist me.

"I'm sure as your friend he is just concerned."

Rogue rolled his eyes but before anything else could be said, Father Michael appeared.

"Well, I am glad to see that she hasn't killed you yet."

Rogue grinned. "The night is still young."

Father Michael stepped forward and took my hand before leaning over and pressing a kiss to my cheek. "It is good to see you again, Mrs. Delaney."

My eyes shot up at the unfamiliarity of the name.

"Still not used to being married, I see. You will get more accustomed to it."

I smiled brightly, feeling a bit more myself again. "I'm not sure there will be enough time for that." I glanced back at Rogue whose frown had become more pronounced then wrapped my arm through Michael's. "I am told that you are an excellent chef."

"Lies, all of them. I do enjoy cooking from time to time, but it is nothing to brag about. Tonight, since you are my special guest, I tried something different, chicken marsala. I hope you like it."

"I'm sure I will love it."

He escorted me inside the church. "Do you live here?"

"I have a small apartment in the basement. I find it is convenient."

I felt Rogue's presence behind me even before he spoke. "And sparse. I have offered him other options, but he refuses and continues to martyr himself by living in poverty."

"I prefer a simpler life."

My arm was still linked through his as we walked down the narrow passageway to the church basement. It was a typical basement, with stone walls, cold floors, and a tad bit damp and musty smell, but the living quarters that Father Michael had there, while plain and simple, also gave off a sense of peace, a sense of home.

I breathed in the scents coming from his small kitchen. "Hmm, smells delicious."

He escorted me over to a small round table and held a chair out for me. Rogue sat opposite me, and Michael began serving us.

"I know our meeting yesterday was brief, Brielle. But I would like to get to know you better. Tell me a little about yourself."

I immediately picked up the glass of red wine before me and took a drink. I wasn't comfortable talking about myself or sharing my past, and I could feel Rogue watching me. He had never asked a lot of questions about my life before Chicago other than my relationship with Tony. "I hope you weren't counting on me for lively stories. I haven't lived the exciting type of life that the two of you have. I don't have a lot of family and spent most of my time since I was fifteen working a full-time job and going to school."

"Rogue had mentioned that you were from Colorado. What made you want to start a new life here in Chicago? I would think it must have been difficult to leave behind the beauty of the Rocky Mountains."

I picked up my fork. "It wasn't that difficult. I mean life is all about change and who of us knows how long we will be in one place."

I looked up at Rogue, his expression had not changed.

I took a bite of the chicken, it was good, really good. "This is delicious, Father Michael. I think you could open a restaurant."

"He would go out of business in a month," Rogue said, his voice indifferent and distant.

Michael laughed. "Rogue is right. I don't have the head for business that he does. Do you have plans to go back to the club tonight?"

Rogue swallowed the food he was chewing. "As soon as we leave here, but I will not be there for long. I have other plans for the evening."

His eyes were intently fixed upon me, and I took another drink hoping the wine would help soothe the tickle in my throat.

Father Michael cleared his throat. "I was hoping Blaze would come tonight."

Rogue wiped his mouth and swallowed the remaining contents of his glass. "He is occupied with other things."

I watched as Father Michael's face fell. "After dinner, I would like to speak with you, if you have time. One of my parishioners brought some information to me and asked me to tell you. It concerns a man named Petros."

I immediately scooted my chair back. "I can leave the two of you alone."

Rogue's hand grabbed mine. "No, finish your dinner. Michael and I can step out."

I watched as Father Michael and Rogue left the kitchen. I wasn't sure where they would go and while a part of me wanted to follow and hear what was said, another part of me said to mind my own business. It wasn't about Tony, so it didn't concern me. I continued eating, licking, the final remnants of sauce from my fork before pouring myself another glass of wine. But my curiosity finally got the better of me, and I couldn't resist moving closer to the kitchen door, hoping to catch a little bit of the conversation.

Rogue

"What do you know of Petros?"

"I know that he is dangerous," Michael said as he leaned back against the wall. "One of the young men who attends church said that he heard a man of that name asking questions about you. He is trying to discover your habits, the places you frequently attend, and your shipment schedules for your merchandise or whatever it is you deal in. I don't want to know so don't tell me. He has men watching the building where the penthouse is downtown as well as the club. I know he is working on a much smaller scale than you, but remember, a snake is a snake, and can easily take down a giant with one strike. Don't underestimate your enemy, Rogue."

"I'm not underestimating him. I already knew he had me under surveillance. What he doesn't know is that Blaze is watching him as closely as he is watching me. Nik is also aware of him, as is Alessio. The fool has no idea the trouble he has started. His arrogance and pride will lead to his downfall."

Michael looked back toward the kitchen door. "What of the men from yesterday? The ones looking for Brielle."

I sighed heavily and motioned for him to walk farther away from the door with me. "The man that sent them is Tony Galante."

I watched his eyes narrow as the name ran through his head. "It is not familiar."

"I didn't think it would be, but his stepfather is Frankie Ballentine. I'm sure that name will ring a few bells."

"The mafia hitman? That Frankie Ballentine?"

"The same."

I watched as he started pacing the room. "That is an entirely different problem. What does his stepson want with your wife?"

"Before she came to Chicago, he attacked her. He beat her and nearly raped her before someone heard her screams and came to help. That fact alone would have been enough for me to end him, but now that he has followed her to Chicago, I not only will kill him, but I plan to make him suffer."

Michael's face turned ashen. "You can't kill Frankie's son, it will be signing your death warrant, as well as your wife's."

"So, I am to let it go? Allow him to continue to torment her, or perhaps I should call a meeting and return her to him." I thrust my hands in my pockets, trying to control the anger threatening to explode from me. I seldom lost my temper with Michael but tonight I felt it beginning to flare.

"I'm not suggesting anything of the sort, and you know it. My

God, Rogue, you know me better than that. I am just trying to get you to think rationally. There must be another way."

I shook my head in disgust. "Even if there were a way to buy him off, I still wouldn't do it. He hurt her and for that, he is going to die by my hand. It's as simple as that."

Michael blew out a slow ragged breath. "Well, if you are determined to do something so foolish, you will need help. Tell me what I can do."

I stepped forward and placed my hand on his shoulder. "You are a good friend, Michael, but you left this world a few years back and started a new one. I will not be the one responsible for pulling you back into the depths of my sin and immorality."

"I wasn't asking permission, Rogue. You are faced with two equally dangerous threats and as your friend, I will not allow you to face them alone."

I nodded knowing how stubborn he could be once his mind was set on something. "Thank you for supper tonight, Michael. But I must get back to *Sinners*. I have been neglecting it the past few days for obvious reasons."

I walked back into the kitchen and saw Bri sitting in the same place where I had left her, but her face was pale and her eyes wide. "Haven't I already cautioned you about listening at doorways?"

"You should have told me."

"Told you what, love?"

She stood up and threw her napkin on the table. "You should have told me that Tony's father was a mafia hitman!"

I moved quickly, wrapping my arms around her. "It never came up in conversation and how would you knowing have benefitted the situation?"

She struggled against me. "You are crazy."

"Maybe so, but you really should have more trust in me. I didn't get to where I am in life by being careless. Now, would you like to spend the rest of the night arguing about something I will not change my mind about or hurry to the club so I can finish my business there before I give you the surprise I have planned?"

Her lips thinned into a straight line and her eyes narrowed just a fraction. "You could have just sent me away once you found out who Tony was and the people he is connected to."

"I could have, but where would be the fun in that?" I leaned forward and kissed her quickly before she could utter another word. "Come let's go before Michael tries to feed us dessert. Blaze will be at the club waiting for us."

I took her hand and led her from the kitchen. Michael was waiting for us by the stairs that led out of the basement back up the sanctuary of the church. "Thank you for supper, Michael."

He nodded toward me before taking Bri's hand. I had a brief moment of jealousy course through me as they locked eyes. It was as if some sort of silent communication passed between them, and I found myself envious of the bond she seemed to be forming with Michael and Blaze. I wanted her to have faith in me, to trust me, as she was beginning to them.

"Brielle, thank you for coming with Rogue tonight. I hope you have a pleasurable evening and if you ever need anything, I will be here."

She smiled sweetly. "Thank you. But perhaps you will still be able to talk some sense into him."

Michael laughed as he shook his head. "I have never been successful in making Rogue see reason. Once he has set his path, he doesn't deviate."

"We have to go. The two of you can talk about saving my life or my soul another time. I have work to do."

I took Bri's hand and together we began walking up the stairs. When we stepped out onto the street outside the church, I took my coat off and draped it across her shoulders as it began to rain. I hurried her to the car and climbed in beside her. She was quiet but I could tell that hearing the news of Tony's stepfather had her worried. If I wanted to see more of her smiles, I would have to settle this matter quickly, because my angel would have no peace until her fears were laid to rest.

. . .

Bri

Knowing that Tony's stepfather was a hitman should have been more of a shock to me, but instead, it felt like just another piece of the puzzle coming together. His cruelty, the things he had said in passing when we were together, his having the connections to find me, and being mixed up with the type of people he claimed to know all started to make sense. What I couldn't understand was why he wouldn't give up, why he continued to search for me. Was it his pride because I had refused him, or was he just that sadistic? Either way, now the man sitting beside me had vowed to kill him if he tried to hurt me again, which puts his life in danger.

I watched as the rain droplets slid down the window of the car as it moved through the streets, taking us back to where it all began, his nightclub, *Sinners*. I turned away from the window to find him watching me.

"Come here, Angel?"

The driver raised the partition between the seats giving us complete privacy.

I wanted to turn away, ignore the command in his voice, but there was something about him that compelled me to submit. As I moved closer to him, his hands spanned my waist to lift me so that I sat straddled across him, my hands instantly going to his shoulders.

"What do I have to do to erase those pesky worry lines from your beautiful face?"

His hands had already moved under my skirt and I knew what I wanted from him, what I craved.

"Tell me that you want this, that you want me. I want to hear it from your lips, Bri. I want to know that you have finally accepted your fate." His hands continued to move up my thighs before moving around to cup my ass. I had to bite back a grin as his expression changed.

"You aren't wearing panties, sweetheart."

The expression on his face was a mixture of anger and sheer unadulterated lust.

"I thought it would save time."

The growl emanating from deep in his chest was proof enough of his approval. The sharp smack to my bare ass caused me to suck in a deep breath.

"You were going to walk into the club like this?"

I nodded slightly, eagerly waiting to see his reaction.

"My naughty little angel. There will be consequences for this behavior." I felt his fingers moving across my hips and dipping between my thighs. "Does the thought of being so exposed turn you on, little minx? I am curious to see."

My head rolled back as his fingers slid over my clit and through my damp folds. I could hear my breathing increase in the quietness of the car. When he slipped two fingers inside me, I couldn't hold back the sounds that broke free from my lips. He knew just where to touch me.

"That's it, baby. Spread your legs wider for me. I want to watch you while you come."

My eyes flew open, unsure how I felt about him watching me.

He lifted the skirt of my dress higher, over my hips. I looked down and watched his fingers move over me. I could see moisture glistening on them. It was...exhilarating. I had not expected to be so entranced, and as his fingers moved, I began to match his rhythm.

"Oh, baby." His voice was deep and throaty. "You ride my hand almost as good as you ride my cock."

I knew my cheeks had turned scarlet by now, but his words, his touch, and the way his eyes seemed to flame as he watched me made me bolder, more daring. I gripped his shoulders tighter and leaned forward, wanting to bury my face in the side of his neck.

"No!"

He pushed me so that I was leaning back against the seat in front of us. With his other hand, he pushed my dress higher. "Wider baby."

I complied with his request and at that moment it washed over me. I was having trouble catching my breath, my knees were weak, and I was glad I didn't have to stand right away.

When he removed his fingers from inside me, I swallowed the pouty whimper that moved past my throat. He was still watching me. I closed my eyes as his hand moved to the back of my neck and roughly pulled me up to him.

"Now I know exactly what to do to ease your anxiety, sweetheart. Every time I see your brow furrowed with worry, anytime I see that the light in your eyes has dimmed because something has upset you, I will make you come so you can forget it all."

His lips came down onto mine and I was fully aware that I was still straddling him. His tongue played with mine and I found myself waiting, certain he would free his dick from where it strained against his pants and thrust inside me. I wanted it, I needed it. Hell, if I had to unzip him myself I would do so. But when he broke the kiss, he lifted me from his lap and put me back on the opposite seat. The sense of disappointment I felt was borderline overwhelming.

I quickly adjusted my dress, looked at my reflection in the window, and sighed heavily. There was no hiding it.

The car came to a stop.

"Stay here, Bri. The business I have inside will not take long and there is no way in hell you are going to walk into my club not wearing panties. I'd have to kill too many men tonight." He winked at me.

He must have seen the concern on my face and pressed a quick kiss to my lips.

"I am not leaving you unprotected. Steven will stay in the car. He is armed and quite proficient. I will also have four more men sent out to watch the car. Blaze will be with me, but my men will not let anyone get within twenty feet of this car. Stay here. When I am done, I have something for you that hopefully will make you smile."

I saw his eyes drift to my lips.

"I love to see your smiles, Angel."

He kissed me once again and then quickly left the car. I heard him barking orders but soon he disappeared into the club. I drummed my fingers against the seat, wondering just how long he would be, and if the surprise he had planned for after included me being naked. A thrill washed over me at the thought. Maybe I could survive a relationship built entirely on lust. My heart seemed to skip a beat at the thought.

CHAPTER
fourteen

ROGUE

L eaving Bri behind in the car, looking flushed and entirely too desirable, was harder than I had anticipated. But tonight, I didn't want her in the club. She was still too anxious and scared of the man who had attacked her, and I was concerned that even the mention of his name would cause her to have more nightmares. Tonight, I was to meet with the person responsible for sending the two men to follow us the day I married her at the church. If the man was smart, which I wasn't overly convinced of, he would give up Tony Galante to save his own skin. But over the years, people have surprised me at every turn with their stupidity. It would be interesting to see how this played out.

When I walked into the club, I immediately saw Blaze leaning against the bar, a waitress in one hand and a class of whiskey in the other. He was whispering into the unsuspecting woman's ear, no doubt telling her the things he would like to do with her once the club closed.

Every waitress or dancer that was hired at *Sinners* was given ample warning about Blaze and his lecherous habits. If they chose to play with fire after that, I considered it their problem. He was a player, as we all were at one time, but Blaze was different. He was rough, brutal, and uncaring, but for whatever reason, the women he lured into his bed could never get enough. Unfortunately for them, Blaze only slept with a woman once. It was a rule I had never known him to break, no matter how hard a woman tried to attract his attention again.

As I got closer to the bar, he lifted his head, grabbed one more handful of ass, then strode my way.

"Where's the little one? Don't tell me you tired of her already."

I took a minute to look around the club. Nothing seemed out of the ordinary. "Hardly. She is waiting in the car. I want to keep her as far away from any conversation concerning Tony Galante as possible."

He nodded in understanding. "Well, she may be waiting awhile."

My eyes narrowed at this unwelcome news. "He is not here?"

"No, but I have already sent men to retrieve him."

"You know where he is?"

The look on Blaze's face was one of frustration. "You had two of our men follow the two idiots from the other day. They went straight to their boss, if you can call him that. His name is Petey Guzman." His lips lifted slightly. "Not exactly the name you would expect a wanna-be drug dealer would have. Since I was afraid he wouldn't have the balls to face you tonight, I sent a crew to stake out his hangout."

"His hangout?"

"Yeah, he runs drugs from the bar down the street from his apartment." He shook his head again in disgust. "I still can't believe we are dealing with someone so inconsequential. It's ridiculous."

I nodded toward the bartender to fix me a drink. "We aren't going into business with him. I just want to know how he knows Galante and where the bastard is hiding. After I have the information I need, he will be useless to me. What he is willing to share will determine how much mercy he receives. Not showing up for a meeting with me is not the best way to get on my good side, especially considering I have Bri in the car."

A deep humorless laugh came from Blaze as he welcomed the promise of violence, but just as quickly, his smile faded as he narrowed his gaze. I turned to look back toward the door to see four of my men practically dragging poor Petey behind them. They came to a stop before us, and I could see that the man was sweating profusely. His eyes were red and bloodshot, not certain if it was from crying or if he had snorted his own product before my men showed up to take him.

"Where do you want us to take him, boss? To the suite upstairs or the office?"

I stepped closer, my imposing presence sending shivers of intimidation over the man cowering before me. "Take him to the office, he doesn't deserve the luxury of the suite."

Petey raised his head and the strong smell of cheap whiskey and sweat swirled around him. "I don't know nothing, Mr. Delaney. I swear."

My reaction was swift. I wrapped my hand around his throat, squeezing until his eyes bulged and his air was cut off. Spittle and foam began to form on the corners of his lips.

"Lying to me is a mistake. Do so again and I will gut you myself and sit back and watch you writhe in pain for hours with a smile on my face before death comes for you."

"Watch out, Rogue." Blaze's voice caused me to release my hold. "He is pissing his pants. Don't want it all over your shoes."

I stepped back in disgust. "For Christ's sake. Take him to the office."

I walked over to the bar where a glass of bourbon was waiting for me.

Blaze came up behind me. "You want me to handle this? For once, I think I may have more patience than you."

"It's not patience I am lacking, it's restraint." I turned up the glass and drank, hoping the liquor would have a calming effect on me.

"I will send a few more men to watch over the little one. Then I suggest we go to the office and get this shit over with. You aren't the only one that has pussy on the brain tonight."

I looked back to where the waitress from earlier was watching us. "Why does it always have to be the women that work here?"

He shrugged his shoulders. "Don't blame me because the waitresses you hire can't get enough of me. Besides, if I remember correctly, you married the last woman you hired to work here."

I smiled at his remark, knowing that Bri working here was never part of my plan, just an easier means to have her to myself. An image of her from earlier popped back into my head and my smile faded.

"Hurry up before Petey pisses himself again."

Blaze walked away and gave some instructions to a few more men. I didn't like leaving Bri behind, but knowing my men were there protecting her allowed me to focus on what had to be done. I started walking toward the office at the back of the club, ignoring everything that was going on around me, the music, the laughter, the women dancing on stage. I was focused, and unfortunately for Petey, he was the object I had in my sight.

When we walked into the office, we were met by a sobbing Petey on his knees. "Mr. Delaney..."

"Stop! Before you open your mouth again, remember the warning I gave you about lying to me earlier. Now stay on your knees and only open your mouth to answer the questions I ask."

Blaze came up beside me at that moment with what looked like a scalpel. I watched Petey's eyes focus on the razor-sharp weapon in Blaze's hand, and he started crying again.

"For fuck's sake, man! Have some pride." Blaze said, disgusted with the loud blubbering coming from the man kneeling before us.

"Tony Galante hired you to find a girl, correct?"

He nodded.

"Speak!"

"Yes, he came to me and said that he met a woman in Colorado. He said the bitch wouldn't put out after leading him on for weeks."

I nodded toward Blaze who quickly swiped the scalpel across Petey's chest. He didn't even flinch until red started oozing through his shirt.

"Ah, fuck," he said before weeping again.

"The 'bitch' you are referring to is my wife, Petey. Disrespect her again, and I will slit your throat. Make no mistake, I don't need you to find Galante. Your cooperation will make it easier, but it is not essential. Do you understand?"

He nodded, his bloody hands shaking.

"Let's start again then. Galante paid you to find my wife?"

"I owed him a favor from a few years back. He said that if I could find her and report back to him where she was hiding, he would cancel my debt to him. I didn't know she was your wife, Mr. Delaney, I swear."

"That I do believe, Petey, otherwise you would already be dead. Now, did you report back to Galante?"

"No, when the two men I sent came back to the bar saying that the girl was with you, I told Tony we couldn't find her." He held up his hands in surrender. "I swear to that. I wouldn't go against you."

"But yet you ignored me and tried to hide instead of coming here tonight. Where is he now?"

His eyes widened. "Do you know who Tony is? He will kill me if I tell you."

I stepped closer. "And I will kill you if you don't. So, it's either die right now or take your chances, Petey."

I watched his eyes widen. "He was in Chicago, but I don't know where he is now. If he is still here, I have no idea where he is staying or anyone else that might know him. I swear! I haven't seen him since the first day when he asked me to find her. He did leave a number for me to call with any information."

"The number?"

"It's written on a sticky note behind the bar where your men grabbed me. I can give it to you."

I stepped back from him, hoping the stench of piss and sweat didn't rub off on me. "I hope you are telling the truth, because if you aren't, my friend here...," I motioned toward Blaze. "He will make your torture last for a very long time...and enjoy every second of it."

I looked at the other two men in the room. "Take him back to the bar where he operates and get the number. You know what to do if he tries anything stupid." I looked back to where Petey was being helped to his feet. "Oh, and Petey, I think it's time you made another city your home. Do you understand?"

He nodded as his knees wobbled in fear.

"Go now." I stepped back as the two men began dragging him from the office.

"It always disappoints me when a man is that weak. I prefer it when they have a bit of fight, spit curses at me, or swear they will kill me when they get free, but that was pathetic."

I agreed with Blaze. "When you get the number, do whatever it is that you do. I want to find him before he has a chance to find her."

"Where are you going? The club is busy tonight. You should stay. There is plenty of pussy for the both of us."

I shook my head as a smile curved my lips. "I have other plans for the evening, but feel free to fill your bed with as many women as you like."

He laughed as we walked from the office. "I will take that as a challenge. I do have a personal best to beat."

The thought of having another woman in my bed no longer interested me. All I wanted was her, my angel.

Bri

Rogue had made certain that I couldn't leave the car even if I had wanted to. From what I could see, there were at least six men standing guard, each one of them looking like a cross between a secret service agent and a club bouncer. While I hated to admit it, the extra security did make me feel safer, especially since I was so new to all of this.

I slipped off my black heels and pulled my legs underneath me as I waited for Rogue to return. I leaned my head against the window and watched the people standing outside the club. It was a busy night but *Sinners,* being the premier club in the city, was busy every night. When I worked at the hotel, I heard lots of talk about the club and its owner. I never imagined I would have become so entangled with him.

The rain had slowed to a misty drizzle, but that didn't deter the people waiting in line to get inside. The windows in the car were growing foggy and I took my hand and wiped it clean so I could see better. Then I sat up quickly. Was that?

A woman was on the opposite side of the street. She was wearing a green coat. Allison often wore green and had a green coat that looked a lot like that one. While I couldn't see the woman's face, she was the same height and build as my friend. *Could Allison have traveled to Chicago to find me?* I had not tried to call her back since our last conversation, and it would be just like her to rush here and try to bring me home herself. I quickly put my shoes back on and opened the car door, ready to dash across the street.

Stephen, our driver, quickly intercepted me. "Mrs. Delaney! You can't leave the car."

I tried to move around him. "I think I saw my friend over there across the street. I have to see if it is her." I pushed against him and tried to go around again, but now there were more of them. "Ok, this is ridiculous. You are supposed to be watching over me not holding me prisoner. I am just going across the street to see if the lady in the green coat is my friend from Colorado. Now move aside before she gets so far out of my sight that I can't find her."

My speech sounded much more powerful to my own ears than it did to theirs since none of them moved. I huffed out a deep breath. "Fine, I will do this your way." I pushed hard against Stephen who was surprisingly easier to move than I expected. Once I saw a hole in their ranks, I bolted, only to be grabbed around the waist and hauled up against a strong muscular chest. I knew immediately who held me without seeing his face.

"Let me go!"

The arm that was around my waist tightened like a band of steel as he lifted me off my feet to pull me back over to the car.

"What the hell are you trying to do, Angel?"

I kicked my feet out hoping to connect with something, but all I managed to do was kick the side of the car, causing me to shriek in pain.

"Stop fighting me!"

His voice was harsher than I expected and for some unknown

reason, whenever he used that commanding tone with me, I had the urge to comply. It was the most irritating thing.

"Let me go! I may still find her."

He set me down on my feet but spun me around so that I was pressed between his body and the car. "Who? Who are you trying to find?"

What fight I had in me was quickly dissipating. "Allison. I saw a woman across the street who looked a lot like Allison. It could be her. She was wearing a green coat that looked a lot like the one Allison wears frequently. She must have come to Chicago to find me when I didn't return her call."

Rogue still held me against him with one hand while he reached into his pocket with the other and took out my phone. "Call her."

"What?"

"Call her. If your friend is in Chicago, call her. Make certain before you run off into the darkness chasing after someone you don't know. If she is here, I will help you find her."

I eagerly grabbed the phone and dialed her number. It rang, but Allison didn't pick up. I immediately tried again. "Why isn't she answering?"

Rogue continued to stand in front of me preventing any opportunity I might have to bolt free.

"I know it was her. Why didn't you let me go to her?""

"If it was your friend, we will find her once she answers the phone and tells us where she is. Call her again."

I rolled my eyes and dialed the number; I was just about to hang up when I heard Allison's voice. "Allison? Where are you?"

"I just stepped out of the shower, why? Are you alright? Did you quit your job yet?"

I looked up to see Rogue's eyes narrow slightly. "I just saw you in Chicago."

She laughed softly and my stomach sank. "Chicago? It wasn't me, Bri. Do you not think I would have called to tell you I was coming? I wouldn't have just shown up."

I didn't know what to say. I had been so certain. "I saw your coat, the horrible green one I tease you about wearing all the time."

"My goodness, Bri. I am not the only woman in the world who likes the color green." She paused. "Are you alright? I don't feel good about this at all. You sound different."

I shook the fog from my brain. "I'm just disappointed that it wasn't you. A little homesick, I suppose. I miss you."

"I miss you too, Bri. You need to come home. We will figure something out when it comes to Tony. You can't stay in Chicago forever."

I looked up at Rogue, his face set in stone. "I have to go, Allison. I'll call you back tomorrow or the next day. Trust me, I am alright. No worries."

I hung the phone up and handed it back to Rogue.

"Keep it. It is yours until I buy you an updated version."

My head dropped and I turned to open the car door, but Rogue beat me to it. He helped me inside and then moved to the other side of the car. *Could I have imagined it? I was a little tired, but was I so exhausted that I was starting to hallucinate?*

Rogue's hand covered mine and I turned to him. "I was so certain that I saw her. How could I have been so wrong?"

"It could have been a coincidence, perhaps the lighting made you think you saw something you didn't. It was dark and sometimes the shadows and light from the streetlamps play tricks with your eyes."

I knew he was just saying this to placate me, but I felt really stupid right now. "I feel like an idiot, and I suppose I owe Stephen an apology."

"He was doing his job. He doesn't expect apologies."

I snorted a short laugh. "His job is to keep me from running around Chicago like a mad woman?"

"No, his job is to protect you at all costs. He and the other men that work for me are paid very well for that."

I shook my head, trying to push all of this from my mind. "I suppose I am just tired and a bit strained."

He pulled me closer. "Too tired to enjoy the surprise I have for you?"

I couldn't help the small smile that crept up my lips. "I guess that depends on the surprise."

The car came to a stop outside the Field Museum. I looked out the window and then back to Rogue. "Were you going to take me to the museum? If that is your surprise, I'm afraid it is closed."

He grabbed my hand and brought it up to his lips before turning it over and kissing my palm. From there his lips moved to my wrist, up the bend in my elbow, and finally to my shoulder. "Darling." His lips pressed against the pulse point beating rapidly in my neck. "I have told you before that you don't wait in line for anything...not anymore...not since you became mine."

He opened the car door and stepped out before turning to offer me his hand. He interlaced his fingers with mine and together we walked up the stairs to the museum entrance where we were met by an older man wearing a three-piece suit and a thick white mustache that curled up on the ends.

"Mr. Delaney." He offered his hand to Rogue who promptly took it. "I was so pleased to hear of your interest in touring the museum tonight and of course, your generous donation is most appreciated."

My mouth fell open slightly as I watched the exchange between the two men.

"As you requested, you have access to the entire museum. There are security officers on hand, but they have been instructed to leave you alone. If there is anything you need you have my cell number."

"Thank you, Mr. Greer. I was very pleased that you were so accommodating with my request."

The older man's smile widened as he stepped off to the side, allowing us entrance into the world-famous museum.

"You rented the entire museum? For me? How did you manage that?"

He continued to tug me along beside him. "You would be surprised at what I can do, baby. A substantial donation will get you into many locked doors. Money is powerful. You mentioned that you had wanted to visit the Field Museum but because you didn't have the money or the time, you had not had the opportunity. Now you have both."

He pulled me into his arms and kissed me...deeply. A kiss that made my toes curl and my heart flutter.

"I will give you more than you could have ever dreamed of, sweetheart. This is just the tip of the iceberg."

I slowly opened my eyes to find him watching me and my cheeks pinkened.

"Well, we have all night. Where do you want to start?"

My lips curved into the widest smile of my life. "Are you kidding? Dinosaurs of course!"

I took his hand and began dragging him to the Prehistoric Hall. He may be a monster, a criminal, even a killer, but right now he was the man making my dreams come true.

Rogue

I watched as Bri eagerly moved through each of the exhibits, reading every placard, and studying every piece. Her smile had stabbed me right through the heart when I told her that I had rented the entire museum just for her. It made me want to see her smile more often, to take her places and let her experience things she never had before. I wanted to hear her laugh, I wanted to watch her lie on the beach of a private island, I wanted to watch her expression as we walked the streets of Rome and toured the vineyards of Tuscany. This woman made me want more in life, more beyond making money and building an empire. She made me want to live.

But as much as I enjoyed the joy and exuberance with which she roamed through the museum, something didn't feel right about tonight. She had been so adamant that she had spotted her friend Allison in the street. It had been dark and after the rain, there was a light misty fog. But it was too much of a coincidence and I didn't believe in chance. Had hapless Petey lied to me? Was Tony Galante in Chicago still seeking to take her away from me, even after knowing that she was mine? That was ballsy. The man was either brave or stupid. My money would be on the latter.

I walked out of hearing and called Blaze.

"There was an incident tonight outside the club."

I could hear his heavy intake of breath over the phone; he was either irritated about having his liaison disturbed or he was already aware.

"One of the men told me."

"Take some of the men and search..."

"Save your breath. I have already done that. One of them did find a green coat waded up in a garbage can two blocks from the club. Inside was a business card for a cheap hotel in midtown. I am on my way there now. Not sure if I will find Galante there waiting, but I might get information from the clerk at the front. I will keep you posted."

"Send me the address. I can take Bri back to the penthouse and meet you there."

"Don't ruin her evening for what might be a wild goose chase. If I discover anything of importance, I will text or call."

"If you do find Tony there..."

"Don't worry, I will not deprive you of the pleasure of killing him yourself. Besides, after hearing what he did to the little one, I wouldn't mind watching him suffer for a long time."

That's what I liked about Blaze. He was cunning, brutal, and a bit psychotic, but we thought alike. He already knew what I needed him to do. I looked back to where Bri was moving toward the Egyptian exhibit and I knew that if Galante was unlucky enough to be at the hotel when Blaze got there, I would be sending him to hell sooner rather than later.

I moved up behind Bri as she was leaning over a glass case staring down at the face of a three-thousand-year-old mummy. I moved her long hair off the side so I could have access to the sensitive skin right below her ear. My lips pressed against her flesh as my arms wrapped around her waist.

"You know what I would like to do?"

I felt her body lean back against mine, and I nuzzled my nose into the side of her neck breathing in her scent.

"I would like to sit you on top of this case, push your skirt over your hips, and fuck you right here. I bet your screams would echo through these empty halls. Would you let me, sweetheart? I don't know how much longer I can stand here and watch you move about the room reading every little description of every piece. Images of you naked riding my cock or lying on your back with your knees over my shoulders keep popping into my head." I spun her around to face me. "Spread your legs for me. I want to see how wet you are." I gathered the skirt of her dress and slipped my fingers through her folds. Her pussy was weeping for my cock.

"We can't do this here, Rogue."

I leaned closer and whispered in her ear, "I can fuck my wife anywhere I please."

"No, you can't. There are more than likely alarms on the glass case, and I would prefer that we not unleash some ancient Egyptian curse on us for desecrating a sacred mummy. That's all I need right now. An Egyptian mummy chasing me through Chicago. I have enough stalkers, I don't need another."

I sighed heavily, hating that I was being denied what I wanted so desperately but she was right, this was not the time. "Fine, you do have the entire museum for the night, but just so you know, for every hour I give you here, is an hour you will give me naked, and after feeling just how wet that sweet pussy is, I'm not certain I can wait until we reach the penthouse."

I was expecting her to roll her eyes or come back with a sarcastic comment, but she surprised me again when she leaned closer, her plump red lips hovering over mine, her long lashes resting against her pink cheeks, and whispered, "If that is to be my punishment, I may stay here until the museum reopens in the morning."

I stood there rooted to the spot imagining having her to myself for hours and all the things I could do to her. My dick grew hard as granite as she sashayed away to another exhibit. *Holy Fuck!* An image of her on her knees before me, taking my cock into her mouth, her tongue moving up and down the length of me before her lips closed around my shaft was enough to make me damn near come right then.

I clenched my hands into fists to keep myself from marching over to her, throwing her over my shoulder, and carting her back to the car. I would make it up to her, hell I would take her to every fucking museum in the country if that was what she wanted. I took a few steps toward her when my phone rang. I hesitated, not wanting anything to ruin this night, but if Blaze had found Galante I wanted to know, I wanted to finish it. I wanted to give her the gift of knowing that she had nothing else to fear, no more nightmares.

"Tell me you have him."

"No, but he was here. I got his description from the hotel clerk. He has been living in this shithole for about three weeks and there is more. I will send you a few pictures."

I pulled the phone away from my ear and looked down at the screen. There were photos of Bri's old apartment before I had everything boxed up, photos of her with me outside the club and again outside the penthouse.

"That fucking bastard. Have two men stationed outside the hotel in case he returns there tonight. And pay the clerk off. I don't want him to warn Galante that we were there. Leave everything like you found it."

"Since you have taken to giving me orders, I have some for you. Get her out of town, take her to the estate, or send her to New York to stay with Alessio. I have a bad feeling about this man. We have too much that can go wrong. Petros and his Armenian thugs are poised to make a move any day now. While I know they aren't much to worry about, they could cause just enough of a distraction that Galante could capitalize on it. I don't want another incident like we had with Alessio's Cara Mia. We were lucky that night; it could have gone much worse and if we had been thirty minutes later to rescue her, it would have. I don't want a repeat of that scenario. Heed my warning and take her away from here."

I heaved a heavy sigh. "I will have Brenda make sure the estate is properly staffed. It will take a few days but once everything is in order, I will take her there. But I want that bastard found! I don't want her to even have to see his face again. See if the hotel has any security footage of him and have every man look at it so he can be recognized."

"This isn't the kind of hotel with security cameras, but I will ask. But Bri was right, it either was him outside the club or he paid someone to wear the coat, hoping he could lure her away. He may have had plans to grab her tonight. This makes me question if he has friends inside the club, not one of your employees, but maybe someone posing as a patron. Someone sent to just watch what goes on and report back to him."

I wanted to punch the wall; my anger was growing by the second. "There are too many 'what ifs' and I don't like it."

"Me either, but it's what we have right now. Let's just hope that we can find Tony before Petros makes his next move."

CHAPTER
fifteen

Bri

I would remember tonight for the rest of my life. I never imagined anyone having the power or money to rent out an entire museum, but Rogue had done exactly that for me. A gift to me simply because I mentioned wanting to visit but never being able to afford the luxury. As I strolled through the different halls, admiring the ancient treasures and exhibits on display, not one time did I think of Tony or the trouble that followed me. It may be only a short reprieve, but I was happy to take it.

Things had changed between Rogue and me. I wasn't sure exactly when this transformation occurred, but I no longer felt like a captive looking for the first opportunity to escape. I no longer was afraid or angry with him, and the flame of desire that burned between us only seemed to burn hotter the more we were with each other.

I glanced over my shoulder, expecting to see him hovering behind me or staring at me, but he had walked away to stand across the room to take a call. Something had happened to change his demeanor. He was angry. And just like that, the reality of our situation returned. The fragile but twisted fairy tale that I had woven into my brain was now broken. I was not living with a prince or a knight in shining armor. I was living with a dangerous man in a world where death and peril were commonplace.

The desire I had to continue my exploration of the museum deserted me along with any hope that this could turn into a normal relationship. The steps I took drawing me closer to him alerted him to my presence. An intense feeling of dread swept over me, and I knew that the phone call that had disrupted our evening had to do with Tony and his search for me.

He looked up and put the phone back into his coat pocket. "Finished so soon, Angel?"

I nodded my head. "I am just a little tired and while I feel foolish and hate to admit it, my foot hurts a little bit from where I tried to kick you and instead kicked the car."

He stepped forward and before I could utter a protest lifted me into his arms and I felt that fairy-tale feeling threatening to take over my senses again.

He carried me over to the information desk and sat me on top of a stack of maps and brochures.

"You should have told me your foot was hurt. I had not realized you kicked the car hard enough to injure yourself."

He slipped off my black heel and held my foot in his hand as he examined it.

"I am not injured. You just saw me walking all over this place. My foot is just a bit sore. There is no need to be concerned."

His hand slid over my ankle and slowly up my calf. "It doesn't appear to be sprained, but we really should be certain."

I saw a hint of amusement flicker in his eyes.

"I told you it was just a little sore."

His lips lifted into a small smile. "Let's be sure."

I shrieked as he raked a finger down the bottom of my foot and nearly jumped from the desk. I tried to pull my foot free, but he held it tighter and raked his fingers across the bottom of my foot again, causing me to burst out in a shrill giggle.

"Stop! I can't stand anymore."

He laughed and released my foot before placing a quick kiss to my lips. "You are ticklish. That is an important bit of information that might prove useful in the future."

"Don't you dare!"

He laughed and then swept me back into his arms and started for the museum entrance.

I wrapped my arms around his neck. "You don't have to carry me. You know my foot is not injured to the point that I can't walk."

"Perhaps I just like the way it feels to hold you in my arms."

I squeezed my eyes shut tight and pushed those pesky feelings away. Feelings that threatened to hurt me far more than anything I had physically experienced. This wasn't real. It couldn't be, and I had to shield my heart from feeling anything for Rogue Delaney.

A security guard was stationed at the front entrance and held the door open for us. Once outside I saw the men that worked for Rogue waiting. "You can put me down now. I don't want everyone to think that I am incapable of taking care of myself."

Even from his profile, I could see his lips curve up a bit.

"After the way you fought tonight outside the club, I'm sure they are well aware."

I felt the blood rush to my cheeks. "Yes, I should apologize. It was embarrassing, especially now that I know I was wrong. I don't know why I would think Allison would be here in Chicago." I felt his muscles stiffen. "Rogue? I was wrong, wasn't I?"

"Darling, you had a natural reaction to what you saw or thought you saw. Anyone that had been through the shock that you have over the last few days would have done the same thing."

"My shock is one thing, but can you imagine how shocked the person would have been if I had managed to break away from your security detail and catch them? They would have thought I was a crazy woman."

"They might think it, but never would they have the balls to say it in my presence. Now get in the car, Angel. My restraint is reaching its limit."

I knew exactly what he was talking about. Since our little talk at the mummy case, I had thought of little else but being in bed with this man. A man who frightened me but at the same time brought me to new heights of desire and lust. The darkly enchanted and wicked world I was living in now was fragile. At any moment the bubble could burst, and I could be on my own again, but here and now, I wanted every moment of pleasure I could steal before life hit me like a brick wall, before danger crept back into his world, before he grew tired of me as Blaze had suggested he would.

Rogue remained silent, never turning his head away from the window as the car drove us through the streets, the reflection of the city lights twinkled against the wet pavement. A part of me didn't want to know what he was thinking, or what was said on the phone to cause his mood to change so drastically. Whatever it was I didn't want it to spoil the evening. Even if Tony was waiting around the corner to grab me, I didn't want to know, not tonight. Tonight, I wanted to pretend that I could love this man and he could love me. I wanted to live the fanciful tale, and pretend to be his princess. Tonight, I didn't want anything to disturb the fragile peace I was feeling.

The car came to a stop, and he got out, took my hand, and silently we entered the high-rise building and walked toward the elevator that took us to the penthouse. Although we never spoke, I felt his fingers lightly caressing my hand. The expectation of what we both knew was coming excited me like nothing before.

When the elevator doors opened, I expected him to walk directly to the bedroom, but instead, he went over to the sofa and took a seat, sighing heavily as he looked at where I was still standing.

"The green coat you saw someone wearing tonight was found inside a trash can two blocks away from the club."

I felt my heart sink a little. I didn't want to know this. I wanted to pretend it had all gone away. "So, I was right."

He breathed in deeply. "You were right about seeing the green coat, but wrong thinking it was your friend."

I shook my head in confusion. "I know it wasn't Allison, who was it?"

"Blaze found a business card in the pocket to a hotel here in Chicago. When he went there, he confirmed that Galante had been there."

I pinched the bridge of my nose and closed my eyes. "So, it was Tony the whole time and I almost ran right to him."

My knees felt wobbly and when I felt Rogue's strong arm wrap around my waist, I was grateful for the support.

"You should have let me leave Chicago when I discovered Tony was here. He is going to find me. There is nothing anyone can do to stop it. Now that he knows where I am, he will not stop."

Rogue put his hands on either side of my face and forced me to look up at him. "Open your eyes, Angel, and listen carefully to what I am going to say to you."

My eyes fluttered open and the intensity I saw as he stared back at me sent chills down my spine.

"I don't know why I am having to address this again with you, but I will try once more. You belong to me, Bri. You are my wife, and I will protect you. I didn't tell you this so you would cower in fear, and believe me, I was conflicted when deciding if it was the right thing to do. I told you so that you would make better decisions and think before you act rashly. Tonight, if, and I emphasize if, you had been able to break away from the men I had protecting you, you would have run headlong into danger. This is a lesson. Something that you need to learn and fully understand. It's not just about Tony. There will be others, other dangers you will face, you have to make better decisions."

I felt my temper rising above my fear. "Are you seriously chastising me right now?"

"If that's what you want to think of it, then yes." He gripped my arms to keep me from turning away. "You are in my world now, Angel. It's a world in which you are afforded many privileges but cannot always do as you please."

I tried to pull away, but he refused to release me. "What if I don't want to be a part of your world?"

He wrapped a hand in my hair and tugged my head back sharply. "It's too late for that now. You are already a part of it. The first moment I laid eyes on you, the second my lips touched your skin, once I made the decision to claim you as mine...it was already too late. Trust me, Angel, to keep you safe."

"I don't want to always rely on others to keep me safe. I want to be able to do so myself."

He shook his head. "No, protecting you is my job."

I squeezed his arms harder to make him listen to me. "Can't you see that me knowing how to defend myself can only be an asset? I don't want to play the damsel in distress. I don't want to always be fearful. If I had known some sort of self-defense moves on the night that Tony attacked me, I might have avoided a stay in the hospital. Teach me to shoot, teach me something that will allow me to save myself if the need arises."

I could see that he was considering it by the way his eyes searched my face.

"The thought of you having to defend yourself doesn't sit well with me. I don't want you to ever be in a situation where those types of skills are needed, but if you are determined to learn, I will consider it."

"Blaze could even teach me if you are too busy."

He grinned. "Blaze would turn you into a cold-blooded killer if given half the chance, but Father Michael might be able to assist."

"Thank you."

His lips came down hard on mine, and I felt any anger or fear I was holding onto swiftly dissipating. I didn't know how he managed to make me melt in a puddle of desire with just a kiss, but he did every time.

When he pulled away, I felt strangely bereft.

"You looked beautiful tonight. Now take off the dress."

My brow furrowed. "Excuse me?"

"You heard me. Strip for me, Angel. I have wanted to see you naked before we arrived at the museum. So, you have two choices, take it off or I'll rip it off. Your choice."

He moved back to the couch and took a seat as if waiting to watch a show.

"Here. Not in the bedroom?"

"Right here. The clock is ticking, baby. Better get started."

My fingers moved slowly to the straps of the dress. It was strangely disconcerting to undress while he sat there watching. I could feel the heat in my face as the straps slowly slid down my arms. His eyes darkened as the tops of my breasts became visible and what at first made me feel awkward and uncomfortable, suddenly became very erotic. I shimmied the dress down a little slower, stopping just as my nipples became visible. A muscle in the side of his jaw flinched as my hands moved up to cover my breasts.

"You want to give me a show, Angel? Go right ahead but know that I will not be held responsible for my actions."

The threat emboldened me. I pushed the dress down farther so that it hung low on my hips. My hand glided slowly over my stomach before dipping lower, the dress still obscuring my actions. Rogue's eyes were watching every move I made, his lips set in a straight line.

When the dress fell to the floor, my hand stilled. It was one thing to be hidden, but with Rogue's hungry gaze fixed on my hand, watching every movement I made was another thing altogether.

He stood from the sofa and walked toward me, every nerve ending in my body tingled in anticipation of his touch.

He raised his hand, letting the backs of his fingers gently graze over my skin. "You truly are perfection."

Then something snapped in him. He became urgent and aggressive. He gripped my hair in his fist and pulled my head back sharply. His head dipped lower, and he pulled my nipples between his teeth while his other hand moved over the curve of my ass. His urgency grew. He lifted me in his arms and carried me over to the bar and sat me on top of the cool granite surface.

"Lie down and put your feet on the edge."

I did as he asked and felt him press my knees farther apart. One of his hands moved over my stomach toward my breasts. He rolled my pebbled nipples between his fingers, squeezing them enough to elicit a gasp from my lips. As his hand slid lower, I felt his fingers spread apart my folds.

I closed my eyes under his inspection and waited in anticipation for his mouth to cover me.

"Keep your eyes closed, Angel."

He pressed one finger inside me.

"Stay there. I have another surprise for you."

I leaned up and pressed my knees together. "You want me to stay here?"

"Don't move. I will be right back."

I pulled my lower lip between my teeth, my eyes remained closed as I waited.

"Do you trust me, Angel?"

I nodded my head, eager for him to get on with it. I was burning for this man. I heard a small humming noise, but before I could question it, my body jumped at the vibrations against me. My eyes flew open, and I leaned up to see the device in his hand.

"Lie back down, Angel."

He moved the device over my center, and I nearly came off the top of the bar. The vibrations were intense, and I felt my body jump with every stroke. But when he inserted it inside me, I felt a rush of liquid. The feelings were so strong and so powerful that I tried to close my legs and scoot away. But he held me firm as he continued moving the vibrator in and out of my pussy.

My body began to tremble and convulse violently. "Fuck!"

"Do you like toys, baby?"

I was almost beyond speaking, my body gushing. He removed the device, and I heard the sound of his belt and zipper. I cried out as he shoved his hard cock inside me, both hands gripping my breasts as he slammed into me.

Another scream escaped my lips as he pulled me to an upright position. I wrapped my legs around him as his mouth sucked in my breast. I convulsed again, feeling weak and satiated.

"That's it, baby. But we aren't done yet."

He ripped off his shirt and kicked off his pants that were around his ankles, then swept me into his arms and carried me to the bedroom. He kicked the door open, it banged loudly against the wall.

He carried me to the bed. I had no idea what he had in store for me until he pulled out 4 black sashes.

"What are those for?"

"Do you trust me?"

I nodded but inside my stomach fluttered a little. He took the sashes and tied my hands to the headboard before moving to my feet. The sashes were wrapped around my ankles before he spread them wide and secured them to the bed.

He walked away and I started to rethink my decision to allow this. I pulled on the restraints, but they were secure. There was no way I would get out of this until he released me.

"Rogue?"

He walked back into the room with a glass of ice.

"You must learn patience, Angel."

He moved over me on the bed and placed a cube of ice in his mouth before lowering himself to my breast. I inhaled swiftly as his tongue swirled the ice around my nipple, causing it to harden even tighter while his fingers glided down my stomach to caress my clit. I bucked and pulled against the restraints as his fingers worked their magic.

"You can't free yourself so you might as well enjoy the moment."

He slid another ice cube down my belly and between my thighs. My eyes closed as my body shivered.

"Please."

"Please what, Bri?"

"Stop teasing me."

His chuckle reverberated against me as his mouth closed around my center. His tongue swiped over me while his fingers explored further. Being restrained was frustrating, but also exhilarating. There was something about being so exposed, so vulnerable that I found exciting. A tremor rolled over me as he brought me closer to the edge.

"Rogue! I need you."

He raised his head. "Then tell me. What do you want?"

I was beyond caring about embarrassing myself at this point. The need to have him inside was stronger than any hesitation I had about speaking the words out loud. "I want you to fuck me. I need you inside me."

I didn't have to wait long. His thrust was fierce, making me cry out and immediately I felt my muscles clench around him. I pulled against the restraints again, wanting to touch him, wanting to wrap my legs around him as he roughly took me. My orgasm was building and I couldn't control its release. I watched as his eyes closed in pleasure as my moisture moved over him. He continued to thrust inside me almost violently until he found his release.

My breathing was hard, and my body felt like jelly. When he untied me, I lay there unable to move. He pulled me to his side and lightly feathered kisses over my shoulder.

"Get some rest, Angel, because I am not nearly finished with you tonight."

My body trembled at the promise. The man was a beast, but I loved every minute of it.

Rogue

Watching her sleep was one of the most peaceful things I had ever done. There had been no nightmares last night. Of course, after several hours of making love to her in every conceivable way possible, she was quite literally exhausted. I wasn't certain if it was the fatigue or the fact that she finally felt safe, but whatever it was, I was glad to see her sleep serenely.

She was lying on her stomach, her brown hair to the side and the sheet had slipped down to her waist. I marveled at the perfection of her skin. I leaned forward, pressing a kiss to the top of her spine and the most delicious-sounding moan passed between her lips. I let my hand slip under the sheets to caress the soft curves of her ass before dipping between her thighs.

The craving for this woman couldn't be adequately explained. Never before had I been so obsessed, but Bri was like an addiction, a habit I was unable and unwilling to give up. Her warm body stirred as my fingers found what they were seeking. She breathed in deeply as I pushed two fingers inside her. I leaned over her pressing kisses down her spine to its base and pushing the sheet aside so I could see her, so I could watch her body take me in.

When another soft whimper escaped her, I couldn't wait any longer. I flipped her to her back and settled between her legs so I could thrust inside her.

"Damn it, Bri. I should have let you sleep. I should have already left for work. There are things I must get finished today but all I can think of is how good it feels for my cock to be inside you."

I pulled out slowly then pushed in faster, her swollen pussy growing wetter with each thrust. I knew I had so little control when it came to this woman but after last night, I wanted to take it slower, to make it good for her, but when her legs came up to wrap around my waist, I knew she wanted more. She wanted me to take her fast, hard, unrelenting. She liked it that way and whatever my princess wanted, she would get. My thrusts became more powerful, her cries grew louder, and it was not long before I could not hold back any longer. As I filled her fully, I kissed her, and for the first time in my life, I felt a cold chill of foreboding pass over me. I could not lose this woman. I could not be without her and as that was the case, I needed to up my search for the man that hurt her, the man that was still seeking to take what was mine. And when I found him, I would enjoy every second of torture I would reap upon his black soul.

I heard the notification beep on my phone, but I was reluctant to pull away from her body. I propped up on my elbows so the weight of my body would not crush her and brushed a few tendrils of hair from her face.

"You are even beautiful when you sleep, Angel."

Her eyes held a look of sleepy satisfaction, and it made me even more hungry for her.

A soft smile brightened her face. "Can we stay in bed today?"

"As tempting as it is to say yes, I do have some business to see to today. Blaze will be waiting for me here at the office downstairs and then tonight I will need to make an appearance at the club."

"Can I stay here? I don't feel like leaving the penthouse."

I could tell from the look in her eyes that she was still driven by fear. "You may stay in bed and sleep while I go downstairs. Sleep, take a shower, or a bubble bath if you prefer. I will have breakfast delivered to you, whatever you are in the mood for. But when I leave the penthouse, you come with me."

"But I..."

I pressed a quick kiss to her forehead. "We can't let our lives be ruled by fear, Brielle. You can't hide away from the villains and monsters that stalk the world. But you will not have to face them alone, that is my job."

I threw the covers back and stood from the bed. Her eyes looked their fill of me as I grabbed my phone and headed into the bathroom. Another notification came through and I looked down at the screen. When I saw Nik's number as well as about a dozen calls from Blaze, I knew something had gone wrong.

I called Blaze back first. Nik could wait.

"It's about fucking time!"

I was not in the mood for a lecture from Blaze this morning. "Save it! What the fuck happened?"

"Petros made a move last night against Nik in Vegas."

"Fuck!"

I heard him scoff.

"I would say you have done enough of that."

I wanted to tell him to mind his own damn business, but in a way he was right. I had not been taking the threats seriously. Petros was a punk thug who had been given too much power with no one to stay his hand. He was reckless and foolish, but he was still dangerous. My obsession with Bri and my drive to find and rid the world of Tony Galante had caused me to take that fact for granted.

"I'll be showered and dressed in thirty minutes. Meet me at the office downstairs."

"I'm already here."

He hung the phone up and I cursed inwardly. This was exactly what we had not wanted to happen. We wanted to make the first move and for Petros to strike the Bratva first showed not only his arrogance but his ignorance.

Steam rose from the shower as I let the hot water clear my head. I showered quickly and dressed. Bri had fallen back asleep, and I did not want to wake her. The last thing I needed right now was for my head not to be in the game. I needed to speak with Nik and make plans should Petros try something against my organization.

CHAPTER
sixteen

ROGUE

When I stepped into my office, I expected to see Blaze pacing back and forth uttering a stream of curses under his breath, but it was empty. There was an intense pounding in my head that was increasing in intensity by the minute, and I couldn't shake the feeling that this was my fault. I should have acted before allowing Petros to make the first move. For the first time in my life, I had allowed myself to be distracted, to let lust for a woman affect business and now because of my lack of focus, Petros, a man that should have been of no consequence to any of us had dealt the first blow, drawing first blood.

I was angry, angry at myself for not listening when Blaze tried to convince me to take the threat seriously. I still didn't know exactly what had happened, how bad the attack had been, or if there were casualties. I was hoping Blaze would be there to fill me in, but I couldn't wait any longer for him. I had to call Nik. He picked up on the first ring.

"Hmm, glad to see you were finally able to free yourself from your more pleasurable pursuits. Don't take offense. If I had a woman that looked like your little kitten, I would have a hard time thinking with something other than my dick too."

I bit back the angry retort on the tip of my tongue. Nik meant nothing by his words, he was just naturally an asshole. "Blaze informed me that Petros made an unexpected move against you last night but did not give me any details."

"Unexpected, yes. Successful, no. Let me give you the abbreviated version. The young Petros made two attempts last night, both attacks were synchronized clusterfucks. A group of his men tried to rob one of my casinos, conveniently at the time we were getting ready to transport funds, while another group almost simultaneously ambushed me and some of my men when we were across town away from the strip, at a place I am fond of for conducting more private business. We were just concluding...let's just say that I was finishing up negotiations with a competitor. Anyway, as we were cleaning up, Petros and twelve of his men opened fire. Really a sloppy attempt, I'm surprised he was even allowed the power that he has been given. I understand he was his father's heir, but for fuck's sake, either his father refused to train him in the way of things, or he is just a fucking idiot."

I pinched the bridge of my nose and closed my eyes, hoping I could summon whatever patience I had. "I have already surmised that. What the hell happened? Did you lose any men?"

Nik huffed a short, abbreviated laugh. "Do you truly believe a man like Petros would be a worthy opponent? No, the men who attacked the casino were killed as soon as their intentions were known. Unfortunately, we were not able to eliminate the threat entirely. Petros and a few of his men did manage to escape. It would have been nice not to have to concern ourselves with the fool a second longer, but it also wouldn't have been fair for me to have all the fun for myself. At least Blaze is excited about the prospect of violence."

"Yes, I'm sure he is. It is bothersome at times, but useful. Are you certain Petros will be headed to Chicago?"

"There were a few of his men left behind that did survive the bloodbath. After intense interrogation, they admitted that Chicago is the next target. Although, after losing the majority of the men foolish enough to follow him, I'm not certain if he will continue with his plans or if he will regroup. Whatever he decides, I think it wise to find him before he finds you. Petros is a reckless bastard that needs to be stopped, but reckless bastards have been known to get lucky a time or two."

"Yeah, I will handle it."

"Are you certain you can manage?"

The fact that Nik felt he could ridicule me made me furious. "Are you trying to insinuate that I can't?"

"No, I never insinuate. If I thought you couldn't handle it, I have the balls to come right out and tell you. But perhaps I can offer my assistance in another way. Your young beautiful bride, is she safe with you? I could come to Chicago and take her with me, bring her here to Vegas where I would employ all the resources of the Bratva to take care of her until you are free of Petros. And what about Tony Galante? Is he still searching for her? From what I hear, he is more of a threat than Petros. If you wish, you can think of my offer as a belated wedding gift."

"There is no way I would allow your lecherous hands anywhere near my wife. I don't need your help where she is concerned."

"Very well, my friend. But I have seen firsthand the brutality of Frankie Ballantine. He is not a man you want to piss off."

I was swiftly losing my temper. "I don't give a fu..."

Nik quickly interrupted me. "I also know that he does not have a loving relationship with his stepson. To say they are estranged is an understatement. It has been reported to me that he has threatened to kill Tony himself. So, you may be free to do as you please. While I am confident in my sources, I would check this information with Alessio since his father knew Frankie personally."

"Why were you looking into Tony Galante?"

His laugh was brief. "I thought it would be in my best interest. Besides, if something happens to you, I would like to think I would be there to comfort and console your grieving widow."

I hung the phone up before I said something that would destroy a relationship that couldn't be repaired.

"Nik is just fucking with you."

I turned quickly at the sound of Blaze's voice. "You were right. If I had sent her away as you suggested, I would have been able to deal with Petros before he had an opportunity to strike Nik. She distracted me."

He walked over to the bar, poured a glass of bourbon, and held it out for me. "Yes, I was right, but I believe Petros still would have struck Nik first. I think after the failed assassination attempt outside the club, he had his mind set on it. At least he is hurting from the losses Nik and the Volkoff Bratva inflicted on him. He will be easy enough to sniff out, the wounded always are."

"Contact Sevan and find out if he has any information as to his whereabouts. I think we should go for the kill now before he has time to regroup. I will send out feelers and once we find him, I don't want to hesitate. I want to attack and finish him. I'm tired of this son of a bitch causing problems in my circle."

The sadistic grin on Blaze's face showed me that he was on board and more than ready for a fight; he always was.

"What are you going to do with the little one?"

I took another large gulp of bourbon from my glass. "I already discussed with Brenda the arrangements to make the estate ready. It should only take a day or two. I will take her there until I have finished with everything."

He nodded, but I could tell that he wanted to say more. "Go ahead, say it. We have never held back with each other."

"I had no plans on holding back. Has it occurred to you that Petros could be the pawn in this game, that he is merely a puppet whose strings are being pulled by someone else?"

I narrowed my eyes as I took in his words. "Do you have someone in mind or is it just a hunch?"

He took a few steps forward before sinking back into the chair in front of my desk. "Think about it. A young fool with an ass load of ambition. His father dies before he could be trained to take the reins. Could there be someone else whispering in his ear, telling him that he is stronger and mightier than he is, hoping that he will be humiliated or taken out by either you or Nickolai, setting the stage for a takeover of his inherited right to rule the family?"

I heaved a sigh as my hand moved over the day-old stubble on my face. "Sevan. He was the one to seek us out and was so supportive of our taking Petros out."

"Yeah, and we paid the old bastard well for the information he brought us. It may be just my inherent distrust of people, but I would bet money that once Petros is out, Sevan and his sons move in to seize control."

I threw the glass I had been holding against the wall. I didn't like being played for a fool and if what Blaze was thinking was true, that was exactly what Sevan had attempted to do. "Dig deeper and find out what you can. If Sevan is behind any of this, it's not just Petros who must be stopped. I will burn down everything, taking it all."

"I will see what I can discover, but at risk of furthering your sour mood, the men stationed outside the flea-ridden hotel that Tony Galante was staying in reported that he still has yet to reappear."

"Fuck!"

"He will eventually come out of hiding. Unless he saw that we were on to him and decided to give up to save his own skin. He can't be that stupid to think he can target Bri and you will let him live."

I walked over to stand along the windows. The sky was gray, another day of no sunshine. "He hasn't given up. He is the type of man whose pride won't allow it. Eventually, he will appear again and when he does, I will be there. But now I need you to focus on Petros. There are too many factors that are unknown with the Armenians."

Blaze nodded. "I will have information for you tonight at the club."

"That quick?"

His eyes narrowed. "Don't insult me. Did you expect less? Just don't question my methods."

He closed the door behind him loudly. I took advantage of the few minutes of quiet to clear my mind. It had not been that long ago that I had been bored and wishing for some sort of excitement to break the monotony. Since finding Bri, the thirst for danger and blood was not nearly as strong.

The solitude didn't last long. My phone vibrated in my pocket. I took it out not in the mood for conversation, and I wondered if Alessio had already garnered information about the attack in Vegas.

"Tell me you have information about Tony Galante."

"As a matter of fact, I do. It was the reason for my call this morning. I invited Frankie Ballantine to lunch. You owe me one for that. The man eats like swine. I could barely stomach sitting at the table with him."

"Other than his grotesque eating habits, what else can you tell me?"

"Frankie said that he hasn't seen or heard from Tony in a few months."

I wanted to throw my phone across the room. "That's rather helpful."

Alessio chuckled on the other end of the line. "Don't be a dick, Rogue, because I can be an even bigger one. Now, where was I? Frankie said that Tony had always been a bad seed. The last time Tony was in New York, he attacked and beat the shit out of his mother. Frankie threatened to kill him then, but he respected his wife's wishes not to do so. After hearing about the trouble Tony has started with you, he said that he would actively seek to find him and get him out of Chicago. He doesn't want problems with any of us and would make certain that Tony gave us no more trouble. I believe he will follow through with his promise."

"It would still be nice to know where the bastard was. And I hope you know that I will find and kill Tony when I get the chance. I will not let what he did to Bri go unpunished."

"Yes, I know that, but it allows you to do it on your own time. Frankie did say that Tony had a few friends in Chicago that he could be staying with. I know that doesn't narrow down your search, but it does let us know that he could have people working with him. And if that is the case, he could be even more dangerous. My plane lands in Chicago tomorrow. No need to thank me, I owed you one."

He hung up before I could object, but honestly, with everything I had going on, it would be nice to have extra reinforcements. Plus, since I would be spending more time dealing with other matters, I would have less time to spend with Bri. With Eden in town, she would not be alone, and I could count on Alessio's security to protect her while I was taking care of eliminating the threats around us. I picked up my glass and took another sip of bourbon before moving to the wall safe hidden behind a large oval mirror on the opposite wall.

I took the mirror down and typed in the combination. What I was searching for was exactly where I had placed it ten years ago. A yellowed tattered business card from a restaurant that had been closed down for at least fifteen years, but it was what was on the back that was important. I stared down at the faded numbers, numbers I had sworn never to call, but now, with Bri's safety on the line and the nagging feeling that there was more to Petros' attacks and planned takeover than what was on the surface, I knew it was something I needed to do. I blew out a long breath and drank the remainder of the bourbon in my glass before dialing the numbers and making the call. A part of me wondered if the number was still good. Who the hell still had a landline now? But it only rang twice before a gruff voice with a thick Irish accent answered.

"It's about time ye called, lad. Your da would be pleased."

I could feel the tension in my jaw as I clenched my teeth tighter. "I didn't call to talk about him."

"Aye, I know why yer calling and a fine mess ye have now."

"What do you know of Sevan Avagyan?"

My uncle's raspy cough and a brief pause were the answer I received.

"I shouldn't have called."

"Don't ye be hangin' up on yer uncle now. You should have called fifteen years ago. If ye had, ye would be sittin' in your rightful place with even more wealth and power than ye have now."

Regret and anger poured through my veins. I should hang up, I should burn the card, and block the number. This was a waste of time.

"Very well, I'll tell ye what I know. Sevan and young Petros' father were not the close friends he is tryin' to portray to everyone. It had been planned for Sevan and his sons to take power once Hyak died, but the old man was always chasin' the skirts. Even at the age of sixty-five, he managed to coax a young waitress into 'is bed and after several attempts, his seed took hold, and young Petros was born. As ye can imagine it didn't sit well with Sevan who had been waiting for his chance to gain power for years."

"So, Sevan has been fostering and playing on Petros' foolishness and convincing him that it is in his best interest to take on me and the Russian Bratva. All the while, feeding us information on how to kill him. He doesn't want to see Petros succeed, he wants him dead."

"Aye, but don't mistake what I'm sayin' to ye. Petros is unstable and a fool to boot. He doesn' have what it takes to lead a group of men or run a family enterprise. His foolishness makes 'im even more dangerous. But he never would have been able to maintain power for long. Sevan is tryin' to cement 'is lineage by havin' you and your associates do his dirty work for 'im. Looks bad for 'im to kill and destroy the family from the inside, best to let ye do it for 'im. That way he can come in lookin' like a champion instead of the traitorous bastard that he is."

I sighed and took a deep breath to control the rage inside me. "The old man tried to use me and for that, he will pay. I can't let that kind of deception stand."

"Nor should ye. Ye have built up a fine organization on yer own. You can' expect to hold onto it if you don' rule with a firm hand. I expect now that ye have a wife, ye will have sons and yer sons need to be trained."

"Trained the way my father trained me? Left to fend for myself on the streets?"

"Your da did wrong by ye, that's a truth, but once I knew of yer existence, I 'ave tried to do right by ye. Once I discovered I had a nephew, I tried to bring ye into the family. But ye refused, ye were stubborn and determined to make it on yer own."

"And I did. Thanks to Alessio Messina I learned to be the man I am today."

I heard him scoff loudly. "That's a shame, it is. But I can't say the man did wrong by ye, and he has proven to be an ally. You built an empire, and the city is yours, but ye can have more if ye would accept it."

This was the conversation I didn't want to have. "I don't need more."

"Nonsense. You have a wife now and if ye are lucky, she will bear ye many sons. You are buildin' a dynasty for them."

My eyes narrowed as his words sank in. "How do you know I have a wife?"

His laugh was short and breathless. "You don' think I haven' been watchin' ye for the past fifteen years? I may be old, but I know more than ye think. I don' understand the rush behind it, but I was impulsive when I was a young man too."

"She needed protection and being married to me was the best way I could assure that she had it. Nobody would dare touch her knowing she belongs to me."

I don't know why I felt the need to explain. The lie was an easy one to tell. Protection may have been the excuse I had given Bri for pressing a hasty marriage, but the truth was that after having her in my bed, I knew that having her walk away, giving her up, was no longer an option.

"Protection, huh? Ok, lad. It had nothin' to do with a nice ass and long legs."

"I appreciate the information, but I did not call to discuss my wife with you."

"Nothin' comes without a price, lad. Ye know that as well as anyone. When all this is over, I want ye to join me for dinner. We have much to discuss. If ye need additional resources, they are yours. Just make the call."

I twisted my neck from side to side relieving the tension. "I have my own resources."

"Stubborn. It's a family trait I'm afraid. Take care, Rogue."

I put my phone down on the desk and took a few steps away as I twisted the card I still held in my hand. I moved back to the safe and put it inside in the same place as before. Sevan had tried to use me and now not only did I have to find and kill Petros, but Sevan and his sons would need to be dealt with too if they were involved.

But something my uncle said kept ringing in my ears. He had spoken of Bri and having sons. I had never asked her if she was on any kind of birth control because I didn't care. I certainly had not taken any precautions against getting her pregnant. Even now, my baby could be growing inside her. The thought pleased me more than I would have first anticipated.

I couldn't think of that now, though. There were too many other things that demanded my attention. I moved behind my desk; there were calls to make and plans to be made. Petros was about to meet his end, and Sevan would not be far behind him.

CHAPTER
seventeen

BRI

Rogue had been gone much longer this morning than I expected. Breakfast and lunch had been delivered to the penthouse. I had eaten very little, my stomach still in knots with the anxiety I was feeling about what was to come. Rogue's penthouse was very luxurious, but when you were alone, the extreme quiet gave your mind time to think up the worst scenarios imaginable. I had always had an active imagination so not having anything to occupy my mind was never a good thing.

When the elevator doors opened, I was surprised but happy to see Father Michael walking toward me. He didn't look like a priest now. He was dressed for the gym in navy workout pants and a gray tank top. He had a smile on his face that made him appear carefree, content, and quite handsome.

"Father Michael, I wasn't expecting you this morning."

He came farther into the room and held out a bag to me. "Rogue called me early this morning and said you were interested in learning some self-defense moves."

I tried to hide my excitement as I reached for the bag he was holding. "I was afraid he would forget. Yes, he said you could help me."

He tilted his head a bit. "I will try. It's a good thing for you to know. I wasn't sure if you had any workout gear, so I stopped by a

Lulu store on my way here. I guessed at the sizes, but I figured you would need more than the designer dresses and clothing Rogue has bought for you. I'll wait here while you change and then we can go to the gym on the top floor."

My face couldn't hide the excitement I was feeling. I had not expected to start training so soon. Last night Rogue still seemed a little put off at the thought of me having to protect myself, so I was surprised to know he had already contacted Michael about it. "Thank you. I won't take long to change."

I rushed into the bedroom so happy to be able to slip into the leggings and crop top that were in the bag. I pulled my hair into a ponytail and hurried back to find Michael sitting on the sofa waiting patiently while drinking a glass of what I presumed was bourbon.

He took another sip. "Rogue always has the best liquor in his bar. Even as a teenager, he never settled for subpar liquor."

I smiled thinking that Micael was the most unusual priest I had ever met. "Thanks for thinking about the workout clothes. The leggings fit perfectly and feel great."

"You are welcome. Well, I know Rogue is planning on going to the club tonight so we should get started."

I eagerly followed Michael into the elevator excited for my first lesson, but that excitement quickly turned to apprehension when I realized how seriously Michael was taking the assignment. He had no plans of taking it easy on me. After a two-hour session teaching me a few basic ways to get out of submission holds, he decided I needed to learn how to hit a man properly. He showed me how to correctly make a fist to protect my thumb and let me hit the bag a few times.

My knuckles were a little bruised already when Michael suggested I try what I had learned on him.

"When a man threatens you, the first thing a woman thinks of is to kick him in the balls. It's extremely effective but also expected. Most trained men will know how to counter and if they can manage to flip you onto your back, you are screwed. So, the best thing is to take them by surprise, punch the throat, shove the heel of your hand into their nose, anything to take them off guard before you bring them to their knees with a swift knee or kick to the ballocks."

He demonstrated the techniques a few times, then nodded at me to try them. He straightened his shoulders and stepped closer. I took a deep breath, balled up my fist the way he had shown me earlier, and took a swing. He caught my fist in midair, spun me around, and wrapped his arm around my throat.

"You hesitated. It gives your opponent time to anticipate your moves. You have to think quick, be quick, get angry, and put all your weight into that punch."

He walked away to grab a bottle of water from his gym bag and tossed it to me. "You aren't confident enough but that will come with time. Are you tired or do you want to continue?"

The water felt refreshing, but I wasn't about to admit defeat now. "Let's keep trying."

He grinned as he walked back over to me. "Don't be discouraged. This is just your first day of training. It takes time to be proficient."

He lunged for me, and I sidestepped, but when I tried to hit him, he swept my legs out from under me, and I landed hard on the mat. I covered my eyes with my arm and took a few breaths. "Maybe I should just learn how to shoot."

"You should, but I don't know how Rogue will feel about that. You might get mad and shoot him one day."

He smiled to let me know he was teasing me and reached out his hand to help me back to my feet.

"Ok, let's try again."

He narrowed his eyes. "Focus all your anger on me. Imagine I am the man who hurt you. Think back to what he did to you and how it felt. Are you going to allow it again? Are you going to be a victim or a fighter?"

When he stepped closer, I didn't hesitate. I reached up and punched him right in the nose. His hand came up to cover his face and I immediately felt remorse. I stepped closer. "I'm so sorry, I..."

His arms shot out before I could finish my sentence and I found myself on my back once again with him looming over me.

"Don't ever feel remorse. And if you can disable or distract your attacker, even if it is only for a little while, run. Run and don't stop running until you can get to safety."

"Ok, but at least I connected this time."

He took his fingers and wiggled his nose. "Not bad for the first time. Next time I will be more prepared."

"Should we try again?"

"No." We both turned our heads at the gruff voice on the opposite side of the gym.

Rogue was walking toward us now and from the frown on his face, he wasn't very happy.

Michael helped me back to my feet and I took a second to wipe the sweat from my forehead. "Did you see? I finally got in a punch?"

Rogue's eyes flicked over me and then back to Michael. "I saw." He looked back at me, and I watched his lips turn up slightly. "I hope you are pleased with yourself, hitting a priest." He snaked an arm around my waist and pulled me closer to him. "I hope you know that if I had seen any other man abusing you the way I have watched Michael throw you around for the past twenty minutes, they would have already been dead by now."

My eyebrows arched as I looked between the two men. "You are being overly dramatic and don't be mean to my teacher. Besides, you aren't always around."

He leaned over and kissed my cheek. "Well, you have had enough for one day. Blaze is waiting just outside the door to escort you back to the penthouse. I need to speak with Michael."

I nodded, not at all disappointed to have my session cut short. I hated to admit it, but I was exhausted and a little sore.

"Thank you again, Michael. When will we have another session?"

"I will discuss my schedule with Rogue, and he can let you know. Soak your knuckles. I'm sure they are a little bruised."

I glanced back at Rogue before walking toward the door where I could see Blaze waiting for me.

"Did you have a good time with the priest, little one?"

"It was a lot harder and more challenging than I thought it would be. I'm sure I will feel it tomorrow. Why does Rogue look so angry?"

A deep brief chuckle escaped his lips. "He doesn't like the idea, and he wasn't overly fond of seeing you manhandled, even if it was by Michael."

"I know Rogue doesn't like the idea of me having to protect myself, but if I do find myself in a situation where I am forced to defend myself, doesn't it make sense for me to be prepared? I'm just tired of being afraid, always looking over my shoulder, expecting to see him come after me."

He held up his hands. "I never said I thought it was a bad idea, little one. I think it's smart and once Michael finishes training you on how to punch and get yourself out of submission holds, I will teach you how to handle a knife."

"You will?" I asked excitedly

"Just don't tell Rogue."

I gave him a sly smile. "It will be our secret."

The elevator doors opened, and while I hoped that I never needed the training Michael was giving me, I did feel more empowered, more sure of myself, and hopefully in time, that would translate into less fear and anxiety.

Rogue

"How is your nose?"

Michael's smile widened. "I barely felt it."

"That's what I thought. You let her hit you, didn't you?"

He looked away. "Yes, I felt she needed a win today."

My eyes narrowed. "I don't want her to be deceived into thinking she is more powerful than she is. It could very well get her hurt."

"A confidence boost isn't going to hurt her, Rogue. Besides, we are all hoping she never needs to use any of what I am teaching her. The security detail you assigned to her will quickly take care of any threats that may arise before she even has a chance to become aware of any danger."

I knew my security was strong but with her, I wanted more. "I could use an extra man watching over her, a man I can trust. At least until I am free of Petros Sargsyan."

His face darkened and his smile slipped into the frown I had seen so often in the past. "Are things really so serious?"

My shoulders shrugged. "As I have said before, it is nothing I can't handle. But I would like to take extra precautions where Bri is concerned."

His expression turned quizzical. "You love her, don't you?"

I scoffed at the suggestion. "Don't be ridiculous. If you are unable to step aside from your duties, I will assign one of my other men to the task."

He stepped away and bent over to pick up his gym bag. "I will give it some thought."

That's all I could ask.

"Let Bri know I will stop by tomorrow for another lesson if she is free."

I stayed behind while he walked to the elevator, wondering how my concern for Bri's safety could be interpreted as love. Love was an emotion more dangerous than any of the threats I had faced. No, Michael was too much of a romantic. Lust, desire, and the urge to possess her and protect her, yes. But love?

Bri

After soaking for a good thirty minutes in the hot whirlpool, letting my sore muscles relax and recuperate, I closed my eyes and let the water attempt to wipe away the tension in my body. Unbidden images of Rogue and how he touched me floated through my head. My hand involuntarily slipped between my legs to find the place he always knew just how to touch that would make me come unglued. A short soft sigh passed through my lips as my fingers moved over me, but it was nothing like the feelings Rogue elicited when he touched me. Just the thought of him and how he made me feel was almost enough for me to reach a climax.

"While I would love to continue watching you, or better yet, become an active participant in your explorations, I'm afraid that I have a meeting at the club in about an hour, and I need you to come with me."

My eyes flew open as embarrassment rushed over me at being caught doing something so intimate to see Rogue standing over me, a fresh towel in hand.

I instinctively crossed my arms over my breasts and scooted farther down into the water.

"No need to be shy or embarrassed now, sweetheart. Not after last night."

I pushed myself up from the tub and reached for the towel. "I wasn't embarrassed, just startled."

His arm snaked around my waist as he lifted me from the tub with no concern for the water or soap bubbles dripping from my body. The material of his shirt was rough against my skin, and I had an intense desire to feel his skin against mine. But before I could put thought into action, he set me on my feet and stepped away.

"We need to leave for the club within the hour, will that be a problem for you?"

I wrapped the towel tighter around me. "No, I can be ready."

He nodded and walked away back toward the bedroom, presumably to change his clothes since what he was wearing now was wet from where he had lifted me from the tub.

By the time I had dried off and styled my hair, he had already changed and was no longer in the bedroom. I selected a simple but elegant royal blue dress, grabbed a pair of Louboutin heels, and went in search of Rogue. I found him wearing a tailored gray suit, his back was to me as he was standing by the windows looking down at the city below. He looked to be deep in thought, and I contemplated going back into the bedroom and giving him time alone.

I turned, careful not to make a sound, but his deep voice stopped me.

"There is no way for me not to know when you enter a room, Angel. I can sense your presence long before my eyes lock on yours."

I turned to find him looking toward me. "I was trying not to disturb you. You looked distracted."

He nodded and held his hand out to me. "Nothing distracts me more than your presence. Come, there are things we must discuss."

I felt my stomach flip at his words. His demeanor was different. Whatever he was about to tell me was not going to be something I liked. Could he have tired of me already as Blaze suggested he would? Or perhaps he was just tired of the drama that seemed to follow me. Either way, I took a short breath and stepped toward him, trying to prepare myself for whatever he was about to say.

When I was in arms reach, he took both of my hands in his and raised them to his lips, kissing my bruised knuckles.

"What is it that you wanted to talk to me about?"

He released my hands and stood a little straighter. "Things have occurred that will require more of my attention than I would have liked. I am not certain how long it will take, but you will be seeing a lot less of me. I may have to leave the city."

I listened but resisted the urge to wrap an arm around my waist. A wave of nausea washed over me, and I felt as if I would be sick. My head bobbed in acknowledgment to let him know that I was listening.

"You will no longer be able to stay here at the penthouse."

I felt my knees wobble, but I managed to keep it together. A part of me knew this was coming and while I thought I was prepared for it, I guess I wasn't. My heart began to hurt, and a million thoughts ran through my mind. Had I fallen in love with Rogue? Had I been stupid enough to lose my heart to a man that I knew would hurt me eventually? Or was he simply my safety net, protecting me from Tony?

I squared my shoulders and said a silent prayer that my voice wouldn't crack when I spoke. "I understand. I will be alright. There is no need for you to worry about me. I can be packed and out of here in a few minutes."

I turned to walk away, glad that the moisture gathering in my eyes had not leaked down my cheeks. That would be the ultimate humiliation, to cry in front of the man who was breaking my heart. *Damn, how could I be so stupid?*

But before I could take more than two steps, he grabbed my hand and pulled me back so hard that I slammed into his chest. I tried to look away, not wanting him to see the pain on my face, but he would have none of that. He gripped my chin and turned my face up to his, refusing to let me look away.

"You misunderstand what I am telling you, Angel. I have no intention of sending you away unprotected and certainly not with the idea that I am casting you aside." His thumb moved over my trembling bottom lip. "How could you have thought something so absurd?"

I didn't know what to say, the shock had stolen any words I might have formed.

"I have made arrangements for you. A place for you to stay outside the city. It will be safer for you there until I can take care of the business at hand."

"You will not be with me?"

He shook his head, his lips forming a firm straight line. "No, I will be staying here, as will Blaze."

My eyes fluttered and I shook my head. "No, this is my fault. Tony is coming for me! This is because of me! I will not let you..." He placed a finger over my lips.

"Enough! I have already decided, and it is done. This isn't just about Tony Galante. There are other things at play, things that are equally if not more dangerous. You are in my world now, and you will do as I say."

He kissed me hard as if he were hoping to quell any more arguments I might have had.

"Now, the car is waiting downstairs. Once I have concluded business at the club, I will explain more about where you will be going and who will be responsible for keeping you safe. You must trust me, Bri. I told you if you married me, I would protect you and I will."

He took my hand and pulled me along behind him as we made our way to the car waiting downstairs. When he told me that he was not simply casting me aside, the rush of relief was intense, but there was more going on than he was saying, and I had to bite my tongue to keep from pressing for more answers. But aside from that, I had a feeling of foreboding sweeping over me, like something was about to happen, something that could change everything.

The ride to the club was quiet and when the car came to a stop outside of *Sinners*, I wondered if Rogue would expect me to wait outside like last time. But when the door was opened for him, he took my hand and tugged me alongside him. His arm wrapped around my waist to hold me close to his side as we moved past the crowds waiting in line. I noticed the increased security, a few of the men I had not seen before, and something else I had never noticed, they were all wearing protective vests.

"You are expecting serious trouble, aren't you?"

Rogue's hand squeezed a little tighter where it rested on my waist. "I'm not sure why you would say that, but regardless, it is nothing you should be concerned with."

I scoffed at his comment. "Not sure why I would say that? You have a lot more men tonight and all of them are wearing protective vests. I'm not so clueless that I don't notice things. I bet they are all armed too."

He laughed quietly. "Surprise, darling. The men who work for me are always armed. That is not exactly a startling revelation."

I rolled my eyes at his sarcasm. "You don't seem overly worried."

He stopped and turned to face me. "I'm not. I don't live in fear, Angel. I make decisions and take precautions. The only concern I have is making certain that you are not involved."

"I'm already involved. You made sure of that when you refused to let me leave the day I walked into your office for my bogus interview."

The loud music and flashing lights made it difficult to hold a serious conversation and since he never responded to my comment, I wasn't sure if he even heard me. We walked to the back of the club to a large booth set back in a secluded corner. Blaze was already there, but as we approached, he stood and began walking toward us.

"You are looking good, little one. No obvious bruises from your session with Michael."

"Thanks." The mischievous smile on his face made him look less intimidating.

Rogue nodded toward some men standing off to the side and they came forward. "Stay here, Angel." He led me to the booth, and I took a seat. "I am going into the office with Blaze, but I have men stationed throughout the club and these two will stay with you. I will not be gone long."

My eyes flickered to the men who were stationed on either side of the booth. Both stoically staring in front of them. I watched as Blaze and Rogue walked away, and I settled back against the cushions in the booth and observed the crowd moving about the club.

One of the waitresses came forward. Both of my guards instantly became more alert, hands positioned over the weapons I was certain were hidden beneath their jackets.

"Can I get you a drink, Mrs. Delaney?"

"Just a water if you don't mind."

She smiled. "I'll bring it right over."

She walked back to the bar, and I continued my study of the people in the club tonight. Most were partying pretty hard. Barely clothed young women danced in the cages overhead and some on the stage. There were a few guys by the bar that were getting loud, looked to be a bachelor party. Another group on the dance floor started getting a little rowdy and I saw security step closer to them. As I continued to scan the crowd, my eyes locked on a man standing by the door. He didn't look familiar, but he was staring at me as if he knew me. It was beginning to creep me out.

"Mrs. Delaney, I brought your water. Is there anything else you need?"

"No, thanks." I watched as the waitress smiled flirtatiously at one of my bodyguards then turned back to where the man was still watching me, but it was what he was holding in his hand that caught my attention...a pistol.

I grabbed the arm of the man the waitress was flirting with. "There is a man over by the door. He has been staring at me and I think I saw that he had a pistol in his hand."

Both guards immediately became alert.

I raised my hand to point toward the man. "He is over by the... door." But he was no longer there. I scanned the room, hoping to catch a glimpse of him again. "He was just there!"

Something wasn't right. The air around me seemed to thicken and I felt a powerful urge to run, to hide. What if the man was there to kill Rogue? He needed to be warned. That's what I had to do. I needed to find Rogue! I was about to stand and tell the men beside me to take me to wherever Rogue was, but I never got the chance before chaos ensued.

CHAPTER
eighteen

BRI

I frantically scanned the room looking for Rogue, hoping he would materialize at my side. It struck me as funny that the man I had been so afraid of was now the only person in the world that made me feel safe. The club had erupted in chaos. The blaring sound of the fire alarms going off everywhere and flashing lights illuminating the exits had caused the crowd of revelers to get nervous. The sounds of people murmuring buzzed in my ears as I watched some of them slowly move with uncertainty toward the exits. My eyes scanned the room, searching for the man who had been staring at me earlier. A part of me knew he was to blame for the disruption, and he had to be among the crowd somewhere.

"It's time to go, Mrs. Delaney."

The hulking bodyguard to my left grabbed my arm and pulled me from the booth. My legs felt weak, and I reached out to take hold of his arm as the crowd bumped into us. When the sprinklers went off overhead, the crowd of people who had been scared but orderly began to panic. We were pushed and shoved. The two men at my side did their best to shield me, but when people began running, I became separated from them and was swallowed up by the flow of the crowd. Fear propelled me forward.

My eyes continued to search the area. I flinched when a hand touched my arm, expecting it to be the menacing man from earlier, but it was a younger girl trying to steady herself as we pushed through the exit door with the others. Once outside, my fear escalated. Fire trucks and ambulances were on the scene; they were directing the crowd to move away from the building. I placed my hands over my ears as the sirens blared. Images, noises, and people all whirled around me. Every face began to look like him. My hysteria began to consume me. I had to get out of there. I had to escape. With every step I took, I could almost feel the monster closing in on me.

When an arm reached out and grabbed me from behind, I screamed only to have a hand close down hard over my mouth.

"Shh, come with me. We need to get out of here."

Even through my state of shock, I recognized the voice and sank against him in relief. "Father Michael..."

He was barely recognizable, dressed in black and wearing a black jacket with the hood pulled over his head.

"Come on, we can't talk here."

He wrapped a hand around my waist as he quickly pushed our way through the crowd. Once we were free of the chaos, his pace slowed.

"Where are we going?"

"There is a safehouse we have used on occasion not far from here. You and I will wait for Rogue there."

I still didn't understand what was happening. "Why were you at the club tonight?"

"This morning Rogue shared with me his concern that you needed extra protection. He asked if I would be willing to watch over you. I was coming to the club tonight to let him know I would do that. But before I went inside, the alarms went off and people were running around like damn idiots everywhere. When I saw you, I knew something strange had happened and my instincts said that the best thing to do was to get you away from there. I will call Rogue to let him know that you are safe and with me as soon as I am able."

My hand reached over and grabbed his arm pulling him to a stop. "I saw the man that did this! I don't know who it was. I didn't recognize him, but he was staring at me while I was seated at Rogue's booth. When I tried to tell the bodyguards about him, he was gone, then the alarms went off and everyone began to scramble out of there. I know he had something to do with it. I wanted to find Rogue and warn him. I was afraid that he had been sent there to kill him. But I got separated from the men Rogue had guarding me and I couldn't find him."

I looked up to see the intense dark frown on his face.

"I don't know who is behind it, but I do know that Rogue was right, you do need extra protection."

"I know Rogue has enemies and things are in motion that I don't understand, but do you think it could have been Tony, the man who has been trying to find me since I left Colorado? I honestly don't think he will ever stop until he kills me."

Father Michael came to an abrupt stop and turned me to face him. "Tony Galante has never come against a force like Rogue before. You have not seen that side of him, but trust me, he will never allow that bastard to get to you, Bri. He will make sure that Galante gets everything he deserves and more. Now, let's hurry and get off the street and out of sight. I will feel better once Rogue knows where we are and sends reinforcements."

Rogue

While I didn't like the idea of leaving Bri behind inside the club while I conducted business, I did not want her to hear any of the information Blaze had discovered. There were things that I was involved in, things that I wanted to shield her from. I wasn't only protecting her from outside threats, in a way I was protecting her from myself, from the darkness in which I resided.

"Sevan? Did you find him today?"

Blaze closed the door behind us, leaving us alone in the office. "No, I contacted him via text, asking him if he was aware that Petros had made a move against the Bratva in Las Vegas. He pretended to know nothing of the attack. When I asked if he knew where Petros was at or heading to, he said he would find out and get back in touch with me." He scoffed as his eyes narrowed. "The old bastard even wished us his best saying he was worried for our safety. It was all I could do not to call him out for the liar that he is. I have already decided that I am going to cut out his lying tongue when the time comes."

I moved to the desk and leaned back against it. "It will be no less than what he deserves. I made a call of my own and received confirmation that Sevan is indeed behind Petros' aggression. He has been playing us for fools."

Blaze's face darkened. "Who is the source?"

Blaze probably knew me better than anyone. We had seen each other's most dangerous sides and taken on many challenges backing each other up, but even he didn't know of my past, of the connections to my father's family. I wasn't ready to reveal anything about my ties to the Irish mafia or my father and uncle. I wasn't sure if I would ever let anyone know. I had spent years denying them after my father abandoned me on the streets. I had made my way without them, created an empire without their name or connections.

"They are a reliable source." I recounted the details I had learned from my earlier conversation with my uncle and waited for Blaze's reaction.

"Hmm, so we will need to kill Petros and the scheming Sevan."

It was a statement, not a question. "If his sons are involved, they will have to be dealt with as well. I can't let this kind of deception go unanswered."

"Did you call Nik and let him know what you discovered?"

I shook my head. "No, they will not dare attack him again. Once they regroup and form another plan, they will go after us, but we will be waiting for them. But until we have taken care of Petros, we must play Sevan's game. I don't want him getting word that we know of his treachery. You know how much I love surprises."

Blaze grinned as he sank into the seat in front of the desk. "How did Bri take the surprise you had for her?"

"I haven't explained everything yet. I told her that I would not be able to spend time with her until this business with Petros was over. I haven't told her about the estate, just that she would be leaving the penthouse. Speaking of surprises, I should warn you that Alessio will be arriving tomorrow."

Blaze abruptly stood up. "I suppose that son of a bitch Tomas will be coming with him."

I tried to bite back the smirk forming on my lips. "Alessio is bringing Eden. You know as well as I that he has assigned Tomas as her personal guard. Besides, Tomas can be handy. Maybe he would be willing to help you plan out a strategy for capturing Petros."

"Fuck you, Rogue, and fuck Tomas! I don't want nor do I need that arrogant prick's assistance with anything."

I never flinched. "If that is the case, we need to come up with something before he arrives. I can take Bri back to the penthouse and we can meet at my office there in the building."

The mention of Tomas had blackened his mood and while Blaze was dangerous any day of the week, when he was angry, he was positively lethal.

"I have a liaison scheduled upstairs, but as soon as I have had my fill, I will meet you. That will give you more time with Bri before you take her to the mansion. You should enjoy what time you have left with her because we have no idea how long it will take to find and rid the world of Petros and Sevan. Then we have that damn Tony Galante to take care of, but that will be more fun than work."

I frowned at the thought. Not having Bri with me, not being able to put my hands on her whenever I wished would be difficult, but it had to be done. Blaze was right, I should make wise use of the time we had together. "I will meet you later then."

I stood from where I had been perched on the edge of the desk when the fire alarms began blaring in my ears. The security lights flashed, and the ear-piercing screech of people yelling and screaming filled the air. Blaze and I exchanged worried glances and rushed for the door just as the sprinklers went off.

"What the hell? Sprinklers don't go off unless there is a fire," Blaze yelled over the alarms, but I couldn't think of anything but getting to Bri.

We rushed through the office door and down the hall back into the heart of the club where chaos and panic had already taken hold. People were screaming and running to the door. Pushing and shoving each other in the pandemonium to reach safety and get away from the streaming water being sprayed on top of everyone. I couldn't see over the crowds, but I pulled my pistol in case I needed to be ready. Blaze was shoving his way through the mass of people toward the booth beside me. When we reached it, she wasn't there. Neither were the two guards I had posted to watch her.

"She probably ran with the crowd. Maybe the guards took her to the car," Blaze said as I continued to scan the club looking for any sign of her.

The sprinklers were still going off and I heard sirens from fire trucks in the distance. *Fuck!* I didn't need this shit right now. I looked around, there was no smoke, no sign of a fire. Nothing that would have set off the alarms and the sprinklers.

"This was intentional. Find Bri!"

A sickening feeling began to settle in my stomach. I rushed to the doors, pushing everyone out of my way. Once outside, I looked toward the car. The windows were tinted, and I couldn't see inside. I ran forward and opened the door to find the back seat empty. She wasn't there. I frantically began searching the crowd of people that were flooding out the door. I didn't see her. Blaze rushed forward.

"She wasn't in the car. Where is she? Where are the two fuckers that were supposed to be watching her?"

Blaze's face was hard. "I found one of them inside searching the bathrooms. When the alarms went off, they grabbed her and headed for the exit, but in the mayhem, they were separated. They were pushed and somehow lost their hold on her. She was carried away in the crowd of people and vanished. The other man is still searching for her among those that left the club."

Anger threatened to take over any rational thoughts I might have had. My wife had disappeared in the chaos, the two incompetent assholes that were supposed to be watching her had lost her. They would be lucky if I didn't kill them for this mistake, and if I didn't find her soon, that was exactly what I would do. I would not tolerate this kind of uselessness in my organization.

A million thoughts rushed through my head. Had Petros taken her? Was this what he had planned all along, or was it Tony Galante? Both men were dangerous, and my angel could be in their hands right now. The thought infuriated me as much as it terrified me. But I couldn't focus on that right now, I had to find her and when I did, I would bring hell down upon the person that dared take her from me.

Three Hours Later

The fury raging inside me grew with every second that I didn't have her with me. I had searched everywhere for her, but she was nowhere near the club.

Blaze walked to where I was standing, both of us still wearing the wet clothes we had on earlier. "The fire chief confirmed that the sprinklers were tampered with; this was an intentional act. I paid him a cool grand to keep the information under wraps. I have one of the men handling things. He will take care of hiring a cleanup crew. I checked the cameras and I think you should see them."

I followed Blaze into the IT office where one of the men had the security cameras pulled up on the monitors. My eyes were fixed on the screen where Bri was sitting at the booth before the fire alarms were pulled. One of the waitresses brought her a glass of water but from the video, I could see Bri's eyes were focused on someone or something across the room.

"What the hell? Go find that waitress and bring her to me. Now!"

The man I had directed the order to didn't hesitate. He rushed from the room.

"Zoom in."

Even in the video, I could see the concern on her face.

"Where the fuck is the damn waitress?!"

"She is right here, boss."

I turned to see a short little blonde clutching her hands together tightly. She looked as if she would burst into tears at any moment. "You took my wife something to drink. Was there anything said or unusual when you were at her booth?"

I stalked toward her, and she backed away as if she were afraid.

"I took her a glass of water. She didn't say anything to me but before the alarms went off, she did tell one of the men standing guard that a man was staring at her. When she tried to show them where he was, he had already disappeared. She seemed nervous. Then the alarms went off and everything went to hell from there."

"Is that all you know? Did you see what happened to her after the alarms went off? The direction she went or if anyone was with her?"

She shook her head and clasped her hands nervously in front of her.

"Go, but if you think of anything else, I want to know. Do you understand?"

"Yes, Mr. Delaney."

She didn't waste any time getting the hell out of the office.

"Fuck! I found her on the camera, boss. Someone took her."

I moved back over to the monitors and watched him replay the video. Bri had run outside with the crowd, the fear still evident on her face when a man wearing all black came up behind her and grabbed her. His hand covered her mouth as he dragged her away from the camera angle.

While my blood turned cold, and anger was threatening to consume me, I felt a rush of relief when I saw the security footage. I turned to Blaze. "Bring the car around."

"It's already waiting out front."

I threw open the door to the office, almost knocking down some workers in the hall as I made my way to the front. Blaze was behind me.

"Where are we going?"

"To the safe house. I know who took her."

Blaze easily caught up to me. "Do you want to share?"

"She is safe, thankfully. Michael has her. He was wearing a crucifix around his neck, and I noticed it on the camera. However, this was an orchestrated attack, and I don't know if it was meant for me or a means to get her."

"So, why was the priest at the club?"

"After his self-defense session with Bri this morning, I asked if he would be willing to step back into our world long enough to keep her safe. He said he would think about it; I guess he made his decision."

Blaze scoffed loudly as he opened the car door and got in the driver's seat. "You don't think he will be a bit rusty. Are you sure he is prepared to send souls to the devil without taking the time to try to save them first?"

"You sound offended, but you will be dealing with other matters. Michael is the only other one I trust with her. Besides, before he gave up this life, he was very efficient. He just doesn't have the bloodlust that you do. I am confident that given the situation it will all come back to him."

"I hope you are right, but I have my doubts. But I suppose who better to protect an angel than a priest."

Bri

The safe house was nothing like the penthouse in the heart of the city, and it was much different than what I had seen in the movies. However, it was still nicer than my old apartment. There were two modest-sized bedrooms, a kitchen stocked with nonperishable food as well as several bottles of liquor. The bathroom was fully equipped with medical supplies, enough for several small emergencies, and there was another room Michael had not shown to me, but while he was busy making sure everything was secure, I peeked in. I had never seen anything like it before. It was an arsenal equipped with everything from knives, several different types of guns, loads of ammunition, and even some grenades and flash bangs.

I quietly moved away from the room and sat back down at the kitchen table and realized that I truly didn't know the man I had married.

"Would you like something to drink? I could make some coffee or if you prefer something stronger. Rogue has a nicely stocked bar."

I shook my head and pulled the blanket Michael had given me when we first arrived tighter around my shoulders. "No, thank you."

"You look a bit pale. Are you sure you are alright?"

I almost laughed at the observation. "No, I'm not alright. I know we only had one session this morning, but I had hoped it would make me a little stronger and braver. But tonight, when the alarms went off, I panicked. If you had not been waiting for me outside, I don't know what I would have done. My first instinct was to run, to escape, not to fight."

He moved closer and took a seat across from me. "It was one session. It isn't realistic to expect to be a master at self-defense so soon. It takes years of practice and after what you have been through, it is only natural that you were afraid. Don't beat yourself up over it, and don't underestimate your instincts. It was instinct that urged me to go to the club tonight. If you sense danger and something inside you is telling you to run, do it. The self-defense moves I am teaching you are meant to be used as a last-ditch effort, not to prepare you for battle."

"How long do you think it will be before Rogue discovers I am gone?"

His eyebrows rose. "I'm sure he knew it immediately. Not much gets past Rogue. I just feel sorry for the men he had stationed to protect you; they will not receive much leniency."

"It wasn't their fault."

He stood and moved over to the window. "Rogue will not see it that way. They had one job and they failed at it, miserably I might add." He pulled back the curtain. "I knew it wouldn't take him long to find us."

I jumped from my seat when the front door banged open. Both Rogue and Blaze were wearing almost identical frowns, but when Rogue's eyes met mine, the intensity I saw made me take a step back. He crossed the room in three strides, grabbed my wrist, and pulled me down the hallway to the closest bedroom. I jumped as the door shut loudly behind us.

Once we were alone, he yanked me hard until I crashed into his chest. His hand gripped my chin and turned my face up to his. "Are you alright, Angel?"

"I'm alright, but I think I saw the man that did this. He was staring at me while I was sitting in the booth at the club. When I alerted the two men you had guarding me, he disappeared and then the alarms went off."

His hands came up to my face. "Why didn't you come find me? You ran."

"I didn't run. I wanted to find you. I was afraid that the man was there to kill you, but when the sprinklers went off, I was carried away with the crowd. Michael grabbed me outside and brought me here."

He continued to look over me as if he were inspecting me for injuries. "I'm getting you out of the city. I'll have your things packed up and brought to you, but it isn't safe for you here. But first, we need to get you out of these damp clothes."

"I am fine. There isn't anything for me to wear here and I'm not going home naked wrapped in a blanket. I can change at the penthouse. But I don't want you to send me away, not unless you can come with me."

"I should have already taken you there. I never should have allowed you to stay with me when so much danger surrounds me. Don't worry, it won't be anything like this. You will be in luxury and have everything you could want or need, but I won't be staying."

I took a deep breath, surprised at how the thought of Rogue not being with me made me feel when only a few days ago I was trying to find any way I could to escape him. "Then I won't have everything I want or need." I took a step back. "How long will you be away?"

"It depends on how easy it will be to kill the men that threaten me."

He took my hand, opened the door, and pulled me back to the kitchen where Blaze and Michael were waiting.

"Why didn't you call me and let me know you had her?"

Michael shrugged his shoulders. "Dropped my phone outside the club when I grabbed her."

"Thank you for being there tonight. The men that were responsible for her safety will be dealt with."

Michael nodded his head slightly. "I have a few things to take care of before I can leave the city, but I will meet up with you in the morning." He looked over at me. "I'll see you soon, Bri."

I wasn't given a chance to respond before Rogue began pulling me out the door and into the waiting car. There wasn't another driver, so Blaze jumped in behind the wheel and Rogue sat beside me in the back.

"It wasn't the men who were watching me that should be blamed for tonight. They did all they could; it was an accident."

Rogue's eyes narrowed as he turned his face to me. "They lost you, Bri. You could have been taken tonight. It was most definitely their responsibility to keep you safe."

"In that situation, anyone could have lost sight of me, even you."

He huffed out a deep breath. "Will it make you feel better if I promise not to kill them and only remove them from your security detail?"

"Yes."

"Fine, it's done. Blaze, don't kill the two idiots that were tasked with keeping Bri safe."

Blaze grumbled something under his breath, but I couldn't tell what he said.

Rogue pulled me across the car to sit on his lap.

He brushed back a strand of hair that was hanging near my face. "Your clothes are still damp, too. Are you cold?"

"I'm too nervous to be cold."

"When we reach the penthouse, we can take a warm shower. Now, tell me, did you recognize the man you saw at the club? Did he look familiar at all?"

I shook my head. "No, he didn't. The way he kept staring at me was unnerving and I thought I saw a pistol in his hand, but now I am not certain. Maybe it was my imagination. I do think he is the one that set off the alarms, but no, I have never seen him before tonight."

"Hmm, I will have security footage sent to my computer and have you look over it. Hopefully one of the cameras caught him and we can identify him."

I snuggled against him relishing in the warmth his body offered mine. This man who I had hated a few days ago was now the only thing I craved. His touch, his voice, his smell, the strength of his arms around me. I yearned for it, but I couldn't help but wonder when Rogue sent me away, would he ever come back for me?"

CHAPTER
nineteen

ROGUE

I didn't waste any time getting Bri upstairs once we reached the penthouse. Her skin was chilled from the damp clothes she was still wearing. I carried her straight to the shower and turned the water on as hot as we could stand it.

I stripped her out of her clothes and followed suit with my own. The need to get her warm outweighed my desire to fuck her until the morning brought the cold reality that I would have to send her away until all the threats had been disposed of and it was safe for her.

When I joined her under the hot stream of water, her hands reached out to me, and I felt a tightness in my chest like nothing I had ever experienced before. This one woman had power over me. More power than anyone. When I couldn't find her after the chaos at the club tonight, the feeling of terror that coursed through me was almost paralyzing and I didn't like it. I had allowed Bri to become embedded into my soul as if my very existence depended upon her, and it disturbed me to think that she had that kind of hold on me and how easy it would be for someone to take her and destroy me.

"Rogue, I don't want to go. I don't want to leave you."

I looked down into her upturned face, her bright eyes pleading with me as water cascaded down her back and shoulders.

My hands moved over her arms, my fingers tracing the same path as the rivulets of water down her spine, and pulled her closer. "It is better this way. The farther you are from me, the safer you will be."

She crossed her arms over her breasts. "I don't care. When I am not with you, I don't feel safe. You are the only thing that keeps the nightmares away. I don't want to wake up in a bed alone, wondering where you are and what is happening. Besides, there has to be something I can do to help."

Her hands moved over my chest as her breasts pressed against me, but I couldn't let lust override logic. I knew what had to happen. My hands gripped her wrists, and I walked her backward until she was against the tile. The power she had over me was strong, and I was close to giving in to anything she asked simply because I wasn't sure how long I could go without her. I leaned down closer, letting my lips press against the throbbing pulse in the side of her neck.

"Like I said before, this isn't just about you, Bri. There are other matters at stake. You are a distraction, an encumbrance. The one thing in this world that could destroy me. I need you to be where I don't have to worry about you, where I don't see you."

Her eyes widened at my words, and I had not meant for them to be so sharp, but I was still wrestling with the crushing feeling of need for her. I had never felt this attachment to another living person before and it bothered me.

"You don't want to see me? Well, you must be taking romantic advice from Blaze." She rolled her eyes and tried to move away from me when I chuckled at her suggestion.

I pulled her back into my arms. With one of my hands anchoring in her hair, I yanked her head back, eliciting a shocked gasp from her lips. "Don't think that you are going to walk away from me in a fit of pouty anger because you can't get me to change my mind."

I spun her around and braced her palms against the tile as I nudged her feet farther apart. "When I see you, I can think of nothing but having you naked, and then my mind is consumed with tasting you, feeling your flesh against mine, and fucking you until you are screaming and begging me to stop. I meant what I said, Angel. You are a distraction, an obsession from which I can't break free."

My fingers slipped between her legs where I found her pussy weeping for me. When I roughly pushed two fingers inside her, she shrieked. "But make no mistake, you are mine!"

I entered her swiftly and violently, bringing her off her feet to her toes. "I will end these threats and once I have, I am going to take you somewhere far away so I can have you naked and all to myself with no distraction. I am going to fuck you until there is no doubt in your mind as to where you belong." I leaned over her shoulder and let my teeth sink into the long column of her neck. "Don't ever make the mistake of thinking I would ever let you leave me. You are already embedded too deep into the darkness, but until it is safe, and the dangers eliminated, you will go wherever I say and stay there until I bring you back."

My hands went to her hips, and I continued my thrusts. I felt her muscles tighten and squeeze my cock and I came undone. But this wasn't over. I didn't know how long we would be apart and if I was going to be denied access to her body, tonight, I would feast my fill. It wouldn't be enough. I wasn't sure if I would ever get enough of her. The cravings and desires I had for this woman would rival any known drug. I longed for this to all be over so that I could have her to myself without the dangers that were lurking closer every day.

I turned her back around and lifted her so that she was settled down over my dick again, her legs wrapped around my waist as I carried her from the bathroom to our bed where I would fuck her until the light of morning brought me back to cold reality.

Bri

My eyes felt heavy, and I was still so incredibly sleepy, but after spending another passionate night with Rogue, I was not surprised. I blinked a few times, trying to adjust to the bright light streaming in through the windows. My arms reached out to discover the bed empty. Rogue wasn't there, but that wasn't the most disturbing thing. This wasn't the same bed I had fallen asleep in, and I was dressed. When I fell asleep, I had been most definitely naked and curled against Rogue's side, his arms around me. I scrambled up to a sitting position to take in the room as the sun's brightness filtered in through the large floor-to-ceiling windows. My head felt heavy and there was an intense pounding right behind my eyes. I put a hand over my forehead, trying to make the pain stop.

This was most definitely not the penthouse. My heart began to beat faster as fear began to settle over me. *Where the hell was I? What had happened?*

"Oh good, you're awake."

A soft feminine voice on the other side of the room drew my attention. I stared at her for a few minutes and her smile widened.

"I know you must be confused, and I am sorry that our first meeting had to be this way."

"Where am I?"

She stepped closer to the bed, and I quickly pushed aside the covers ready to run for the door if necessary.

She sighed heavily, clasped her hands in front of her, and stopped moving. "I want you to know that I told Rogue he never should have done this. But he is just as stubborn as my husband."

I squinted my eyes and tried to get my brain to focus. "Who are you?"

"I know you have a lot of questions and trust me when I say that I know exactly how frightening it is to wake up and not know where the hell you are, but if you will take a few minutes to calm down, I can explain everything to you. It may not make you feel better, but it will at least take away some of your confusion as to how you got here."

My eyes darted around the unfamiliar room, hoping Rogue would walk through the door and explain everything himself. Or, I would wake from whatever weird dream I was having.

"I don't think calming down is an option at this point."

The small pretty blonde nodded. "Trust me, I get it, but give me a few minutes to explain. Then if you still want to scale the walls and run, I will completely understand. I'll even help you."

"Fine. Start explaining."

"Would you like something to drink or eat first? I can have one of the housekeepers bring something up for you."

I shook my head, growing more impatient by the second. "Where is Rogue?"

"Let's start with something less complicated, shall we? My name is Eden Messina. My husband Alessio is a friend and business partner of Rogue. They have known each other for a few years, Blaze too. We flew in this morning to help with whatever situation those two are mixed up in. But before we could get to our hotel suite in the city, Rogue called and asked us to meet him here. We arrived just as he was carrying you inside the house."

My eyes squinted as I tried hard to listen and understand what she was saying. "Why don't I remember anything? How could I not remember getting dressed or driving here? You say he carried me inside. How did I not wake up for that? I have never been that sound of a sleeper."

She rolled her eyes and her pretty smile slipped. "That's the part you aren't going to like. Rogue was worried about how you would react to him bringing you here and then leaving. He mentioned that you were anxious about it, and he thought if he gave you something to help ease your anxiety it might help make it easier for you."

I couldn't believe what I was hearing. "Rogue did this to me?"

She nodded sympathetically. "He put something in your drink last night. It was meant just to relax you, but it knocked you right out. You have been sleeping soundly for hours. Rogue's personal physician was called, and he said there would be no strange side effects and that you should wake up within a few hours. Sedatives affect people in different ways." She took another step closer. "Be grateful that he didn't use chloroform. Unfortunately, I know firsthand that it gives you a horrible headache for several hours after you wake up as well as nausea. You are feeling alright, aren't you?"

I put a hand to my forehead, trying to comprehend what she was saying. "Yes, I'm fine except for the fact that I have been drugged. I can't believe he did this to me." I thought back and vaguely remembered him bringing me some juice just before we went to sleep.

She nodded a sad mixture of sympathy and pity on her face. "If it makes you feel any better, I gave him an earful letting him know exactly what I thought about it. I felt it was the least I could do, considering you were unable to do it yourself."

I sank back down on the bed letting her words sink in. "Why? Why would he do that? I still don't understand." I looked around the room still confused. "Where am I?"

"I am not sure why he did it. The excuse he gave me was that he just wanted you to have something to relax. He never imagined that the medication would affect you the way it did. I am not defending him, just letting you know that I truly believe he had the best intentions. As to where you are, you are at Rogue's estate outside of Chicago. I have to say, I am rather impressed. This is the first time I have ever been here, but it is quite lovely."

"Rogue owns an estate?"

She nodded. "Yes, a rather large one."

"Where is Rogue?"

"That is the complicated part of all this, and I am not exactly certain what is going on. My husband doesn't tell me very much about his business and to be honest with you, I'm not sure I want to know."

"Your husband is...."

"Don of the Messina family."

I rolled my eyes. "Of course, another mafia connection. The second I have met in the past week."

My eyes closed, and I pinched the bridge of my nose with two fingers. The headache I had when I woke was beginning to get worse. "Let me see if I have this correct and please forgive me if I get the events confused, but you are saying that Rogue drugged me, brought me to his estate, where I have never been before, and left me here to wake up alone with a stranger. He really thought that would ease my anxiety and make this transition easier for me?"

"What can I say, men like Rogue and my husband are impulsive and don't always make the most rational decisions, especially when they are in love. But we are not alone. They left us well-protected. My constant shadow Tomas is here, as well as a man named Michael. I have never met him before, but he seems capable. He said he was a priest although I have never seen a priest that looks like him before."

She winked and gave me a cheeky grin. "He and Tomas are downstairs having breakfast. I thought it would be best if you saw a friendly face when you woke, someone who understands what you are going through. I am sorry you had to find out this way. I know Rogue never expected the medication he slipped into your drink to be so effective. If it makes you feel better, he was very worried."

I narrowed my eyes in frustration. "He should be worried because I am going to kill him."

Her eyes twinkled as she giggled at my comment. "I was hoping you would have that reaction, now I know we can be friends. I don't blame you. I have been in a similar situation and Alessio is very lucky I was never able to get my hand on a weapon."

I know she was doing her best to make me feel more at ease, but I wasn't sure that was possible. "I would like to speak to Michael."

She motioned toward the door. "You are free to do as you wish."

I stood from the bed and walked quickly to the door. As I stepped into the hallway, I realized just how expansive Rogue's mansion was. There was a dual staircase that led down to a large entryway. I continued walking as I looked around, surprised at the differences between the penthouse and the mansion. Where the penthouse was dark and masculine, this house looked like something out of a magazine. Professionally decorated with lots of large windows letting in the sunlight, the color schemes were lighter, not nearly as menacing as I would have thought Rogue preferred. It was beautiful.

"The kitchen is to your right once you get downstairs. Just follow the voices."

I looked over my shoulder to where the woman was standing along the railing. She was exceptionally beautiful, like a real-life

Barbie. She was the type of woman men noticed, and I wondered if
her husband was as protective of her as Rogue had been with me.

I made my way down to the kitchen, my bare feet not making a
sound as I followed the voices and the rich smell of coffee brewing.
When I peeked around the corner, I was relieved to see one familiar
face.

Michael jumped down from where he was sitting on the coun-
tertop talking to a man I didn't recognize, but whom I assume was
there to protect Eden Messina. He had a darker complexion and dark
hair. His eyes followed me into the room and like all the other men I
had met recently, he looked as if he could kill someone and not think
twice about it.

"Brielle, I'm glad you are awake. Come have a seat and I'll get you
some coffee and something to eat. Are you feeling well?"

I walked farther into the room, my eyes darting between Michael
and the tall broad-shouldered Italian man standing on the opposite
side. My mind was still reeling with everything that had happened and
I kept thinking that I wake up from whatever kind of *Alice in
Wonderland* dream I was having. "I don't want coffee. I want to
know why the hell Rogue drugged me and brought me here."

Michael looked back at the other man, who had lowered his head
and looked away with what I thought was a suspicious grin on his
face.

"With as angry as you look, Rogue should be glad that he is not
here."

"Anger is just one of many emotions I am feeling now. Why
would he do this to me?"

Michael held a cup of coffee in both hands as he moved closer to
me. "Rogue did tell you that he was bringing you someplace safe away
from the city."

"Yes, but I wasn't aware that he would drug me, drop me off, and
leave me to wake up with strangers."

Michael at least had the good sense to look ashamed. "I know you
may not believe me, but that was not Rogue's intention. The medicine he gave you was supposed to relax you and help you sleep.

Instead, it had an anesthetizing effect and knocked you out. And while I am not condoning it, he refused to leave until I got here just in case you woke up. He wanted at least one of us to be familiar. He was really worried."

I narrowed my eyes. "How considerate."

Michael grinned but wisely didn't try to take up for Rogue again.

"As a priest, I know you have to preach forgiveness, but right now I am firmly on the retribution side of things."

The young woman from earlier walked into the kitchen. "I like her."

Michael took a sip of his coffee. "At least with Rogue being away for a few days, it will give us ample time to work and practice more self-defense moves."

At this Eden stepped closer, obviously intrigued. "Self-defense? You are teaching her self-defense moves?"

I looked up at her. "Yes, I thought it would be wise and give me something to do. Michael graciously has been teaching me the proper way to punch and how to get out of submission holds if someone tried to grab me. I thought it would make me feel more secure."

"Oh, that sounds awesome! I want to learn to. Do you mind if I join in on a few of your lessons?"

The other man who had remained silent the whole time immediately spoke up. "Not on my watch, princess. You expect me to allow you to be manhandled and then for Alessio to return to find you covered in bruises or hurt while learning these moves...no, it's not going to happen."

She crossed her arms over her chest and rolled her eyes. "I'll handle Alessio. It will be fun, and you can't tell me that it is a bad idea, especially considering the trouble all of you get into on a regular basis."

Her mention of trouble reminded me of the reason Rogue had sent me away. I looked back to Michael. "Where is Rogue?"

"He and Blaze received word on the whereabouts of the Armenian, Petros Sargsyan, who has been attempting a takeover of both Rogue and Nickolai Volkoff's businesses. He was behind the attempt on Nickolai's life the day you went to the club for your interview."

I folded my hands together, trying to hide the anxiety I was feeling. "Rogue had told me that there were other factors, things that didn't concern me. I suppose that was what he was talking about."

Eden took a seat beside me. "It is always distressing when Alessio puts himself in danger. I often have a hard time keeping my mind free of everything that could go wrong, so I understand exactly what you are feeling. But since we are together, perhaps that will make it better. We can distract each other, and now we have Father Michael to teach us some of his skills."

"Fuck, Alessio is going to kill me, princess. I'm going to walk around the perimeter and check security so at least I will have an alibi," Tomas said as he walked from the room, leaving the three of us alone.

"I think I would like that coffee now."

Michael immediately got up and walked over to the coffee pot. After settling the cup in front of me, along with cream and sugar, he put a hand on my shoulder. "Everything will be alright, Bri. I may have been away from this life for a few years, but one thing I know hasn't changed is Rogue's ability to take down anyone who opposes him."

"When will I see him? When will he come here?"

"I don't know. He was insistent that it would be easier for you if he stayed away until he had taken care of everything. I tried to change his mind, but he was already set on this course. To be honest with you, I'm not certain if he is trying to make things easier for him or you." He winked. "Stay here and rest. You still look exhausted. Later today if you feel like it, we can practice. The entire house is at your disposal. It is quite large so it may take you awhile to learn your way around." He glanced over at the beauty beside me. "Mrs. Messina, it has been a pleasure to meet you."

"And you as well, Father Michael."

I wrapped both hands around the warm mug of coffee and pondered everything Michael had said.

"If you would prefer to be alone, I can find something to do. I saw that the house has a library as well as a large media room. I am more than capable of entertaining myself."

I gave her a small smile. "No, I wouldn't mind the company. The past few days have been crazy. I'm sure you wouldn't even believe it if I told you everything."

She laughed at that. "You think you had an unusual courtship and marriage? I will have to tell you about how I met Alessio."

After talking and laughing hysterically for two hours while sitting in the media room, I knew that I liked Eden Messina. She was as sassy as she was beautiful, and it was good to know that someone like her had adapted so well to her unconventional marriage and the life she now led. She made it look easy as if being married to a dangerous man, a killer, was nothing out of the norm. It gave me hope.

Before dinner, Michael took both of us to the gym where he showed Eden some of the moves that he had tried to teach me earlier. It was all done under the watchful and disapproving eye of her body-guard, Tomas.

After a delicious dinner prepared by the private chef who had been hired to work here at the estate, all I wanted to do was take a hot bath and climb into the large bed in the master suite and sleep. But once my head hit the pillow, I was reminded of how it felt to be alone, of the nights I spent in my old apartment, waiting for the sun to rise because I couldn't sleep, or watching old reruns of *Seinfeld* or *Friends* to fill the silence. I plumped up my pillow and turned to my side, looking at the empty side of the bed, and I began to worry. I didn't need confirmation from Eden Messina or Father Michael to know that what Rogue was involved in was dangerous or that it was not uncommon for the men he called his friends to be surrounded by death. What I wasn't sure of was if I could meld into this world as Eden had done. Could I get used to going to bed alone knowing there was the possibility that Rogue may not come home? Eden seemed so at ease with all the danger that surrounded them, but I wasn't sure I would ever be.

CHAPTER
twenty

ROGUE

I had not intended on returning to the mansion until I had concluded the business of killing Petros Sargsyan and then of course there was the score to settle with the lying snake Sevan who had used me as a tool to get rid of his rival because he was too cowardly to do so himself. But after a long day of nothing, no sign of the Armenians, and no word from Sevan, all I wanted was her. It was an inherent need. To see her, touch her, hear her voice, and know that she was mine and that she was safe.

The house was dark and quiet when I arrived. Security was in place, but mostly out of sight as they had been instructed to be. I made my way up the dual staircase toward the master suite. I seldom came here. It had been a few years since I had stepped foot inside the mansion. I kept a small staff to take care of the house and to keep it ready in case it was needed, but I had always preferred to stay in the city, closer to the club, closer to my assets. The house was purchased as an escape or for times when I needed to entertain business associates away from the loud boisterous nights at the club.

While I enjoyed being surrounded by hedonism, I felt a strong need to keep my innocent angel away from it. She was the only thing pure I had ever possessed in my life. This house, with its light airy feel, soft color schemes, and gardens suited her. I could picture her strolling the grounds, working in the gardens, and making this a home. It was an illusion I had never allowed myself to believe could exist for me.

The door to the master suite opened noiselessly and I stepped quietly toward the bed. The room was dark except for the small sliver of moonlight pouring through the white sheer draperies, giving just enough light that I could see her face. She was peaceful. No nightmares tonight, no hint of the fear she had felt at the hands of Tony Galante. I removed the coat I was wearing and unbuttoned the sleeves of my white shirt as I walked over to sit in the large chair by the window. As much as I wanted her right now, I didn't want to wake her. Seeing her was enough...for now.

As I watched her sleep, the realization came to me that I would do whatever it took to keep this woman safe, to make her happy, to give her all the things she had been denied. And while a part of me knew the only way to truly keep her safe would be for me to stay away from her, to let her go. I knew it couldn't be done; it was an impossibility. I didn't have that kind of willpower. So, being the beast that I truly was, I would drag her light into the darkness with me.

A sweet sound from the bed drew my attention as she rolled over in her sleep, her long slim leg slipping from beneath the covers. My dick hardened as my eyes followed the length of it from her ankle to her upper thigh before it dipped beneath the sheets, shielding the rest of her from me. She was perfection, everything I was not.

I settled back into the chair, wishing I had brought a glass of whiskey upstairs with me. Her sleep became restless, and she rolled over again, this time giving me a view of the gentle slope of her breasts. My fingers itched to touch her, and I was almost ready to give in to my desires when I saw her eyes open. At first, I thought she might still be sleeping; she didn't react right away as if she wasn't sure she was seeing me, then she sat up quickly.

"Rogue?"

I walked toward her. "Shh, it's just me, Angel. Go back to sleep."

"I thought you weren't coming back."

Against my better judgment, I took one more step closer. "I

wanted to see you. I needed to see you, but I am perfectly content to watch you sleep." *That was the biggest lie I had ever told in my life.* Contentment was far from the emotion I was feeling now as my eyes raked over her perfect form.

My hand reached out to trace the curve of her cheek, then my thumb pulled at her bottom lip.

She pushed my hand away. "Don't. I'm still pissed at you."

My lips turned up slightly at the spark I saw in her eyes. "You seem unharmed."

She jumped from the bed and poked me hard in the chest. "You can't just drug me every time you want to shield me from your world! Was that your plan; to keep me in a hallucinogenic dazed state just so you can spare your conscience? I will not live that way, Rogue. If you ever do anything like that to me again, I will leave and never come back."

I didn't like to be threatened, even by her. I grabbed her arms and tossed her back on the bed before following, pinning her to the mattress with a hand on her throat, not enough to hurt, only to get her attention. "Don't make threats you can't keep, Angel. You gave yourself to me and the moment I took you, took your virginity, your fate was sealed. I will take whatever punishment you want to dish out for drugging you, and I will even promise not to do so again, but don't ever threaten me with leaving or denying me. Run and I will chase you."

Her breathing increased and my grip on her throat loosened as my fingers slid lower over her chest down the valley between her breasts. My voice lowered to an almost imperceivable whisper. "You confound me. Desire rages inside me when I think of you. Tonight, I tried to stay away, I wanted to stay away, but I couldn't. It's a physical impossibility. The hold you have on me is too strong."

My hand slipped lower, pushing the silk chemise she was wearing above her hips. I slipped my hand between her legs and frowned when I felt the silk of her panties instead of the warm, wet flesh that I craved. With one fierce tug, I ripped the offending fabric from the body I was so desperate to sink into.

Her chemise suffered the same fate. I was eager to see her nakedness, to feel her skin, to explore every inch of her, and nothing would stop me. I took a moment to admire the perfection laid out before me. Tonight, there was a force driving me. I didn't want to be gentle or take things slow. I wanted to fuck. I wanted to fuck hard. I wanted her screams to wake the house. There was a need to brand her, mark her, drive into her, and take everything she had to give.

I quickly freed my cock and pushed her legs apart. I didn't take the time to make her ready; I slammed into her, and a gasp or half scream escaped her lips as I pulled out and repeated the action. She felt so good, so incredibly tight as if she were made just for me. I leaned down and took her lips as the desire to taste her swept over me.

I felt her hands reach for me, but I pulled them over her head, immobilizing her. I needed to control her. I needed to feel power over her, to command her, to dominate. Something, anything to make me believe that I wasn't losing my authority, because when I was with her, I felt powerless, as if I were drowning. When I thought I couldn't hold back anymore, I pulled out. Her eyes were filled with lust, and it spurred me further. I yanked her from the bed, pulled her over to the sofa, and pushed her down so her perfect round ass was exposed. I entered her, bringing her nearly off her feet, unashamed at the ferocity in which I needed her tonight. Her cries got louder with every thrust, and I finally could hold back no more. I pumped into her, my cum running down her legs. Her body convulsed at the same time as pleasure swept over her. I lifted her in my arms, her knees no longer able to hold her up, and carried her back to the bed. I stripped the remainder of my clothes off so that I could feel her skin against mine. Her cheeks were flushed, her chest was heaving, and her legs trembled, but we were not done. I needed her in every way possible before I was faced with the uncertainty of what tomorrow may bring.

The Next Morning

. . .

Bri

Before I could open my eyes, the warmth of being held in Rogue's arms melted my anger away. I wanted to stay in bed with him; I didn't want him to leave. I didn't want the phone to ring with information that would pull him away from me. I snuggled closer against him, relishing the safety I felt when I was wrapped in his arms.

"After the way I took you last night, you must be sore and tender in certain intimate areas. So, I will give you one warning and one warning only, if you wiggle your little ass against my cock one more time, you will find yourself on your back with your legs thrown over my shoulders."

I turned in his arms to face him. "I am still mad at you."

His deep chuckle reverberated through me. "I can only imagine how mad you were when you finally woke up yesterday. I'll know next time that you don't have a very high tolerance for medications."

"Next time! There better not be a next time, Rogue. I don't want you to think that I am so fragile that you must medicate me when things get difficult. I meant what I said last night. You won't give me up or let me leave so you have to trust that I am strong enough to handle things."

He pressed a kiss to my forehead. "I was only trying to make things easier for you, but if it makes you feel better, I promise to never drug you again." He pressed a kiss to the corner of my lips. "I am more partial to the handcuffs anyway."

I pushed against his chest, even as his lips spread into the most handsome smile. "None of that either, Rogue."

He sighed heavily and rolled to his back. "Now that is something I won't promise you. Stop trying to take all the fun out of everything."

"What happened yesterday that you were so worried about me anyway?"

His face turned serious, and he stood from the bed and slid on his pants that had been tossed to the floor. "Yesterday, Blaze received information that our enemies were planning something against us. We had every intention of stopping it before they could strike. But it didn't happen, now we wait."

"Wait? Just wait for whoever this person is to attack you."

He put on his shirt but left it unbuttoned. "No, sweetheart. We wait until the first opportunity that is given to kill him."

I knew he noticed my face pale.

"Don't ask questions that you don't want to hear the answer to, Angel. That's why I brought you here, that's why I gave you the medication to keep you from being worried. Arrangements have been made for you. Michael is here to protect you and I'm sure Eden being here will help keep your mind off things."

I wrapped the sheet around me and stood from the bed. "Arrangements for me?"

He stepped closer but didn't reach out to touch me. "I do have some good news. Alessio received word that Tony Galante's stepfather forced him to return to New York. You no longer have him to worry about. He is no longer in the area and according to Alessio, Tony was given an ultimatum to leave you alone or be left on his own. His stepfather will not intercede for him."

I pulled the sheet tighter over me. "Tony is gone, and he agreed to never come for me again? I find that hard to believe."

"That's right, sweetheart. Tony is no longer your problem, but know this, once I have disposed of the threat from the Armenians, I still have every intention of finding him and killing him for what he has done to you. I promise that you will forever be free of the fears that haunt you, Angel."

"If he has left Chicago and has no plans to return or seek me out, there is no need to kill him. Will that not cause trouble between you and his stepfather? He is a hitman for God's sake. You shouldn't antagonize him."

"There is no need to argue with me. Tony's fate was sealed the minute he hurt you, and for that, he must pay. But all of that can wait. You are not to worry. Once the Armenians are dealt with, I plan on taking you away somewhere special."

I wanted to know more, but his phone rang on the other side of the room, and he quickly walked over to grab it. His eyes narrowed and I saw the muscle clench in his jaw.

"Give me an hour."

He grabbed the phone tighter. "Go back to bed, Bri. I'll have the chef prepare breakfast and one of the maids will bring it to you in an hour or so."

I didn't get the chance to ask where he was going or when he would come back before he hurried from the room. It didn't matter. I knew he wouldn't answer me and a part of me didn't want the truth. I crawled back into the bed, but I knew I wouldn't be able to sleep now.

Rogue

The video Blaze had sent to my phone showing Petros and Sevan meeting on the same day that Sevan had told Blaze that he had not seen or heard from the young fool confirmed our suspicion that Sevan was using us to take Petros out so it would be easier for him to take control. It still pissed me off that I didn't see through his ruse sooner, but his machinations would not go unpunished. Anyone who attempted to play me for a fool would pay for their mistake.

I stopped my car in front of the high-rise building expecting Blaze to be waiting for me. After meeting with Michael and double-checking the security around the mansion, Alessio had agreed that Tomas' skills would be more useful in helping take down Petros and Sevan. The fact that Tomas would be joining us on the hunt was bound to put Blaze in an even fouler mood than usual. Hopefully, we could find and eliminate our targets before the two of them killed each other. Normally I enjoyed watching the animosity between the two of them fester, but not today. There was too much to be done.

Before I could step from the car, I caught sight of Blaze walking out of the building, a deep frown on his face and a fresh cut above his right eye.

"Drive!"

I didn't hesitate. "Where the fuck are we going?"

"My place. Petros and his men are about to make a move. They plan on burning the warehouses off of 14th after dark and then hitting the other warehouse out of the city right after. There are only twenty or so of his men left, but we don't know how many Sevan has with him."

I nodded. "And as soon as we take down Petros, Sevan will show his true colors."

Blaze didn't bother to confirm my suspicions.

"Where are Tomas and Alessio?"

"Alessio will meet us later. Tomas is tending to a black eye and it's not my place to keep track of him anyway."

"The two of you couldn't hold back until this was over. Does the cut over your eye need stitches?"

He didn't bother responding.

When we arrived at Blaze's apartment, he gathered his favorite weapons, the ones he preferred when violence was necessary. If everything went as expected, Petros and all the men who worked for him would be dead before the night was over. Then I would deal with Sevan myself.

Seven Hours Later

Alessio and Blaze were on the south side of the warehouse covering the rear entrance, and Tomas was set up on the east end with a sniper rifle covering me. I planned on facing Petros head-on. The area around the warehouses was dark, the security guards that were normally on duty had all been dismissed and sent home. I didn't want anyone other than the four of us here tonight.

I was dressed in my favorite black suit, I felt that being professional was always important regardless of the circumstances. I just hoped it wouldn't be covered in blood before the night was over. My phone vibrated with a notification from Blaze alerting me to the fact that Petros and some of his men had arrived on location. It pleased me to know that Petros was so easily walking into the trap we had set. The man truly wasn't worthy of the responsibilities that had been passed down to him from his father.

A dark car drove toward the building where I waited patiently. Six men got out of the car, one holding a black duffle bag, all of them armed. I watched for the others to show or to get in their positions. Tomas texted that there were about twelve of them. Another car pulled up, and I needed Petros to be in it. He was known to often send his men to do the work while he hid, I hoped tonight was not one of those times. One of the men ran to open the backdoor, and I was relieved to see Petros step from the vehicle. He was wearing dark sunglasses even though it was midnight. *What a prick.* His black hair was slicked back, and he was wearing a black hoodie underneath a black wool peacoat. He adjusted his coat as he looked around the warehouses, trying to portray confidence that this would be an easy task for his men.

I knew Blaze was positioned on the other side of the complex prepared to handle an assault from the rear and Tomas was an excellent sniper, so I stepped out from behind the large shipping container where I had been waiting and walked out into the open. Petros and his men looked confused. Some pointed their weapons at me, while others darted around looking for the ambush they were now realizing they had walked into.

Petros moved confidently to the center, two men flanking him as I walked forward...alone.

"I had heard that you were a dangerous man, Delaney, but I didn't think you were stupid," he stated loudly in a thick accent before laughing and slapping one of the men beside him on the back.

I ignored the insult. "It was ambitious of you to try to take on the Volkoff Bratva, Petros. Some might say even ballsy, but to think that you could come into my city and take from me was the mistake that will end your life."

His laughter stopped as he stepped closer. "You are just like my father, unable to see what I am capable of, thinking that you know better than me." He held his arms out wide. "And now I will take it all. Once I have killed you and taken over all your holdings and businesses, I will move on to New York, Los Angeles, Las Vegas…"

I held up my hand just to get him to shut his mouth. "You have already tried Vegas. That didn't go as you had hoped."

I watched his face redden. His immaturity showed at that moment. In this world, you learn how to hide your emotions. Petros just showed a weakness; he could be goaded into making foolish mistakes. It was probably how Sevan managed to control him.

His lips curled into a snarl. "You talk big for someone about to die."

"You are a puppet, Petros. Sevan has been pulling your strings the entire time, feeding me information about your attacks and hoping I would take you out so he can take control of your father's organization."

He took another step closer, but I held my ground.

"You know nothing! You are spouting lies, hoping to save your miserable life. You should be on your knees begging me to at least make your death swift."

The sound of one of the men behind him falling to the ground drew his attention. He turned just in time to see another one fall. Chaos moved through the ranks of his men as others fell to the ground. Tomas's sniper skills were impressive. It only took a matter of seconds until Petros was the only one left.

He was shaking now with both rage and fear.

"I am not alone! I have other men with me."

I shook my head. "You think I was not prepared for that. The other men who came with you are already dead. Although, I'm sure they were not granted the easy death these men were. So, it's just you and me, Petros. How do you want to play it?"

His hands curled into fists. "I'm going to kill you, Delaney."

He rushed forward, a blade in his hand, and swiped at me. I shifted to the left and easily avoided his attack. The fool still thought he could win. After wiping out the remaining men that followed him, Petros still thought he could beat me. It almost felt as if I were doing something especially evil by killing this man. The neurons in his brain were obviously not firing as they should.

He lunged for me again, this time almost nicking the sleeve of my coat. While a part of me enjoyed this, I was most anxious to end it. I still had Sevan to deal with, and I wasn't quite sure how I wanted to handle that.

"Let me make it easy for you, Petros. You are already destined to die tonight. Throw down the knife and I promise to make it quick and clean. I have other things I need to do and playing cat and mouse with you is beginning to bore me."

The young man's eyes narrowed as sweat beaded across his forehead. "You are the one that will die tonight, Delaney. Or maybe I will keep you alive just long enough for you to watch me force your pretty little wife to her knees to suck my cock."

The fury I felt at that moment couldn't have been contained if I had tried. I swiftly grabbed the hand holding the knife while gripping his throat with the other.

His face began to turn red then purple as the air flow was cut off, his windpipe crushing beneath the force of my fingers.

"Speaking of my wife was the one sure way to make certain your death will not be either neat or painless."

His strength was fading as I twisted the hand in which he still held the knife between us. Spit began to pool in the corner of his mouth as he struggled to draw a breath. I thrust the knife forward into his belly, his eyes widened, and I loosened my grip around his throat, allowing him the opportunity to breathe even if was only for a moment. I didn't want him to slip away so easily. The knife was still embedded deep into his stomach. I jerked it to the side, and I stepped back and released him. He fell to his knees, his hands immediately going to the wound where his guts were now visible.

At that moment, Blaze walked around the corner covered in blood, a look of surreal satisfaction on his face. "Is he dead, yet?"

I bent down watching the shallow rise and fall of his chest. "No, but he soon will be."

Blaze stood over him, blood dripping from his hands. "Finish him so we can be done with this."

Tomas stepped forward. "Why are you in such a hurry? Do you have another lady waiting to be left disappointed and unfulfilled tonight?"

I stood up and placed a hand on Blaze's chest to stop him from going after Tomas.

Alessio moved in front of Tomas. "That's enough. While the two of you may have nothing better to do than spit insults and spar with each other, I would like to end this and be back in bed with my wife before the sun rises."

Blaze looked down at the man lying in a pool of blood at my feet. "This mess needs to be cleaned up."

I stared at Petros as he took his final breaths. He was beyond comprehension now. It wouldn't be much longer. "Daniel and a crew of men are waiting for my text. He will make sure everything is handled here." I pulled my cell phone from my coat pocket.

"Now that Petros is no more, should we go visit your friend Sevan and give him the good news?" Alessio asked as he stepped over Petros' lifeless body.

Blaze lit a cigarette and took a deep drag. "I'll give him a call."

"No, don't call. It is better if he doesn't know we are coming. We don't want to give Sevan any advantages."

CHAPTER
twenty-one

ROGUE

Blaze discovered that Sevan was no longer in Chicago but had returned to his home outside Albany, New York. Distancing himself from Petros' downfall no doubt. If he thought that leaving Chicago would save him, he was mistaken. Alessio made a call, his private jet was refueled, and we landed in Albany just before dawn. A car was waiting for us at the airfield to drive us to Sevan's home outside the city.

It was easy to gain admittance into the house. The lack of security or any alarms was surprising but not as much as the look of shock on Sevan's face when I walked into his kitchen. He was wearing a robe and eating scrambled eggs looking very pleased with himself...until he saw me.

"Mr. Delaney, I did not...I was not expecting a visit from you."

I walked over to the coffee pot, grabbed a mug from the stand beside it, and poured myself a cup. It had been a long night, and the caffeine might help improve my mood.

"I'm sure you didn't, but I wanted to deliver this news personally. Petros and all the men that were with him are dead."

He dropped his head in mock sorrow. "It is a shame that the young man could not be controlled. So young and foolish. If only his father had lived longer."

He spoke his lies with such confidence.

"Yes, it is. Young and foolish is never a good combination."

He nodded in agreement. The fake sympathy on his face was nauseating.

"I'm curious though, who will take his place? With no one at the helm, how will the organization move forward?"

I couldn't suppress the grin on my face when he nervously took a sip of his coffee. His hand was shaking slightly.

"I'm sure the family will come to a wise decision when appointing a new leader. Someone with more experience."

"Perhaps, but I am curious as to if you will be considered for the position."

Sevan's eyes widened as Blaze came into the room, blood still staining his clothes.

"I am not certain. Although, I would consider it an honor."

I took another sip of the coffee and shifted my gaze to Blaze.

"Hmm, well the new leader should be careful who he trusts. The puppet master pulling his strings might set out to see him killed...just as you did Petros."

His eyes flashed with the realization that we knew of his schemes.

I stepped closer. "Was your plan to simply have Blaze and I do your dirty work and kill Petros so that you could step in as the one meant to save the family? Petros' father was your friend. Did you swear to him on his deathbed that you would guide his son? You guided him right into his grave. Do you wish to know how he died or is that too much for you? Literal blood on your hands is not as bad as the blood on your conscious."

His face reddened. "I did everyone a favor. It was always understood that I would take power after Hayak's death, but he could never keep his dick in his pants. I was not worried. He had been with countless women through the years and never produced a child. I thought he was sterile, but the young waitress he fell in love with changed everything. When she became pregnant, Hayak was determined that the young Petros be his heir, even after it became obvious that he did not have the brains nor the will to be a leader."

"Getting rid of Petros wasn't any of my business, Sevan. You made your mistake by lying to me. You were the one behind the threats. You were the one whispering in Petros' ear that he should take on Nickolai and the Volkoff Bratva as well as my organization. You endangered everyone around me with your scheming, including my wife, and that is something I will not forgive."

"I can give you whatever you want, Delaney. We can be partners. Together we can increase our holdings and power. I will give you a large percentage of the profits."

I shook my head. "I don't need you to do any of those things, Sevan, because I am going to take it all. Did you think that my services would be free?"

Sevan knew he was beaten. I could see it on his face. His eyes were downcast as he nervously moved around the table. Blaze and I both knew what he was about to do and were ready when he lunged for the gun he had hidden in a drawer. By the time he had turned to point it at me, I already had mine leveled at his forehead.

The pistol he was holding clattered to the ground as my shot went through his brain.

Blaze stepped forward. "Well, that was anticlimactic."

"I don't have the time nor am I in the mood for dramatics."

Blaze grinned. "Tomas and Alessio made certain we didn't miss anything, no security cameras, there was no one else in the house, nothing to connect us with being here, and I have some of Petro's blood and his identification to leave somewhere here in the house. I can easily make it look as if the two of them argued and Petros killed Sevan before fleeing the country and as Petros' body will never be found, it should be an easy sell."

I sighed before putting my pistol back inside my coat. "Let's just get it done and get back to Chicago."

About thirty minutes later my phone rang. "I know you are impatient, Alessio, but you could give us just a bit more time."

"You need to get back to the plane now!"

The urgency in his voice caused me to immediately pick up my pace toward the waiting car. "What's happened?"

"I just received a phone call from Frankie Ballentine. It's Galante, he doesn't know where he is. He discovered that his safe had been broken into sometime yesterday and Tony stole somewhere around a hundred grand. Frankie wanted to warn you. He doesn't think he will return to Chicago and go after Bri, but I wouldn't want to take that chance if I were you."

I hung up the phone and immediately tried to call Michael, but the call failed. Something was wrong. I could feel it. I had given Bri her phone when I left, but when I dialed the number, the call wouldn't go through.

I sprinted the rest of the way to the car with Blaze right behind me. I had promised Bri that I would protect her, keep her safe. I had told her that Tony wasn't a threat anymore, that he had left Chicago. And now I wasn't there to protect her from the monster who had hurt her. The prospect of that bastard putting his hands on her, hurting my angel again was enough to make me commit murder a hundred times over. My fury intensified at the thought. If Galante was foolish enough to go after Bri again, I would show no mercy. His death would not be an easy one.

Bri

I had spent most of the day learning my way around Rogue's ridiculously large mansion. He did not return that night and I had not heard anything from him since he left me. Michael had assured me that I had nothing to worry about, but how could I not worry?

"Did you want to change and practice some of the moves you have been learning? It might help take your mind off things."

I turned and saw Michael walking toward me. It was odd seeing him dressed normally, not as a priest.

"Have you heard anything?"

He shook his head. "No, but my phone hasn't worked all day. There must be a tower down somewhere."

I took the phone from my pocket and stared at the blank screen. "Yeah, mine isn't working either."

"I normally would try to be more sympathetic and understanding but you look as if you could use some tough love. Go get changed and meet me in the gym. If you can manage to hold your own, I will teach you something new."

"Something new?"

His grin stretched wider across his face. "Rogue has a target range in the basement. I thought you might like to try your hand at shooting. You did say you wanted to learn."

I returned his smile. "Rogue knows that you are going to teach me to shoot?"

"No, but he isn't here right now. But just so we are clear, you only get to go to the range if you manage to hold your own on the mat, and I have no plans of letting you off easy."

I slipped my phone back into my pocket. "For a priest, you certainly aren't being very encouraging, but I think I might surprise you. Will Eden be joining us?"

"She is napping and since Tomas is not here to supervise, I think I will steer clear of throwing around Alessio Messina's wife. It could be dangerous to my health. Now go change, I'll be in the gym."

While I missed Rogue, I did enjoy spending time with Father Michael. He made me laugh and there was something about him that made all of this feel normal. "I'll meet you there in fifteen minutes."

I hurried up the stairs to the master suite to change, tossed my phone on the table by the bed, and turned back toward the closet.

"Hello, Brielle."

The voice from my past caused me to freeze in fear. "Tony."

He took a step closer, and I felt as if my feet were glued to the floor.

"I thought you had forgotten all about me, sweetheart. You gave me more of a chase than I expected."

His hand reached out toward my face and my senses returned. "How did you get in here?"

"It was difficult, I will give Delaney that. His security was almost impenetrable...almost."

"Then you should also know I am not alone."

A mocking smile stretched across his lips. "I'm not foolish enough to come alone either, Bri. Right now, there are two men downstairs taking care of the man Delaney left here for your protection."

I felt sick that Michael could be hurt because of me. "Leave him alone! He hasn't done anything to you."

His eyes darkened and I could almost feel the evil radiating from him.

"What would you do to save his life?" His hand went to his zipper. "Get on your knees and open your mouth. Suck my cock, Bri and if you do a good job, I'll spare your friend."

A wave of nausea swept over me as he stepped closer.

"You are sick, Tony."

My head jerked back as he backhanded me. The coppery taste of blood from where my lips was split hit my tongue.

"Shut the fuck up, bitch. You are coming with me."

My hand covered my stinging cheek. There was no way I was going to willingly leave with this psycho. "I'm not going with you, Tony, and if you try to take me, Rogue will kill you."

He moved with lightning speed and before I could step away, he had his hand wrapped around my throat and painfully squeezed, causing me to gasp for air. "I don't want to hear another word about Rogue Delaney, the man you so easily spread your legs for when you denied me."

He began dragging me toward the door, but I wasn't going to make it easy for him. I kicked at the back of his knee and his grip loosened enough that I could break away and I ran just as Michael had said I should do. Run until I was safe.

Tony tracked my steps, and I heard him mutter something under his breath. He was right behind me, but I ran even though I knew he would catch me, and he did. I was halfway down the stairs when he kicked my legs out from under me, causing me to lose my balance. I screamed as I tumbled the rest of the way down the stairs. My head hit the floor hard, and I could feel blood oozing down the side of my face.

I tried to get up, but I was dizzy and fell back down again.

Tony flipped me over to my back and stood over me. "Why do you make me do this to you?"

He roughly pulled me to my feet and snaked his arm around my waist, and I could feel his breath against my neck. I squeezed my eyes shut, pushing back the fear that threatened to consume me.

"We are going to finish what we started, Bri. You are going to give me what you were so quick to give to Rogue Delaney."

Another wave of nausea and dizziness moved over me, but I pushed it aside and summoned what little courage I had. I was not the same girl that Tony had terrorized back in Colorado. I was stronger now. I slammed my heel down hard on his foot. His grip loosened, but it wasn't enough for me to break free again, and even if I had been successful, the dizziness that had my head swimming probably would have taken over.

"Fucking bitch!"

He spun me around and punched me hard in the face. The force of the hit made everything go a little dark for a few seconds and everything around me seemed to spin out of control.

"Keep it up, Bri. The fighting just makes my dick harder. Now start walking."

I struggled to keep myself conscious. I had to keep fighting. My head lolled to the side, and I blinked a few times.

"Brielle!"

I saw Michael running toward me with Eden right behind him. Through my dizziness, I could see blood on his hands and shirt. Tony's fingers were digging into the side of my neck, and I knew that if he managed to get me out of this house, I would die. I looked at Michael once more before trying to jab my elbow into Tony's gut. I connected but with my strength fading, it didn't have much of an impact. Eden's eyes were wide as she watched. I squeezed my eyes shut and pushed back the tears. I would not give this man the satisfaction of seeing me cry.

Just before I thought all was lost, a loud crash caused me to look up, and what I saw made my heart leap. Rogue was standing in the doorway looking fiercer than anything I had seen before. His eyes flicked over me briefly before meeting Tony's and then they seemed to blaze with fury. The severe anger radiating from him caused Tony to take a step back. While I felt a rush of relief at seeing Rogue, the rage in his eyes made him look like the devil himself. The last thought I had before everything went black was that the devil had come to save his angel.

Rogue
A Few Minutes Earlier

When the car pulled up at the gates of my estate, I saw that two men were already dead. My security must have found them. Hopefully, they were smart enough to ask them a few questions before ending their lives.

I jumped from the car. "Where is she?"

"There are three men in the house. We found these two lurking around the perimeter."

I didn't wait to hear more. I ran toward the house, hoping I had gotten there in time before Tony could hurt her. When I threw open the front door, the sight I saw made my blood turn cold.

Tony had his hands on Bri. There was an open wound on her head with blood oozing from it and her right cheek was red and swollen from where the bastard had hit her. I saw Michael from the corner of my eye, but I couldn't fully take my eyes from my angel. Her eyes were filled with fear, then to my horror, I watched her go limp in his arms.

"Let her go."

He laughed. "You think I am a fool? If I let her go, you will kill me. No, she is the only way I have to get out of here." His arm moved around her throat as he held her against his chest as a shield. "So, unless you want to see me choke the life out of her before your eyes, you will step aside."

I didn't have to turn my head to know that Blaze had come to stand beside me, I could feel his presence. Alessio and Tomas had probably gone around back. Michael took a step closer to Galante, and I noticed that he was covered in blood. He must have already taken care of the other two men in the house. That left just Tony.

"There is no way out, Tony. Let her go, and I will have some mercy."

His bitter laugh made my skin crawl. I looked at Bri's face. Her eyes fluttered as she began to regain consciousness.

I moved forward, needing to close the space between us so that I could reach Bri quickly if things didn't go the way I planned. Tony continued backing away. Bri began to struggle, and he tightened his hold, causing her airway to be cut off. Her hand reached up to grip the arm that was around her throat, but she was weak. I needed to get her away from him.

I saw her eyes dart over to Michael and the small nod of her head indicating that she was about to attempt something. But before I could stop her from doing something that might get her hurt, she reached up and raked her nails deep into Tony's face. The hold he had on her loosened, and I rushed forward pulling her free and shoving her behind me before I tackled the man that had dared to touch her. All the anger and fury I had inside me came to the surface. My fists pounded against his head until he no longer moved beneath me. I would have killed him right then and there had Blaze not stepped forward and pulled me off him.

"Stop! Killing him now is not what he deserves."

I looked down at his bloody face. "Get him the fuck out of my house. I don't want her to have to see his face again."

At some point, Tomas and Alessio had made their way to the scene. Tomas helped Blaze drag Tony from the room while Alessio swept his Cara Mia into his arms.

I turned to find Bri slumped against the wall, her arms crossed over her chest. I immediately walked over to her, scanning the injuries on her face. I picked her up, cradling her in my arms, and headed for the stairs. I wanted privacy to make certain she was alright and find out what Tony had done to her before I arrived.

When I had her behind the closed doors of the master suite, I put her back on her feet and held her a little away from me so I could further examine her injuries. "Where are hurt?"

Her hand went to the cut on her head. "I'm fine. Just a few bumps. He tripped me when I was running from him, and I fell down the stairs, and I will have a few bruises on my face from where he hit me."

I took out my phone.

"What are you doing?"

"I'm calling my physician. If you fell down the steps, I want you examined."

I braced for an argument from her, but she never uttered a word as she walked away to sit on the edge of the bed. I could tell from the wobbliness of her steps that she needed to sit before she fell.

Once the call had been made, I went into the bathroom and came back out with a hot washcloth and gently washed the blood from her forehead.

"I'm sorry that I didn't get here in time."

A heavy sigh passed through her lips. "But you did."

I tilted her chin up so I could see into her eyes. "It's over now. No more nightmares, Angel."

I leaned down and kissed her softly. "The doctor will be here soon. Take a shower, and I'll bring an icepack for your cheek."

"Where will you be? You aren't leaving again, are you?"

Her hand clung to mine.

"No, baby. I am just going downstairs to talk to Michael and make certain all of this is handled. I'll come back when the doctor arrives."

She nodded and walked into the bathroom on her own power.

Once I heard the shower running, I hurried downstairs, hoping Michael could give me more details of what the fuck had happened.

I found him in the kitchen with Alessio and Eden. "I don't want to burden Bri with a shit ton of questions so tell me what you can." It was then that I really took notice of his appearance. His shirt was torn, and he was coated in dried blood. "I sent for the doctor. He can examine you too."

"No need. None of this is my blood."

I glanced over at Alessio who still had Eden wrapped in his embrace.

Michael knew I had never been patient and thankfully didn't make me wait for an explanation.

"Bri had gone to the bedroom to change. She was to meet me in the gym to practice more self-defense moves. On my way there, I heard glass break here in the kitchen and came to find Eden fending off two men. She was armed with a knife in one hand and a coffee mug in the other and seemed to be holding her own, but you know me, I hate to see a lady in distress."

"You killed them?"

"Yes, their bodies are in the dining room. I moved them out of sight."

I looked at Eden. "Are you alright?"

"Yes, thank goodness Father Michael was here. How is Bri?"

"Other than a few cuts and bruises, I think she will be fine. We will know more after the doctor examines her. The hard hit she took to her head when she stumbled down the stairs worries me."

Alessio stepped toward Michael. "I am forever in your debt, but since the two of you seem to have everything in hand, we will be returning to New York."

Michael shook his hand, but I could tell he was uncomfortable with the situation.

Alessio and Eden left the room, and I turned back to Michael.

"If you don't need me for anything right away, I'm going to shower. But before I do, what happens next?"

"Blaze has taken Tony to the chambers. He will wait there. You know what his fate will be and don't try to convince me that I should show mercy."

His head dropped and looked at the blood staining his hands. "I don't think I have the right to tell anyone how they should live. I just killed two men and the sad part is that I have no remorse."

"Some men don't deserve to live, Michael. You are merely God's outstretched hand of vengeance."

He rolled his eyes. "Don't start being philosophical. Go be with Bri. I'll see you later."

I made my way back up to the master suite. I could still hear the shower running and I walked into the bathroom to see Bri sitting on the floor underneath the hot water. Her knees were pulled up to her chest and her arms were wrapped around them. I took off my clothes and stepped into the shower with her. She didn't even notice me at first. I sat on the floor behind her and pulled her closer so that my arms could wrap around her body.

She didn't speak, nor was she crying, but I did think she was in some kind of shock. "Angel? Are you hurt anywhere else?"

She shook her head but still didn't speak.

"The doctor will be here soon, love, and once he has made certain you are alright, I will put you to bed and have the chef cook whatever you want to eat tonight."

I continued holding her until the water turned cool, then carried her back to the bedroom and wrapped her in a blanket. "I'm going to change clothes and go downstairs. The doctor should be here in a few minutes, and I'll bring him up. Do you need anything, Angel?"

"No, I'm fine. But how is Father Michael? I saw him and there was so much blood." Her voice was small and quiet.

"Not a scratch on him. He will be trying to save my soul again in no time. Alessio and Eden have already left for the airport. He was anxious to get back to New York and Blaze will likely head back into the city."

I leaned over and kissed her forehead. "Just rest and when the doctor leaves, if you feel up to it, we will make some plans."

I walked toward the closet, dressed quickly, and went downstairs to make certain everything was being taken care of. I didn't want Bri to see any more of the blood and death than she had already. The sooner I could erase what happened from her mind the better off she would be.

Bri

The doctor arrived not long after Rogue had left the room. Other than a slight concussion and a few cuts and bruises I would be fine. He suggested I take a day or two to rest and left some pain medicine if I needed anything stronger than Ibuprofen.

Rogue had not returned upstairs since the doctor had left. With everything that went on today, I wouldn't be surprised if I didn't see him for a few hours. I had no idea what getting rid of a body entailed, but I assumed no police would be involved. It was probably best if I didn't know anything.

None of that was what was bothering me though. Now that everything was over, I knew things would change. Rogue had even mentioned making plans once I felt better this evening. It was the prospect of what those plans entailed that made me nervous. I had grown accustomed to being with Rogue now. The thought of him no longer being in my life hurt. Not to mention the fact that I was certain another man would never be able to make me feel the same way he did, nor would I want another man to touch me.

Rogue's ideas for the future and what that meant for us kept going through my mind, making me crazy. So, I left the bed, against the doctor's orders, and walked over to the balcony. I opened the French doors letting in the fresh air. The cool breeze felt good. I took a deep breath and moved over to the railing.

"What the hell do you think you are doing, Angel?"

I didn't bother to turn around. "I was tired of being in bed and wanted to get some fresh air."

He moved behind me and wrapped his arms around my waist

before pressing a soft kiss to my neck. "You should have waited for me. The doctor said that with your concussion you could experience dizziness."

"I wasn't sure how much longer you would be, and I think the doctor is being overly cautious. I feel much better now."

Rogue turned me around to face him and I watched as his eyes scanned over my injuries. "Regardless, the doctor said for you to rest and that is what you are going to do. Don't make me get the hand-cuffs, sweetheart."

The smile on his face made my heart twist. "You said we were going to talk about plans, and I think I would feel better if we did so now."

His eyes narrowed as he stared down into my face. "What's on your mind, Angel?"

I took a deep breath and decided it was best just to get it over with. "Is the danger gone? The men that attacked Nickolai, the ones that you said were watching you and would take me if given the opportunity, they are gone?"

"Yes, sweetheart. It has been handled. The threat is over."

"And Tony?"

His fingers came up to lightly brush across the bruise on my cheek. "Gone. No more nightmares."

I closed my eyes, trying to shut out the way his touch on my skin made me feel. "If there is no longer any danger, I just want you to know that I will understand and not make a fuss."

His fingers stilled and his eyes darkened.

I pulled away from his embrace and turned around knowing it would be easier for me to say what needed to be said if I wasn't looking at him.

"What are you talking about, Bri?"

"I heard you on the phone a few days ago reiterating that the only reason why you married me was to protect me, to keep me safe. It only makes sense that now the threat is gone, the marriage is no longer necessary."

I heard him inhale deeply. "Is that what you want?"

"It doesn't matter what I want. You did what you promised. You protected me and saved me from the biggest monster I have ever encountered. It wouldn't be right of me to try to hold you to a commitment you didn't want."

At first, I didn't think he would say anything. It seemed like time had stopped. He made no move to touch me.

"Turn around and look at me."

I did as he asked and the stormy expression on his face made me quiver.

"What are you trying to say, Angel?"

I looked away. "You married me with the sole purpose of protecting me, you did that. I assumed now that the danger has passed, you would want things to be as they were before."

He fisted a handful of my hair and forced me to look at him. "I asked you a question and I expect an answer. Is that what you want?"

I felt my heart race. No, it wasn't what I wanted. I wanted to stay with him. I wasn't sure how I would walk away if told me that was what he wished. I shook my head as one whispered word passed through my parted lips.

"No."

His frown turned up slightly. "Then why would you suggest something so ludicrous?"

His arms wrapped around me, and he pulled me close.

"You said we would make plans when I felt better, and I thought that was what you wanted to talk about."

He kissed the top of my head before sweeping me into his arms and carrying me back inside to the bed. "I wanted to make plans for a honeymoon, Angel, not dissolve our marriage." He sat me back on the bed and stood a few feet away from me. "What am I going to have to do to convince you that there is no escape, that you are mine forever? Do I seriously need to rethink the idea of chaining you to my bed?"

The joy I felt as his words was so overpowering that I couldn't help but smile at his reference to the handcuffs. "No, I get the idea. Besides, I did sign a contract."

He pressed me back against the pillows and hovered over me. "Damn straight you did, and don't think for one minute that I will not use it against you if that pretty little head ever thinks of leaving me again."

I wrapped my arms around his neck and pulled his head closer for a long, slow kiss.

"Darling, the doctor said that you should rest for a day or two, but if you continue to kiss me like that, it will be difficult for me to heed his advice."

"Would I be more convincing if I were naked?"

His smile instantly became predatory. His lips claimed mine and his hands made swift work of the chemise I was wearing. "You know an angel should never tempt a devil, darling."

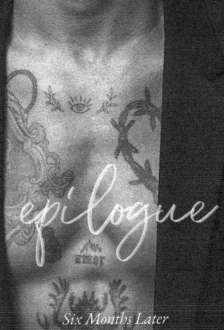

epilogue

Six Months Later
Sinners Night Club, Chicago

ROGUE

Sinners was exceptionally busy tonight. It was the grand reopening since the night Petros had tampered with the fire alarms, setting off the sprinkler system which had caused a great deal of water damage. And while we could have opened three months earlier, Alessio had suggested shutting down for longer. He thought it would build anticipation and allow us to make a few changes. One of which was the exclusivity of the club. While the main floor and upstairs rooms were open to the public, we added an exclusive section. The benefits of membership included a secluded private entrance that protected members from being identified giving them a certain anonymity. Once inside the members-only section of the club, they could immerse themselves in the most sinful and pleasurable acts money could buy. The finest liquor, the most beautiful women eager to disappear into the shadows with a patron, smuggled Cuban cigars, as well as other delicacies not readily available to others. It was a high-class, glitzy, palace of immorality. But membership was exclusive, and the annual fee was $150,000. It kept the clientele list small.

The public side of *Sinners* also had a few changes and with the number of people clamoring to get inside tonight, it seemed as if Alessio's business sense had been correct again. Blaze had complained about waiting so long to reopen, but now that he had at least three women demanding his attention, he seemed rather pleased.

I sat alone in my private booth, wishing I was back at the penthouse with Bri. I had wanted to bring her with me for the reopening tonight, but she had not felt well all day and had elected to stay behind. The noise and lights would not have helped her headache, but I missed her.

We had stayed at the estate for about three weeks after the incident with Tony, but when I mentioned needing to return to the city to take care of business, she was more than happy to come along with me. As if I would have ever left her behind.

The pleasure-seeking life of debauchery I had always craved didn't have the same appeal as it had before she walked into my life. The bourbon in my glass didn't ease the burning desire I had raging through me every single day. I couldn't be without her if I tried. She was an addiction and even now, I just wanted her.

I drank the rest of my bourbon, fully intending on speeding up the evening and returning to the penthouse. That is until I saw someone unexpected walking toward me.

Michael moved through the crowd, his height making him easy to see as he pushed through the people on the dance floor.

"I was not expecting to see you here tonight. Taking the evening off from saving souls?"

He sat in the booth beside me. "I came to talk to you about something."

His tone instantly concerned me. "Certainly. Whatever you need, I am here for you."

Michael smiled at the waitress who brought over two glasses of bourbon. "I am leaving the priesthood. My replacement arrives tomorrow."

My eyes narrowed as I watched him sip the liquor. "Leaving? As in taking a sabbatical?"

"No, I am leaving for good. It isn't for me anymore."

I shook my head, confused as to what had changed for him. "Is this about what happened at the mansion? You were acting in self-defense, Michael. I shudder to think what would have happened to Bri and Eden if you had not been there."

He nodded. "I realize that, but it doesn't change the fact that I killed two men that day. How can I stand in front of a congregation of people and preach redemption, forgiveness, and honesty when I am guilty of the things I have done?"

"None of this makes sense. Those were not the first men you have killed, Michael."

He sipped the bourbon. "I know that, but they are the first ones that I didn't feel guilty about."

"You shouldn't feel guilty. They were evil men that were about to hurt an innocent woman." I watched as his eyes scanned the room and I knew he was resigned to his decision. "What are you going to do? You know there is always a place in my organization for you."

He grinned. "I appreciate that, but I have other ideas. I would like to start a few money-making enterprises of my own. Alessio has offered me a chance to invest with him, and since you decided to split up the Armenian spoils you took from Petros, I thought I might give a try at being more hands-on. I am leaving for New York this afternoon." He drank the remainder of the bourbon in his glass. "Besides, a change of pace will be good for me."

"If this is what you want, you know I support you, but I will miss the monthly spaghetti dinners."

He chuckled. "I'm sure you will. Give Bri my best and tell Blaze that I'll see him around. Take care, Rogue."

I shook his hand. "I'm sorry that I pulled you back into this world, Michael."

"No worries. Everything is as it should be. I have come to accept that for what it is."

I watched as he turned and walked away, pushing through the crowd. When Michael had set a course, very little could deter him. I just hoped he wouldn't live to regret this decision.

"What was the priest doing here?"

Blaze had managed to shed himself from the eager ladies from earlier and was standing before me looking annoyed.

"He came to tell me that he is leaving the priesthood and going to New York. Alessio has an opportunity for him, and he wants a change of pace."

Blaze scooted into the booth. "Fuck, I would have never thought he would have done something that drastic. Guilt can make you do crazy things, I guess."

I stood from the booth. "It's the absence of guilt that is driving him." I grabbed my suit coat. "I am going to visit our mutual friend. Would you like to join me, or do you have a woman waiting for you?"

He grinned. "Can you give me an hour?"

"No, I want to get this over with and go home. Bri and I have an early flight tomorrow."

He stood from the booth. "Fine, give me twenty. The little blonde by the bar is more than eager and it won't take much to get her to lift her skirt, and I would bet everything in my wallet that she isn't wearing panties."

I rolled my eyes as he walked away to defile another unsuspecting woman who thought she would be the one to tame him. I would wait twenty minutes and that was it. I was anxious to get this evening over with and get back to the angel who was waiting for me.

The Chambers

The chambers were an underground bunker I acquired some years ago. It was just outside the city in a remote area, undetectable, and its existence was known to only two people, Blaze and me. It had at one time been a bomb shelter, but I had remodeled it to be more of a dungeon, a place to take those that most offended me. Blaze used it more than me, but recently it had been extremely useful.

The cold dampness sank into my bones as Blaze and I descended the steps into the chambers. The smell of blood, anguish, and despair was overpowering. Those who managed to find themselves here knew there was no escape. When we stepped farther into the room, the sounds of rattling chains drew my attention away from the water dripping overhead and down the walls.

"Good evening, Tony."

It took all his strength to raise his head. "Just kill me, Delaney, and get it over with. I'm tired of seeing your face."

I walked closer to him. I had kept him imprisoned here in the chambers since the day he tried to take Bri from the estate. Alessio had encouraged me to kill him then, but when I thought of the many days and nights my angel had lived in fear and the nightmares where she had to relive what this man had done to her, I couldn't see giving him an easy death.

"I wouldn't be in such a rush if I were you."

Blaze stepped closer and released him from his bonds. He collapsed onto the concrete floor.

"You are letting me go?"

I knelt before him. "Do you really believe that I would allow you to walk out of here alive after what you did to my wife? No, I am here to grant your request. I am going to kill you. My wife and I will be leaving for Europe in the morning, and I want to tidy up any loose ends before our flight, but in the spirit of fair play, I am going to give you a fighting chance."

His glossed over gaze moved from me to where Blaze stood on the other side of the room. "Nothing about this is fair."

"Take it for what it is. It is the only chance you will have and more than you deserve."

Blaze stepped forward and set a pistol and a knife within arm's reach.

"You even have your choice of weapons, choose wisely and do be quick about it. As I said, I have an early flight tomorrow."

I stepped back and waited for him to make a move. His eyes flicked between the knife and the pistol. At first, I didn't think he would reach for either one, but eventually, he summoned what little courage he had left and lunged for the pistol. But I was prepared. I moved forward quickly knocking it in the air just as it fired before I snapped his neck. His lifeless body fell to the floor at my feet. The nightmare for my angel was finally over.

My head snapped around to see Blaze smirking. "Seriously! You gave him a loaded pistol?"

"I thought you wanted to give him a fair chance. Besides, I only put one bullet in it. Don't be a baby." Blaze heaved a heavy sigh. "I still don't believe he got what he truly deserved."

"No, maybe not but it's finally over. Bri is free from him. She will never have to look over her shoulder wondering if this piece of shit is waiting to torment her again, and I got some retribution."

Blaze took a cigarette out of his jacket pocket and lit it. "Retribution is magical, but so is something else I would rather be doing right now. Let's get this mess cleaned up so we both can enjoy the remainder of the evening."

My phone rang. I took it from my pocket and silenced it. The same number had been calling a few times a day for the past month.

"When were you planning on telling me that your uncle was the leader of the Irish mafia?"

I should have been surprised that Blaze knew of my connections, but he always managed to be a step ahead of everyone. "How long have you known?"

He rolled his eyes. "Since the day you gave me inside information about Sevan. Did you think I wouldn't research to find out who your sources were?"

"I never wanted to acknowledge it, not after what my father did."

"I can understand that, but the old man isn't going to give up."

I walked a few steps away. "I have had my uncle's number for years, but never called it until I wanted information about Sevan. That information came with a price. My uncle wants to meet with me. He seems determined that I take my rightful place among the family."

"You don't want it, don't take it."

"It's not that simple."

The phone rang again.

Blaze's eyes narrowed. "For fuck's sake, just answer the damn thing and get it over with."

I took my phone out of my pocket and answered the call. "I'm a little busy at the moment."

"Aye, but ye will make time for me tonight. I am waiting outside the building that houses your penthouse. There are things we must settle before I fly back to Boston."

The phone went silent.

"Go, I'll finish up here."

I nodded toward Blaze, thankful he didn't ask for an explanation.

Driving from the chambers back into the city seemed to take twice as long as usual. I was angry. Angry that my uncle refused to take no for an answer and even angrier at myself for considering the offer he had made.

When I pulled up in front of the penthouse, I tossed my keys to the valet and strode toward my uncle who was standing beside a man who looked to be about my age and height, wearing a near identical menacing expression on his face.

"Do you wish to conduct business on the street, or do you prefer to follow me to my office?"

"Yer office will do."

My uncle and the man escorting him followed me inside the building to the elevator. Once inside my office, I walked over to the bar and poured myself a drink. "Would either of you like something? I don't have Irish whiskey, but I'm sure I have something that meets your tastes."

My uncle used his cane to walk forward and take a seat. The man with him stayed beside the door.

"No, we don' have long, and I want to get business over with. Perhaps we can toast to the future another day."

I took another sip of bourbon. "Why are you here?"

He sighed heavily. "I know that ye are not eager to embrace yer family. After what your da did to ye I can't blame ye for the hard feelings ye harbor, but regardless of the past, ye are indeed a Delaney."

I had heard this speech before and was not impressed.

"Before we talk business or family, or whatever reason has brought here, shouldn't we have some sort of introduction?"

The man standing by the door stepped forward, but his expression didn't change, and I got the impression that he was sizing me up as much as I was him.

"This is Colin Quinn. Colin is my sister's only child and therefore yer cousin."

"Cousin?" My entire life I had never had family, now suddenly, they were coming out of the woodwork, and I wasn't sure I liked it.

I glanced from my uncle to the man he claimed was my cousin. He had an arrogant grin on his face that I didn't like.

My uncle coughed into a handkerchief and took a few deep breaths before continuing. "The doctors are not giving me more than a year left to live and I will not stand by and see ev'rythin' that I worked for lost or torn apart by greed. Havin' no sons of my own, I will be leavin' ev'rythin' to the two of ye." His eyes squinted as if he expected me to argue. "Colin will assume all the responsibilities that come with the business interests in Boston and the East Coast. Ye will take over the few business interests that I have in Chicago as well as all international affairs. The funds in my accounts will be split between the two of ye. It is the fairest way I can see things done, and the only way I can make things right."

He stood slowly from his seat. "My lawyers will be in contact with ye soon. Accept what I am offerin'. There is no reason to refuse."

I watched as he walked toward the door. Each step seemed harder than the last. The other man came forward and offered his hand.

"Nice to meet you, Cousin."

I shook his hand. "I'll reserve judgment for the time being."

He nodded. "As will I."

I escorted them down to the lobby but went no farther. I wasn't sure what to make of my uncle's request. I had never wanted anything that belonged to my family, nor did I need them. And then there was the cousin. There was something about him that made me uneasy. Hopefully, it was just my suspicious nature, but time would tell.

The stress of it all was beginning to give me a headache and I knew of only one thing that would relieve that stress. After the day I had, all I wanted was Bri.

It was late, and I expected to find Bri already in bed, especially since we were flying out for Europe in the morning. But my angel was not asleep, she was curled up on the sofa reading over another travel book she had purchased for our trip.

I stepped forward and took the book from her hands, causing her to finally notice my arrival.

"Why are you still up, Angel?"

She smiled and I felt my chest tighten.

"I was too excited to sleep." She stood from the sofa and wrapped her arms around my neck. "Besides, you know I don't like going to bed without you."

I lifted her so she could wrap her legs around me as I kissed her lips. "I'm glad you are awake."

My fingers slipped over the short lacy silk gown she was wearing. After the day's events, I needed her. She was the one constant in my life. I set her on her feet and stripped the silk gown over her head, smiling because she was still following my no panties rule.

I took a moment to admire her beauty and knew I would never grow tired of it, and just like always, the overpowering need to be inside her took over. I should try to make love to her slowly, but it was never that way between us. There was always an urgency, a burning need to be close, to bring her pleasure. It was intense and something I was unable to suppress. Tonight would be no different. I carried her to the bedroom, knowing she was as eager as I was, knowing she would be accepting of anything I wanted from her. She was mine, all mine, and it would be a cold day in hell before I ever gave up my angel.

.

Three Days Later

Mykonos, Greece

Bri

I had never seen anything more beautiful in my entire life. When Rogue had told me that we would be traveling through Europe for the next month or two, I had not imagined how wonderful it would be. I had never even had a passport before now and certainly never imagined that I would be flying in a private jet or staying in luxury suites at five-star hotels. It was like a dream.

Rogue was so attentive and treated me like a princess. He still stepped away to take calls in private and every once in a while, I would catch a slight nod of his head toward one of the men that worked for him, or he would speak softly so I wouldn't hear what he was directing them to do, but I tried not to think of it.

Eden and I talked a few times, and she convinced me that while our husbands may be monsters to some, they were the men we loved and that was all she needed to know. At first, I couldn't imagine turning a blind eye to the things Rogue was involved in, but he assured me that he did not traffic women or children, nor did he make money from drugs. The men that he killed were all deserving of their fate, and he would never do anything to hurt me. I never asked any more questions after that conversation. It wouldn't matter anyway. Rogue would never allow me to leave him, thankfully I didn't want to.

As I stood on the balcony of the house Rogue had rented on the island of Mykonos off the coast of Greece, I couldn't imagine being with anyone else.

I heard footsteps behind me and closed my eyes as his strong arms wrapped around my waist and pulled me into his chest. His lips pressed against the sensitive skin right behind my ear.

"Standing here, with the ocean breeze whipping your hair behind you, and the way the sun shines on your face, you look very much like an angel."

I smiled as I turned around in his arms. "An angel would not have done the things we did last night in our bed."

He chuckled as his hands moved up along my sides, barely grazing the sides of my breasts. "Hmm, if she was in the arms of a devil, she would." He kissed my lips and my whole body warmed. "The yacht has been made ready for us to sail tonight, but I will inform them that we will be late."

I grabbed his hands before they found their way up my skirt. "There is something I want to talk to you about first."

He stepped back and concern washed over his facial features. "Is something wrong? Are you unhappy here in Greece?"

I couldn't help but smile. "No, I love Greece. It has been a magical place, and I am having a great time."

"Then what do you want to talk about, sweetheart?"

I pulled my lower lip between my teeth, hoping what I was about to say didn't make him upset. It was something we had never discussed and I had no idea how receptive he would be to the news I was about to share with him.

His hands moved up my arms. "You're nervous, Angel. Tell me what has happened to make you look as if you are afraid of me."

I tried to smile. "I'm not afraid of you. I'm just afraid that you are about to be unhappy with me."

He grinned. "Darling, what could you do to make me angry with you?"

"I have been keeping something from you."

His expression changed instantly, and I felt a chill move up my spine.

"I know every move you make, Bri. What could you be hiding that I don't know?"

I took a deep breath. "I was going to tell you before, I swear. But every time I worked up the courage, something would happen to make me chicken out. And then you planned this trip and I so wanted to go, and I was afraid you wouldn't let me go if you knew."

His grip tightened and I could see the frustration on his face. "Bri, what the fuck is going on?"

"I'm pregnant."

I watched his face, waiting for his response. At first, there was no reaction, and I thought I had made a mistake by telling him, but suddenly he pulled me closer.

"My child is growing inside you?"

I nodded, trying to hold back tears. "Yes. Are you upset?"

He gently wrapped his arms around me. "Darling, why would I be upset?"

"We never talked about it, and I wasn't sure it was something you would want."

He grinned. "We never talked about birth control either. And I certainly never did anything to prevent it."

"So, you are happy?"

He picked me up and cradled me in his arms. "Very much so, but we will have to be careful now."

My eyes narrowed. "Don't you dare try to cut this trip short. If you do, I will handcuff you to the bed while I traipse across Europe on my own. Women do all sorts of things while pregnant, and I will not have you put me in a protective bubble."

"I don't give a damn what other women do. I only care about you. Protecting you has become a habit, darling. I'm not sure I can break it."

"I love you, Rogue."

He bent his forehead to mine. "It's a good thing, Angel, because I am irrevocably, irreverently, and unpardonably in love with you."

I felt tears glistening in my eyes, then his lips covered mine in a kiss that stole my breath and claimed my soul. And I knew I would forever be his angel and he would eternally be the devil that claimed me.